WIND RIDERS

OAKEN

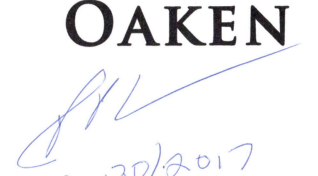

R.P. WOLLBAUM

First Published in Canada by Midar and Associates Ltd. 2017

Copyright © R.P. Wollbaum 2017

While some of the events and characters are based on historical incidents and figures, this novel is entirely a work of fiction.

ISBN 13: 9780995253766

Cover and Book layout by www.ebooklaunch.com

All rights reserved. No part of this publication may be reproduced, stored in a retrieval system, or transmitted, in any form or by any means, electric, mechanical, photocopying, recording or otherwise, without the prior permission of the publisher.

www.bearsandeagles.ca

To all the members, past and present of the
Kings Own Calgary Regiment (RCAC)

Prologue

THE PRE-GRADUATION MIXER had started an hour earlier. Megan was sitting at a table for eight by herself. All the rest of the graduation class had full tables and her friends in the class kept asking her to join them, but she repeatedly refused. She kept looking out the window and hoping. All the other graduates' relatives and friends had arrived. The dress was casual, so the graduates were out of uniform, but dressed tastefully. Megan was wearing a business pantsuit and most of the rest of the room were wearing sports jackets or business suits. The room was filled with happy people, but everything was low key, not overly boisterous.

A commotion at the registration desk at the entrance to the banquet room drew her eyes toward it and she smiled and rose. There were seven people trying to make their way past the undergraduates manning the entry. Some were dressed in blue jeans and polo shirts, others in cargo pants and polo shirts, some with cowboy boots on their feet and others sneakers. One short man had on cargo-pant style Bermuda shorts, a T-shirt and flip flops, and a tall man had boot-cut jeans held up by a belt with a huge buckle, a denim shirt, cowboy boots and a black Stetson hat on his head.

"It's okay," Megan said, as she came up to the table. "They're with me."

"Sir," one of the undergrads, all in scarlet uniforms said. "I am afraid you will have to remove your head gear, Sir."

"That's okay, son," the man with the Stetson said. "I know what it means to walk in the mess with head gear on. You just keep the drinks coming and charge it to this room number."

He handed the undergraduate a card with his room number and a note from the hotel manager authorizing any charges.

"Uncle Duncan," Megan said hugging him and then Karen. "This is going to cost you a lot of money."

"Honey," Duncan said. "The tradition is, as long as I have this hat on, I'm buyin'. Unless somebody plans on trying to knock it off, it ain't comin' off. Where's the table? I'm dyin' of thirst and turning into a skeleton from lack of food."

Duncan gestured at CT, Carol and Diane to follow him and headed to the bar where each of them grabbed four beers and joined Megan, Barb, Dave and Karen at the table. As they sat down Barb was just finishing explaining why they were late. The transportation they had ordered to meet them at the airport had trouble accessing the airbase and then there had been a mix-up at the hotel check-in desk. But everything had been worked out and they had made it, just in time. The band started to play background music and Megan's friends came by and were introduced to her parents and the rest of the group. No last names were given.

At first, the small group of Western Canadians was left to themselves, but, as the night went on, more people gravitated to them. They seemed to be the only ones actually enjoying themselves. Soon, other people from the other Prairie Provinces joined them, followed by some from the Maritimes, especially after the band played a few country songs and the westerners started to two-step to the music. There was a lot of laughter and good times being had in that group.

Most of the others were not impressed at the unseemly behavior of those people. But, unfortunately it was a democratic country and sometimes the underclasses had to be tolerated. Why, Megan's party had actually sung so loudly to a song called Ghost Riders in the Storm that they had overpowered the band and the words were not even right. Well, they had only come because it was expected of them and they left as soon as they could.

The fun-loving group and all but the most well-connected of the graduates stayed and partied until early the next morning.

At the graduation ceremony the next day, all but Barb and Dave from Megan's party were missing from the crowd of friends and relatives. Dave was dressed in his robin blue Air Force uniform and Barb in an Army one. Curiously, Dave had a black beret on his head, instead of the Air Force fore-and-aft cap, as did Barb. Few of the friends and relatives were aware; those that were, did not recognize the unit the berets belonged to, or the unit crest on it.

Seated with the graduates and facing the friends and relatives, Megan scanned the crowd and saw the other five standing in a small group at the rear. The group of five had grown to twenty-five and they were all in full dress - not mess dress like all the rest of the military people present, but the dark green uniform. At the end of the ceremony, they moved away and none of the other guests or graduates noticed they had been there.

At the graduation banquet, only Dave and Barb had been present at Megan's table and there were five empty tables around hers. Her table was at the front center just below the head table, which was on a small stage. After the meal and the obligatory toasts to Queen and country, the speeches began. Barb and Dave excused themselves and did not return, leaving Megan sitting by herself.

The dean of the academy finished his speech and made his way back to his seat. Now would come the speech from the keynote speaker, who had not been announced. The lights in the hall went dark, the only light in the room coming from the exit signs and a dim projected picture of a military crest on the white wall to the left side of the stage.

Then, in single file, twenty-seven people marched onto the stage from the right. That they were soldiers was clear. The black silhouettes all had berets on their heads and when they stopped, they had formed in groups: two groups of four to the left and right ends and two groups of five in the center, with one soldier in the front alone. This soldier marched up to podium and, as he did so, the others assumed the position of parade rest: feet shoulder-width apart, both arms tucked into the back. When he stopped, a spotlight shone on him while other spots illuminated the other troopers.

They were dressed in dark green uniforms, black stripes down the trouser legs, and jacket seams in black. Black berets were on their heads, the brims just above the eyebrows and the unit crest on the berets centered on their foreheads. All of them were wearing their qualification and rank badges and full medals, not ribbons or miniatures, on the jackets. There were two colonels, two majors, two captains, six warrant officers, five master sergeants, five sergeants and six master corporals. All of them had parachute wings, the sixteen on the ends boasted pathfinder wings. Two had pilot wings, and a female in the far-right rank of four had a brass eagle on her right collar. A number of the men and women in the groups of four on the ends had wound stripes, some with more than one. The female colonel had a ranger badge and an expert combat infantry badge on her jacket, both American decorations; the group of four troopers on the far left also had the combat infantry badge and force recon badges. Each and every trooper had an expert marksman badge and a commander-in-chief unit citation.

The man behind the podium was the cowboy from the night before. He was a master warrant officer. He had pathfinder wings and pilot wings. An expert combat infantry badge and a ranger badge were above a bronze star, with silver star and a purple heart medals on the right side. Around his neck was the member of military merit medal, a medal of military valor, a meritorious service cross, a cross of valor and a medal of bravery, mention in dispatch medals and a number of medals depicting where he had served under combat.

"Congratulations to this year's graduating class," Duncan said. "Few of our fellow citizens are willing to make the sacrifice of being in military service, and fewer still take the route you have chosen, to be our future leaders. Sacrifice it is, because, for at least the next five years, while your civilian contemporaries are building careers in the private sector, or enjoying their lives, you will be protecting them. For those of you who will be going into combat arms, life is seldom pleasant. Even for those of you who have been selected for technical or service positions, the first few years will see you serving far from homes and families."

"You have just joined a magnificent brotherhood. Right now, you have only just begun to realise how special this bond between us is. No one outside this brotherhood will ever really understand why you feel the way you do. They don't have to.

"When you first join your new commands, you will have people like me or the people behind me serving under you. Pay attention to what we have to say. It might save your life. In time, I might even listen to you. Stranger things have happened. Our community is small and I am sure we will run into one another at some point in the future. Most of the time you will never know we are around.

"My unit is the very tip of the spear. People call us the Wind Riders. We are attached to the Kings Own Regiment out of Alberta. Who are they? I can hear you ask. The Kings Own Regiment is a light armoured cavalry regiment. We are reservists. We are one of the most active reserve units in the country. We serve as your recon and intelligence people."

The picture on the wall changed to show four troopers on a high point. One had high-power binoculars to his eyes, while another was peering through a powerful spotting scope. Another had earphones on her head and a boom mike coming off the earphones. None of them had flak jackets or helmets on.

"Ninety percent of the time, we are dying of boredom. We monitor radios, we scan terrain for signs of enemy. We relay messages to the troops in our area from the command posts. Sometimes we provide coordinates for artillery strikes, or laser targets for air or drone strikes. But most of the time we spend just sitting, looking and listening."

A picture of cheerful troopers getting into a clean G-Wagon comes on, followed by another with the same troopers coming out of a dusty and dirty vehicle, uniforms dirty and worn and no smiles.

"We deploy in teams of four and my unit is generally deployed until we run low of water, fuel or rations. And then sometimes, we run out of ammunition and we do something to deserve these."

Duncan pointed to his medals and the picture on the wall changed to show four separate images. One showed all four team members shooting, another with a G-Wagon in full flight with the C-9 gunner standing in the open and firing his weapon. The next image depicted that same gunner, now firing while facing backward, the rear hatch open and a pair of legs dangling out, sparks flying on the vehicle as it sped toward a transport plane that was also under fire, its rear cargo door and ramp open and extended and one engine smoking. The final picture was of a single trooper advancing on a large group of armed men with his C-8 raised like a baseball bat.

"And sometimes we die," Duncan said at the last picture.

"Very few of you will be chosen to lead combat troops and even fewer to lead groups such as the Kings Own Regiment. Maybe, one of you may be asked to join us; who knows?"

"It is the custom for the top graduates to be allowed to pick which regiment they wish to start their service with. All of you but the top graduate has done so. What is about to occur has never been done before and most likely will never be done again."

Duncan took four steps back and two to the right and in his parade voice yelled, "Attention to Orders!" All the uniformed people in attendance rose and came to attention.

"Ensign Megan Kline, front and center."

Megan marched up to Duncan and he had her turn to face the crowd. On her jacket were the decorations she had put on when the room went dark. There were pilot wings and parachute wings, a mention in dispatch award, the medal denoting 180 days of service in Southwest Asia medal, a gold eagle on her right collar and an expert marksman badge on her uniform jacket.

"As the top Air Cadet in the Prairie Region, Ensign Kline was allowed to take flight training where she received her flight wings. As the top cadet in the country, she received three months of the most intensive special forces training this country and NATO offer, and she received that brass eagle for that. Those things were accomplished before she came here. When she disappeared from here last year for six months, she was flying a surveillance aircraft as one of only four people qualified to fly that aircraft. She studied her lessons at night and in off-duty times. Ensign Kline parachuted in to help save our asses when one of my teams came under heavy fire and needed medical assistance and ammunition until the US marines came to our rescue. That is where she earned the mention in dispatch and the parachute wings."

"Ensign Kline, are you brave enough?"
"Yes, Master Warrant."
"Are you determined enough?"
"Yes, Master Warrant."
"Are you tough enough?"
"Yes, Master Warrant."

Duncan turned Megan to face him again, and held his hand behind his back. Jane came forward and placed a black beret in it and he put it on Megan's head, then took two steps back and saluted her. Then he and Jane rejoined the Wind Rider formation, leaving Megan alone by the podium. As the top graduate, she would now address the crowd and the lights in the room came up.

"The last four years," she began, "We have been challenged physically and mentally almost to the breaking point. Some of those who began this journey with us could not endure and are no longer here. Most of the time, we will wonder why we went through all of this. Then will come a time when this will seem like child's play and all the discipline and training we have received will seem insufficient. But it has to be, and we have to endure, because our troopers will expect us to lead. Our troopers will be looking to us to guide them.

"During my six-month deployment, all but one day was spent doing routine matters. Flying in circles for eight hours a day, sometimes dropping supplies from the air or landing on a remote airstrip to deliver or pick up troops or supplies.

"One day, a US Marine Corps company came under heavy fire. A Wind Rider Team was in the area and I was flying cover for them. At first, we vectored in artillery support for the Marines and then air strikes, but it was not enough. They were being attacked by around one thousand enemy. Yes, they the bad guys were not well trained, but what they lacked in training, they made up for in bravery and numbers. The Marines were in great danger of being overrun and, as they always do in situations like that, the Wind Riders went into action. Because no one usually knows they are around, our attacks come as a surprise and are usually enough to break the attackers, but not this time. This time there were too many enemy forces. The Wind Riders found themselves surrounded and running low on ammunition, and the C-9 gunner was wounded. There were two of us in that plane and it only needs one to fly, so I first dumped out the spare ammo we always have on board, then I jumped out to help.

"Yes, the Marines came and saved us. But that was after we had drawn most of the enemy on ourselves. For, you see, we have a reputation in those parts and we always say a few words in Arabic and English on the radio before we attack.

"We are the wind rustling through the leaves and the grass, bringing fresh air and comfort.
We are the babbling brook, bringing refreshment and soothing.
We are the sun in the sky, bringing warmth and sustenance.
We are the Wind Riders, bringers of Peace, Hope and Justice.

We are the torrent that rips trees from the ground.
We are the raging flood waters that destroy homes.
We are the burning sun that devastates crops.
We are the Wind Riders, bringers of Despair, Death and Destruction."

"If you ever find yourself in a position where you hear those words, know that we are on our way and we will do our best. For we are wolfhounds and killing wolves is what we do."

Chapter One

AFTER A VERY LONG NIGHT of celebrating, Duncan, Karen and the rest of the gang had gone back to their rooms. They would be flying back home the next night and everyone wanted some sleep.

He didn't know it, but he was tossing and turning in his sleep. His vivid dream was of a huge herd of sheep under onslaught by a huge wolf pack. The swift lean herd dogs were valiantly trying to keep the herd together, moving it away from the wolves, sometimes trying to defend themselves from the larger, more powerful wolves and dying.

Bigger shaggy white guard dogs were operating in pairs like they did against smaller packs. They were effective, but not effective enough. Wolves were getting through and killing sheep, forcing more and more of the guard dogs to the herd to drive off those wolves. Duncan sat on a hill, but he was alone. If he had help, he knew he could defeat this wolf pack, but there was none. So, he stood, saying to himself, it is a good day to die, and he launched his four paws straight for the largest group of wolves, intent on killing as many of them as possible before they killed him.

Duncan's eyes snapped open and the dream dissipated. He was laying on his back looking up at the sky, not a hotel room ceiling. The sky was not blue, but the violet that sometimes comes before a large storm. He sat up and looked at his combat-booted feet. His tan combat pants were tucked into the boots and, as he levered himself up to stand, he could tell from the weight that he was carrying a full combat load around his body. His Sig was by his left shoulder and his C8 lay at his feet. He picked it up, ejected the clip, saw it was full and put it back in the rifle. The other three members of A Troop were laying as he had been, on their backs, beside their G-Wagon.

Looking around he saw it was a full deployment. Four other G-Wagons and two Coyotes, with their crews lying beside them, were haphazardly parked in a small clearing surrounded by strange trees that were more yellow than green. From the position of the reddish sun in the sky, it looked like it was late afternoon. At first singly, then in groups, the other Wind Riders woke up, all just as confused as Duncan.

"Okay," Duncan said, more as a test of their personal comms system than anything else. "Get these vehicles in a proper laager. Get a perimeter set up. Drivers and gunners, ammo, fuel and food status. Coyotes, start searching frequencies and coordinates and see where the hell we are."

Training took over and troopers deployed to all points of the compass with weapons at the ready, scanning the treeline. The Coyotes moved to a position ten yards apart, noses facing opposite each other, then deployed their large antennae arrays, both satellite and surveillance. G-Wagons formed a circle around them, broadside to the outside.

All the vehicles had full fuel tanks and four spare jerrycans, also full. They had full loads of rations and ammunition and each vehicle had, in addition to four full jerrycans of fresh water, all of their sleeping gear, medical equipment and spare clothing. After deploying the remote sensors for the Coyotes, Duncan called the security teams. CT and Jane reported no human or animal activity in the area, so Duncan called them all together for a meeting.

"So," he said. "We have no idea where we are or why we are here. All I can say for sure is that we ain't in Kansas anymore, Toto. Anybody got any ideas?"

Before anyone could say anything, they heard a rash of sizzling in the distance followed by some deep booms and screaming. Duncan motioned for his troop to follow and everyone else deployed into defensive positions as he and the rest of A Troop cautiously made their way through the trees, going to their bellies at the edge of the tree line. They crawled forward to the edge of a hill and looked down.

About five hundred grey armoured troops were attacking a town. There were twenty-odd looking large vehicles with them, which in ten-second intervals fired a stream of red into the town, exploding it. Highly outnumbered defenders in light blue armour were engaging as best they could, but they were quickly outflanked by another hundred troopers on each side who only seemed intent on capturing women and dragging them back to a penned area.

"Well," Duncan said over the radio. "I don't know who the bad guys or the good guys are, but I don't like what I see the attackers doing. Bring all the vehicles forward and spread out on this hill."

The G-Wagons spread out, two to each side of Duncan, and the two Coyotes placed themselves ten yards back of the line, one to each side. Duncan had everyone but the drivers and the gunners deploy twenty yards in front of the vehicles, each troop's snipers with their long-range rifles in hand. They would first take out any obvious officers, then the snatch teams and finally the prisoner guards. The two Coyotes were to fire a sabot round at the biggest of the opposition vehicles and see what happened. Hopefully that would draw the attackers' attention and take some heat off the defenders.

The weapons the others were using looked like they only had about a hundred yards of good range and were not much good over two hundred. If they were attacked, the Wind Riders would engage at three hundred yards with only C8s and slow single shots first. Then three-round bursts and only as a last resort full-auto with the C9s joining.

Duncan switched frequencies on his radio and all the PA systems on the vehicles went live.

"We are the wind rustling through the leaves and the grass, bringing fresh air and comfort.
We are the babbling brook, bringing refreshment and soothing.
We are the sun in the sky, bringing warmth and sustenance.
We are the Wind Riders, bringers of Peace, Hope and Justice.

We are the torrent that rips trees from the ground.
We are the raging flood waters that destroy homes.
We are the burning sun that devastates crops.
We are the Wind Riders, bringers of Despair, Death and Destruction.
I am the Ghost in the Wind, the bringer of justice, prepare to die!"

He had spoken the words in Arabic and as he switched his frequency back to the command net, he noticed that the attackers had seen them, but disregarded them.

He deployed his bipod at the end of his .50 caliber sniper rifle and lay down behind it, sighting on a man directing troops in the middle of the attackers' formation. Then he began a five-second countdown speaking aloud and as he hit one he squeezed the trigger and the big gun went off along with the five others and both 20mm guns in the Coyotes' turrets.

"Holy shit!" Brett said, "those two vehicles just blew right apart."

Duncan was now sighting on a trooper that was dragging a woman on the ground by her hair. The grey armour blew apart in small pieces as the big bullet hit it and drove the man onto his face. Duncan shot one more and the others dropped the women they were carrying and ran, then Duncan and the other four shooters concentrated on the guards who ran after only one shot each.

All the women were sprinting back to their comrades and now a group of twenty-five grey clad troopers and one vehicle were advancing on the Wind Riders position in line abreast. They held their fire until the attackers were at 300 hundred yards, then twenty-five shots rang out and twenty-five troopers were down. Only then did Jane's 20mm gun fire once, and the vehicle exploded in spectacular fashion.

The next attack was more ambitious. Two lines of a hundred, with two vehicles in each line, approached. This time the Coyotes spoke first, the exploding vehicles taking out many of the troopers on foot, then the C8s began to fire in single fire. The snipers had changed to the smaller caliber weapons now. After three shots each, the few attackers still standing ran for their lives. The defenders had now consolidated, not having to deal with flanking attacks any longer, and were taking a toll on the attackers. Townspeople, male and female, were joining the fray, with what looked like bars of steel, lengths of wood, hammers, axes, almost anything that had weight and that could be swung. The attackers had enough and ran.

Duncan dispatched B and C Troops with Jane's Coyote in support to follow the retreat with orders to not let them stop for ten miles at least, and then to watch until nightfall or recalled. Duncan ordered D and E Troops to conduct a perimeter check with their G-Wagons while A Troop and CT's Coyote kept watch for any stragglers and on the town itself.

"Notice anything weird about that sun?" Brett said.

"Ya, it looks like it's almost noon now," Scott said.

"This is getting weirder by the minute," Duncan said.

D and E Troops came back in and dismounted. Everyone was relaxed but alert. Jane reported that the people in grey had linked up with vehicles and loaded up and took off in the opposite direction, fast. Duncan called his people back in and now they all sat around and waited for something to happen.

They redeployed in their laager formation with a trooper manning the C9s in each vehicle while the rest reloaded clips and cleaned weapons. Someone had a camp stove going with two pots of water on it to boil water for their MREs and Bob handed Duncan a cup of hot coffee. There were grey-clad bodies all over the field below them and broken pieces of vehicles littered the ground in a large radius. Blue-armored troopers and townspeople were gathering their own dead and wounded, with many hasty looks at the tan-uniformed Ghost Riders and their tan vehicles on the hilltop.

Duncan sat on the hood of his G-Wagon sipping his coffee and Karen sat beside him. She was paler than usual and her eyes were darting all around the field below them. Duncan put his arm around her waist and kissed her neck. She sighed and laid her head on his shoulder.

"What now?" she asked.

"We wait," Duncan said. "Somebody is bound to come up and talk. We didn't expend too much ammo and I want to keep it that way until we get more information. If this gang comes at us, we hit them, then fall back. CT is going to get one of the birds up to look around for some place to fall back to. Right now, this is as good a place as any. We outgun anything these guys have."

"Duncan," CT said. "I'm picking up some traffic on a weird HF band in some weird language. It's on an AM commercial frequency."

"Visitors coming," Dianne said.

Seven blue-armored figures were making their way forward, five of them armed. Duncan told the C9 gunners not to waste the bullets and they picked up their C8 rifles and laid them across the roofs of the G-Wagons, pointed at the seven figures as they walked toward them. When the seven reached a distance of two hundred yards, the gunners jacked a round into the breaches and activated the laser sights, putting red dots in the center of each of the blue chests that were carrying weapons. The seven stopped on the spot. The five with weapons kept them at port arms, weapons angled across chests, while the two unarmed figures advanced forward with their arms low by their thighs, away from their bodies and palms forward.

Duncan and Karen watched them make their way forward, he still with his arm around her shoulder and she with her head on his. As the visitors reached a distance of a hundred yards, Duncan took a last sip of coffee and slid off the hood. Karen followed. They chambered a round into breaches and started to walk toward the approaching visitors. Both flicked off the safeties, but kept their fingers on the outside of the trigger guards and the barrels pointed down and away. They stopped walking when they were two yards away from the visitors. The visitors stopped at the same time, came to attention and hit clenched fists on their chests.

Duncan and Karen took right hands off the rifles and saluted.

"Master Warrant Kovaks, Commander of the Wind Rider Squadron," he said in Arabic.

The two figures before him looked at each other, then back at them, and shook their heads. The strangers were about five foot ten. Their heads were covered in full face helmets with dark visors so their faces were not visible. The blue armour covered their whole bodies, so it was impossible to determine their body size, but they had five-fingered gloves. The armour was smooth and shiny and looked ceramic. The figure on the right spoke in a language of some sort. It sounded female, but other than that was indecipherable.

Duncan tried German, she tried something else. He tried Spanish, she tried something that sort of sounded similar. He tried French, she tried something he might be able to work with.

"Well if this doesn't work, I'll try French," Duncan said to Karen in English. "We can maybe work something out in that."

"Sir, I speak this can," the figure on the right said. "Say many thanks we come."

"Your accent and form are old," Duncan said slowly. "But I can understand you. I am the commander of my group, and this is my third in command."

"Assistant to Commander I," the figure on the right said. "Commander he." She pointed at the one on the left who nodded at Duncan. "Not speak this he. Speak I for he."

"We consider it very impolite to talk with our faces covered," Duncan said.

The figure on the right spoke to the commander in the Russian-sounding language. He undid the chin strap and removed the helmet from his head. She followed suit. They both had humanoid faces, with short cropped black hair and green eyes. Their complexion was dark, almost Mediterranean.

"Thank you," Duncan said nodding at the commander, who spoke to the woman but looked at Duncan while he spoke. Duncan was catching about every third word he said.

"Sir, sorry say commander," she said. "Intend not insult. Thank you help for intend. Understand you well I. Speak well not. Learn only school I. Speak seldom I."

"You are doing fine," Duncan said. "What can I do for you?"

She looked at him and spread her hands palm out to her side.

"What do you require from us?" Duncan rephrased.

"Require not you we," she said. "Offer feed and sleep you we."

"Ghost!" CT's voice came over his earphone. "Airborne fast movers inbound!"

"Defensive NOW!" Duncan said and he and Karen went to one knee and brought their rifles up to bear on the man and woman before them. Multiple red laser dots appeared on each of the five armed troopers, the gunners on the G-Wagons dropped their rifles and armed the C9s while the two Coyotes moved forty yards apart, the rear weapons pods deploying 50 caliber chain guns that automatically started tracking the inbound aircraft. The 20mm cannons mounted on the turrets were all on automatic tracking now.

"Kill not! Kill Not!" the female yelled. "Friends are! Friends are! Please! Kill not!"

She was down on her knees, her arms outstretched. The commander followed suit.

The aircraft were smaller and nimbler versions of the larger vehicles the attackers had used. They came to a hover behind the line of five troopers and landed. Five people exited each craft. Ten were armed and armoured, five were not. These five made their way forward, while the guards had red dots appear on their chests.

Duncan and Karen stood, rifles still in hand but pointed at the ground. Three women and two men approached them, all of them human looking, wearing colorful clothing of rich fabrics. Their black hair was longer than the soldiers', reaching their shoulders, and their skin the same color as the two soldiers'. None were as tall, but all were a uniform five foot six in height. None of them were overweight. One of the men approached Duncan with his hand outstretched.

"Mr. Kovaks, so glad to meet you in person," he said. "I am your employer's representative. Impressive, very impressive."

Duncan made no move to greet the man, but pointed his rifle at him instead.

"Oh my," the man said dropping his hand. "I do not see what we have done wrong. We have followed standard Guild practice and you have proven your competence with your employer who is willing to provide you with a higher fee for your services."

"What the hell are you talking about?" Duncan said. "I don't know who you people are, where the hell I am, or how the hell I got here. I have signed no contract to provide services to you people and don't know what the hell you're talking about with this guild shit."

"Mr. Kovaks," a woman with grey streaks in her hair said. "I am your employer. You are on our planet. I am the ruler of this country. We are being invaded by an unscrupulous neighbor who has employed a group of mercenaries to attack us. We contacted the Mercenary Guild to provide us with a counter measure and here you are."

"Listen, lady," Duncan said. "I have no signed agreements with anyone at this moment. I have two contracts under review, but they will not be conducted until the end of the year, if I decide to accept the offers. It is very unlikely I would accept this kind of contract anyway."

"On the contrary, Mr. Kovaks," the man said. He pulled an envelope from beneath his jacket and gave it to Duncan. "This is a signed contract between Chinook Winds International GMBH and Mercenary Guild Interplanetary, to provide security consulting services for a retainer of 20 pounds of silver per year. In addition, Chinook Winds International agrees to provide a security force when required or otherwise not employed. We require your services and by your own admission you are not currently employed. Therefore, we are exercising our option. At our own expense, we have equipped and transported you here for an audition of your capabilities. Your new employer has agreed to your employment and has reimbursed the Guild for its costs."

Duncan looked over the contract and could see why the investment banking arm of his multinational, multi-company assets would agree to it. Easy money from a bunch of crackpots. If they needed some security consulting, there were a number of freelance ex-military types that could be contracted to do that. At the current silver exchange rate, it worked out to $150,000 a year, for doing nothing.

"Well sir," Duncan said. "I would suggest you take this up with Chinook Winds International GMBH. It is an investment bank, not a professional security firm. My people and I belong to a company called Wind Riders Security and, as I said, I have signed no agreement with you people. I would recommend that you return the fees you have obtained from this fine lady, pay my firm 25 pounds of silver for services rendered and return us from whence we came."

"Oh my," the Guild man said. "This puts us in a terrible quandary. You see, Interplanetary Law states that once formal war has been declared and the belligerents have agreed to contract Guild members to fight for them, for the period of one year, or the cessation of hostilities, only one inbound transportation of personnel and no outbound transportation of any kind is allowed. Oh my."

"Please, Mr. Duncan," the female ruler said. "Can we not come to some form of agreement, you and I?"

Duncan looked at Karen, who shrugged her shoulders. "We can at least listen, Duncan."

"Bob," Duncan said to his microphone. "Have you got some shade set up yet?"

"Ya, Ghost, all set," Bob said.

"Right, I'm bringing some guests into the perimeter for tea," Duncan said, then he turned to the female ruler. "Ma'am, if you would come with us, we will hear your proposal. Guild man, you come along with your two soldiers. Everyone else stays put."

Someone had made a fire pit and gathered wood, as a campfire was going underneath a fifteen-by-twenty-foot dark tan tarp attached to Jane's Coyote on one end and collapsible tent poles on the other. Eight collapsible camp chairs with side-mounted tables were placed around the fire pit. The four visitors sat together on one side of the pit, with the ruler and the Guild man in the center chairs and the two soldiers on the outer. Duncan sat down, Karen on his right, Bob to her right and Jane to his left.

"I would offer you some food," Duncan began. "But, unfortunately, all the Guild provided us with was field rations, which are nutritious to be sure, but taste completely horrible. They did, however, provide us with a substantial quantity of a fairy tolerable alcoholic beverage which I can offer. If that will not offend you."

The ruler smiled and nodded, and Duncan ordered up a beer and four mugs. Scott brought out a case of twenty-four beers, popped the tabs on four of them, poured them into the cups and handed them to the visitors. Bob reached over and tossed a can to each of the Wind Riders and sat back down. The four of them made a show of popping the tabs and gesturing to the four in front of them before taking a deep pull from the cans. The other four made the same gesture and took tentative sips from the cups, then the ruler smiled and took a much bigger drink.

"This really is fine Pilsner beer," she said, then drained the cup and motioned to the case on the ground. "Just toss me one. I am not a pampered court lady."

"As I mentioned," Duncan said, as Bob tossed her another can. "It is tolerable. Like everything else on this operation, the Guild got it almost right. Now, why don't you tell me your story?"

The ruler popped the tab and took a deep pull right out of the can. "Ah, much better," she said.

Sensing what was about to occur, Scott brought another case and put it by the visitors.

The ruler began her story with the stranding of five thousand strangers on their planet two generations earlier. She described how her people had given them land, helped them settle and survive, and how these people had prospered and had now grown to be almost fifty thousand people. They had approached her husband for more land. Her husband had explained that the district they had would accommodate one million people easily and that they did not need another district. But then these people had attacked the next district and killed everyone in it. Her people had only a small armed force, designed really as a police force, not an army. They were overwhelmed easily and then the people attacked the next district. This time they killed everyone but young girls and children. Her husband had rallied all of the policemen and demanded the people return to their own district. These people had then declared war on her people and contracted a large contingent of mercenaries. Her husband and his troops had confronted these mercenaries and had been killed, to a man.

For the last year, this group had taken district after district, and now they controlled almost half the planet. Along the way they had killed all the people, excepting the very young and the prettiest of the women. She had used a lot of her resources in obtaining weapons and training for her people and had contacted the Guild about hiring mercenaries herself, but she had limited funds and the Guild had recommended Duncan as the best solution. She was informed that they were small in number, but highly skilled and able to handle this situation. What she had just witnessed had proven it.

"How many troops am I looking at to fight?" Duncan asked.

"Twenty thousand mercenaries and ten thousand indigenous troops," the Guild man said.

"Jaysus," Bob said. "We're good, but not that good. That's ten thousand to one odds against."

"One of the things my people are good at is negotiating settlements in situations like this," Duncan said. "Is there any way the Guild can arrange a meeting between me and the other people?"

The man took a box out of pocket and hit a button on it.

"Done," he said. "You have a one day truce, starting now. I will transport you to meet with them."

"Right," Duncan said. "Everyone stay put until I get back."

In less than half an hour, Duncan and the Guild man were in the commander's quarters of the enemy camp. Duncan explained that he would like to come up with an agreement that would end the conflict without any more loss of life. The man from the Guild translated his words into a Slavic language that Duncan found he could understand. The mercenary turned to the man next to him and in archaic French relayed Duncan's words. After much back and forth, which Duncan followed easily, the enemy presented a proposal.

Duncan would be allowed to surrender after providing a token resistance. His women would only be used for one night by five men each and returned to him otherwise unharmed. The men would be entertained by a feast and the next day they would be allowed to leave unharmed.

Duncan asked for five days to bring the proposal to his people and to plan for how to make it look like they would be defending vigorously. To his surprise, he was given twelve days and that a truce would be in effect for that time. Duncan assured them that they would have his answer at the end of the truce period and then he and the Guild man returned to his own camp.

"Interesting how you people twist things to suit yourself," Duncan said.

"I do not approve of these methods," the man said. "But my hands are tied if both of you agree."

"Somehow, I don't think that jackass will honor any agreement," Duncan said and he stayed quiet for the whole trip back.

Duncan rejoined the group around the camp fire, his face grim.

"I accept the assignment," he said without preamble. "You will pay us twenty-four thousand pounds of silver. Nonnegotiable. You will deduct forty pounds per month which you will pay me at the first of every month. You and your people will do exactly what I say, when I say to do it. You, Mr. Guildsman, will provide me with whatever supplies I require at your, not the planet's, cost. Nor will you demand or receive any commission from me or the planet. It was your screw-up, not ours. I will do what I can to wipe those assholes off the face of the universe. They give no quarter, so no quarter will be given in return. If the Guild does not like it, tough shit."

The ruler swallowed hard and nodded her head in agreement. As did the Guildsman, as Duncan had named him.

"Okay," Duncan said. "I have bought us twelve days. This is what we are going to do."

Duncan told the ruler to immediately evacuate this district and to wreck as many of the buildings, machinery and crops in the fields as they could. Then, he urged they do the same in the next two districts.

Next, he wanted one hundred of the townspeople and one hundred of her troopers to be transported to the capitol. He wanted the male commander to oversee this. Ten of his people would train them starting in fifteen days. Until then, the townspeople were to be instructed in close order drill. Jane would supply them with the weapons required before the fifteen days were up.

Next, he wanted another one hundred troops to be trained in defensive and offensive tactics by ten of his people, also in fifteen days. Lastly, he wanted one hundred of their best troops commanded by the female trooper to be trained in the Wind Riders tactics. They would start immediately.

"The people we will be training will in turn train one hundred more after we are done. By evacuating these districts, you are buying time to train and arm. By the time the enemy start into the second district, my troopers and I will be doing what we do best as will the one hundred we train. You may not have seen it, but I noticed that the enemy troops are not high-quality troops. They are brutes with weapons. We will show you how to, first, negate their weaponry advantage, then how to attack and defeat them using simple weapons and superior tactics.

"If we don't win, well, I guess you won't have to pay us the final amount." Then Duncan laughed. "Tomorrow morning at daybreak, Assistant Commander. You be here with your one hundred. Now all of you get out of here and let me think."

"Russia, 1940?" Jane asked after the visitors had left.

"Ya," Duncan said. "Scorched earth to buy us some time. Then we start hitting supply lines as they start getting over-extended. We will also do harassment raids more or less constantly. I think I have figured out their weapon systems and how to defeat them. Did you notice how the townspeople grabbed what they could for weapons and came into the fight? They are not scared to do battle. Shield wall and phalanx, I think. Simple weapons, like long axes, spears, hammers. That armor is ceramic. We will find out their manufacturing capability, but it looks like they have a high metalworking skill set."

"Now, here is the surprise we are going to give our friends down the way twelve days from now…"

A high-pitched whine the next dawn heralded the small surveillance drone's takeoff to obtain intelligence of the area surrounding the target. It was out of earshot by the time the female commander and her one hundred troops appeared.

"So, Commander," Duncan said. "Are all of your troops going to be able to communicate with us?"

"Sir," she said. "All better than I."

"Well, then," he said. "You had best pick it up fast. Now please demonstrate to me how your weapon works."

The woman demonstrated how to operate and handle the weapon, which, as Duncan had suspected, was a high-energy light device. Or laser. He took the weapon from her, sighted on a beer can he had set up about a hundred yards away, and fired. The can was blown away a distance and he sent Brett to retrieve it for him. Other than some scorching and a small dent, the can was intact. Then he aimed it at a G-Wagon, with the same result. Now he focused it at CT's Coyote, which was just over a hundred yards away and fired. It didn't even scorch the paint. Then he moved closer and fired again at the same spot and finally at twenty-five yards he fired the last shot. That one scorched the paint.

"OKAY, score one for us," Duncan said. "Grab me a rear-view mirror and set it up down there a bit."

All the Wind Riders were watching now as Duncan fired at the mirror and the light bolt careened off of it in another direction. Finally, Duncan tossed a smoke grenade and fired into it. Nothing came out of the other side of the smoke.

They had retrieved four sets of body armor from corpses left on the battlefield the day before and Duncan had set them up as targets. He pulled a ball-peen hammer out of his G-Wagon's toolbox and showed it to the armor-clad troops. Then he walked over to one of the targets and swung the hammer at it, shattering it into pieces.

"We are going to show you how to defeat your own weapon system so that you can get close enough to use this simple tool to kill your enemy," he said.

He pulled a clip out of a pouch on his weapons belt, pulled a cartridge out of it and passed it around to the trainees. Then he put it back in the clip, put the clip in his rifle and shot one of the armored targets. The rear of the armor exploded as the bullet exited it.

"I can do that just as easily at six hundred yards," he said. "I can do it at night, under any kind of lighting conditions, in the rain and through smoke. Each one of these clips holds twenty-five of these bullets and, if I have to, I can fire the whole clip rapidly." He fired the rest of the clip at full auto, hitting and destroying that piece of armor. Then he pulled out his sniper rifle and sighted on a block of wood six hundred yards away and fired, blowing a huge hole in the block of wood.

"I can target three troopers at eight hundred yards with this weapon. Fire the first two shots and be firing the third, before the first man drops and the third will just be figuring out what has happened to his two buddies when the third bullet hits him. Essentially, I could kill all one hundred of you, by myself, before you even got close enough to me to even fire your weapons."

"But we will be teaching you how to use your own weapons and simple weapons like this hammer," then he pulled his combat knife from his boot and held it up, "and this knife to kill quietly and efficiently. We will be teaching you how to attack and retreat without being detected. This is how we begin to defeat your enemy. By hitting them when they feel they are safe. First lesson, take off the armor; it slows you down and won't help you anyway."

They spent the rest of the day demonstrating how to overpower opponents in hand-to-hand combat. They had already had some training in this area, but were being taught new and different techniques. While they were doing that, Duncan and Scott learned the capabilities of the laser weapons. They smiled.

"Piece of cake," Scott said.

By the tenth day, they had all the information they needed to make their raid. Duncan would take the female commander and nine of her troopers with them, but just as observers. The plan was simple. The enemy troops were so confidant of their superiority that they were not conducting patrols, nor had they posted any sentries. Duncan had split his vehicles into two groups. His plan was for one to hit from the north; the other from the west. Two four-man teams, Duncan and A Troop being one, would wreak havoc among the sleeping men for twenty minutes first, then the vehicles would attack. After five minutes, they would all withdraw, leaving what was left of the camp down in the valley to the enemy.

It was all knife work for the infiltration teams. They entered a tent and killed all the occupants, then moved to the next tent. Then the vehicles attacked, spitting fire from roof-mounted weapons on full auto. The chain guns on the Coyote's spit fifty caliber bullets at fifteen hundred rounds per minute, every third round a tracer. The 20mm main gun was firing high explosive rounds as fast as it could fire. Both Coyotes stopped in front of a large tent and fired smoke grenades into and around it, then enemy troops came out of the back as Duncan's troops entered the front, firing the entire time. Soon they emerged with large boxes, tossed them in the back and went back in. They did this four times, then the Coyotes left with the G-Wagons, stopping only long enough to pick up the two infiltration teams. They left behind devastation and destruction, bodies lying everywhere and tents on fire.

The enemy commander looked at the piece of paper that had been laid on his desk. "This is my answer. No deal," was written in his own language.

Chapter Two

IT WAS PAST NOON when they returned to the hilltop and the original laager position. The town below was a hub of activity as machinery was being demolished and buildings and homes were prepared for demolition. The farm fields around were all ablaze, smoke filling the air. People were loading personal and public transports, and some large open-backed vehicles were filled to overflowing with people and possessions.

Duncan ordered Jane and E Troop, with all their support people, to accompany and provide security for these townspeople on their way to the capital. Once there, Jane would start training the first group of civilians. The rest of them would proceed to the next district and help with security while that district was evacuated.

After nightfall, the small drone was brought back in and refueled. Carol had decided it was her responsibility to care for the little beast and she started to go over it, inch by inch.

Somebody started a camp stove and pot of water going, while others made a campfire, or pulled camo netting across vehicles. Remote sensors were set up to monitor the perimeter from the Coyote and perimeter guard posts were manned. Technology was fine, but nothing beat a pair of ears and a nose. Boots on the ground were still required. The C9s were still armed, and a trooper was in the Coyote's turret ready to man the guns. All the troopers had their C8s close to hand or draped across chests with clips loaded.

Duncan tossed his sleeping bag to one side of A Troop's G-Wagon, grabbed his camp chair in one hand and a case of beer with the other and walked to the fire pit, setting up next to CT who was already sitting down, sandaled feet stretched toward the fire.

"Just what we needed," Duncan said as an errant wind gust blew smoke from the fire in his face. "More smoke." He handed a beer to CT.

Duncan had given up admonishing CT for wearing shorts all the time. They came to mid-calf anyway, were the same colour and had the same cargo pockets the combat pants had. When it got cold, CT would put on a pair of knee high socks to keep his California blood warm.

"CT," Duncan said. "I know it's safe here right now, but I want you to be wearing combat boots all the time now. You will be with us up front from now on, not safe in the rear like you are used to. Get in the habit now of wearing the boots. Changing footgear under fire will get you killed."

CT was one of the Wind Riders' technology people and, while he was certified expert on all their weapons systems, last night's raid had been the first actual combat he had been on.

"You okay?"

"Ya," CT said. "A little more intense than operating a drone or watching a vid screen, and a whole lot noisier, but ya, I'll be okay. Watching the vid screens doesn't prepare you for the screams and the smells."

Barb brought Duncan a small pot of hot water, a towel and a bar of soap. Her hands and face were newly scrubbed, but her uniform had dark patches all over it. Looking at Duncan, that's when CT saw the blood stains going up to Duncan's elbows, covering the right side of his face and his whole shirt front.

"Megan okay?" Duncan said. "That was her first time at hand-to-hand."

"I don't think it has sunk in yet," Barb said. "I'm keeping my eye on her. How's Karen?"

"She'll be fine," Duncan said. "She was manning Jane's twenty mike. She's done that before. I'll check up on her in a bit. I think it will be after dark before that bunch is ready to leave."

He finished towelling himself off and Barb took the cleaning utensils and pot and, as she walked away, tossed the red-stained wash water to the side. Duncan reached into the beer case, pulled out two and tossed one to CT.

"Tough lady," CT said.

"Not any tougher than the rest of us," Duncan said. "Barb and Dave have each other; they'll handle their shit in private. Just like all of us will. It's Megan and you I am worried about."

"Don't worry about me," CT said. "Dianne and I talk a lot. I'll be okay. Dianne has sort of adopted me as her long-lost brother. Wish it was otherwise, but there it is. Lots of babes in this new place, anyway."

CT told him that the enemy were in disarray, running all over the place expecting a new attack at any time. Duncan smiled and nodded his head. That was the whole purpose of the raid, to put the enemy on guard. Then CT told Duncan he had isolated the radio band the enemy was using and they could monitor it anytime. Duncan smiled again.

"Good," Duncan said. "Tonight, I'll be wanting to have a chat with them."

"Speaking of babes," CT said nodding to the approaching female commander. She and her ten troopers had arms full of what looked like food with them.

"Sir," she said. "Eaten your food have I. Disgusting it is. Better food make we for you."

After putting his load down, a male trooper relieved the commander of hers.

"The Commander's cooking is as bad as her Standard," the trooper said, which rewarded him a dirty look that he laughed off.

"Oh, thank Christ," Brett said putting his arm around the trooper. "It's Duncan's turn to cook tonight and it's usually downright inedible."

Duncan tossed the empty beer can in his hand at Brett, hitting him on the back of the head .

"See what we have to put up with in this chicken shit outfit?" Brett said laughing. "Your commander throws dirty looks; our commander throws whatever he gets his hands on."

"Oh, ours would like to," the trooper said. "But being an officer, she is not allowed to."

"Ah that makes sense then," Brett said. "Ghost is an officer, but not a gentleman. Come on, while I show you how to work these camp stoves, I'll tell you the difference between a commissioned and non-commissioned officer."

"What means he?" the commander asked. "You always gentleman are."

"Where we come from," Duncan said. "There are two types of officers. Commissioned and non-commissioned. Commissioned officers are like you and have higher and lower ranks. They are called officers and gentlemen, or, in your case, ladies. Even the lowest ranked commissioned officer, like Megan, outranks even the highest rank non-commissioned officer. In theory. In practice, an ensign is tolerated, barely, and the other ranks will make suggestions to her as they can't order her to do anything. In combat, she follows orders and any she gives will most likely be ignored."

"Yes, we a similar system have," the commander said.

"I am what is called a Master Warrant officer," Duncan said. "That is the highest rank a non-commissioned officer can reach. There are only four of us in my whole army."

"Don't kid yourself," CT said. "Ghost could be a colonel if he wanted it."

"Well," Duncan said. "I thought we told you that lieutenants were to be seen, barely, and not heard, ever. Sir."

"What?" the commander said. "Even out ranks you he?"

"Yes, Commander Ma'am," CT said. "I outrank him, just as you outrank me, Ma'am."

"Ya well," Duncan said. "We have a loose command structure here. Sometimes you will see me defer to CT or anyone else if they have a better idea."

"But he is the boss," CT said. "What he says goes, all the time."

"I...have...much...to learn?" the commander said.

"Yes, you do," Duncan said. "You said that correctly. Now calling you Commander and Ma'am all the time is a bit of a pain in the ass. I assume you have a name other than Commander? Something your parents gave you when you were born?"

"Horschak, family is," she said. "Katarina am I."

"Dasvidania, Katerina," Duncan said in Ukrainian. "I thought I recognised your dialect. It is close to this one."

Her eyes went wide and she rattled off a fast stream of words that Duncan only caught a third of.

"Sorry," Duncan said in English. "If you are going to speak that language to me, you are going to have to speak much slower."

"Hardly anyone speaks this here anymore," she said slower. "I can understand you fine, yours is much purer than mine. Where did you learn this?"

"It and several other dialects like it are in common usage where I come from," Duncan said in Ukrainian, then switched to Russian. "This is the most common dialect."

"That I hardly understood," she said.

Duncan held his hand up as his earbud broke squelch.

"Alpha One, Echo One," Karen said.

"Go ahead, Echo One."

"We might as well call it a night and come back to the laager. They will not be ready to leave until morning."

"Roger Echo One, RTB. Alpha One, out."

"Yo, Brett, Echo and Foxtrot are RTB for the night," Duncan said. "Make some room for them."

Katerina was looking at him funny.

"E and F Troops are coming back for the night," Duncan said. "On long-range open frequencies, we use call signs instead of our names. It makes it harder to figure out who is whom. Each of our teams is broken up into groups of four or five which we call troops. Each troop is designated with a letter of the alphabet and each team member has a number. For instance, I am Alpha One. Or A Troop one. If we were with a larger group, we would be called a squadron. In our case it is Wilco Squadron or W Squadron. But you will mostly hear Wind Rider Squadron, and that is because we have a certain reputation and we usually want the bad guys to know we are here. When we use it, that is. Mostly, we don't."

Jane's Coyote and Karen's G-Wagon came into camp and shut down. Karen dragged her sleeping bag out of the rear of the G-Wagon and tossed it beside Duncan's, then came and sat on his lap and stole his beer.

"Commander Katerina Horschack, my wife Karen," Duncan said.

"Pleased to you meet," Katerina said.

"Dasvidaniya, Katerina," Karen said. "And before you start talking Ukrainian at me, I am just learning it from the Neanderthal here."

"Neanderthal?" Katerina said.

"Big, hairy muscle-bound beast." Karen said. "Now give us a kiss, you beasty. I've missed you all day."

"Yes Major, of course, Major Ma'am," Duncan said and he did.

"Very well Master Warrant, now why don't you be a good little trooper and go find yourself another chair and some more beer, hmm?"

Duncan stood, made an exaggerated salute at a belly-sticking-out attention, belting out, "Yes Ma'am, right away Ma'am." And he strolled off in the opposite direction from where he was supposed to go.

Karen laughed. "Are your troopers just as disrespectful?"

"Not as blatantly," Katarina said. "But I am relatively new here."

"Well, I am sure they are being instructed properly." Karen pointed at where several of Katerina's soldiers were talking with Wind Riders.

"Are you involved in a lot of actions like the one we did last night?" Katerina asked.

"Ah, as the booze takes hold, her English gets better," Karen said, making Katerina blush.

"Oh, I think it's getting better because CT just left," Jane said plunking herself down in CT's vacated chair. "Toss me a beer, hon."

"Commander Katerina Horschak, my mother, Colonel Jane," Karen said as she grabbed a beer from the case and tossed one first to Jane, another to Katarina and one for herself.

"Katarina, Karen and I are usually behind the lines monitoring what the assault troops are doing. That was the first time for us. It's always Troops A, B, C and D that do the hard work. Ah, Barb! Welcome to the cats' club."

Barb had changed out of her bloodstained clothing and was dragging her camp chair behind her and another case of beer in the other hand. She plunked both down, saluted and stuck her hand out to Katerina.

"Major Barb," she said. "Or Voice. Take your pick."

"Barb here has been on a few ops, though," Karen said. "But here come the real pros."

Dianne, Carol and Amanda were walking up. They had their camp chairs in one hand and C8s draped across chests, barrels down with righthand trigger fingers on the trigger guards.

"Commander Katerina here was just asking if this was normal for us, and I told her you guys were the real pros," Karen said.

"So is Ann, but she is hanging out with that jarhead husband of hers for a while," Dianne said. "She said she'd be by later. Hi, I'm Captain Dianne, that's Captain Carol…"

"All you females are officers?" Katarina said.

"Hey! Speak for yourselves," Amanda said. "I work for a living. Master Sergeant Amanda, Ma'am. Master Sergeant Ann has apparently discovered she has had enough testosterone for the day."

Ann was making her way over to the little group just as the other three had, C8 at the ready and her head on a swivel.

"Ma'am," Ann said after being introduced. She pulled a bottle of clear liquid from under her jacket. "Second batch," she said. "It's not half bad." The bottle went around and each woman took a healthy pull. Karen passed it to Katerina but held on to it.

"Now go easy Katerina," Karen said. "This stuff has a big bite."

She took a tentative sip, then looked up and took a strong pull.

"That is the best Waska I have ever tasted," she said. "Where did you get it from?"

"You're calling this good?' Ann said. "The boys just made it this morning. They are having trouble getting the mixture correct with your vegetables. I guarantee the next batch will be almost perfect."

"You make this yourselves? What can't you people do?"

"Wash dishes," Ann said.

"Make beds," Dianne said.

"Wash windows," all of them said and then they all laughed.

"The other ladies want to spend the night with their men," Ann said. "Can't say as I blame them. Was their first time last night."

"Ya, no more virgins in this squadron," Carol said. "Speaking of which?" she was looking at Dianne.

"CT will be okay. We've already talked."

"I am a little worried about Megan," Barb said. "She only had that one action before and it was long-range, not hand-to-hand."

"Looks like Uncle Ghost has it in hand, Voice," Karen said. "Okay Katerina, spill the beans. Our hotty single girls want to hear all about your cute guys."

• • •

Duncan found her sitting ten yards in front of B Troop's G-Wagon. She had her arms around her knees and was staring off into the distance toward the site of the fight the night before. He could tell from the darkness on parts of her face, arms and uniform that she hadn't cleaned up yet. He quietly sat down beside her and also looked off into the distance.

What he was seeing was different than what she saw. He was seeing the farmlands in flames and picturing where he would be placing his ambushes soon.

"I made four mothers lose their sons last night," Megan finally whispered. "Four wives are widows tonight. Four sisters no longer have brothers…"

"Four sons and daughters lost their father," Duncan said. "Ya, I get it. I killed six with my knife and about a dozen with my C8, not including the hundred or so here last week. So what? Shit happens."

"How can you be so callous!" Megan was almost shouting. "I killed four men last night. I felt their blood, I heard them scream, I felt them take their last breath and watched the light go from their eyes. How can you just sit there and say shit happens?"

"So, hitting a button and launching a six-inch rocket, or lasing a target for a 500 pound smart bomb or vectoring in artillery rounds is somehow not killing people?" Duncan said. "You probably killed a thousand in Iraq doing that. But that was not real to you. That was killing little green or red figures on a screen. Last night you heard, saw and felt what it really is for the first time. We kill people, honey. That's what we do. Last night was up close and personal. Those men at least had a chance to fight back. A drone strike? Those people had no chance at all."

Now it all came crashing down on her and she started to shake and cry hard. Then she flung her arms around him and really cried. Duncan held her close with his left arm, stroking her hair with his right hand, his cheek against her hair and cried, too. He wasn't only crying for her. He had also killed the night before.

She finally stopped and looked up at him. Seeing the tears on his cheeks she rubbed them away with her fingers.

"Look at us," Duncan said putting a smile on his face. "The mighty Wind Riders - a bunch of bawling pussies."

"I thought it was only me," Megan said.

"No luv, it's all of us. Your mom and dad will be consoling each other later. Karen will come to me tonight. Some of us, me included, usually go off on our own someplace. But all of us go through this. Otherwise we turn into animals, like the ones we killed last night. They needed killing, but I don't have to enjoy it."

They sat in the darkness for a while, arms around each other's shoulders. Then Duncan nudged her in the ribs.

"Go join the cat club," he said. "They need someone to pick on and you're the rookie."

He watched her go to the group of women by the fire and could tell she was getting some ribbing; then each of them but Katerina hugged her. Barb was the last and held her the longest. Then Carol tossed a piece of firewood at them, Dianne tossed a beer at Megan and Barb walked toward Duncan.

He rose as she came near and tears were streaming down her cheeks as she rushed into his arms and muffled her wails into his chest.

"I've lost my baby girl, Duncan," she finally whispered.

"Ya, that tends to happen," he said.

"Ach, and what do you know?" Barb said, thrusting him away. "Bloody men!"

She started stomping back to the cat group, then stopped and looked back. She smiled and blew him a kiss, then walked to where Dave was standing and the two of them wandered away into the darkness. Duncan stood and walked to another campfire. This one was all male. Bob tossed a bottle of vodka at him and Scott a can of beer and they did what most males do when dealing with what they had done: they made jokes at each others' expense with sudden lapses in silence when something said triggered a memory.

It was almost daybreak when wives collected their missing men. Karen was the last and she was very wobbly when she came, clearly feeling no pain. When they snuggled under the sleeping bags she let out her grief and then they made passionate love.

•••

"Come on you bums, up and at it!" Brett yelled, kicking the feet of the one hundred soldiers as he passed them. "If you're gonna drink like men at night, you're gonna work like men in the morning! Come on, get up, ya bums!"

"Ah, so good of you to join us, Commander, Ma'am," Duncan said. Katerina had just kicked away her blankets and looked around her.

"If you're going to drink with the girls, luv," Jane said. "You're going to have to work like the girls the next day, dear."

All the squadron was up and working. Gear was being stowed in vehicles, camo netting being taken down, rolled up and stashed, weapons being checked. The remote sensors had already been retrieved and stowed away and the large antennae were being collapsed to the sound of hydraulics into their stowed positions on the Coyotes.

"Oh God!" Katarina said. "How can you people be so chipper?"

"The diction is correct," Duncan said. "Now to work on the accent. Unfortunately for you, Commander, you people cannot hold your liquor."

"Speak for your self shithead," Karen said. "God damn Canadians anyway."

Jane and Ann laughed at her.

"Ya well, you two are almost bloody Canadians," Karen said sticking her tongue out at them.

"Come, my dear," she said to Katerina taking her arm. "Let us leave these bloody colonials to their boorishness while we real ladies properly compose ourselves." They linked elbows and sashayed towards the latrine.

"Bloody hell," Karen said as Megan said a cheerful hello to them inside the latrine. "Can't we escape you cheerful people ever?"

Megan only laughed harder and walked out.

"Woah, those two got up on the wrong side of the bed this morning," she said, holding her coffee cup up to Duncan to be filled.

"Ya, just like those other ninety-nine," Duncan said gesturing at the struggling soldiers that Brett, Scott and Carol were haranguing.

"Been there," Megan said.

"Done that," Dianne said.

"Wrote the book," Barb said.

"Starred in the movie and sold the T-shirts," they all said together and laughed.

"More than once!" Duncan finally snorted out and they all roared in laughter again, just as Karen and Katerina walked up.

"Oh, you think this is funny, do you?" Karen said. "I'll show you funny!" She made a fist and advanced on them, which only made them laugh harder. Then she smiled and kissed Duncan.

"Okay, you got me, you bums," she said. "Laugh it up, it'll be for the last time."

"That's what you said the last time," Ann choked out.

"And the time before that," Jane said.

"I ain't saying anything," Duncan said as Karen looked at him.

"Good boy," she said kissing him again. "Next time I'll show you how to control a big hunk like this, Katerina."

"I love you Dunc, please be safe," she whispered into his ear.

"You too," he whispered back. "All right, party's over! Get your asses in gear! We've got miles to make!"

A and H Troops stayed behind as the others left. With them were the one hundred soldiers they would be training and their ten vehicles.

"So, here comes the first lesson for Commander Horshack," Duncan said. "The rest of you will be shown some new weapons. Commander, follow me, please."

He took her into the Coyote, had her sit on a bench and handed her a headset. Duncan selected another.

"Are they up yet?"

"Yup," CT said. "Anytime you're ready."

"Commander of the invaders, this is your enemy calling," Duncan said in Ukrainian. Katerina's eyes went wide.

"I know you can hear me," Duncan continued. "Are you too scared to talk?"

"I'll show you scared the next time we meet," an angry voice replied.

"I am waiting for you. You sure showed us how tough you were a few nights ago. Boring, really."

"We will not be so boring the next time, I assure you. We have logged a complaint against you with the Guild for your unwarranted actions."

"It was after your deadline, Commander. You have no case."

"But, then again," Duncan now said in French. "You had no intention of honoring that agreement anyway, did you? Come on; what are you waiting for? There are only thirty of us and we are getting bored over here."

"I'll show you bored," a different voice said in French. "I will cut your balls off, then force you to watch your woman being humped by ten men before I kill her and then you."

"Ya, tough guy," Duncan said. "I see how you operate against untrained militiamen and civilians. I also see how you run like little babies when real soldiers fight back. Come on, I am waiting for you, coward."

Duncan cut the transmission off as the enemy commander lost complete control of himself.

"Holy shit!" CT said. "Take a look at this!"

A figure in dark armor flung himself out of the command vehicle and started shooting anyone near him, only stopping when his weapon ran out of charges. Then he flung the weapon at another soldier and stalked away. CT and Duncan high-fived each other.

"That, Commander, is called getting the advantage over the enemy," Duncan said. "Now he is so mad he is going to come rushing straight for us. Just like we want him to. Time for the next lesson."

• • •

They had driven toward the enemy for two hours until they came to a portion of the road that went through a cut made into a hill to make the road less steep. The cut was about half a mile long and had large trees growing along both sides. The first demolition charges were set to block the entrance to the cut, then other charges were set at fifty yard intervals. In between, claymore mines were set. and a final set of demolition charges was hidden at the exit to the cut.

Duncan gathered all the troops around him as he sat on his G-Wagon's hood.

"Normally, back home, when we set an ambush like this, I would position dismounted troopers on both sides of the cut," he said. "But there we deal in smaller numbers of troops than what we will be facing today. If I did that today, there would be a very good chance of some or all of the dismounts being captured or killed. There will come a time for that, but today is not that time. This is what we are going to do instead…"

All ten of the planetary vehicles were in line abreast, facing the growing dust plume approaching from the distance. CT had found a way to patch his video feeds into their vehicles and they were seeing what he was seeing. Both the squadron's vehicles were positioned in front of the planetary ones and all were just sitting there, waiting.

"Okay, boss, we've been spotted," CT said. He was monitoring the enemy's radios. "They are deploying a hundred vehicles for us."

"Oh my," Duncan said. "Only a thousand troops and a hundred vehicles against our messy hundred-and-nine troops and twelve vehicles. Whatever will we do?"

"Alpha One to Recon One, wait until they reach five hundred yards, then withdraw to the other side of the cut," Duncan said.

CT confirmed what they had expected, that the enemy was monitoring the planetary frequency. The attackers spread out into two lines abreast and accelerated. Duncan waited until they were almost at five hundred yards.

"Go now!" he said. "A and G to hold until the others are clear."

The planetary vehicles reversed direction and sped toward the cut, changing to a staggered formation of two abreast. The cut was just wide enough for two vehicles to traverse side by side. Brett opened up with his roof-mounted C9, firing three-round bursts. The chain gun on the Coyote was doing the same and slow, single shots were coming from the turret-mounted 20mm cannon. The front rank of the approaching enemy was wiped out.

"Go! Go now!" Duncan yelled into the mike. The Coyote already facing toward the cut took off. A few seconds later so did the G-Wagon. As soon as they cleared the cut they went to the left, out of sight. The Coyote kept going, chasing the dust cloud in front of it.

The enemy came roaring into the cut, two abreast. The front two accelerated as they neared the cut's end and saw the Coyote disappearing down the road. That's when Duncan hit the button detonating the charge at the exit. The trees fell right across the road as planned, completely blocking it, and both vehicles crashed heavily into them. The next two rows of vehicles slammed into the ones in front, before they could stop. Now Duncan blew the trees in the entrance blocking the way out. Then he systematically blew all the charges and the claymore mines the entire length of the cut.

It would take hours to get to the soldiers who had survived, and more hours to clear the mess. But that was not all. Duncan had rigged other charges to blow later. It would be days before the track was clear. And the track was the only way through this ridge for hundreds of miles in both directions. If the enemy cleared the cut or found a way around the ridge, it wouldn't matter. Duncan had just bought them at least two days.

That night, they were camped just outside their next ambush site. This time the road narrowed because of large trees. Unlike the last time, they would be nowhere near the ambush site when the mines went off. They would be triggered by a tripwire low enough to catch the leading vehicle, but high enough so that an animal would not trigger it. Once the first charges went off blocking the road with fallen trees, the others would go off right behind it.

They took their time setting the charges, showing the new soldiers how to do it first, then supervising their setting the last ones. Even so, they had a day's rest before the large dust plume in the distance told them the enemy was coming. Then they leisurely boarded their vehicles and drove through the trees, Duncan stopping long enough to string the trip wire before he followed the other vehicles into the distance. When the mines went off, they were too far to be seen, but they heard the blasts.

They continued toward the next district. Sometimes they would stop and bury a mine or two in the road. This they did at varying intervals, sometimes close together, sometimes a day apart. With the little bird overhead all day, every day, it was easy to see the progress the enemy was making and Duncan planted mines randomly in a field he suspected the enemy would use as a camp spot. They planted all the mines they had left and then drove hard for the rendezvous point at the edge of the third district.

The ruler, the male commander, the Guildsman with another man, Jane and Karen were waiting for them when they came into the camp. Their vehicles were dusty, dirty and battered, as were the people in them. They had been in constant motion for over a week. Duncan looked around him and saw lines and lines of people working with sword and shield. There were shield walls with spears bristling, advancing and withdrawing, and wooden swords, headless spears and wooden long-handled axes, all dueling with one other.

On the other side of the camp, ten vehicles charged one hundred mocked-up vehicles, just shy of two hundred yards away. Then smoke grenades were fired to land fifty yards ahead, obscuring them. Once the vehicles reached the smoke, the ramps went down and ten soldiers from each vehicle sprinted down the ramps and into the smoke. All ten soldiers would fire at the targets as they hit the edge of the smoke, then five ran forward ten yards, flinging themselves on the ground and firing while the other five sprinted past them to do the same thing.

Duncan formed his people up. His troopers mixed with the soldiers, he and Katerina out front. he called them to attention and saluted. All the soldiers responded with the same salute the Canadians made. They stayed that way. Jane leaned over and spoke into the ruler's ear. She turned red and brought her right fist, clenched, to her chest in a return salute. Then Duncan had the formation assume parade rest. Trailed by Katerina, he marched up to within a yard of the ruler, raised his right foot to belt height and stomped it down hard saluting as he did so.

"Ma'am! Training Squadron A, all present and accounted for! Ma'am!"

Once again, the ruler returned the salute, then looked at Jane, who once again whispered into her ear.

"I would inspect my troops, Warrant Officer," she said.

"Yes Ma'am!" Duncan said. "It would be an honour, Ma'am!"

Striding one step behind her, he escorted her down the line of troopers. Jane prompted her, the first time, to stop and speak to a soldier. Then she stopped on her own from time to time. As usual, the diminutive Dianne was singled out. She performed the same belt-high foot stomp and salute Duncan had performed. Then the inspection was over and Duncan escorted the ruler back to her entourage, called his people together and dismissed them.

"It's your turn to cook tonight, Duncan," Carol called out as they walked away. "Steak, medium rare, baked potato and refried beans."

"Hell, that's all he knows how to cook anyway," Scott said.

"You've done a good job here Colonel, Commander," Duncan said. "Those soldiers are looking good."

"My people are highly motivated," the ruler said. "Plus, they have excellent teachers. I suppose we can expect the onslaught a few days from now?"

"I shouldn't think so," Duncan said. "Two days ago, they had not reached the center of the first district. They seem to be encountering severe resistance along the way."

"Yahoo!" CT could be heard yelling from inside his Coyote.

"If I am not mistaken, the enemy has just found some more heavy resistance."

"Holy shit, Dunc!" CT said, poking his head out of the turret hatch. "That was brilliant! They pulled off right where you said they would to camp. Twenty vehicles and occupants, poof! Gone! Two of them were high-ranking command-and-control vehicles. Plus, another twenty or thirty severely damaged by the secondary blasts. I taped it. You have to see this."

"Maybe later, CT," Duncan said. "Get me a copy so we can show the ruler in somewhat better surroundings."

"Oh, no problem, Master Warrant," Katerina said. "We can show it to everyone now. CT, beam the tape to my vehicle, please."

Katerina hit a few buttons on her wrist console and the air shimmered around her vehicle briefly before a life-sized holographic image of what had just happened began to play out. Vehicles were deploying to each side of the road and troopers were beginning to come out of them when the first vehicle hit the first mine, exploding it in a cloud of fire and spraying ceramic everywhere. Then another and another. All that was missing was the sound and the vibration.

"Wow," CT said. "It looks even better on that deal."

"Wow indeed," said the man with the Guildsman. "I take it you have been doing that type of thing for the last two weeks?"

Duncan just looked at the man.

"Oh, excuse me Mr. Kovaks," the Guildsman said. "This is my boss. Actually, The Boss."

"Yes, Sir, we have," Duncan said. "Does the Guild have a problem with this?"

"No, not at all," the Boss said. "You have done much better than we anticipated. All of us, myself included, thought that when you arrived we would be involved in a last-ditch defence."

"Master Warrant Kovaks," the ruler said. "We have something of import and sensitivity to discuss. Would you mind? We will not keep you long. Katerina, you come along."

They moved a short distance away, where a large tent was set up, and entered. The interior was plush and had all the comforts of home. The ruler sat down on a plush chair and motioned the others to sit as well. The plush chairs were arranged in a circle and servants quickly came with pitchers and glasses of pale-coloured drinks for everyone, then left.

"Your health," the ruler said lifting her glass and they all took a taste.

"Nice beer," Duncan said. "Much better than ours."

The ruler smiled at him and nodded her head.

"To business, then we can talk after," she said.

"An offer for a ceasefire, truce and peace has come in," the boss said. "We have to present it and can offer no advice or opinions on it."

He laid a piece of paper on the table in front of the ruler. She looked at Duncan and raised her eyebrows.

"Why bother?" Duncan said. "They broke the last peace deal your husband signed with them. Then misled us as to the reasons for the last ceasefire and truce. We are hurting them, and they want to regroup, rearm, get more troops and hit us again. I say no."

"What would you have us do?" the ruler asked.

"Stay the course," Duncan said. "We have just hurt them, not defeated them. Once we draw them into a pitched battle, we will hit them hard and hurt them badly. Then we will destroy them. While they were negotiating with the Guildsman, among themselves they were planning to kill us without mercy. They had accepted our offer for them to keep what they had gained. At the official signing they planned to kill you, Ma'am, and all the rest of us."

"That is not true," the Guildsman said. "That is not what I heard them say."

"But you do not understand the other language they were speaking, do you? I do."

"Were they speaking this tongue?" the boss said in French.

"Yes," Duncan replied. "I have a recording of the meeting if you wish to hear."

Duncan told CT to play the recording and he turned his volume up so everyone could hear it. As the enemy commander hit the description of the worst of the atrocities he was going to commit, Katerina's breath took a sharp intake and the ruler's face went first pale and then deep red, her fists curled and her arms began to shake. And when the commander of the mercenaries added a few descriptions of his own and both men laughed, the boss's eyes narrowed. Duncan cut the transmission at that point.

The ruler extended her right arm and, shaking in rage, she pointed at the unopened document on the table.

"Get that thing out of my sight," she said. Her voice was quivering with emotions.

"I will personally deliver your response," the boss said as he stood and gathered up the document. "I must remind you, Madame, that the Guild is prohibited from intervening for one belligerent over another. However, the Guild can and will intervene against any Guild member that exhibits this kind of behaviour, when the Guild finds that said Guild member shall overcome his opponents."

"Mr. Kovaks, Madame Horshack, good day." Then he, followed by the Guildsman, left the tent.

"Sitting in the bush, eh?" Duncan said to Katerina in French.

"Yes Mr. Kovaks," Madame Horshack said also in French. "My niece, Katarina, was, as you say, sitting in the bush."

"All aristocrats here are given intense instruction in all the classical languages," she continued in Ukrainian. "Just as you were sitting in the bush, so too was my niece. This, as you know, was prudent until we knew where you stood."

"Unfortunately for us," she said now in English, "all our male aristocrats over the age of fifteen and many of our women perished, along with my husband, two oldest sons and all of Katerina's family and siblings. All that is left of my family are my two youngest sons, one twelve, the other ten, Katerina and me Unfortunately, Katerina must serve in the army. We must have a family presence. I can hardly be risked and my sons are too young."

"I understand, Madame Horshack," Duncan said. "Commander Horshack, you and your people will have the next two days off. Relax, rest, have some fun, because after those two days, the real work begins. Ninety of you people will now train ten of your best soldiers each in what you have learned. Your people will have two weeks, three at best to do that. You and seven of your best will join me three days from now at dawn, where you will put into use what we have trained you to do. Madame Commander, Good day."

Duncan and Jane stood and left the tent.

"Can you hold them for two weeks, Duncan?" Jane asked.

"Oh, we have slowed them considerably already," Duncan said. "They will be much more cautious now, especially after what happened today. We planted a few more delayed surprises for them along the way as well. It won't be until five days until they hit the border to sector two. I'll give them a couple of days then begin stage two. I think I can delay them about a month. But.."

"Yes, I know," Jane said. "Hope for the best; prepare for the worst. Two of their vehicles will be ready for you when you leave. They are fully prepared. Also, we will be swapping yours out for the new ones that just came in a couple of days ago. The weapons and all systems checked out."

"Okay, assemble double loads of everything, including spare barrels for the automatic weapons," Duncan said.

"I think it would be more prudent to establish a cache for you instead, Master Warrant," Jane said. "It won't compromise your mobility that way."

"Good idea, Colonel," Duncan said. "Now, I need a shower, some new clothing and my wife, not necessarily in that order."

Karen walked in on him and joined him in the shower.

It was dark their last night in camp. Duncan and Karen sat snuggled together, looking at the campfire. All of A and B Troops were with them, as were Jane, Barb, Megan, Bob and Dave. There was some light-hearted banter going on, but Duncan was quiet. He was under no illusion of the enormity of the task ahead of them. Nor were the older hands. They had all been on missions like this before or, in the cases of Jane, Dave and Barb, had observed them. Only Dianne's B Troop, Carol and Megan were joking around.

"Do not be alarmed," Madame Horshack said as she and Katerina approached the fire. "We come in peace and bearing gifts."

Both women were smiling and had two large boxes stacked on their arms, which they placed by the fire. They opened two of the boxes and began handing out bottles of beer to the delight of everyone around the fire pit.

"Now, Katerina tells me you have some truly high quality Washka you have been hiding from us," Madame Horshak said.

Duncan reached under his chair and pulled out a bottle he had stashed there.

"Ma'am," he said proffering the bottle to her with one hand and a coffee cup with the other.

She just took the bottle, spun the lid off to fall in the dirt and took a deep pull right from the bottle.

"Oh, heaven in a bottle!" she coughed out. "Tonight, I am Tanya and you are Duncan. There is no Madame Horshack tonight."

"Well, Tanya," Duncan said. "If you don't have a good story to go along with the good beer, you still can't stay and drink with us."

Tanya started right in with an embarrassing story about Katerina and a boy, which had everyone howling by the end. Then Katerina told one about her aunt and the party was downhill after that. After a while Duncan went silent again. He responded when he was addressed and laughed along with the rest, but mostly he sat looking at the fire.

He didn't notice Tanya watching him from across the fire. She too had gone quiet.

"Come Katia, tomorrow comes early," Tanya said. "I have it on good authority that the leader of this group takes a dim view of late and hungover troopers."

That enlisted more comments at Katerina's expense, Brett getting up and mimicking Katerina's movements the last time she overindulged. Tanya got Duncan's attention, motioned her head to the side, and they moved out of earshot.

"Can we win, Duncan?" she asked.

"It will be a near thing," Duncan said. "It has been done before and I am using those tactics. Many people, yours and mine, may die. But yes, I think we can win."

Tanya stood looking at the ground for a minute and when she looked up, tears were staining her cheeks.

"Please bring her back to me, Duncan," she whispered. "I love her dearly."

"I can't guarantee that, Tanya," Duncan said. "She is very good at what she does and we all need her to do her job. When we put on these uniforms we are dead men walking. We all know that. If God wills it, we survive. If not…well, we have a saying, Tanya. It's always a good day to die."

Footsteps coming their way told of Katarina and Karen joining them. Tanya quickly rubbed the tears from her eyes and cheeks and laughed as if Duncan had just cracked a joke.

"Oh, if you were not already taken I would be all over you, Duncan," she said. "Karen, you had best keep your eye on this one. Come Katerina; we must go to bed now."

After a few steps, she turned and watched Duncan and Karen walk away, he with his arm around her shoulders and she with her head on his. Tanya's heart skipped a beat and the tears began to flow again as she remembered her lost husband.

Chapter Three

DUNCAN, WITH KAREN by his side, was tossing his personal gear into the rear of the new G-Wagon. It was dark flat green and was so new that it still had the new-car smell. The odometer showed less than a hundred.

Brett was tinkering under the hood.

"Man, the paint isn't even burnt on the engine yet," he said. "Sweet. Never had a brand-new G-Wagon before."

The upholstery was brand new, not the usual cracked and duct-taped seats, the floor was clean, the paint not scuffed, scraped or missing, and the hatch leading to the pintle-mounted C9 on the roof had all the paint still on it. The roof itself had not yet been marred by C9 ammo belts rubbing on it and the exterior had neither scratch nor dent. The C9 itself was also brand new; its barrel still had the original bluing and the stock was not dented and scratched.

CT's Coyote was in the same new condition. Not a scratch or a dent anywhere on its dark flat green paint. The interior was still a pristine robin's egg blue and smelled of new machinery and upholstery instead of old diesel fumes and sweat.

A ghostly grey silhouette of a wolfhound's snarling head was painted on the rear quarter-panels of both G-Wagons and on both sides of the Coyote's turret. On the front sloping armor of the Coyote and the hoods of the G-Wagons was painted a grey ghostly warrior, sword arm upraised holding a smoking sword, astride a wolfhound in full stride.

"Very artistic," the Guildmaster said as he walked up to Duncan with the Guildsman in tow.

"One of my ladies in the intelligence section is very talented," Duncan said. "We normally don't show any identification markings. But this time, I want the enemy to know who we are."

"We have just returned from informing your opponents that no peace is in the offing at this point," the Guildmaster said. "I will reiterate what I said earlier: the Guild will not become involved between the two belligerents themselves, but will intervene should the Guild determine that its member is winning."

"Yes," Duncan said. "I heard you the first time. I also take it from the wording that you do not consider us Guild members?"

"Technically, that is correct. But, you are considered associate members and thus must follow the same rules of conduct as full members. Would you have a place nearby where we could have a private conversation?"

"Step into my office," Duncan said pointing at the Coyote. The three of them walked into the rear of the vehicle and Duncan motioned CT and his driver to leave, closing the rear door after them. He motioned the Guildsmen to sit on one of the benches, while he sat opposite them.

"We feel it appropriate to double your contingent," The Guildmaster said. "We feel that you require a number of technical people to repair and service your equipment. We have located suitable personnel for this purpose and can have them here shortly."

"Very considerate of you," Duncan said. "Unfortunately, I have some problems with that. First, I do not have the time to train them properly in our primary purpose. Everyone on this squadron is a combat specialist as well as a technical specialist. It takes a lot longer than a month to train even a soldier up to a minimum of competency. Secondly, I pick my own people. That way I ensure I don't end up with unsuitable people and a squadron full of people like my opponents have."

"Very well, I understand, Mr. Kovaks. We will supply you with a list of names to pick from. But you must pick carefully because of what I am about to say next."

The Guildmaster looked at Duncan intently for a moment and then told him: Earth was off limits for the recruitment of mercenary teams. His team had been an exception granted by the Interplanetary Council, because of the uniqueness of the circumstances. Everyone had assumed that the squadron had voluntarily agreed to the terms of the contract, which unfortunately had not been fully disclosed to them.

Or more specifically, to Chinook Winds GMBH in the first place, and, of course, Chinook Winds had not disclosed anything to the Wind Riders or Duncan himself.

Unfortunately, the Interplanetary Council was insisting that the provisions outlined in the contract be enforced. There were several, but two provisions were the most pressing. First, the Wind Riders had to join of the Guild. Secondly, they would never be allowed to return to Earth. Because of the uniqueness of this situation and the fact that the full terms of the contract had never been disclosed, the Interplanetary Counsel had agreed to double the original size of the squadron. In light of Duncan's statement, the Guild was willing to wave the full enlistment membership requirement until after the current hostilities were finished and to give him a year to fill out his squadron strength.

Seething in anger, Duncan only sat and stared at the two men. Then he closed his eyes and laid his head against the cold steel walls of the Coyote, his mind reeling. Finally, he snapped his eyes open and raised his head.

"So, we have nowhere to call home, is what you are telling me?" he said.

"Every reasonable effort is being made to find you somewhere to base out of," the Guild Master said.

"Before I commit to anything," Duncan said. "I want a copy of this Interplanetary Council decision as well as a copy of the original contract signed by Chinook Winds and a copy of your Guild's membership duties, responsibilities and requirements."

The Guildmaster pushed a few buttons on his wrist console and looked at Duncan, eyebrows raised. Duncan leaned over and activated the Coyote's computers and a temporary encrypted wifi connection isolated to one USB port only. Then he plugged a high capacity thumb dive into the USB port and gave the Guildmaster the password. Once the information had been transferred, Duncan shut down the wifi connection and removed the thumb drive.

"I will need time to digest this information," he said. "Then I will have to disclose this to my people and we will inform you of our decision, one way or another. Good day, gentlemen."

He waited until the two men had left, before he activated the squadron wide radio net from inside the Coyote.

"All deployments and training to stop immediately. All Wind Riders to report to the main mess tent ASAP."

Then he flipped to the planet's command and control network.

"This is Wind Rider One. Effective immediately, all deployment and training missions by the Wind Riders are suspended indefinitely. Wind Rider One, out."

Duncan slammed the off switch and angrily walked away to gather his thoughts.

He walked through and around the camp for over an hour, acknowledging no one. Most of the time he was unaware of his surroundings, just walking and staring at his feet. He became aware of someone calling his name repeatedly, and came back to the present. He was facing the squadron's mess tent, about a hundred yards away. The Guildmaster, his second, Tanya and Katerina were standing right in front of him.

"Duncan," Tanya said. "I have just heard. Rest assured I…"

"At this moment Madame Horshack, I am uninterested in what you or those other two have to say to me. We undertook to help you people because it was the right thing to do and that is what we do. We help people. Now I must tell all those people that not only were we brought here without our knowledge or permission, but we can never go home. Never. Now don't you worry your pretty little head. We will complete this mission. We always keep our word. What happens after…"

"Also," Duncan continued. "I have two parents in there that I have to tell will never see their two young boys ever again. So Madame Horshack, Mr. Whatever-the-hell-your-name-is Guildmaster, forgive me or not, but I don't give a rat's ass about your problems right now!"

Duncan walked straight at them, aiming for the gap between the Guildmaster and Tanya. The Guildmaster was a little slow in turning aside and received Duncan's shoulder and right elbow in the gut as Duncan rumbled his way toward the mess tent.

"Auchtung!" Duncan yelled as he walked in and all twenty-nine members sprang to attention and stayed that way while he made his way to the front. When he reached the front, he smartly about-faced.

"At ease!" he continued in German. "Be seated."

That he was extremely agitated was very clear, from his stance at a rigid parade rest to the frown on his face.

"Not only have we been removed from our homes and families without our knowledge or consent, to fight for some damn planet and people we don't even know the names of, I have just been informed that we can never, ever return home again!"

All of the faces before him registered shock to some degree at what he had just said. And as he knew it would, Barb bent down and grabbed her knees and began to cry. Dave remained stoic and Megan stared at her mother, before what he had just said and her mother's actions sunk in.

"Oh my God!" she said in English. "The boys!"

"Yes Megan, the boys." Duncan said also in English as he saw the four planetary people standing at the back of the assembly. "The boyfriends, the girlfriends, the mothers and fathers, the sisters and brothers, uncles and aunts, cousins. We will see none of them ever again."

"We have agreed to fight for these people," he continued, now in German. "Because in our hearts we know that their cause is just. But we should be under no illusion that we are just tools for them, tools that will be discarded the second they do not need us anymore. As for the so-called Guild and Interplanetary Council? Like every bloated bureaucracy we have ever dealt with, they will change the rules to suit themselves, or to cover their asses. We cannot trust them as far as we can spit."

The reality of their situation was beginning to dawn on everyone now.

"For myself," Duncan said. "Everyone who means anything to me is here. I do not know everyone else's situation. It has been agreed that we can have a onetime allotment of thirty additional people. Mechanics and technicians to repair our equipment, they think. Barb and Dave's two boys will be two of them. If you have someone important to you that you want here, you let me know. But it will be a one-way trip. They also will never be allowed to return home. So, make your decision wisely. Remember what we do. Because for the next, for God knows how long, we will have to keep doing that until we have enough money to break off on our own."

"Duncan," Barb said. "Dave, Megan and I have to discuss this. It may be better for the boys to stay home."

"Of course," Duncan said. "All of you: take the rest of the day to think about this and get back to me tonight with your decision. Because tomorrow, I plan to start killing. The planet's people have been trained well enough. It is now time to do what we do best and we do it without mercy and without let-up. They wanted killers. I plan on showing them exactly what they bought! Dismissed!"

Everyone filed out of the tent — everyone but the four planetary people and Karen. Duncan gestured with his chin for Karen to leave, but she just came to attention and stood there. As Duncan marched by her to confront the four, she turned and was by his side when he stopped. The Guildsmaster proffered a large brown envelope to Duncan.

"If you would review these documents and sign them, Mr. Kovaks...."

"You can shove those papers up your ass," Duncan said. "As for you Madame Horschak, we will be returning the fees we have already collected from you and we will not be requiring you to pay us the agreed fee after the completion of the deployment. You will however, deliver supplies to us at a place to be determined. The Guild will resupply us as agreed and the Guild will not charge the people of the planet for those supplies, also as agreed. And if the Guild should even think about changing that deal, I will be supplying Madame Horschak video and audio evidence that will back up that agreement."

He let them stew on that for a few seconds and then told them that the whole squadron would be leaving in the morning to begin operations against the enemy.

"I must insist that members of my planet accompany you," Tanya said.

"If you insist, so shall it be," Duncan said. "But only two small scout troops as we originally agreed." Now he looked Katerina right in the eyes.

"If they are not here when we leave, too bad. If they cannot keep up, too bad. If they get in our line of fire, they will be dead."

"You think long and hard about who it is you send us, Madame Horschak," he said looking Tanya in the eyes. "They will most likely be dead before this is over." Then he and Karen left the mess tent.

• • •

"I am so sorry, Karen," Duncan said. They were sitting on their camp chairs beside the fire pit. Duncan had just started the fire and the flames were rising fast as the dry kindling caught and popped. They had a case of the local beer between them and Karen handed him one as he sat down.

"You don't deserve this."

"All the people I love are here, Duncan," Karen said. "You know that. There is just you, mom and now Bob."

"Oh, I am part of the family now, am I?" Bob was grinning as he and Jane came to the fire, their chairs in his hands, Jane with a bottle of what looked like the local version of wine in hers.

Karen gave Bob a quick kiss on the cheek as he put Jane's chair next to hers.

"Just don't ask me to call you Dad, you old coot," she said.

"What's going to happen to all of our assets?" Jane asked. "I would hate for some low-life relative I have never met or even worse, the government, to get it all."

"Ya, I know," Duncan said. "For me, it will all depend on what Barb and Dave decide."

"What do you need us to decide?" Barb said. The three of them were approaching, along with Dianne, Carol, Brett and Scott.

"You bringing the boys or not?" Duncan asked.

"No, we think it best they stay home," Dave said. "They will inherit the farm and all the money. They will be all right."

"Well," Duncan said. "They are about to become the richest men in Alberta and two of the richest men in the world. I'm going to give them everything I own. The companies run themselves, mostly, except this one. Shelly will keep a good eye on them for the boys until they are old enough to take control themselves. Plus, they, and you, were not only already partners in most of the companies, but have substantial offshore bank accounts. All of you do."

"Ah, the Saudi job," Dianne said. "I was wondering where all that money went. Count me in, I have no one back home."

Both Brett and Scott said the same thing.

"Sorry Barb, Dave," Carol said. "My brothers and sisters need the money. I'm the only one they have."

"Well, with what the Colony will give them and from what they will receive from you, they will never have to worry again," Duncan said.

"Worry about what?" CT asked as the rest of the squadron came up. Duncan told them what they planned to do.

"Well, I don't think it's right to leave my folks on the hook for all my student loans," CT said. "So, I'll give them half and the kids the other half. Yes, I know about the Saudi money, Duncan."

"As well as all of you being shareholders in not only the Wind Riders, but all of my other companies, all of you have twenty million dollars in offshore accounts," Duncan said. "The Saudis were very generous when they looked the other way. There was also the little matter of a few dollars that went missing from two banks a few months before that. You see CT, some of us are a little better than others at hacking into bank records."

That brought a round of laughs, as everyone knew that, try as he might, CT could never hack his way around Duncan and Karen's security systems.

The four Marines and their wives said the same thing that Carol had. All of their extended families were below the poverty line back in the US and could use the help.

"As to how this is all going to happen," Duncan said. "One thing that CT is very good at is hacking into communication systems. He cracked the Guild's codes weeks ago. All of you write out your wills and CT will send them to Shelly. I trust her completely; she will not let us, or your families, down. I am sure the Guild will manufacture some disaster that will have us all killed."

"So, what are we going to do to make sure they don't try that?" Amanda asked.

"Well, it seems that some nasty Trojan Worm was magically introduced into the Guild's computer systems," Duncan said.

Then he explained how he had introduced the same virus into Karen's dad's computer system. It was buried in some minor program data. How it had worked in the background infecting every computer that it communicated with, eventually infecting almost every computer on earth. The same thing would be happening here, except on a much larger scale.

"Karen, Barb and Jane and, to a lesser extent, CT and I are going to be very busy over the next little while designing filters to sort out who and what is important."

"Somebody grab a couple more chairs," Duncan said in English; they had been speaking in German. "And make room for our guests."

"Welcome Tanya, Katerina. I apologise for my earlier behavior."

"No Duncan, it is I who should apologise," Tanya said. "It was I who put you in this mess. I am truly sorry, all of you. I am very, very sorry."

"Ma'am," Dave said. "All you did was ask the Guild to send you some help. The best help you could get for your budget. It would seem that the Guild took advantage of you as well as us."

"Well I insist on paying you the full amount we agreed upon," Tanya said. "It is the least I can do. Also, I will do all I can to see that you are settled in a suitable place after all this is over."

"Now don't you worry about the silver, honey," Jane said. "You are going to need it to rebuild. Besides, we already have double that amount of silver and we plan on adding to it."

"The boxes!" Tanya said. "I was wondering why you went through so much trouble for stupid boxes."

"Yes, well," Duncan said. "Guild rules are very clear about plunder. It was just a shame we couldn't get at the other army's payroll as well."

"Now, I was not joking about tomorrow, Tanya," Duncan continued. "We will be leaving right after daybreak and we will not be returning until just before or just after the main battle begins, if at all. What we will be doing is very dangerous and could get your people killed."

"How can we live with ourselves, Duncan?" Katerina asked. "How can we live with ourselves when you are sacrificing yourselves, while we stay safe at home? No, I will be coming as we agreed and I will keep up and I will not get in your way and I will do my damnedest to kill my enemies where and when I find them!"

"Real fireball you've got there, Tanya," Barb said.

"Good genes," Tanya said and smiled.

"Now, as far as the main battle is concerned," Duncan said.

He spoke about how the main commander knew all the plans, but that he would upload everything to their computer databases just in case and for reference, to work her people hard, just as the Wind Riders had, because in the end it would save lives. This plan had worked successfully many times before. But it would not be easy and many lives would be lost. The troops had to be able to do the moves in their sleep. With endless repetition and practice, everything would become second nature. Every officer and senior non-commissioned officer needed to know all the commands. They should not only practice together, but against each other. Make a competition out of it. Give them an incentive to win. Something like the losing platoon or company had to make dinner for the winners. Split the army in half and once a week have a mock battle and the winners receive a trophy of some kind. Nothing fancy, preferably something cheap and gaudy.

"Like that stupid, oversized cheap tin beer mug we all competed for at the academy," Megan said. "God how we competed to win that stupid thing. It was old and dented and full of holes; wouldn't even hold any beer anymore. But it held the place of pride in every winner's mess."

"It was like that when your mother and I went through all that as well," Dave said. "We had some right good brawls over that stupid cup. It was probably something some commander's wife was going to throw away."

"Yes," Tanya said. "I understand. Like those ribbons we competed so hard for in in university sports. They are cheap and gaudy, but we competed hard for them and I still have all of mine displayed in my trophy room."

"Unit pride and pride in their accomplishments," Duncan said. "That is what means the most. All of the Wind Riders have personal achievement awards. But the awards that mean the most to us are the ones we received as a unit. Because, in the end, I am not fighting for God, or country or an idea. It may start off like that, but when the shit hits the fan, I am fighting for my comrade to the right and my comrade to the left. I will do everything I can to keep them safe, so that they can go home. The worst thing I could ever do would be to let them down. I will die for them and they for me."

Heads were nodding all around the circle, agreeing to his comment.

"We will be doing our best out there," Megan said. "We will try and wear them down as much as we can. But in the end, you will have to stop them, not us. There just are not enough of us."

With her words, Duncan rose and collapsed his chair nodded to everyone and walked to his tent. Karen took another beer out of the case and popped the top.

"Command is a heavy burden," Jane said. "Never more so than just before commencing operations, or in a group such as ours where we know each other so well. He will feel each loss and injury personally, for we are all he has. We are his family, his children if you will. He will never tell us, but he loves us all and we him. And he is right. I will never, ever, let him down."

Then she stood, grabbed first her chair and then Bob's hand and they walked away. Soon other couples were leaving, to spend their last hours together. Leaving only Karen, Tanya, Katerina and the single people beside the fire. Tanya was looking at Karen.

"He needs his time alone," Karen said. "If I went to him now, he would just not be there anyway, if you know what I mean. His body would be with me, but his mind would be a million miles away. I will be there for him when he needs me and he will be there for me, when I need him. Good night everyone. I'm going for a walk."

"They have a strange relationship," Tanya said.

"Duncan loves her more than he loves anything, including himself," Dianne said quietly. "He thought she had betrayed him, a long time in the past, and it almost destroyed him. Even when he got over it, he was a hard and cold man after. I will die for him." Then she walked away as well.

"Yes, men take a woman's infidelity very hard," Tanya said.

"Oh, it's not like that at all," Megan said. "Duncan understands that all of us are human beings that have wants and needs that need to be satisfied. No, he thought she had betrayed his trust. He had given her his all, he can do no less, and he thought she had just been using him. Karen's father had a company much like ours and he wanted Duncan badly. So he encouraged Karen; well, I think she had the hots for him anyway, so it wasn't much of a push. Then when Duncan was doing some charity work in a far-off poor country, Karen's father had some of his men murder Duncan's friends and the whole village that they were staying in. He had hoped that Duncan would think it was a radical insurgent group that had been operating in the area. But he didn't know that Duncan had put hidden cameras all over the camp. And that even though Duncan was getting out of this life, he was still very, very good and had spotted the men before they made the attack. He was alone and only armed with a hunting knife and could do nothing to stop it."

"Later that night," Carol continued for her. "He tracked them down and killed all eight of them. Then he just disappeared. He found out it was Karen's father who was behind the deed and that he had used Karen to get at him. He pretty much self-destructed at that point. Only a young, poor neighbor of his, she was studying psychology at the time, saved him. She didn't do much, just was there and made sure he ate properly once a week, things like that. But it was enough. Duncan got his shit together and over the period of a year, he killed every single one of Karen's father's men, discrediting him from every prospective employer. Karen's mom divorced him and he basically had nothing but his government pension left to him by the time Duncan was finished."

"Meanwhile," Megan said. "Karen had never given up on him. She never believed Duncan was dead. She kept looking everywhere for him. She was calling Mom every week asking for information. She started the company Duncan had wanted to start and moved from her country to ours to be closer to him. But Duncan did not know she was innocent, that she had not known what her father had done. He still loved her, but he was going to kill her just the same."

"It took three years," Carol said. "In that time Duncan had set up a number of investment companies around the world and was making a lot of money from them. He had decided that Karen's father had been correct, that he could make a difference, just not the same way. So, he started the Wind Riders. His first employee was the young woman who had helped when he was down. She had become a lawyer by then, so Duncan started a law firm. Wind Riders is her biggest client. But he insisted that she also charge reasonable rates for regular people in the neighborhood and that they only hire the best people. And they have. The law firm does very well on its own without our business and has an excellent reputation."

"Then he came home," Bob said. "For the first time in three years he used his own identity and our government picked up on it, like he knew they would. I was a member of the original Wind Riders and the only one still in the army. So, the government sent me and a security agent to interrogate him when he came into the country. The first person he talked to when he landed was Dianne. She was a customs agent at the time. She was the only one, me included, that treated him with dignity and respect. The rest of us were a bit hard on him. I drove him home after that and we had a long talk. I quit the army right then and joined him. Scott and Brett came right behind me."

"At first it was just the four of us," Brett said. "Duncan had inherited his family farm after his folks died and we set up shop in an old barn and lived in the old farm house. Barb and Dave were his neighbors and he had grown up with them. He leased the land to Dave, and Barb looked after the house for him. Then she kind of became our den mother and unofficial fifth member."

"Duncan did surveillance on Karen for six months," Scott said. "By then, Jane had moved in with Karen, and Duncan bought the apartment right across the hall from them. He had set it up, so that they would watch him kill the father, and then he was going to kill them."

"When Karen saw him, she was overjoyed," Megan said. "But then she saw the gun he had pointed at her head. Jane stepped between them. She had known what her husband had done, but had never told Karen about it, and she let Duncan know that Karen had not known about it. She said it would be understandable to kill her, but leave Karen alone.

"Karen was devastated. She broke down and ran into her room. Duncan calmed down and listened to what Jane had to say to him. Then he took Jane to his own apartment, hooked his computer up and remote detonated bombs he had set up all around Karen's father's house, killing him. After that, he went to Karen's room, threw the gun on her bed, apologised and told her to kill him. She was very angry at the time and Duncan couldn't live with himself after what he had put her through. She pulled the gun on him and forced him to marry her and here we are."

"Duncan has put his life on the line for us, and he will again," Amanda said. "He was the only one who saw the potential Dianne had. He brought the best out of her, like he does with all of us. Like he will with you, Katerina. Don't think for a minute that just because you are Tanya's niece is the reason you are with us. If he didn't want you here, you wouldn't be here. He sees something in you that you do not see. We all do. Just like with Tanya and your people as a whole. He will die for you. We will die for you. Don't you let us down."

Then, as a group, the rest of the Wind Riders left, leaving the camp fire to the two women.

"For the first time I have hope," Tanya said. "Right now, this night, they have given me hope. If they are willing to sacrifice so much for us, how can we do any less? How can I do anything less. Come, my love, I have much work to begin in the morning."

Chapter Four

THE ONLY PEOPLE LEFT in the mess tent, hovering over a last coffee or tea, were the six vehicle commanders. All the rest were going over their vehicles. Once again these would be new vehicles, the second of the three shipments the Guild had promised. Everyone also had on new uniforms. The vehicles were a little overloaded as much more ammunition had been packed into them than normal. Sleeping bags and duffle bags were strapped to the backs and roofs instead of being stowed inside. Antennae were clipped down instead of being allowed to stand upright. Instead of two jerrycans of water and fuel there were three for the G-Wagons and five for the Coyotes.

This time, the G-Wagons would have their normal components of four troopers: a driver, automatic weapons specialist, electronics specialist and designated marksman. One of them would also be the vehicle commander, another the medical specialist another the marksman's spotter.

The Cougars would have their normal contingent of driver, commander/electronics specialist and gunner. This time they would also have four dismounts, normally the intelligence specialists and the three pilots. The dismounts would be responsible for security for the Cougars as well as assault teams, should it be required. They had a radio/electronics specialist, a designated marksman, an automatic weapons specialist and a medical specialist. They would also be responsible for operating and monitoring the small surveillance drones while the Cougars were in motion. CT had deployed his before daybreak. At this point, none of the planetary people knew they had this capability, or so they hoped. The little remote aircraft had been taking off and landing in the dark.

This would be the last time they would be safe at base for some time. Each of the commanders was lingering over their beverages.

Duncan's briefing had ended five minutes earlier. They all knew the route they would be using, as well as the projected waypoints, the possible ambush sites, camp spots, escape routes, rendezvous points and the resupply point. Once contact was made with the enemy, much of this would have to be changed to suit the circumstances, but initial planning still had to be made. Each commander had to be aware of the plan. Any of them could be killed or badly wounded and the mission had to keep going. Finally, Duncan knew he was talking just for the sake of talking and putting off the inevitable, so he had stood, putting an end to the briefing and they filed out to join their troops.

The eight planetary troops quickly lined up in front of their two vehicles and gave their cross-chest, fist-clenched salute, which Duncan returned with his right hand smartly to his forehead. The planetary vehicles were approximately the same size as the G-Wagons but white instead of dark green. Where the G-Wagons were boxy and all right angles, these were more rounded. The hoods were slightly lower than the rounded front fenders. Instead of a C9 mounted on the roof, the planetary vehicles had a more powerful version of the personal laser weapon systems they all carried. While the vehicles were painted to resemble the ceramic armour the normal military vehicles utilised, these were actually metal. Their uniforms were similar to the Wind Riders, made of cloth, not the usual ceramic armour. They had spare battery packs for their personal weapons mounted on a belt system like the Wind Riders'. They also had small pistol-like weapons mounted in the same fashion the Wind Riders utilised for theirs. The Earth troopers were already having an impact on the planetary way of doing things.

"Brett, you drive that vehicle until the first break," Duncan said, pointing at Katerina's vehicle. "Dianne, you're my driver; Katerina, with me. Okay, everybody, mount up."

Tanya, this time with two security people with her instead of the usual Guildsmen, walked up and gave Katerina a last hug after returning everyone's salutes. Today she was dressed in military clothing. A song started playing over CT's exterior speaker system as the troopers entered the vehicles and engines were switched on. The song was in German, but it was an upbeat tune with a fast beat.

"When can we expect you?" Tanya asked Duncan.

"In three to four weeks," Duncan said. "You can expect the enemy to be in contact with you. We won't be far behind. Don't worry about us or where we are. Follow the plan; you will be fine without us. But the next time you hear this song, know that we are close."

Then he saluted her for the last time, jumped into the front passenger seat and the group moved off down the road leading to the enemy. They were soon out of sight.

• • •

The small company was divided into two sections. The first was Duncan's. His G-Wagon was in the rear. In front of him was the planetary vehicle, then the Coyote and a hundred yards in front of that was Dianne's G-Wagon. The other vehicles were spaced twenty yards apart and staggered to left and right. A hundred yards behind them was the second troop in the same configuration, except that the rear vehicle was a hundred yards behind in a reverse formation to Duncan's, with the planetary vehicle the second from the front and the Coyote the second from the rear. None of the exterior gun mounts were manned at this point; they were still too far away from the enemy, but the Cougars had their turrets pointed to opposite sides of the roadway.

They were traveling fast, but well below the maximum speed that the Coyotes, the slowest vehicles, could maintain. Early on, Brett had accelerated away from them, gone off road, and done some fancy driving, before returning to formation. They had been traveling for four hours and were coming up on an extended ridge line. This was where they would stop, have lunch and rest for an hour. The two groups stopped, one to each side of the road, forming a rough circle around their Coyote. One trooper from each G-Wagon and two from each Cougar went out forty yards from the formation and set up perimeter guard. Both Cougars' sensor antennae extended from the rooftops. The drivers opened hoods to let the engines cool a bit more and everyone grabbed a box of rations and dug out the lunch snacks inside.

Duncan and the other G-Wagon commanders had binoculars to hand, elbows on the G-Wagon roofs, and were scanning the surroundings. Seeing what the Wind Riders were doing, the planetary people did the same. Then Duncan and Dianne climbed on top of CT's Coyote and scanned around again. Carol and Bill did the same on Jane's. Once in a while, one of them would draw or write something down on a notebook.

After about fifteen minutes, Duncan let the binoculars drop to his chest on their neck strap and climbed down. He looked at Dianne and raised an eyebrow; she gave him a thumbs-up. He glanced at Carol and Bill and they responded similarly. Then they all stashed their binoculars in their vehicles and joined their troopers sitting on the ground eating lunch. After half an hour, the troopers on perimeter duty were changed out so they could relax.

The drivers walked up to their vehicles and went over systems, now that the engine compartments were a little cooler, and then slammed the hoods down. Duncan stood and waved his right hand over his head in a circle and headed for his G-Wagon.

"Thank you for your company, Commander," Duncan said to Katerina. "You may return to your vehicle now. Brett, get your lazy ass back in my vehicle."

Katerina had noticed that the Wind Riders were all very quiet this time. They had hardly spoken a word on the whole trip or during the break. But their heads were constantly in motion and eyes were constantly darting everywhere.

"Not very friendly today, are they?" her driver said as they pulled into formation and drove down the road.

"I don't know why they are constantly looking for something," Katerina said. "We are days away from any trouble." Then they started talking about things of interest to them, to break the monotony of the trip down the empty road.

"So, how's their vehicle?" Duncan said.

"Fast, nimble, better than these things," Brett said. "The engine is more powerful. It looks like the metal is a little thicker too. They should be okay. Too bad they have such crappy weapon systems."

"They are the same as the bad guys have, so they will be okay," Duncan said. Then the conversation stopped as each man began scanning the surroundings again.

It was starting to get dark when they pulled off the road. This time they drove for ten minutes to the left of the road and set up one laager instead of two. In addition to deploying the sensor array, the Cougars deployed the more powerful sensors mounted in a large boxy compartment at the rear of the turret. These had a longer range and used radar instead of heat signature technology. Only four perimeter guards were deployed this time and camp stoves were soon in action, boiling water to cook the freeze-dried rations. Everyone but the cooks and guards were walking around stretching muscles that had been too long cramped from sitting down.

All the Wind Riders had their C8s either in hand or very close by and, once again, everyone was scanning every direction as they walked around. Only once the meals were ready did they relax, sit down, and begin to talk, but in low tones.

Not so, the planetary people. They were talking loudly and laughing heartily at jokes. They had lights strung up on the vehicles illuminating their camp area. It looked and sounded like they were on a camping trip. Weapons were propped against vehicles, or, even worse, inside them. Duncan let them be for the time being.

But after he finished his meal, he tossed his kit to Scott, the cook for the day, and walked over to the group of planetary people.

"Having fun, are we?" he said as he came up, startling them. "You didn't see me coming, did you?"

Then he pulled his C8 to the ready position and targeted each of them in turn with it.

"What are you going to do now? Your weapons are nowhere near. I walked up on you from just over there and you couldn't see me coming. It will take ten minutes for your eyes to adjust to the dark. We could hear almost every word you were saying; my sentries most likely did. You have put them, and us, at risk by silhouetting their positions with your lights - which, by the way, can probably be seen all the way from the road. This will not happen again. Now get these lights off and your goddamned weapons, if not in your hands then at least close by your sides. Commander, a word?"

"You are compromising the security of my mission, Commander!" Duncan said after he had taken Katerina ten yards outside the perimeter. "All day your people have been lax! Do you think this is some kind of camping trip, Commander? A delightful little excursion?"

"Master Warrant," Katerina said. "We will not be at the border for another day. The enemy is at best two days farther than that. There is no danger at the moment."

"Oh, so that's when you will suddenly become alert and professional, Commander? In three days? If I was that enemy commander, I would have at least three teams like ours out this far just waiting to spot the enemy's scout troops and chew them up."

"We are the eyes and ears of the army, Katerina. That is our primary job. To watch, observe and report. Not to be seen and eliminated. If that happens, our army is blind and deaf. That job starts the second we leave base. Yes, we are probably safe, for now. But sloppy habits are hard to break. Start being alert now and, when we get in bad guy country, we are already in the habit of being alert."

Katerina was looking at the ground now, scuffing a boot in the dust. Duncan clapped her on the shoulder.

"If we start operating now, like we will be soon, we will save a lot of lives, Katerina. All this is second nature to my people. Yours are still learning. We have a big responsibility, you and I. Soon I will have to order you into harm's way and you may get killed. And while that would bother me a lot, the mission always comes first. If we don't do, or are unable to do, what we are supposed to do, your aunt and most of your people will be dead or enslaved.

"Now, go get your other commander and meet me by my G-Wagon."

The lights had been extinguished by the time they came back, replaced by a single low-intensity light, and weapons were close by as Duncan walked to his G-Wagon. His six commanders were waiting for him.

"Thank Christ for that," Carol said. "Those damn lights were wrecking my night vision."

"It won't happen again, Captain," Katerina said as she and her second in command walked up. They had their weapons with them.

"Enough said on that subject," Duncan said. "Now, Deputy Commander, give me your report on what you observed when we stopped for lunch."

"It was all quiet, Sir," he said. "No activity, except for some birds."

"Our defensive positions were well placed," Katerina said. "We had good visibility for several miles in both directions and there were no movements observed."

"Bill?" Duncan asked. Bill was the least senior of his vehicle commanders.

Bill pulled out his note book and started reporting. The ridge to the west of the road rose rapidly about five hundred yards away and would be impassable to vehicles at a point a hundred yards further on and it was too steep for personnel to traverse, he informed the group. A similar distance to the east, the ridge dropped off to a large lake and swamp area, also impassable to vehicle and ground troops. The ground to the south gradually rose to a fairly steep incline to the crest for about two miles. Visibility from the crest in that direction was ten miles. The crest itself was mostly level and about a half a mile in depth. It sloped down to the rear, or north, in a much gentler decline for about a mile. Visibility in that direction was unlimited. Defending the position would not be difficult, while assaulting from the south would prove a challenge.

"Anyone else with anything else?" Duncan asked. "OK, then, CT, prepare a report with that. I will add my suggestions to deployment options later and you can send it back to command at that point."

He then pulled out a map and spread it across the G-Wagon's hood and went over the objectives for the next day. Right now, they were just behind the border to Sector Two and would cross it early the next morning. He wanted to be at the resupply point twenty miles west of the road by nightfall, so they would not be stopping for lunch the next day.

"Everybody keep an eye out for possible ambush sites from now on," he said. "We are going to be needing them."

The group disappeared back to their troops at that point and Duncan dragged his sleeping gear down off the roof and tossed it to the ground beside the vehicle. He looked over at CT's Cougar and waved, Karen waved back and then he saw that Katerina was still with him.

"You will not stay together?' she asked.

"No," Duncan said. "In the field, we stay with our own troops. Karen is the commander of CT's dismounts. You will also see that we have split all the family members up. Anne is usually Carol's observer, but Megan is taking her spot and Anne is with Jane's dismounts. It's hard enough in battle to concentrate. Worrying about your spouse or kids is a distraction we don't need."

"I am really sorry about today, Duncan. It won't happen again."

"I know it won't, Katerina. Tomorrow you must keep your eyes peeled. Things will have changed since we came back. Any small change in detail may make the difference between living and dying. You will have a lot more experience when we come back this way, but we are going to need every advantage we can obtain. Go get some sleep; it's going to be hard to come by after this."

As she walked away, Duncan called CT over to him.

"Make sure you get those wills out tonight, CT," Duncan said. "We could get hit anytime now."

"Just as soon as the bird comes back in, Ghost. They sped up some today now that they are past our last set of mines. He's also put four scouts about ten miles ahead of the main column, but still no flankers."

"Okay, I'll split off tomorrow and handle the scouts. I'll meet up with you at the next camp spot tomorrow."

Then, with a last look around he laid down, pulled his sleeping bag over himself and took his own advice. He was asleep in minutes.

• • •

A Troop was on the road heading south an hour before daybreak. It had taken them two hours to reach the road using only dim parking lights to light the way. Brett increased speed with the visibility and soon they were rocketing down the paved highway almost at full speed. They reached the spot for the ambush an hour and half before the enemy scouts would reach it and set up. Duncan and Amanda would position themselves on one side of the road about two hundred yards ahead of the G-Wagon, which would take out the four scout vehicles as they came into view around the sharp corner.

Duncan and Amanda were lying twenty yards off the road in the blackened and soot-covered ground, weapons at the ready. Duncan had a grenade in his grenade launcher. They heard them coming before they saw them. The four vehicles were traveling at thirty miles an hour in two lines of two and only three yards apart.

Duncan sighted in on the farthest vehicle from him and tracked it as it came. When Scott opened up on the first of the vehicles with his C9, Duncan fired the grenade to the rear one, then shifted to the rifle and joined Amanda spraying the nearest of the rear vehicles.

No one emerged from the vehicles as they exploded, slammed into each other or went off the road. One vehicle flipped as it hit the ditch. Duncan fired a grenade into each vehicle as everyone else, Brett included, fired into the vehicles. Then they stopped. Duncan and Amanda cautiously approached the devastated vehicles, weapons at the ready, but they were not needed. Everyone in the vehicles was dead.

"They don't smoke much," Amanda said pointing at the one vehicle that had caught fire. The flames were burning high and hot, but there was little smoke and only a barbeque smell coming from it. Most of the bodies were among the shattered pieces of ceramic that made up the vehicles. Shoving vehicles off the road to clear it would not be necessary.

"Gulf One, Alpha One," Duncan said into his head set radio.

"Alpha One, Gulf One, five by six."

"Gulf One, Alpha One, Tango has been eliminated."

"Alpha One, Gulf One, copy Tango eliminated."

"Alpha One, Foxtrot One. No further Sierra your vicinity."

"Oh balls, Foxtrot, I still have half a clip left. Alpha One, out."

"Do leave some for Voice, Wind Rider. I'm hungry."

"Fuk'n Barb," Scott said. "Somebody always has to be a smart ass."

"Reload and mount up," Duncan said, ejecting his almost spent clip and putting a full one in. "I want a look at the main column before dark."

Duncan and Amanda were laying on the rear slope of a small hill overlooking the enemy encampment as they set up. The mercenaries were laid out in an organised fashion, but not in a defensive one. They had a few guards walking around, but not many. No outposts or patrols were established and bright lights were hanging from every vehicle. Other than leaving enough room to move between them, there was not much distance between vehicles. Like the Wind Riders, the mercenaries set up their sleeping arrangements on the ground or on top of their vehicles.

The client's troops were totally different. They parked their vehicles where ever they felt like. Music was blaring and bottles were being passed around. It looked like one huge camping party. Several large tents were erected. The largest seemed to be the commander's.

Duncan and Amanda watched until it was too dark to see anymore and they crawled back to the bottom and made their way back the two miles to the G-Wagon.

"They are going to make it easy for us the first time," Duncan said as they got in and started driving away. They linked up with the rest of the troop ten miles down the road an hour later.

"OK," he said to the troop commanders after they had shut down. "Still pretty lax security over there. The mercenary commander will probably have figured out his scout team is gone by now. He'll probably send out a new crew tomorrow. Dianne, you take them out at the same spot, then fall back to your observation point where they will camp tomorrow night. Make sure they see all of you, then fall back and we'll meet up at our rendezvous point for the night.

"After the scout team passes, my gang will hit the top of this hill and watch them go by us. We'll be far enough back to be no threat, but if they come at us? Well, we need the target practice."

By daybreak, Team Two was on their way. Duncan and Team Two were parked out of sight behind a small hill with Duncan and Amanda laying just below the crest with their heads peeking above. The four scout vehicles, as expected, drove down the road in the same two-line abreast formation as the first one had and at the same speed. Duncan waited until they were a mile down the road, then called the vehicles up.

They parked ten yards apart, broadside to the road, and all the troopers were outside of the vehicles. Doors were all open, just in case. Roof gunners and the Cougar's turret were pointing at the road and everyone had their weapons close in hand, but pointed at the ground. To his credit, as soon as they were spotted, the mercenary commander sent ten vehicles ahead and they spread out beneath the Wind Riders in a ready position. But the Wind Rider paid them no mind and just stood there and watched the column roll by.

Karen started to wave at the passing vehicles and blow them kisses and she was soon joined by all the other females. Although they couldn't hear them, the passing troops were yelling and waving back. Some of the men placing their hands over their hearts and raising their heads to the heavens. It was even worse when the planetary army passed by. They were honking horns, some even dropping their pants and making lewd gestures.

"We'll see what that looks like after I barbeque you," Karen said to one particularly vulgar individual.

The rear guard was a mile down the road before the ten vehicles assigned to keep watch on them cautiously drove away, keeping their roof-mounted weapons trained on them. At that point Duncan had everyone mount up and they drove down the other side of the hill and two miles across country before heading north and ahead of the column once again.

"Alpha One, Bravo One, Sierra splashed."

"Bravo One, Alpha One, copy Sierra splashed."

"Oh poo, Voice is getting bored."

"Voice will get to party tonight."

"Oh goody, Voice has just the right outfit for it tonight."

"Alpha out."

"Bravo out."

"Ghost, what is Voice taking about?" Katerina said over the short range tactical network.

"Tune into the commercial radio network tonight, Papa One. It'll be an education for you," Duncan said. The interior of Alpha broke out in laughter.

● ● ●

"Woah, Dunc, that mercenary commander is some pissed," CT said after they had parked. "He was screaming at his command over the tach nets."

"Ya, seeing eight of your valuable scout troops chewed up in the same spot kind of does that," Duncan said. "Voice will be addressing that tonight."

"They were a lot more cautious after they saw that," Dianne said. "We definitely made them nervous this afternoon."

"So, everyone saw the layout of the column?" Duncan said. "I'm pretty sure the tankers with the orange triangles are the fuel trucks. In the morning, I'll hit the ones in the back squadron of the mercenaries. In the afternoon, Dianne's group will hit the front squadron. At this point and for as long as we can, I want them to think there are only five of us."

"Tonight, we start phase two."

Just after dark, CT turned his exterior speakers on and a song being played in French broke the silence. At the end of the song, there was a subtle click and Voice began to speak in her sultry sexy voice.

"Oh, my poor soldiers," she said. "To see such horrors, it must be such a fright. Voice cries for my poor soldiers. The Supreme Leader is concerned for his boys and has asked Voice to play you a special song."

Lili Marleen in French began to play and all the Wind Riders were cracking up.

"My brave boys," Voice started after the song was over. "The Supreme Leader is sure that his brave soldiers would never let that happen. But we all know the enemy is deceitful. This is why he has placed those hirelings in the front, so that they and not you take the brunt of the attacks so that his brave and courageous troops can come to their rescue and defeat the enemy. All hail the Supreme Commander. Voice wishes you all sweet dreams."

Then the radio switched back just in time for the normal marshal music that followed the Supreme Leader's nightly broadcast to his troops. To all intents, it sounded as if Barb's transmission had come from the Command Center.

Barb came out of Jane's Coyote to see all the troops laughing and made a deep bow and made several sexy poses. Several of the troopers hit the ground rolling and laughing.

Katerina had a puzzled look as she came up to Duncan, who was having a hard time controlling himself; and tears were flowing down his cheeks as he laughed.

"I fail to see how comforting our enemies helps us," she said.

He was still trying to gain control of himself when Barb sashayed up and put her arm around Katerina and he lost it again.

"Oh, my poor girl," Barb said in the same sexy silky voice, except in English this time. "Those poor, poor boys so far from home and lonely. And such a terrible sight. All those dead and burnt, torn up bodies on the road. It was such a horrible thing for those poor babies to see. I am sure they will have trouble sleeping tonight."

Katerina still had a puzzled look.

"Psychological warfare, dear," Barb said in her normal voice. "A hot sexy lady feeling sorry for them and telling them how brave they are. Playing a sad song about the girl back home. Plus, the mercenaries will be pissed they are taking all the casualties. We haven't touched the regular troops at all yet."

"OK, enough. Early morning tomorrow," Duncan said. "Dianne, everything good?"

"Ya, no problems," she said. "See you tomorrow night."

Karen blew Duncan a kiss from her position and pouted, then she and Duncan wrapped up in their separate sleeping bags and went to sleep.

• • •

Once again, the next morning, Duncan waited until the four scout vehicles were a mile down the road before the five vehicles parked on the crest of the hill. This time the vehicles were parked facing the road. The girls started waving and blowing kisses right away this time but everyone was close to the doors of the vehicles except for the Coyote's dismounts who were ranged in a fire line to each side of it. The turret was pointing in the general direction of the ten vehicles that were parked as a blocking force, three hundred yards away. But otherwise everything appeared the same as the day before. Nobody was making any threating moves.

As the command vehicle went by, the commander glassed them and Duncan waved and smiled at him. Giving him a little salute, the enemy commander just glared back at him. All the troops for the light vehicles casually made their way to their vehicles and got in, shutting the doors. The vehicles started up.

Everyone just sat there like that until the last squadron came abreast; then everything changed and changed fast. In one smooth motion, the Coyote's turret rotated and started spitting 20mm rounds into the blocking force, vehicles exploding into flame and broken pieces of red-tinged ceramic. A few of the rounds went straight through, hitting vehicles in the column itself. The fifty caliber chain gun deployed at the same time, targeting the large armored vehicles providing security for the transports, blowing them apart as the five light vehicles sprinted toward the column, the C9s spitting fire from the rooftops at any vehicle that crossed their sights.

Once they were within a hundred yards, Katerina's roof-mounted gun opened up on a tanker and it exploded after the second shot. Then the C9s shifted first to the remaining fuel tankers and then to the water tankers. Duncan fired a grenade into a square transport, blowing it and the supplies in it up. Then he, like the other passenger gunners, worked his C8 over any vehicle he could see. By then they were turning broadside to the column and they raked everything that came into their path before turning again and sprinting back the way they had come. The whole time, the Coyotes dismounts had gone to one knee and were pouring round after round into anything that moved. Now they sprinted into the Coyote, it slammed the rear door shut and, in a blast of diesel smoke and spinning tires, it took off.

This time they didn't stop their high-speed run until they had gone five miles across country away from the column.

"All good, Ghost; nobody is coming after us," CT said over the tactical net.

"OK, find us a place to pull over," Duncan said.

"Gulf One, Alpha One, massive fireball."

"Alpha One, Gulf One, copy massive fireball. Bravo has splashed Sierra. Party will start in sixty mikes."

"Copy, Alpha One out."

The vehicles started to slow and pull into their laager, except for Katerina's, which stopped right beside the Cougar. Katerina flung her door open and yanked the rear passenger door open and a figure fell out of the seat. Amanda was sprinting to the vehicle with her med kit and Karen was jumping out of the Coyote with hers. Carol's medic joined them, gently pushing Katerina away.

"Captain! Get control of those troopers!" Duncan yelled pointing at Katerina's crew. "Commander! Report now!"

He looked around, but all his people were doing their jobs, although glancing back to the action at times. Katerina jogged up to where he was and Carol took her troops farther away. As Duncan received Katerina's salute he looked over her head and saw the medics stand up. Karen looked at him and shook her head. He waved her over.

"Okay, Commander, what happened?" Duncan asked.

"Sir, a beam came in through the rear window and wounded one of my troops, Sir."

"Lieutenant?"

"Hit him right in the neck, Ghost," Karen said. "He was dead before he knew what hit him."

Katerina was pure white and wavering.

"His name, Commander?" Duncan said softly.

She swallowed a couple of times, then got control of herself somewhat.

"Albert," she said. "Albert Clowswitz."

"OK, thank you, Commander. Lieutenant, please escort the commander to her troop and inform them of the loss of their comrade."

Amanda had draped a silver space blanket over Albert by the time Katerina had turned around, at least sparing her the sight of her dead trooper.

"CT, get me a link to headquarters stat," Duncan said.

"Alpha One, Gulf One," came over his head set.

"Gulf One, Alpha One, six by six."

"Alpha One. Major fireball. No casualties. Proceeding to rendezvous."

"Copy major fireball, no casualties. Inform Papa Two One that Papa One Four is KIA."

"Shit, copy Alpha One, Gulf One out."

Karen, Amanda, the other medic and Dave were putting Albert in a body bag by then. They hoisted it to four waiting troopers on top of the Coyote and passed it to them, where it was quickly lashed down.

"Brett, can you handle driving that thing to the rendezvous? Amanda will go with you."

"Ya, its not the first time I've seen a little blood and guts," Brett said.

Duncan keyed Carol's private channel. "Carol, put the rest of that crew in with the Coyote. You just became my new driver. Bring Katerina with you."

"I've got HQ, Ghost," CT said. "Who do you want to talk with?"

"Madame Horshack," Duncan said.

"Duncan, you have done wonderful work today," Tanya said. "The mercenaries are reporting they lost half of their fuel and water supplies plus a hundred dead, two hundred wounded and the loss of a large amount of food supplies and vehicles. Well done."

"Madame Horshack it is my sad duty to inform you that Albert Clowswitz was killed in action today, Ma'am."

"Ma'am?" Duncan said after a prolonged silence. They were on the move by then and he thought they may have lost the link.

"Th..thank you, Mr. Kovaks. I will inform his family myself."

"Ma'am, we will have to bury him in the field, Ma'am. We can't take him with us. I will record the location and we can come get him later."

"No, someone will come for him after the main column has passed, Duncan. Is Katerina okay?"

"Yes, Tanya, she is fine. It was a lucky shot, it went right through the window. He was killed instantly." Well it sounded good anyway, he thought.

"Thank you for telling me Duncan; take care."

"Break it down, CT," Duncan said. Then he turned to Katerina in the back seat. She had her head against the door looking up at the ceiling. Scott mouthed that he would keep an eye on her and Duncan turned back to look out the front.

"The first one is always the worst," Carol said so only Duncan could hear.

"They all hurt, Carol, but, ya, the first one was the worst. Shit. I didn't even know that kid's name."

"My first was my best friend from high school," Carol said. "Sometimes I think it's better when we don't know them."

"Fuck!" Duncan said. "Lucky goddamned shot through the fucking window!" he slammed his rifle into its spring clip on the dash.

He looked back at Katerina again and she was quietly crying, trying not to let anyone see. Scott moved over and put his arm around her shoulder and she turned and buried her head in his chest and let it all out. She didn't see that Scott was crying as well and that tears started in Duncan's eyes.

"Fuck!" Carol said, wiping hers as she was trying to drive.

After half an hour of looking out the widow, Duncan turned back and saw Katerina doing the same, with Scott now back on his side of the vehicle.

"It was a lucky shot," Duncan said. "We were at high speed. Shit, it could have happened to me just as easily. Sometimes shit happens, Katerina."

"He wasn't killed instantly like you told my aunt, Duncan," she said. "It took him a couple of minutes to die. Maybe if I would have radioed it in, we could have saved him."

"No, love," Carol said. "His main artery was severed; his airway was destroyed. We had no way to save him even if we could have stopped to try. He would have been in massive shock and wouldn't have felt anything. He was probably brain-dead already and what you saw was his body reacting, that's all."

"Remember what I said," Duncan continued. "The mission always comes first. If we had stopped just then, we would have put more troopers in danger. We will be linking up with the others in a few minutes. They need to see you have your act together. Yes, you feel like shit; so do I. But we can't let them see that. They want to know everything will be all right, that you are still in control. We will bury him before dark and celebrate his life tonight. Tomorrow we are back to work."

They were waiting for them when they pulled in and joined the laager formation. The hole had been dug a hundred yards away from the formation and all the troopers were lined up and saluted the Coyote as it drove past.

"Go join your people, Katerina," Duncan said. "Have six of them bear the body to the grave."

CT's crew were already undoing the straps holding the body bag to the roof and others had placed three wide tow straps on the ground. They gently gathered the body as it was passed down and placed it on the tow straps and moved away.

Duncan had the Wind Riders form up in double file at attention and they saluted as the body being transported by six troopers holding the three tow straps walked by. Then they followed, marching the slow step reserved for funerals.

They stopped opposite Katerina's troops on the other side of the grave and stayed at attention as the body was slowly lowered into the grave and the tow straps tossed in after it. All of Katerina's troops, except her and her second in command, filled in the grave and then formed up in a line.

"We all knew Albert," she said, her voice strong. "He was a good man, a funny man and a very brave one. Let us not make his sacrifice in vain. Lord, we ask you to give us strength so that we may carry on and defeat our enemies."

"Squadron. Attention!" Duncan said. "Squadron will salute by squadron fire!"

All the Wind Riders raised their weapons and pointed them in the air. Then Duncan pulled his trigger and as the next trooper heard the one before him fire, they did as well and it sounded like a giant sheet of paper being ripped, as the rifles in sequence fired.

"Squadron, order arms. Squadron dismissed."

The Wind Riders moved away and left the planetary people to their own. After a few minutes, they came into the laager and grouped together. All of them were quiet, just sitting in their chairs looking at their feet, at the stars, or anywhere but at each other. Duncan dug into the back of his G-Wagon and found a twenty-four pack of Canadian beer and brought it and his chair over to them. He sat down, took out a beer and tossed it to the person across from him. It landed in his lap and startled him. Then Duncan started tossing beer cans one by one to the other six and finally one for himself and he popped the tab.

"We have a tradition," he said and stood motioning the others to stand. "You have heard us say part of it before, now you will know what it means."

He held his beer up. "To Albert," he said and took a drink. He waited until everyone had taken at least a sip and held his can up again. "To absent comrades." Then he drank the rest of the beer, crushed the can and tossed it to his feet.

Katerina was the first to follow his example and was soon followed by everyone else. Then Duncan passed out another can to everyone and sat down.

"Now, I hear Albert was a bit of a smart ass," Duncan said. "Why don't you tell me some of what he used to do?"

Again, Katerina was the first to tell a story that got smiles and a couple of laughs. Then others stared talking and soon the whole group, including Duncan, were laughing at the stunts Albert used to pull.

Then CT's exterior speakers came alive again at the end of a French song and everyone went quiet.

"Hello, my brave soldiers. This is the Voice again. My brave, brave boys. Once again you have been subjected to the cowardly enemy that refuses to stand and fight. They know, my brave boys, they know they can never defeat you. That is why they run. That is why they pick on those paid thugs instead of you. Because they are afraid of you. Now I will play your song once again."

Now that the soldiers knew what this was about, they all started to smile. For they knew the exact opposite was true. That the planetary soldiers were anything but professional and brave.

"Know, my poor brave soldiers so far from home. Know that your girls and wives are waiting, just like the girl in the song. Waiting for their brave boys to come home to them again. The Supreme Commander is very proud of his brave boys and all the good work you are doing for him. Until tomorrow night, my pretties, this is the Voice wishing you sweet dreams." This time she ended it with some wet sounding kisses, before the feed cut back to the marshal music once again.

This time it was the planetary people that were laughing hard, especially when Barb made her way over to them and blew them all kisses.

"Hey, you bum," she said to Duncan. "Did you save some beer for me? That's hard work you know."

Duncan made a big show of digging out a beer and making like he was serving it up on a platter and bowing after she took it.

"Rightly so, my good man," she said. "Absent comrades." As she downed the beer and crushed the can, Duncan had another waiting for her.

The rest of the Wind Riders made their way over, forcing the circle of chairs to widen. The beer was flowing freely and the stories getting wilder as more beer flowed. Brett and Bob told stories about Duncan back in the day, which got a lot of laughs.

"CT," Duncan said quietly to CT who was sitting next to him. "I want you to take in the rest of Katerina's crew tomorrow. I'll put her in with my crew."

"No Sir," Katerina said. She was sitting next to CT and had heard what he said. "With all due respect, Sir, my people and I function as a unit. We came in together and we fight together. As you said, the mission comes first and being a vehicle down could make a difference."

"Very well, Commander," Duncan said. "I agree. Any volunteers to join the commander's crew?"

"I'll do it," Brett said without hesitation. "Bob's been bitching about being cooped up in the big tin can with no windows anyway."

"Well, kid," Bob said. "I forgot more about driving a G-Wagon than you will ever know."

"Forgot being the operative word, old man," Brett said. And the verbal sparring between the two was on. The stories got funnier each time one was told.

Duncan quietly got up and left while the attention was off of him. He knew somebody from his crew would bring his chair back.

"Duncan," Katerina said before he had gone to far. "Thank you for that. My people needed it, and so did I."

"No problem, Katerina. It's part of the job."

"I'll have someone from my crew clean up the mess in the vehicle so Brett doesn't have to sit in it," she said.

"Already handled," Brett said as he walked by. He had Duncan's chair in hand. "Just going to grab my gear. I'll grab the ammo tomorrow. Not to be picky, but I like a little more firepower than you people have."

"How can you people carry on like this?" she asked. "Like nothing has happened. A man just lost his life today."

"And more will die tomorrow," Duncan said. "Your man wasn't the only one to die today. Kat, we are all soldiers. I have been one for a long time, and so has most of my squadron. When we put on these uniforms, we are dead men walking. It's only a matter of time before our number will come up. I'd rather die like a man than cower like a mouse."

"Live for today," Karen said as she walked up. "For tomorrow we may die. Now if you don't mind I would like to steal my husband for some after-action sex. You should try it sometime Kat, they are really horny with all that pent-up testosterone after a fight."

Bret had his sleeping bag across one shoulder and weapons harness in the other hand as the couple walked away.

"Come over here Kat, I want to show you something."

He took her over to the front passenger door and pointed.

"Two inches higher and it would have been Duncan laying in the ground beside your trooper."

There was a scorch mark just below the window on the door.

"They were not just sitting there and taking it," Brett said. "They were fighting back. If you look, you'll see we all took some hits. Al has a burn on his arm. Like Duncan said. Kat, it goes with the job description."

"What is this 'Kat' business?" she asked.

"Oh, you just got tagged with a nickname," Brett said. "Like Ghost or Voice. Besides, Katerina is such a large mouthful to say. Beautiful name that it is and all. Kat is much easier."

"Why don't you have one, then?" she asked.

"Well, Shithead doesn't sound right," Brett said and they both laughed. "Come on, let's break the party up before it gets out of hand."

• • •

"God, Duncan, that was close today," Karen said holding him close. "You almost got one through the window too and Al got hit in the arm."

"Ya, those guys are tough alright," Duncan said. "They were shooting back for sure. That's what we get for being over-confident.

I don't think we will get closer than a hundred and fifty yards next time. Kat's people are just going to have to make do. Tanya said we took out almost half of the mercenary's fuel and water supply today. I think that tomorrow we will concentrate on the food supplies. Also, your people will hit them first and as soon as you engage, I'll hit the middle."

"You will be careful, Duncan?"

"Hey, you had a few shots your way as well," he said, pointing to the scorch marks on the Coyote. "Sure, they were long range, but your dismounts were in the open. These guys are pros, Karen. We may outgun them, but they are not going down without a fight and tomorrow they will be waiting for us."

• • •

The next morning, they were sitting lined up at the bottom of a hill listening to the traffic go by and waiting for the other section to start.

As soon as they heard the explosions, they were flying over the hill. This time CT was waiting two hundred yards away as the smaller vehicles crested the hill and opened fire, first on the biggest armoured vehicle he could find, then shifting to the transports carrying the food and other supplies. Duncan fired two grenades from the launcher mounted under the barrel of his rifle. He was surprised he hit something, as he had just fired in the general direction, hoping just to cause some mayhem. Then, as he started to fire the rifle, Bob swung the G-Wagon around and they were pelting back over the hill.

Ten of the armored vehicles chased after them. CT waited until they were at the bottom of the hill before he fired the main gun, taking all ten out with it before they had traveled halfway to him. The lighter vehicles didn't even slow down, passing him and, as he was already facing in that direction, the Coyote was on the move chasing them as the last enemy vehicle blew up in a fireball.

That night, Barb laid it on really thick. Because tomorrow would be the planetary troops' turn.

• • •

"Incoming airborne," CT reported over Duncan's earphone. "It is our friends from the Guild."

The small aircraft hovered and landed just outside the laager and the two men exited and walked into the defensive circle, their eyes darting everywhere, taking in everything. They walked right up to Duncan.

"You have done well," the Guildsmaster said. "Much better than expected."

"We do our best," Duncan said. "You have received our expenditures. Have you replenished them?"

"Yes," the Guild Master said. "Madame Horshack has taken control of them and will transport them to your secret supply point."

"Good. Is that why you came all this way? To tell me of this?"

"No, not all," the Guildmaster said. "As a neutral observer, I am to conduct you to negotiations to end hostilities. You have been authorised by Madame Horshack to begin these negotiations on her behalf. Here is her written authorisation."

He handed Duncan a sealed large brown envelope. Opening it, Duncan quickly scanned the document and handed it to Katerina.

"When is the negotiation to begin?" Duncan asked.

"My assistant and I will leave immediately to confer with your opponents," was the response. "You are both under a ceasefire as of this moment."

Then both men walked back to the aircraft and left, headed toward the enemy.

"CT," Duncan said into his mike. "Little bird in position?" he started walking toward the Coyote. "Ya, Dunc. The bad guys haven't moved from last night's camp spot."

"Right. Jane, get Bird Two airborne and over to the cache location. Something doesn't feel right."

"Roger Duncan, ETA about half an hour."

"Everyone on peak awareness," Duncan said. "Deploy all the remote sensors, full circle at max distance."

Both Coyotes' box-like sensors dropped their protective coverings and hydraulically rose to their full height. Small radar domes started revolving and the sensor mast on Jane's Coyote rose to its full height from its stowed position.

"Amanda, grab my laptop from the G-Wagon and bring it to CT's wheels. Intelligence section to your posts; all other troops to perimeter guard after sensor deployment. Fire free if fired upon."

Machine guns were removed from G-Wagons and taken out ten meters from the laager, bipods deployed and weapons belts fed into breaches. Once the remotes were deployed, the troopers returned and started digging two-man rifle pits. One trooper from each troop kept watch while the other two dug.

Duncan walked into the Coyote to find every monitor alive and consoles manned and activated. The gunner had armed both the 20mm cannon and the coaxial machine gun and was watching his thermal scanners, hands on the fire control system.

Katerina had followed Duncan into the Coyote and looked around, her eyes wide. She had never seen all this equipment fully activated before, or the Wind Riders so determined, so focussed. Amanda yelled into the Coyote and Duncan motioned with his hand and she tossed his laptop bag to him. In mere seconds, he had it plugged into a console and was looking around at all the monitors as he waited for it to boot up.

"Commander," Duncan said. "Please man your position. If we require anything from you, you will be contacted." Then he turned back to his monitors.

"CT, you up?"

"Ya Dunc, they transmit, I've got 'em."

"Barb?"

"Monitoring the mercenaries, Duncan."

"Karen, you have my link yet?"

"Working on it, Babe. They have multiple layers. Mom is working on a few, but we really need you."

"Ya, in a bit, I have to handle something else first. Nancy, once I break this down, you keep an eye on this link."

Katerina had not left yet and she was watching as Duncan's hands flew over his keyboard, his head pivoting between the portable computer's screen and a monitor in front of him. Finally, the main monitor showed her aunt's boardroom with her full council around the table. The laptop was burning data across the screen and then finally stopped.

"Madame Horschak," Duncan said. "I see you have your full council with you."

"Mr. Kovaks," Tanya said. "Why am I not surprised? You received the request then?"

"Do you trust them? I don't," Duncan said.

"Nor I. But the rules mandate we comply, Duncan."

"Mr. Minister of Agriculture. I think you will find your ear implant is no longer working. I have disabled it. Your link to the Guild is severed. Also, all communications into or out of that room have been disabled. Madame Horschak, I have summoned your security people and informed them to arrest the minister. I recommend that no further discussions of any kind be conducted until he is removed."

Six security men entered and removed the docile minister and, when the door was closed, Duncan began again.

"Have my supplies been delivered?"

"Yes Duncan, we are loading them in the warehouse right now."

"Unload them; keep them there. Send the vehicles to the cache site empty. Have them enter the warehouse and stay for half an hour and then leave. I don't really need them at this point. I recommend that you fully deploy right now and go comms dark. Shut everything down and keep it down. We will keep you updated from here. I will activate your systems when I need to and send you a message, then shut everything down again."

"Agreed," Tanya said. "Don't agree to anything they propose. I don't trust them."

"Your wish is my command Madame Horshack. You have your comms back."

"Commander! I thought I told you to join your troops? Now get at it."

Duncan's fingers were flying across his key board again and after five minutes Karen came on the comm.

"Okay, I've got in hon," she said.

"Right, take over," he said. Then he shut his computer down. "All yours, Nancy."

He stuffed his laptop back in its bag, slung it across his shoulders and walked out of the Coyote. He headed over to his G-Wagon and stashed the computer once again, then took a look around at the perimeter. Everything seemed to be in order and he started walking over to Katerina's position. Brett, with his more powerful weapon, was positioned in the middle and he was talking with Katerina.

"Commander, I realise you were curious and wanted to know what was going on," Duncan said. "You already knew more than most of my troopers knew. As a commander of two troops, when I give an order to deploy, you follow it and report back to me when it is complete. If I need something from you, I will ask. Right now, I have no time to discuss things with you. Ah, CT tells me the Guild is returning. As the planetary representative, you may join me."

"The meeting has been set," the Guildsmaster said. "I will give the Commander the coordinates for the meeting. You do not have the capability to do that. You, one of your vehicles and its troops, will be the only ones to come within one mile of the meeting. You will leave your long-range weapon behind, Mr. Duncan. You will be allowed your side arm. Your vehicle will stop three hundred yards from the meeting place and you alone will come. The others will do likewise. The Guild member and his client's representative will be present for the meeting."

"But the Commander is not allowed to accompany me?"

"No, she is not. In addition, I must remind you that there is a ceasefire in effect. The first ones to violate that ceasefire will be dealt with harshly. You have two hours to reach the meeting place."

"Well then, I guess we had better get moving. Commander, prepare your people and your vehicle," Duncan said. Then he walked over to his G-Wagon and put his rifle in the spring clip on the dash, pulled his mirrored aviation glasses off of the sun visor and stuck them in his breast pocket, and removed a small thin rectangular silver package from the map pocket mounted on the door.

The Guild men were moving off in the direction of the meeting by that time and Duncan gave last-minute instructions to Jane, who would be in command until he returned. As he walked, he opened the package he was carrying and put on the lightweight Mylar jacket it contained, making sure the shiny side was facing outward.

"Make sure we go no faster than thirty-seven miles an hour when we reach the road," Duncan said as he jumped into the middle rear seat. "I don't want to be too early."

The rear seat had more room and was more comfortable than the G-Wagon's were. The ride was smoother and quieter in the locally made vehicle. The fit and finishes were tighter and did not rattle as much. Brett had his weapon laying on his open windowsill and he was actively scanning his side of the road as they drove. The trooper on Duncan's left was doing the same.

"Where do you get these vehicles from," Duncan said. "They are well made."

"We make them here," Katerina said. "They are very popular and are one of our major exports. The military models usually have ceramic bodies mounted on the same chassis. In this case, we just modified the interiors and added the gun mount on the roof. The suspension and tires have been upgraded. A few little upgrades in the interior for storage, but those are about the only differences between this one and the civilian one."

"I see it has an internal combustion engine," Duncan said. "I would have thought you would be using electric motors based on your advanced weapons systems."

"This is a hybrid system, Duncan. There are four electric motors, one for each wheel. The floor pan is basically a big storage battery. All the engine does is recharge the battery and run the electrical systems, especially when high performance is required. On a road such as this, we could easily do well over a hundred miles an hour with this load onboard. The engine is powered by a vegetable alcohol-oil mixture and we can run for about a week on one tank of fuel at the rate of speed we have been doing with these operations."

"So, why is the enemy so reliant on fuel then?"

"They are using machines built on another planet," Katarina said. "They were designed for a military purpose only and are powered by the internal combustion engine alone. Most planets consider ours far too expensive to use for military purposes, as the ceramic armor adds significantly to the price."

"What else does your planet produce?"

"We primarily have an export-based economy, Duncan. We manufacture most of the consumer entertainment electronic devices everyone else uses. It is cheaper to manufacture them here as we have all the natural resources required. In addition, we have a very large agricultural impact. Most of the land is suitable for grain crops or pasture. On the other side of the planet, there are large forested areas that we harvest for wood, which is also exported. In fact, the planet is named for the tree species that we harvest and replant: oaken. It is a slow-growing tree that produces very strong wood with tight fiber and beautiful wood grains. It is much sought-after."

"Sounds a lot like home," Duncan said in German, drawing a look from Brett.

"Once all this is over," he said in English. "Maybe you can tell me more about Oaken and your people, Kat."

"It will be my pleasure, Duncan," she replied. "Look! Our hosts seem to be early."

An armed transport was parked at the site with the Guild's aircraft parked beside it. Ten armed mercenaries were lined up in front of it and the two enemy commanders were talking with the Guildsmen. As they had been instructed, Duncan's vehicle parked four hundred yards away, then everyone got out. Brett stood behind the vehicle, his weapon out of site, while the other three troopers stood in front, weapons aimed at the ground.

"You see what I see?" Brett said in German.

"Ya," Duncan replied in the same language. "One to the left prone about a hundred yards, the other crouched behind a bush the same distance to the right. You take the one on the left, I'll handle the one on the right. But they fire first, got it?"

Duncan put his sunglasses on and started walking toward the other men, who also started walking toward him.

"Good morning," Duncan said saluting the two enemy commanders. "It is turning out to be a beautiful day."

"We demand you accept this peace proposal," the client's commander said. Duncan ignored him.

"Your people fight hard, Commander," he said. "Harder than we had imagined."

"Why don't you stand and fight instead of hitting and running, then? You are clearly beating us. Stand and fight like real soldiers then."

"Even though you have killed one of my people, you still outnumber us two thousand to one. Committing suicide is not in my job description, Commander. I am authorised by my client to hear your peace proposal."

The client haughtily outlined their proposal, which was almost the same as the previous one. The enemy would keep all the land they had taken. A number of Tanya's people would be required as hostages. Absolutely no harm would come to Duncan's people.

"Mr. Kovaks," the Guildsmaster said. "The Guild feels this is a good agreement. I should also point out that you have broken the spirit of this truce. Your man has one of your weapon systems pointed in our direction."

Brett had his rifle laying across the roof of the scout vehicle, butt to his shoulder and eye at the scope.

"Sir," Duncan said. "The trooper that was killed was from that scout troop. They were a man short and unfortunately, we have not had time to replace the dead trooper from the pool of local people available to us. It was necessary to put one of my people with this troop so that it could remain operational. Had you picked the other vehicle, this would not have been the case. You only specified that I could not bring my long-range weapon, not my security detail."

"I will once again remind you that breaking this ceasefire agreement will be dealt with harshly," the GuildsMaster said.

"I assure you sir, we will not be the ones breaking the agreement, but we *will* be the ones to punish those that do."

Seeing the man to the left suddenly rise and point his weapon, Duncan turned so he was standing sideways to the man on the right and, as he heard the shot coming from the left man, pulled his Sig Sauer from its holster with his right hand. The shot from the left reflected off the shiny Mylar coating of his left shoulder as his left hand grabbed his right wrist and he levelled the pistol at the man on the right whose shot missed him by inches, blazing across his chest. As he pulled the trigger for his first of two shots, Brett's rifle fired three rapid shots. Both of Duncan's shots hit his man squarely in the chest, the first shattering the ceramic armour, the second passing through the body and shattering the rear armor plating. As the man was flung to the ground, Duncan fired twice more, once to the chest, the last to the head, then he swung to cover the two enemy. The client had his pistol half-drawn but stopped.

"Tell your people to stand down, Commander," Duncan said as the mercenaries began to run toward them. "Or they, and you, will be dead before they get in range."

The mercenary commander yelled into his communicator for his people to stop, which they did.

"Now, very carefully, Sir," Duncan said pointing his pistol in the client's face. "Slowly remove your sidearm and toss it behind me." A red dot from Brett's laser sight lit up on the client's chest armor.

A look of disgust was on the mercenary commander's face and he turned to the Guildsmaster to plead his case.

While he was doing that, Duncan replaced the half empty clip with a full one and holstered the pistol. Then he gathered up the spent shell casings and put them in his pocket.

"I think you will find, Sir," Duncan said to the Guildsmaster in the lull, "that those two men, are, in fact, the client's troops. I believe the Commander had no knowledge of this. As for myself, we did not break the ceasefire agreement, they did. We were only protecting ourselves. I intend to inform my client that her enemy is still operating with dishonour and that, in my opinion, any further negotiations with these people would be fruitless. They seem to be intent on breaking any and all agreements that they make. As they have in the past. Have a good day, gentlemen."

"You get all that, CT?" Duncan said on his communicator as he walked back to his vehicle.

"Ya Dunc, it's all recorded."

"OK, short burst it to headquarters. We should be back in half an hour. Get ready to move out. Have you isolated the Guild's surveillance frequencies yet?"

"Ready to start jamming when you give the word, Dunc."

"Not yet," Duncan said as he was getting into the scout car. "Wait until after we start leaving for the next camp area. Home James, and don't spare the horsepower this time."

"That means, drive as fast as is safe to do so, Driver," Brett said.

The next morning, Duncan and A Troop were alone on the hilltop overlooking the road. They were six hundred yards away from the road and in full view of it. The tailgate was down and Amanda had set up her spotting scope on it, but was sitting on the tailgate with her legs dangling. Bob and Scott were sitting on the hood and Duncan was standing behind it with his elbows on the roof and his binoculars to his eyes, watching the approaching column.

Two of the scout vehicles pulled off to the side of the road twenty yards apart and observed them, while the other two slowed down and crept down the road, the observers with binoculars to their eyes scanning all around the area. Two armoured troop carriers approached fast and, as they came to a stop and dismounted the troops they had onboard, the two scout vehicles took off to join the other two. The dismounted troopers quickly set up a defensive perimeter on both sides of the road and the turret mounts were constantly in motion scanning for movement.

"It took them long enough," Bob said. "But they are finally acting like professionals."

The advance guard was fully alert, weapons trained and turrets in constant motion. They were in a staggered formation and shifted position every three hundred yards or so. The main body was also on full alert and maintained a ten-yard distance from each other instead of the bunched up formation of earlier days. As the command group approached and Duncan saw he had been noticed by the enemy commander, he went to attention and saluted the commander and was saluted in return. Then he grabbed his cup of lukewarm coffee and joined Amanda at the rear of the vehicle, leaned up against the back panel and watched the parade.

The rear guard and the rear scout troop passed by and, five minutes later, the gaggle of unorganised local troops appeared. They were bunched together, no security was practised and the troops, instead of being inside the transports and protected, were riding on the tops, most with shirts off and weapons out of view.

Duncan reached inside of the G-Wagon and pulled out his Tac-50 advanced sniper rifle. As he walked ten yards in front of the vehicle, he extended the bipod and the butt piece. Then he laid down and inserted the five-round clip. When the command vehicle came up, he sighted on the bodyguard furthest away and shot him. Then Duncan moved quickly from man to man until all four of them were blown off the top by the high powered fifty caliber bullets. The last shot he placed in the armour just to the side of the commander, blowing it and most of that side of the vehicle to pieces.

"That, Commander, is what a real sharpshooter can do," Duncan said into his radio. "Sleep well."

Then he gathered up his spent shell casings and his rifle, stowed all the gear away and they sped off, leaving confusion behind them.

The next morning, all four sniper teams were deployed in various locations on both sides of the road. All of them were concealed and camouflaged and were at long range. This time they concentrated their fire on any officers or leaders they could spot in the gaggle of local troop vehicles. Twenty bodies were blown off transports in red misted clouds. The only warning the vehicles had that they were a target was when the body was hit, followed by the loud sounds of the shots.

That night, the Voice was very sympathetic to the poor troopers. She commented on their bravery and how the paid professional troops that were supposed to be protecting them were failing in their duty. Right after promising them a special surprise for being so brave, all eight vehicles opened up with every weapon they possessed for a full minute from every direction. The dark night was alive with tracer shells, laser bolts and explosions. Then everything stopped and all that was heard was the screams of the dying and the wounded.

Chapter Five

"You guys have to see this," CT said and the holographic projector on Katerina's vehicle came alive.

Four large armored airborne troop transports landed, surrounding the warehouse that held their reserve supplies and, as the troops came out, multiple barrelled weapons mounted on the transports started firing into the warehouse. While some troops set up a perimeter, others broke into the warehouse with satchels on their backs and, shortly re-emerged without the satchels. Everyone reloaded into the transports, which took off. Minutes later the warehouse exploded.

"Good thing there was only empty boxes in there," Duncan said.

While the rest of the Wind Riders had been involved training, Jane's troop had been using the new Coyotes to relocate all of their supplies to a cache known only to the Wind Riders. While a few supplies had been lost, most of them were safe.

"What are you going to do now?" Katerina asked.

"Oh, we will make do somehow," Duncan said. "Any idea who those guys were, CT?"

"Locals from some place called Arial," CT said. "They have also been funding the rebels."

"What?" Katrina said. "But they are our closest trading partners and friends."

"Apparently not," Duncan said. "Include that in the nightly report, CT, along with a request for the Guild to replace the lost supplies."

"They will not reach here in time, Duncan," Katerina said.

"Maybe. Then again, maybe not. So, this is the plan for tonight…"

• • •

It was all knife and stealth work that night, once again Barb had consoled her poor troopers, vowing revenge. After midnight, the Wind Riders infiltrated the camp, killing any sentries they had found. Then, while some eliminated whole tent loads of soldiers, others planted explosive charges on tankers and supply vehicles. It took two hours to complete all the work.

As the sun broke the horizon, the dead were discovered and an hour later, the charges went off. The next phase of the plan went into action. As the massive column lumbered on its way, the Wind Riders stayed in place, moving further behind the advancing column. They set up their ambush and waited.

...

With their successful hacking into the Guild's computer networks, there was no further need to send out the small drone that each Coyote carried. Instead, imagery from overhead spacecraft was being used to survey the progress of the main column. Intercepted enemy transmissions, voice and text, had told them of the column's growing deficit in supplies. Food and water were running short, but fuel was running critically low.

A fast supply column had been sent out to resupply the enemy invasion troops. The makeup of the column showed how critical the situation was. There were twenty-five each of water tankers and food trucks, but fifty fuel tankers. Guarding this column were four small scout vehicles. The column was traveling as fast as it could, which was about triple the speed the main column was traveling. It had rightly been proved that no resistance was expected until the resupply column reached the main column. The ambush would prove that wrong.

Even traveling at the speed it was, the resupply column would not reach the main column for another two days. It would be at the ambush site the next afternoon, giving the Wind Riders almost twenty-four hours to rest and perform any maintenance necessary.

CT, in particular, needed some rest. He had been going almost nonstop for two weeks. While he did not want to rest and did not realise it himself, he was reaching burnout status and even though he protested vehemently at being forced to take time off, he was asleep almost immediately.

Duncan had set up their camp the usual two miles away from the road. While technically behind enemy lines, there was little danger of being spotted, as the enemy did not patrol its rear. Indeed, they had left no troops behind at all, feeling it unnecessary as no people were left anywhere in the districts. Deploying the remote sensors and monitoring the overheads was all that was required, leaving most of the Wind Riders with not much to do but clean weapon systems and relax. This did not mean that they were totally relaxed. Everyone made sure they had their personal weapons with them always and that they were never far from their vehicles. Nothing was said to the planetary defence force people, as at first they wandered about in a totally relaxed fashion, weapons nowhere near ready if needed. But after a few minutes of glaring looks, they too kept their weapons close by.

"Yes, we are in a secure area," Duncan said in response to Katerina's question about why the Wind Riders were wandering about still armed to the teeth. "Yes, we have sensors out and overhead surveillance. Electronic devices can be defeated, sometimes easily. I think we have demonstrated that to you, just by what we are doing to the enemy. Behind the lines, you cannot afford to be lax. The thirty seconds it takes you to retrieve your weapon from your vehicle could cost you and your troops their lives."

He went on to explain, using their past operations as examples of how hard they were hurting the enemy - an over-confident enemy, that, for the most part, still refused to be vigilant.

"Our little nibbles are beginning to have an effect," Duncan went on. "The mercenary commander has realised it, but the locals have not. Our tiny force has given them a ten percent casualty rate. For them it is an acceptable loss rate. They have a lot of numbers. But it is the type of casualties we are inflicting that matters."

The Wind Riders were concentrating on high-level targets. Fuel, water and food. Also, they were eliminating the most experienced and confident troops. The very valuable scout troops, officers and leading non-commissioned officers. Their constant nibbling was wearing on nerves and causing the column to triple the amount of time it would normally take to travel. Now the stealthy, night attacks would be taking a toll, as were Barb's nightly broadcasts. The enemy was being targeted in every way possible. The small attacks were adding up, pecking away at the enemy's resolve.

Day after day of being hit, but unable to hit back or stop the attacks, was becoming demoralising. Traveling day after day in a bleak, destroyed landscape, devoid of people and buildings, nothing but the sight and smell of burnt vegetation and buildings. No plunder or slaves being taken. Attacks coming out of nowhere, at any time of day and night. All this was taking its toll on everyone, but especially the inexperienced local troops. They had been used to easily defeating everything they had come across. Now they were faced with a determined and skillful foe and their resolve was slowly crumbling.

"But other than being a little tired," Katerina said. "We are not experiencing the same effects. We are losing more than they are."

"You are fighting to save yourselves," Duncan said. "They are fighting, well, the regular troopers are not sure what they are dying for. Plunder? Land? Slaves? There has been none of that for some time, but still they are dying. Tonight, Barb will be talking about the troopers' poor girlfriends and wives back home waiting for them. How they are being well looked-after by the men that stayed behind. While on the surface it sounds just fine, underneath, it will be sowing doubt in the troopers' minds."

"But what about the mercenaries?" she said. "That will not bother them."

"No, they are fighting for money or the thrill of the battle," Duncan said. "Even so, losing day after day, especially when no money or pleasure is in sight, is telling. They will start making mistakes, and in fact they already have. Now they are preparing for small attacks like we have been making. When they confront your aunt's major force, they will be scattered and it will take time to organise a proper response. That was the whole purpose of what we are doing."

"But they could easily defeat us," she said. "They have the numbers. We do not. Even with your different weapon systems, with enough troops they could damage us badly."

"Yes, but then I would modify my tactics and they would pay an even higher price," Duncan said. "From what I have been able to discover, you people engage in fast wars, using overwhelming odds against weaker unprepared foes. My people try to do the same. But I have centuries of experience in this type of thing to rely on, whereas you do not. We always have a small professional army core on hand, schooled in all the techniques and history. This small core will teach new people these techniques, just as we have done here. All we had to do was buy your people some time to learn skills long lost. To give them some hope with our small victories. To prove that the enemy is human and can be defeated."

Now Duncan asked her more about the area these invaders had come from. The more she talked, the more Duncan began to finalise his plan. He occasionally caught the glance of one of the Wind Riders and made a gesture and, one by one, they departed and were soon in conversation with Katerina's troopers. The night was warm, but Duncan began to yawn. It had been a long two weeks, with more to come. It was time for sleep.

"What is going through that mind of yours?" Karen said as they snuggled together under the sleeping bags.

"We need a home," he said. "I have an idea. We will see how the next week turns out. Then I will decide. I'll get CT and your mom working on a few things in the meantime."

• • •

Life was returning quickly to the burnt and devastated land. Fresh shoots of vegetation were thrusting their way through the ash. Back home they would be bright green; here, they were a pale turquoise. But new life, just the same. As back home, avian life forms and insects were the first to reappear. Larger ungulates were slowly making their way back. They would soon be followed by smaller plant eaters and the predators that preyed on them. The circle of life existed here, too, one life form feeding off another to survive.

All five designated marksman were prone, bipods extended under barrels. Some had semi-automatic weapons, others like Duncan, had bolt action weapons. All of them were fifty caliber and, in the right hands, deadly accurate at long range. These five shooters had the right hands. Death would soon be coming. People would die, without hearing or seeing what killed them. Then the 20mm cannon would fire, also at long range. Death would rain down offering no hiding place to those it was coming for and no way to hit back.

The squelch on Duncan's earpiece broke twice, alerting him that the head of the column had passed the concealed dismounts. He opened the breach of his weapon and inserted another round, making a full load of six. Gently pushing the bolt back and locking it, he engaged the safety and put his eye to the high-powered scope. At this range, the vehicles looked like toys. Each of the troopers had a target for the first two shots. Duncan's was a fuel truck. He gently led the target through the scope, eyeing it as it approached the spot where the ambush would begin. His thumb caressed the safety and made the weapon live, then his trigger finger gently began to squeeze and, with a roar, the weapon slammed into his shoulder as the high caliber bullet fired.

His right hand automatically pulled back the bolt and the still-smoking casing ejected, to be replaced by a new one. All the time he was tracking his next target, a water truck. He went through the same sequence. Unlike the other shooters, Duncan looked back at his first target to see the results. The front of the vehicle, housing the power unit, disintegrated in a spray of ceramic, the power unit itself falling on the ground. The vehicle came to a grinding, spark-throwing halt, the rest of the vehicle intact. The same happened to the water truck. Then, as he sighted on another tanker, all hell broke loose as vehicles exploded from fifty caliber bullets hitting fuel tanks and the two 20mm cannon shells started impacting on fuel trucks.

Now the two mortars the dismounts had started spitting high-explosive hell into the rear of the column and smoke trails from antitank rockets started streaking, ending in mayhem among the vehicles. Pieces of vehicles and bodies were rising in the mushroom clouds and the thunder was oppressive, blast after blast echoing over the landscape as man and machine died on that open plane. Even had they been able to see the destruction coming, there was no way for them to evade it.

Having emptied his five-round clip, Duncan removed it, inserted a full one, collapsed the bipod and slung the big rifle across his back, putting his C8 in his hands, charging the weapon and loading a fragmentation grenade in the launcher mounted under the barrel. The other five shooters had done the same and they began to walk in line abreast toward the carnage. Dismounted troops along the sides and to the rear of the column now stood and began to pour automatic weapons fire into anything that still moved or was intact.

By the time the five shooters had walked the mile to the devastated column, it was all over. Smoke dimmed visibility and fires were still burning. The smell of burnt plastics, ceramics and rubber, along with the unmistakable smell of roasting flesh, permeated the air. Bodies and body pieces were scattered everywhere. Even though they all had weapons at the ready, there was no need. There were no survivors.

Katerina's two vehicles were the first to arrive. Their occupants' eyes were wide and their faces pale as the exited and saw all the devastation that had been caused. Then they looked at the Wind Riders and how they were calmly walking through the carnage, making sure there were no further threats, while others set up perimeter guard. The two Coyotes, their turrets in constant motion came next and parked fifty yards apart and dropped rear ramps.

"No threats inbound," CT reported. "No messages got off. No escapees. No friendly casualties."

"Roger," Duncan said. "Commander, bring your two vehicles up here and let's get you refuelled. Two troopers from the Coyote crews, bring up water cans and let's get them filled up."

Katerina's two vehicles came up to the fuel tanker and they soon had hoses filling tanks and spare containers with fuel, while others were filling all the water storage tanks they could. All the while, they kept looking at all the devastation around them, swallowing hard at times. Katerina kept looking from the devastation to the Wind Riders and back again. For their part, the Wind Riders kept doing their jobs, or kicking empty shell casings out of the Coyotes, or wiping down weapons. Once all the fuel and water cans were full, she just looked at Duncan.

"All right," Duncan said into his radio. "Everyone mount up."

Ten Wind Riders entered each Coyote, while the rest climbed up on top for the short trip to the G-Wagons. While that was going on, Duncan walked over to Katerina, who now had a determined look.

"Did you think war was glamorous?" Duncan asked. "That it was all honour and bloodlessness? The whole objective of war is to kill the enemy without getting killed yourself. This is what you hired us for.

This is what we do and believe me, we do it well. This was nothing compared to what we face at home. In an attack like this, conducted like this, I would have lost half my people. This was nothing. I will think nothing of doing it again.

"Now get in your vehicle and follow the plan. You should be in range of the main column in two days. Another day to get around them undetected and another to get to your army and report. We have hurt them as much as we can and delayed them as much as we could. Now it is your turn. Tell your aunt that we will come as soon as we can. We have to rearm; we are almost out of ammunition."

Then he turned his back on her and walked to the nearest Coyote climbing up to the top as the rear ramp was raised, and in a cloud of blue diesel exhaust, the Wind Riders drove off, leaving the two planetary scout vehicles behind.

"Tough lesson for them today," Brett yelled into Duncan's ear as they sped down the highway as fast as the Coyote could go.

"Now they think they have seen all we can do," Duncan said. "Now we are done playing and I'll be damned if any of my people get killed helping these people out."

Even when he got into the G-Wagon several minutes later, Duncan said not another word. He stayed silent for the whole four hours it took them to reach the cut off to where the real cache was. Nor did he speak for the three-hour trip to the cache itself. Even once they arrived, he said little beyond that necessary, concentrating on cleaning his weapons, while his mind was going rapid fire on what needed to happen next.

"Uncle Duncan?" Megan said and Duncan came to the reality of here and now from his mind swirl. It was rare that Megan talked to him anymore. She spent most of her time with her crewmates or her parents.

"Hey kid, what's up? Need anything?"

"Yes, and no," she said. "What's wrong? Did we do something to upset you?"

"What are you talking about? Everything went according to plan, better even. Why would I be pissed?"

"You're just sitting here staring off into the distance," she said. "You snapped at Kat and basically threw them out. You only grunt when we report to you and you have been sitting here alone. It's getting dark. Everyone, including Mom and Karen, is too scared to say anything. Duncan, you are scaring us. What do you know that you are not telling us?"

"That I am a human being, just like the rest of you,'" he said after a moment of thought. "I am not a machine or Superman or a god. I make mistakes, just like you guys do. But see, I have you guys to rely on. So, when I do screw up, somebody, like a wet-behind-the-ears ensign comes along and clues me in."

Now he smiled sheepishly.

"Look Megs, I've been doing this for a very long time. I don't even really know how many people I have killed, or caused to be killed. To be honest, it never really mattered. It's my job. Before, I just had to worry about my team and followed my orders as best as I could. Then with the company, well, I just had to make sure I took the right jobs, prepared everyone with the best information and equipment I could, and usually everything went okay."

"Just like today," Megan said. "We made a good plan and it worked. Nobody got hurt and no equipment losses. A perfect operation."

"Ya, I know Megs," he said. "Classic textbook stuff. Superior tactics, weapons and the element of surprise, bla, bla, bla. I am happy with the results. Then I looked over at Kat and her gang and the looks they had and saw the carnage through their eyes. I think, for the first time, I really saw what we had just done and it all just came crashing down on me. Back home, we at least have a semblance of normalcy. When the mission is over, we go home, relax, visit friends and families. Here? This is it, only the thirty of us and we have nowhere to call home."

"We still have each other, Duncan," Megan said. "Karen is with you."

"You know, I was out," Duncan said. "Karen and I were going to start a tech company. Do something positive for the world. Something we could be proud of, have some kids, live on the farm like normal people. Then I thought, well, we will do this for a while, pick the safest jobs we can, make a pile of cash and retire. The Saudi job put us over the top, Megan. All of us were extremely wealthy, one or two more jobs, crucial jobs, and we would have been done. Now?"

"You'll figure it out, Duncan. You always do."

"Ya, sure. What's up, CT? I thought I told you to take a break."

"You gotta come see this, Dunc." CT said over the earbud.

"On my way," Duncan clapped Megan on the shoulder and stood. "Thanks for letting me bend your ear."

CT showed Duncan what he had found. It was the roster of another mercenary company that was ready to deploy to Oaken. There were two thousand names on the list and CT had highlighted one of them.

"No way," Duncan said. "Are you sure about this?"

"Ya, I can link you to his comms and a video feed. It's tight and all secure."

A video feed came on the screen. It looked like a mess hall and Duncan saw more faces he recognised. Men supposed to be dead.

"Whiskey Romeo Three One, Whiskey Romeo One One, how copy," Duncan said. A puzzled look came on the man he was watching.

"Whiskey Romeo Three One, Whiskey Romeo One One. If you copy, rub your right index finger on your nose."

The man brought his hand up and scratched his nose.

"This is a secure channel, Wind Rider. Nobody but you can copy. If you can find a way to get your fat square head someplace where you can talk, that would be a good thing."

This time the man took his left middle finger and slowly and deliberately rubbed his nose with it.

"Now, now," Duncan said. "It's a good thing Voice is not here to see that. She would be cross with you."

"Excuse me, my friends," the man said to his companions. "I have a ghost whispering in my ear and I need some air."

The man stood up and casually made his way outside. CT followed him with the security cameras and soon the man stopped and leaned against a wall.

"What the hell, Ghost," he said. "How in the hell did you find us? That damned Guild said there was no way anyone from Earth could find us."

"They are probably right," Duncan said. "We are not on Earth. How the hell did you end up out here?"

"My platoon and I were deployed on a mission. We all fell asleep and wham, next thing we know we are on some desert planet fighting some insurgents for some mining company. Just like everyone else in this bullshit company."

"Sort of the same thing with us," Duncan said. "We are someplace called Oaken working for the local government. The Guild is promising to keep us supplied. Good thing, we would be heavily outgunned otherwise."

"Ya, well that's all bullshit, too," Klaus said. "All our resupplies magically got destroyed and so sorry, but resupply is now forbidden, they said. All of us are the same, using local stuff now."

"I kind of figured that," Duncan said.

"Look, Duncan. We are being deployed to Oaken in a couple of months," Klaus said. "We will either be mopping up if you fail, or absorbing you into our unit if you don't."

"Well, I don't think you will be doing any mopping up," Duncan said. "Nor do I think you will be absorbing us."

"That's been tried before Duncan," Klaus said. "My commander has a habit of removing dissenting officers. Permanently. They have the largest contingent of us, four hundred ex Foreign Legion guys, all from the same unit. The rest of us are in small groups of twenty or so. He was the Chief Sergeant and killed all his officers to get control."

"Well, one thing at a time," Duncan said. "We will probably be out of supplies by the end of this deal. Somehow all our supplies were destroyed by the enemy. We might as well link up with you guys. What's the pay like?"

"Half a pound of silver a month in garrison and a pound on active duty," Klaus said. "Better than most. We own three transport ships and are leasing-to-own two more. All the crews are on our payroll, as are the maintenance and medical people. Five or ten years of this and I can retire someplace nice."

"Ya, sounds good," Duncan said. "Okay, I'll see you in a few weeks then. Have to break this down now before the Guild discovers us."

"No way the Guild would discover us Dunc," CT said after he broke the link down.

"I know that," Duncan said. "You know that. But he doesn't. Just like I didn't tell him none of our supplies were destroyed. Right now, the only people I trust are right here with us. We need a home, CT, but first, we have to finish this job. Keep to the plan. If we get out of this fight, we will have our home. Then I will deal with this other stuff. Shut it down CT, and let's get out of here. Not a word of this to anyone."

For once they had a big bonfire going. They were many miles away from anywhere and there was no danger of the fire being seen. Everyone was grouped around the fire and Duncan sat down beside Karen and took her hand. She looked over at him and smiled, then leaned her head on his shoulder, as he leaned his against hers. They just sat there and listened to the stories going around the fire. After about an hour, Duncan kissed her, rose and walked away. His passage was followed by every eye at the fire.

Karen found him two hours later curled up under the sleeping bags they shared. She undressed and climbed in with him and gently kissed his neck, putting her arm around him as she snuggled into his back, forming herself to him. He took her hand with his, she had thought he was sleeping, and he held it tight. Then his shoulders started to shake and she realised he was crying. She held him closer, stroking his hair with her other hand. He said not a word and soon the crying stopped and his breath slowed down and she knew he had fallen asleep. She kissed him gently on the neck again and turned over and her tears began. Tears for the man who took all their pain and shared none of his own.

Duncan was the first one up the next morning. If they had been back home, he would have thought it was about to snow. It felt like it. He could see his breath and it was cold. He dug into the fire pit and brought up some live coals and added kindling to them. After a few breaths on them, the kindling caught fire and he slowly built it up until it was burning hot, then sat back and looked at the flames.

A coffee pot was plunked down on some rocks and Duncan looked up to see Dave sitting beside him. Like Duncan, he had his jacket buttoned up and his hands in his pockets, jacket collar pulled up to cover his neck.

"Damn," Dave said. "Feels like snow."

"Ya," Duncan replied. "I had the same thought. You know, I bloody well forgot to ask about the seasons and weather here."

"Me too," Dave said. "We have been kind of occupied with other things lately."

CT joined them next. "Goddamn it's cold," he said.

"He says still wearing his shorts and flip flops," Dave said and laughed.

"Hey CT," Duncan said. "You think you could find some weather info for Dave here? Better yet, just show him how to find it. Dave, as the most experienced pilot around here, you are the most qualified to interpret weather data. It would be nice to find out what the seasons are like around here and what we can expect."

"Hell of an idea," Dave said. "Put some of that expensive training I have to good use for a change."

"Ya, you're kind of wasted as a common rifle man," Duncan said.

"Well you know these zoomy types," Barb said sitting down beside Dave. "If it's not going Mach 1 at 30,000 feet they are not happy."

"I'll bet he didn't even know what his feet were for until he got here," Duncan said. "All he's ever had to do was walk to the plane and back."

"Are you kidding me," Bob said. "All he ever did was walk from the jeep to the plane and back."

For the next half hour, it was Dave's turn to be picked on and everyone was smiles as they saw Duncan was back to his normal smartass self.

The rest of the day was spent mounting weapons systems to the Light Armoured Vehicles, or LAVs, and testing them. They also had to ensure all the propulsion, guidance and radio equipment worked. Then they started loading munitions in all the vehicles. As much as they could carry. Now came the rituals each of them performed before battle. Most of them centered around the cleaning of weapons. The camp was quiet while all the activity was going on, but it started to liven up as, one by one, each of the Wind Riders finished their tasks and once again grouped around the campfire.

As Dave had predicted earlier in the day, it started to snow as the sun went down. At first it snowed lightly and soon it was large thick flakes. None of them were too worried. It wasn't all that cold, not compared to what they were used to, anyway. The fire was warm, the clothing was up to the task and their sleeping gear definitely was. CT had donned his knee socks and sneakers. He also was the only one wearing a toque. But he did that every time the temperature went lower than ten. Born and bred in California, he was not used to rapid temperature changes or cold weather. Not like the rest of them, used to the harsh Canadian climates.

The snow had stopped overnight, but a lot of it had fallen. The vehicles were piled high with it and it was up over the tires in depth. Duncan decided to leave right away instead of waiting until the next day. Even with the all-wheel drive and off-road capabilities they had, the snow would still slow them down. It was better to arrive a little early and wait than to arrive late. There was too much at stake.

Snow was pushed off the tops of the armored vehicles and engines were started. Troopers entered the vehicles, hatches were shut, heaters turned up and the Wind Riders headed out toward the road that would take them into battle. Even with the temperature warming up and being on a paved road, the snow was still deep and they stayed well below their normal speed of travel.

Chapter Six

"Ma'am, there is activity along the front!" The aide had come rushing in to disturb Tanya's lunch.

She hurriedly stood and rushed for the door, another aide handing her a jacket as she passed. She pushed her way out of the large tent and ran to a nearby guard tower and quickly climbed to the top. Looking toward the front, she saw a series of flashes coming from rapidly approaching dots in the distance. She grabbed the proffered binoculars and focused in on the dots.

Two of her scout cars were flying at high speed down the road, snow flying behind them. They were being pursued by five enemy scout cars. As she watched, a laser hit the rear of one of her scout cars, the beam dissipating and reflecting upward. Right after that, this same scout car shot back, scoring a direct hit on the enemy, blowing that vehicle to bits.

The scout car in the rear appeared to accelerate, as the one in front moved to the side, slowing to allow it to pass and then slotting back in behind, taking its place in the rear. It immediately started to fire, targeting one specific enemy vehicle. Both scout cars were heading directly for the gap left in the defences.

Five of her precious armoured vehicles roared out of the camp to lend assistance. She only had ten. They drove about half a mile away from the defensive line and made a line across the road, turning sideways to allow all the weapons to fire, but leaving a gap wide enough for the two scout cars to drive through. Another enemy vehicle exploded and now the enemy was out-numbered and dropped the pursuit, electing to stop and observe.

The two scout cars blasted through, only slowing once they reached the gap in the first defensive formation. Once they were safely inside the second ring, they slowed to a crawl and two of the armoured vehicles came back inside the perimeter. The other three moved back to guard the first gap. One was in the center of the road, the others to each side.

"Have that scout troop commander report to me immediately," Tanya told her aide. "And make sure the troops get some warm food in them." Then she made her way down and back into her large command tent.

"Prepare some hot food for one more, please," she said to the aide in the tent as he took her coat from her.

Katarina marched into her presence, came to attention and slammed her right fist into her chest in salute. Tanya looked her over as she returned the salute. She was not wearing armour. Her uniform was dishevelled and dirty. White sweat stains were under the armpits and down her chest. Her hair was akimbo, her face streaked with dirt and grease. She had dark circles under her eyes and instead of a helmet, she had a soft cap under her left arm. A headset and microphone combination was hanging around her neck and she had obviously not had a change of clothing or a shower for some time. She was still wearing her well-worn weapons harness, complete with grenades and a hand weapon attached.

Tanya shot her well groomed and immaculately dressed aide a glance as he wrinkled his nose.

"Report, Sub-commander," Tanya said.

"Ma'am," Katerina replied. "The main enemy column is less than ten miles away and advancing rapidly. The advance guard should be in view shortly. We were able to slow them down somewhat and were initially pursued by ten of the enemy vehicles. We left the slower vehicles behind and destroyed five of the enemy scout vehicles. We have no casualties and no damage, Ma'am."

"What of the Wind Riders?" Tanya asked.

"Ma'am, three days ago we ambushed a resupply column two hundred miles from here. All enemy vehicles and personnel destroyed mam. We refuelled at that point and Master Warrant Kovaks ordered us to proceed here and report while he headed to his resupply point to refuel and rearm, Ma'am. They were very low on ammunition at that point, Ma'am. He reassured me that the Wind Riders will return here in time to join the defence, Ma'am."

"You have been gone for several months, Sub-commander. Surely you did more than just destroy one supply column?"

"Yes Ma'am," Katerina replied. "We previously had destroyed an estimated eighty percent of the enemy supply vehicles and an estimated twenty-five percent of enemy personnel and fighting vehicles, Ma'am. We sustained one casualty, Ma'am."

"Very well, Sub-commander," Tanya said. "At ease, take a seat."

"Leave us please," she said to her aide.

"We have retrieved Albert's body and sent him home, Katerina," she said. "You look tired. Have something to eat."

Katerina tossed her hat and headphone set on the table and sat down. First, she gulped down a glass of orange juice, then tied into the hot food with relish.

"Oh, I have died and gone to heaven," she said. "Fresh food!"

"How are the rest of your people?"

"We are all tired, Aunty," Katerina said. "But a day's rest in a real bed and not having to stand guard will do wonders. Also, some real food."

How things have changed, Tanya thought. She calls this rough camp luxury.

"The Wind Riders? How are they holding up?"

"They amaze me," Katerina said. "They just keep going and going. Laughing and joking at night or when nothing serious is going on, then very deadly when it is. Duncan was a little out of sorts after the ambush on the supply column, though. He was a little abrupt when he ordered me home. Only to be expected though; he has a lot on his mind."

"Duncan thinks the enemy will sit and make a plan for a few days once they get here. We have taught them to be cautious and to expect the unexpected. The heavy snow has concealed much of your defensive plan nicely. I knew what to look for and still had a hard time seeing it."

"Well I hope you are right," Tanya said. "Now go get a shower and change uniforms before my aide faints."

"Yes. I suppose I must smell very ripe," Katerina said. "We are all going to need new uniforms. These are the only ones we have."

"Well, let's get you settled in then," Tanya said and motioned the aide to escort Katerina, giving him instructions to obtain new uniforms for the scout team and to escort Katerina to her barracks.

Then, followed by her guard detail, Tanya, the ruler, exited the command tent and walked over to where the team's vehicles were parked. They were hard used and very dirty. Scorch marks from laser hits marred the paint almost everywhere. The interiors were also dirty, but otherwise well-kept. And then she saw the dark bloodstains on the rear upholstery of Katerina's vehicle and she sucked in a deep breath. It was all becoming real to her now.

As Katerina predicted, the enemy's advance guard arrived just after midday. Except for outposts scattered across the open plain, the main body of the advanced guard set up positions about a mile-and-a-half away. The command and control vehicles came screeching up about five minutes later and soon figures were on top of the vehicles looking at Tanya's positions with powerful spotting scopes and binoculars.

They saw two distinct lines of defence. The first was a quarter of the way up the hill. Except for the guarded entryway, the whole front of the position, from the inaccessible big hill on the right, to the cliff dropping off to a lake on the left, was blocked by concrete and steel barriers hardly wide enough to pass bodies through. Definitely too narrow for vehicles to pass through.

Behind that, the road was intermittently blocked by concrete barriers that a vehicle would have to snake its way through to the next set of barriers a hundred and fifty yards further back. These were thick, sharply pointed poles stuck in the ground at a thirty-degree angle to end just at chest height. Again, a person could fit between the poles, but not a vehicle.

Beyond that was the camp itself. One thousand conventionally armed and armoured troops were in that camp, protected by wire defences and tall guard towers. At the peak of the hill was the large command tent, with even taller observation towers beside it.

All the rest of the day, the main column of enemy troops arrived and set up their camp until, at nightfall, the plain below was covered by enemy tents, parked vehicles and troops. There would be no escape for the defenders. They would have to fight and die. There was nothing to stop the invaders behind them. The road to the capital, a hundred miles away, would be wide open. This was it. The war would be won, or lost, right here.

• • •

It was cold and snowing slightly in the grey predawn light as the enemy commander clambered up to the top of his command vehicle. For two days, he had observed his enemy, trying to locate anything that would betray other than what he was seeing. He had been constantly harangued by the client's commander to attack, but had held off. He had to be sure that the massive firepower they had faced on the trip here was not in place across from him.

All the evidence suggested that that powerful force was far behind them. They had destroyed a large relief supply column many days behind them and except for two small conventional scout vehicles, nothing had come past them from the rear. It would take weeks to take another route around this geographical feature. If that small but powerful force attacked them from the rear, despite their overwhelming firepower, he had the numbers and this was just the right place, where he could overwhelm them anyway.

Today would be the day. He would lose a lot of people, but common troopers were plentiful and he had a long waiting list wanting to join. The attack would come at daybreak and he had no doubt he would win.

• • •

"Your Highness," Tanya's aide had just rushed into her quarters. "The enemy is massing for an attack, Ma'am!"

Tanya flung the blankets from her, jammed her feet into the slippers that were by the bed and hurried toward the exit, stopping only long enough to throw a heavy jacket around her shoulders over her nightdress. She rushed up the steep stairway to the top of the observation tower and saw that Katerina was already there, fully armed. Tanya did not need the binoculars being handed to her to see what was going on. Even with the light snow falling, the mass of enemy forming lines was visible.

"A full-out assault then," she said matter-of-factly. "Very well, Sub-commander, fall your troops out to preliminary positions. Commander, sound general assembly if you would."

Then she went back down and re-entered the command tent, walked back into her quarters and ordered her body servants to bring her armor and weapons. When she re-emerged, she was wearing a complete set of lightweight metal scale armour, highly burnished and shiny. She had a narrow sword strapped to hang from her waist at her left. One aide held out her rectangular shield and another her plumed polished metal helmet. Her long hair was bound tight and high and she rapidly climbed to the top of the observation point once again and ordered her flag to be raised on it.

A ten-man troop of bodyguards were stationed all around the observation tower, armed with swords, war hammers and spears. Looking at the reverse slope, she saw the massive war engines being prepared for action and her troops gathering in their formations. At the front, her ten armoured vehicles had positioned themselves abreast in the centre of the roadway and the one thousand conventional troopers ranged in front of them. They would have to take the brunt of the attack at first.

A red flare burst overhead and the enemy lumbered into motion. The fight of their lives was about to begin.

• • •

All was going to plan. His troops were closing on the first barriers. Even with the snow and long range, his overwhelming numbers of attack vehicles would demolish the puny forces facing him. His ground troops began to spread out. The barriers would only slow them down, not stop them. They would easily outflank the enemy troops. Just as his armoured vehicles were reaching their maxim engagement range, a series of thumps was heard and a hundred large projectiles arched from behind the hill to impact his vehicles with great accuracy. The ceramic armour designed to defeat laser weapons exploded into fragments as they were hit. Every thirty seconds anther hundred would fly, not only aimed at his vehicles, but at the close-massed troops on foot. Bodies and parts of bodies flew after impact.

Then, just behind the barriers, oily, smoky fires began to burn inside deep trenches that had been concealed by the snow. The whole line, except for a one hundred-yard area in the center, erupted in flames, forcing his ground troops to merge to the center in a tight mass. The large projectiles concentrated their fire on this area and many troops were lost as the projectiles smashed into the tightly packed men.

The commander heard strange noises and looked up to the top of the hill where he saw oddly clothed troops coming over it. They were in tightly massed square formations of a hundred, ten wide and ten deep. They were wearing shiny armour and had large rectangular shields on their left shoulders. In the shield-hands were also three long light poles with long metal points attached to them. As they marched down the hill, they spread out and merged into ten groups of a thousand and, as they came, the conventional troops and vehicles raced to cover each flank. These tightly packed groups of a thousand came to a stop behind the second set of barriers and waited. The line stretched a quarter of a mile long and as his men formed up opposite them, they were continually hit by the large projectiles, ripping holes in the lines.

As his men came into range, the enemy's vehicles on the flanks opened fire, spraying his men with heavy laser fire and causing them to bunch up in the center. Now his massive numbers were working against him, as men jammed closer together to escape the laser fire coming from the flanks. All the while, every thirty seconds another hundred heavy projectiles piled into his massed troops.

Now the enemy commander joined the lines just behind them, with her one hundred troop body guard and her battle banner flying high. She was followed by two thousand non-armoured troops holding long thin bent sticks with strings attached to them and they ranged out behind the massed armored troopers.

At a bugled command, the armoured troops marched forward as one to stand in front of the barrier. After they halted, the front two lines passed their poles to the line behind them and with a crash of metal, locked their shields to their neighbors, creating a massive metal-clad wall. Then a load crashing noise was heard as every trooper banged the large hammer in his right hand on his shield in a slow rhythm.

Bang, Bang, Bang, Bang.

Just as his men were reaching maximum range for their lasers, the two thousand troops to the rear put long thin sticks to the stings and pulled them back to their ears and elevated them and, at a command, the sticks went flying in the air and a soft thrumming sound came ever closer. The sticks impacted his troops easily, penetrating or shattering the ceramic armor and piercing the men. Every ten seconds another two thousand of these missiles hit his men.

Then with a load roar, the shield wall began to advance. The large projectiles stopped falling at that point, but not the small missiles. His men began to fire their weapons, but the bolts just reflected off the metal shields and exposed armour they hit and the enemy kept coming and coming. At thirty yards, the long poles were flung, the sharp metal points devastating every man they hit.

Then with a loud crash, the shield wall hit his leading troops and the slaughter really began. The men in front could not retreat, they were being pushed by the men behind them. Now the long war harmers began their deadly work. His men had no defence, other than arms flung up to deflect the hits, which resulted in broken arms and worse. At regular intervals, the shield wall would push forward hard a few paces, then break off and file back between gaps left for them in the lines behind. Then the next front line would lock shields and fresh troops would come into the fray.

The arrows shifted to hit the rear ranks with their deadly missiles. His men began to edge backward, away from this carnage and he was about to order the ten thousand of his client's troops into battle, when his headset crackled.

"We are the wind rustling through the leaves and the grass, bringing fresh air and comfort.
We are the babbling brook, bringing refreshment and soothing.
We are the sun in the sky, bringing warmth and sustenance.
We are the Wind Riders, bringers of Peace, Hope and Justice.

We are the torrent that rips trees from the ground.
We are the raging flood waters that destroy homes.
We are the burning sun that devastates crops.
We are the Wind Riders, bringers of Despair, Death and Destruction
I am the Ghost in the Wind, bringer of justice, prepare to die."

Rapid loud explosions to his rear came at the end of the broadcast and he knew all was lost and ordered his men to withdraw. He hoped he could survive the next few moments.

"Keep at them! Keep pushing them; they are ready to break!" Tanya yelled. Her armour was scorched in several places from hits she had taken and her blood lust was up. Her bodyguard had to work hard to keep her from joining the front lines. She had her sword in hand and was in constant motion. One enemy trooper, who had miraculously escaped severe injury and been feigning death, sprang up to attack and, before her bodyguard could intervene, Tanya had rushed forward and taken the man's head from him with one swipe of her sword, adding bright red blood streaks and spatters to the scorch marks on her armour.

The battle lust she had transferred to her troops and they remembered the horrors these enemy had done to them in the past when they were weak. No mercy was being shown anywhere.

They felt the line in front of them begin to edge backward and surged harder against them. Then they heard the words in their headphones and the explosions coming from the rear of the enemy and as one yelled a mighty roar and all sense of cohesion broke down as the enemy turned and ran.

• • •

As Duncan exited the LAV he had been riding in, he saw the dark masses of the battling combatants on the hill two miles away. He joined the other dismounted troopers and began to walk toward the rear of the enemy formation. As he had expected, all the attention was toward the front where the battle was being fought. The light snowfall had covered their approach and now the four LAVs and two Cougars spread out. Gunners traversed cupolas to bear, the remote weapon stations pivoted and vehicle commanders manned the machine guns mounted on the exterior of the vehicles.

"Gunners," Duncan said. "Remember, I only want the command and control vehicles and those four large transports disabled, not destroyed. Everything else is fair game. Everyone. Hit them at long range. When they break, as long as they keep away from us, let them by. At all costs, we stay alive, people! Open the channels, CT."

As he spoke the last word, he pulled the trigger on his grenade launcher and all hell broke loose. Within thirty seconds, the command and control vehicles were out of action and then vehicles began exploded into pieces as 20mm cannon shells and 40mm grenades began to hit them.

Bodies were being flung on their backs in crimson-tinted explosions of shattered ceramic. Duncan was firing his rifle in semi-automatic single shots. Each shot hit a target and then he methodically moved to the next. As he switched out an empty twenty-five shot clip for a full one, he loaded another grenade in the launcher mounted beneath the rifle barrel and fired it.

His dismounts were in a rough firing line, down on one knee three hundred yards from the enemy and poring fire into them. The Minimi machine gunners were lying prone and firing three-round bursts, rapidly breaking up any formations that threatened to assault.

The munitions from the automatic pods on the LAVs were expended, but high explosive 20mm rounds from the cannons kept impacting the enemy everywhere.

At first, the enemy at the rear tried to escape toward their comrades up front, but then saw them running in panic away from howling shiny aberrations pursuing them and vehicles pouring laser fire into them as they ran. Then a few tried to surrender, but were cut down. Some sprinted to the sides away from the mass of destruction and found they could run away behind the large hulking vehicles spuming fiery death. They also found that, if they tossed their weapons away as they ran, they were not killed.

As Duncan was changing yet another clip, he saw Brett frantically changing the barrel on his Minimi and covered him until that was done and Brett started firing again. Now he stopped and stole a look around.

Had it been anything else, it would have been beautiful. Flames and smoke coming out of barrels as bullets and shells came out of barrels. His troops with grim expressions on their faces as rifle butts hit shoulders repeatedly. Cartridges from the machine guns mounted on the vehicles flying over and around gunners' heads. The overpowering noise of the main guns as they chunked, chunked, chunked out their high caliber munitions. The spectacular secondary explosions as a cannon round occasionally set off munitions or fuel in an enemy vehicle.

Few shots were returned by the enemy and they came nowhere near hitting any of them. It was pure slaughter. Duncan had two clips of ammo and one grenade left when he ordered the ceasefire. They were running out of targets anyway.

"Dismounts, form a perimeter around those four transports. LAVs, proceed to the transports and start loading the booty. Cougars, perform over-watch," Duncan said on his radio.

The local troops that could were running away from them. Everyone else was dead or would be soon. After what they had done and promised to do, none of the Wind Riders had any compassion for the enemy wounded. Any of them that came too close were shot.

As expected, the large transports were loaded with silver bars and those bars were being rapidly transferred into the LAVs. Now Duncan had another concern. The mercenary troops were coming toward them. Right on their heels were Tanya's people.

The command group and about five thousand of his troops had opened a large distance from Tanya's troops and had kept their cohesion, forming a line and firing as others moved through them and then falling back. They were not in full flight, but under order and control.

"Wind Riders, Wind Riders, this is the commander of Bishop's Marauders. I surrender, I surrender and ask you to honour the Guild's requirements."

"Bishop's Marauders, this is Wind Riders. I accept your surrender. Have your troops drop their weapons and place their hands behind their heads. Any who fail to do so will be shot out of hand. Keep advancing."

All of the enemy dropped their weapons, put their hands behind their heads and began to jog towards Duncan's lines. A great roar erupted from Tanya's troops as they saw this and they sprinted to catch up to their prey.

"CT! Jane! Shots across the bow at those people coming at us!"

The two Cougars opened up with their 20mm and machine guns twenty yards in front of the howling advancing troops who skidded to a stop.

"Assemble your people behind my vehicles, commander," Duncan said. "I will deal with you directly. Wind Riders! Skirmish line in front of the LAVs. You will shoot anything that comes across that line CT has just drawn.

"Jane, Bob, Karen, with me. Dave, you are in command. Weapons free if they attack us."

The dismounts quickly fanned out in front of the armoured vehicles and cupolas traversed and cannons covered Tanya's people.

As his command group joined him, Duncan began to walk forward. His rifle was pointed at the ground, trigger finger just outside the trigger guard.

Tanya joined her frontline troops and advanced on him with her one hundred strong bodyguard around her. She was furious. Duncan stopped a hundred yards from her and his troops and waited for her to come. His vehicle's cupolas traversed to cover the rapidly approaching ten vehicles.

Duncan saw Tanya had no intention of stopping. She and her troops were brandishing their weapons and in tight formation. He lifted his rifle and fired three rounds ten yards in front of her. Then three more as she kept coming. Finally, he let loose with the rest of the clip and one of her bodyguard took a hold of her sword arm and stopped her.

"What the hell are you doing!" she yelled at him. "I order you to kill those people! Do it now!"

"Enough, Tanya," Duncan said. "Enough. How many more people must die this day? We have won. Enough."

"No, damn you!" she yelled back. "They must all die!"

Now Katerina was beside her. She pried the sword from her hand and swung her around, looking into her aunt's wild eyes.

"Enough Aunty, enough," she said softly. "If you order me to, I will attack Duncan. But you and I and everyone else here will die. He will not like it, but he will kill us, Aunty, and you know it. You have your revenge; we have won. No more death today, Aunty."

The soothing tone of Katerina's words seemed to sink in and the fire went out of Tanya's eyes. She looked around and heard the screams and the moans of the wounded for the first time. Then she looked at the blood staining her hands, arms and sword.

"Very well," she said. "Have our troops withdraw back to our lines. Warrant Kovaks, you may have your prisoners. You will report to me in my headquarters in three hours. Dismissed!"

Then she turned around and orders were shouted out to disengage and return to base. Her guards surrounding her, Tanya began to march back to her positions and her troops began to cheer as she passed between them.

"Thank you, Kat," Duncan said. "The blood lust had her hard."

"I know, Ghost, I know," she said. "I know you had to accept their surrender and to protect your prisoners. I also know you would have killed her if you had to."

"I like her a lot," Duncan said. "And you. But ya, we would have gone down fighting. We would have taken most of you down with us."

"Most? Not all?"

"No, love," Duncan said. "We are down to two clips each. You might have got us, but you would have paid a big price for it."

"We would have helped him," the enemy commander said. "We all may have died in the end, but the honour of the Guild would have been upheld and many of you would have died with us."

"Go home, Kat," Duncan said. "Be with your people, especially Tanya. All this is going to hit her hard, real soon. She is going to need you."

She gave him a hug, then hugged Jane, Karen and Bob. She saluted them and jogged after her aunt.

"She's got a good head on her, that one," the enemy commander said. "Much better than the people we were fighting before."

"She should," Duncan said. "She's been with us fighting you people all this time. CT, tell me the beer survived."

"I think there is some water in some of those transport trucks, Commander. Your people can probably use it. I'll try and scrounge up some rations for you."

"We have enough with us for a few days," the commander said. "But more is always better." He ordered one of his men to start searching for food and water and to make camp.

"If you and your officers would care to join us?" Duncan said. "I think we have enough for a couple of drinks each if there are not too many of you."

Only ten of his officers had survived and there was more than enough beer for everyone. Except for the six manning the guns on the vehicles, the rest of the Wind Riders joined them.

"Is this it?" the enemy commander asked. "Only thirty of you? Surly there are more hidden away."

"Nope this is all of us," Duncan said.

"Shit," the enemy commander said.

"So, I am Duncan. Duncan Kovaks. You are?"

"James Bishop. Commander of Bishop's Marauders. What is the meaning behind the wolves painted on your vehicles?"

"Where I come from there are four animals," Duncan said. "The sheep, who are vast in number but not fierce. The wolves that prey on them. The guard dogs that protect them and then us, wolfhounds. We don't guard, we kill wolves. Those are wolfhounds, not wolves."

"And we were the wolves," James said. "Good analogy. I suppose you also taught the sheep and the guard dogs how to fight? And very effectively, too, I might add. I have never seen those weapons or tactics before."

"That would not have worked where we come from," Duncan said. "These weapons and machines would have ripped them apart just like we did to these guys. But against you, ya, no problem. Those tactics and weapons are old and are taught to everyone back home. Even the tactics we used against you are not new. You were not just fighting me, James. You were fighting two thousand years of warfare."

"The Guild has brought in other groups like yours," James said. "I have heard about them, but you are the first I faced. We had no defence against your weapons or tactics. But I warn you. Don't believe everything the Guild tells you. For instance, they told us all your spare weapons and ammunition had been destroyed and that you would not get further supplies. Yet I see that not only do you have a lot of weapons and ammunition, but you also have more powerful fighting vehicles."

"As far as the Guild is concerned, they were right," Duncan said. "An airborne assault took out our resupply base. Fortunately, we had moved it weeks before."

"This war was over before you guys hit us in the rear," James said. 'This is my inner core of troopers. I think we would mostly have survived without your help. They would have gotten tired and backed off, but the war was won. I think I have around five thousand troops left. I have a big rebuilding job ahead of me."

"Not as big as mine," Duncan said. "We don't even have a base of our own and we can't go home. Like you said, I have no doubt the Guild will cut us off from our supplies of vehicles, weapons and ammunition after this. They are already sending a group of my home world's people to assimilate us. We will talk about that among ourselves later. Right now, I have to finish this contract. If we don't get fired, that is."

"Hell," James said. "You guys can join me. I pay top wages and benefits and I can surely use you and your tactics."

Before he could answer, CT warned him about incoming Guild craft. Shortly after that a Guild craft landed and the Guildsmaster exited it with his guard group.

"You have done well, Master Warrant," he said. "I see not all of your machines were destroyed in that attack."

"Ya, a few had not been transferred to the supply depot yet. We got lucky."

"Once the ransom has been paid by Commander Bishop, we will transport his troops away," the Guildsmaster said. "Until that time, you are responsible for them."

"Should not be a problem," Duncan said. "Anything else?"

"I assume your contract is finished now? We have other work for you."

"We have a meeting in a few hours," Duncan said. "This war is not finished yet. I will contact you when we are ready. I am sure Commander Bishop can help me in that regard. Some of his communication devices should have survived."

"Very well, we will be waiting to hear from you," he said. He re-entered his vehicle and in a cloud of dust he was gone again.

"Hey, they are paying us well for this job," Duncan said as he saw the look James was giving him. "Plus, I have the silver I took off you and what we just took off these other guys today. So, we don't really need the work all that badly. In any case, I pick the jobs I go on and I am very picky."

"The Guild has ways of getting what they want," James said.

"Well, one job at a time," Duncan said. "This one isn't finished yet. Get your people settled in. My command group and I have to go meet Her Highness now. Things might change by then, but I don't think so. Jane, we will take your Cougar, I think."

Duncan, along with Jane, Karen, and Bob as driver, weaved their way through the extended battlefield. The snow was beginning to cover the bodies strewn on it and on a few occasions, they roughly bumped over them as there was no other way to carry forward.

It was impossible to pass through the main entrance into the defences. The bodies were stacked two or three feet high in places. But at the edge of the defensive wall, the barricades had been designed to swing away to allow the defenders' vehicles to attack. They chose the left one beside the cliff leading to the lake and made their way to the top of the hill and the command tent.

Tanya's people had suffered casualties. Not many compared to the enemy, but casualties just the same. Wounded troops were being ferried to the rear and the dead were being collected. Medical staff had set up a hospital complex on the reverse slope of the hill and were plying their trade. Other troops were gathered in their camping area. Six troop teams sat by their tent or in section and platoon strength. Some had already removed armour, others were in the process and still others were just sitting looking at their feet or the sky.

Three vehicles were already parked in front of the command tent and Bob parked with them. The Wind Riders exited the Cougar armed only with their side arms, leaving the rifles inside it. The guards posted outside the tents entrance barred their entry, refusing to let them pass. The four of them stood there for ten minutes, waiting, arms crossed on their chests and refusing to leave.

"Fine, be that way!" Duncan yelled out finally. "We don't really want to talk with you stuck up assholes anyway."

He waved for his people to follow and jumped back into the Cougar. Bob started it up and they drove out of the camp and back toward their own.

"CT," he said over the radio. "Load ten of Bishop's people on each of our vehicles and ferry them up to their own. Then escort them back to camp. Tell Bishop I want to talk with him. Drive up the left side of the battle field, where it is mostly clear."

They passed this group on the way back, traveling at a much faster pace and were soon back at their original position.

"James," Duncan said the second he came out of the Coyote. "Grab whatever tents and gear that you need and load them up in your vehicles once they get here. We are moving two hours down this road and set up camp. I don't want to be around here much longer. Scavengers and predators will be coming for all this easy meat and I don't want to be anywhere near here when they do."

In a short time, the original camp area was a hub of activity as Bishop's people broke down tents and loaded them and supplies into the fifty vehicles that came back and in just over an hour, the column flanked by the Wind Riders set off back down the road. Having nothing to worry about, they were traveling as fast as the vehicles could manage on the snow-covered road.

They blew past the enemy stragglers as they made their way slogging through the ankle-deep snow, once in a while bumping their way over a snow-covered body. As they reached the main column of dejected troops walking down the road, they did not slow down, running a few down who were not fast enough to get out of the way. No one, not Duncan's or Bishop's people, had any sympathy for these men. To a man, they were brutes and inhumane and deserved no pity. Soon predators would be picking off the weaker ones and Tanya's people would finish off the rest. None of them would ever reach home.

After two hours, they were eighty miles from the battlefield. They pulled off into a field and began setting up their camp. In short order, the smell of food cooking over portable stoves was scenting the air, which was alive with the buzz of conversations.

The sun was setting and dinner was over when Bishop and two of his people came up to where Duncan and his crew were sitting.

"It would seem my employer is less than pleased with me," Duncan said. "No matter. My contract is until the enemy has been removed as a threat to the planet and I intend on honouring my end of the contract. I intend on attacking, overwhelming and capturing the enemy capitol."

"With only thirty of you and six vehicles?" James said. "You guys are good, but not that good."

"You will be joining us," Duncan said.

"It doesn't work like that," James said. "I can't just switch sides in the middle of a war. The Guild will not allow it."

"When was the last time you were paid?" Duncan said.

"Other than the down payment, we haven't been paid at all."

"Nonpayment of fees," Duncan said. "Not supplying you with essential materials while in the war zone and abandoning you at the height of the battle. Your employer is in breach of your contract and you are free to seek other employment. I checked the rules and your contract, James."

James and his people just stared at Duncan, looks of disbelief on their faces.

"My people are quite good at manipulating computer and communication systems," Duncan said. "So, I will pay you what you are owed by your previous employer. We will deduct that from your ransom payment. In addition, I will pay each of you ten pounds of silver per month while on active duty. If you choose to join us and the rest of my people agree, I will pay five pounds of silver per month while in garrison. If any of you choose not to join us, we will arrange for transport off planet."

"We join you?" James said. "Not you join us?"

"Correct," Duncan said. "I just defeated ten thousand of their troops. Easily, I might add. Their total population was only fifty thousand to begin with. A large number of the remaining population will be children and non-combatants. So, I don't really need you. The capitol itself only has about ten thousand inhabitants in total. We will be hitting them hard and fast. We cut all their communications last week, so they have no idea what is going on.

"So, are you in, or out?"

The four looked at each other and shrugged their shoulders.

"Hell," Bishop said. "You're paying double what we normally get. Why not. I keep command of my people, though?"

"Of course," Duncan replied. "We will also give equal shares of any plunder we gather from now on. One stipulation on plunder. All of it, and I mean all of it, is to be collected for us all. I find anyone holding out, they get kicked out. Clear?"

"Also, no looting, and especially no raping or outright killing of civilians. We catch anyone doing that, they will be shot on the spot."

"Agreed," James said.

"How much fuel do you have?" Duncan asked. "We have to travel two hundred miles tomorrow."

"At the speed we were traveling?" James said. "About three hundred miles' worth."

"Okay, no problem," Duncan said. "I have enough fuel for my people at our supply depot. I also have enough of your weapons on hand to arm about half your people. The next day, we should link up with that supply column we hit and you can refuel from the tanker we did not destroy. You should be able to find more weapons there as well. We didn't destroy any of them at any rate."

After a few more details were hammered out, Bishop returned to his own camping area.

"CT, see what information about the capitol you can dig up," Duncan said. "But tomorrow, not tonight. Everyone get some sleep tonight; we need it. Put the sensors on automatic. I'm not expecting any surprises, but better safe than sorry."

"Okay, boss," CT said. "Planetwide jamming of all comm systems is in place and working. Also, I have blanked out anything the Guild has monitoring us. We are invisible."

"Good," Duncan said. With that he walked over to his sleeping bag and was soon asleep.

Chapter Seven

THE WIND RIDERS WERE UP and about before dawn the next morning. It had stopped snowing at some point during the night and cocoons of snow-covered sleeping gear were cracking open as the inhabitants woke up and clambered out. Drivers and commanders gathered up their gear and entered their vehicles, firing up engines and performing systems checks, while others cleared snow from critical components and the cooks for the day began breakfast.

The noise of all this activity stirred the Marauders into motion and soon the whole camp was buzzing. In short order, they were on the main road again and, by mid-day, had swung off the main highway and were heading across country to the supply depot.

The tents and camouflage netting were all covered with snow, but soon, smoke from woodstoves was pouring up out of the tents' chimneys. The camp's generator was started and the hot water tanks for the showers and laundry were fired up.

The Marauders set up their own tents, and electrical lines from their vehicles were attached to each tent. Duncan checked out one of these tents and was amazed at what he saw. A lighting system and heating grid were incorporated into the fabric of the tent. After just a short time, the interiors were warm and the troopers were discarding jackets. While the Wind Riders had been shivering under sleeping bags and tarps the night before, the Marauders had been warm and cozy.

The rest of the day saw long lines for the showers and the laundry. While the Wind Riders had sufficient new, dry clothing in place, the Marauders did not. As with the weapons, Duncan had some local clothing on hand, but even handing out their own spare uniforms, not all the Marauders were able to obtain new uniforms.

It took the entire day to refuel vehicles and load up full ammunition loads. The Wind Riders attached small portable tanker trailers to both

Coyotes and one LAV. While fuel was readily available for the local vehicles, a diesel fuel alternative for the Wind Riders' needs had not been found yet. They had to take their own with them. Most of the work was completed two hours past mid-day and the majority of the troops had begun to relax. CT and Karen were getting street plans for the capitol city and Duncan and James worked out a travel plan. It would take four days to reach the capitol and James agreed that there would be little in the way of resistance until they hit the capitol itself.

At daybreak the column was on the move again. Returning to the highway was faster as the trail they had blazed through the snow was still clear. Once they were on the main road, Duncan turned his radio on and tuned in the frequency they used to communicate with Tanya's people. At the top of the next hour, someone from there called them, then told them to wait a further transmission.

Ten minutes later, a curt clipped voice that Duncan did not recognise demanded their location and to hold in place for further instructions.

"Negative," Duncan said. "Wind Rider Regiment will proceed to the final destination as planned and carry out its part of the agreement with, or without, local authorities' participation. Wind Rider Regiment will halt for one day at location of supply column ambush. After that, we will be proceeding without delay to the final objective. Wind Riders out."

Then he shut off the radio.

There were a few hours of daylight left when the column reached the supply column ambush site. The Wind Riders set up their laager and lit their camp stoves for dinner and coffee just off the road, about two hundred yards away. Taking their lead from the Wind Riders, the Marauders followed suit, making ten larger defensive formations and setting their tents up inside.

In groups of ten, the vehicles moved down to the still intact fuel and water tankers and refuelled. Other troops were scrounging through the wrecked vehicles, loading up on weapons, uniforms and unspoiled food. They even found six undamaged tents, which they gave to the Wind Riders, who promptly set them up. Brett found a way to use their vehicles' battery systems to power up the heating and lighting grids of the tents. For tonight at least, they would be warm and dry.

"Whiskey Romeo Alpha One, Whiskey Romeo Poppa One, how copy?" A crackling transmission came over Duncan's headset. He let Katia call twice more.

"Whiskey Romeo Poppa One, Whiskey Romeo Alpha One, copy five by four, send traffic."

"Alpha One, Poppa One, requesting rendezvous coordinates."

"Alpha One is at ambush site. Alpha One will be departing at daybreak."

"Imperative Poppa One link up. Request Alpha One hold in place."

"Negative Poppa One. Whisky Romeo will depart at daybreak. We will be easy to find. We are a column of fifty-six armoured vehicles. Whiskey Bravo Task Force, change to Comm Plan Delta."

Duncan hit a series of buttons on his communicator which put the unit on a specific frequency hopping scheme. Unless they were extremely lucky, Katia and her group were unlikely to figure it out and then only for a minute before the frequency would shift again.

"From the signal strength," Karen reported. "I put them at least a day behind us."

"Right," Duncan said. "Carol, make sure a bird is ready for the morning. Karen, I want you and Barb flying and monitoring it. Maybe get Megan some flying time, too. Obtain and keep contact with that column."

The rest of the night passed uneventfully. It started snowing again during the night and was still snowing gently at first light. But the column was on the move at daybreak. The snow was not deep on the uncleared highway, not hampering the Marauders much and the Wind Riders not at all.

"A guy could get spoiled with those new tents," Scott said. "Snug as a bug in a rug."

"Which is why we were able to hit those guys so easily," Duncan said. "Don't get used to it. We'll use them tonight, but after that, we hit the border the next day and are in bad guy country. Nobody uses tents after that."

Duncan did not have much do while they were on the move. They were the only ones on the road, except for some local wildlife.

They drove past the village where they had first encountered all this and the landscape changed rapidly after that. Burnt-out farm buildings and lands were replaced by abandoned ones and the roadway was soon lined with trees and shrubs. Cattle and sheep were grazing in fenced pastures and several fairly intact villages were passed along the way. But other than wildlife and domestic herd animals, the landscape was empty.

That night, they camped just outside one such village. Karen reported that Katerina's column would be arriving in about three hours. They were traveling fast and in addition to their own ten vehicles, were accompanied by ten of the Marauders' vehicles.

Duncan was going to treat them as hostile until proven otherwise. He stationed the LAVs a half-mile outside the village, facing the direction of the column's approach, and had the Marauders already with him set up flanking positions around the village. If they were attacked, it would not be pretty for Katarina's column.

"Ten miles out, Dunc," Barb reported. "They are coming hard. ETA ten mikes."

Duncan switched frequencies on his radio.

"Poppa One, Alpha One. Estimate link up in ten mikes. Be advised, any threatening movements will result in immediate commencement of hostilities. Copy?"

"Alpha One, Poppa One. Copy. Link up in ten minutes. We are a column of twenty vehicles. No hostile intentions. Request a meeting. Three of our vehicles will approach. The others will stop two miles outside your perimeter. Copy?"

"Copy, Poppa One. Scott would really hate messing up your hairdo, Kat, but he would do it."

"I know Ghost, I know. See you in a few minutes. Poppa One, out."

Diesel engines fired up and as soon as the electronics came online, cupolas were rotating and stayed moving as fire coordinates were fed to them from CT's and Jane's Coyote systems.

The Wind Riders might not all like it, but they would destroy Katerina's column if they had to.

The column stopped two miles away, as she said it would, and stayed in column formation, not fanning out or forming defensive postures. One Coyote covered the three vehicles that approached at reduced speed, while the other vehicles fed targeting information into weapons systems for the remainder.

"Far enough," Duncan said over his radio as the three vehicles came to three hundred yards away.

Twelve people came out of the three vehicles, four to a vehicle, but only three advanced on foot. All of the Wind Rider dismounts were ranged in front of their vehicles. Weapons were in hand, but not pointed at anyone. Duncan walked out to meet them alone, with only his holstered pistol with him. He wasn't worried. Carol and the other sharp shooters laying prone out of sight would take out any threats before his visitors could get a shot off.

"Nice to see you again, Your Highness," Duncan said. He saluted, but did not wait for a return salute before he dropped it. Nor did he stay at attention or at parade rest. "You wanted this meeting; say your piece."

"How dare you address Her Highness in such fashion," the man on the left said. "You should be shot for such insolence!"

"I don't know who the hell you are," Duncan said. "But if that is going to be the tone of this conversation, it is over. Good luck on trying to shoot me; you'll be dead before your pistol clears the holster."

Duncan turned around and started walking back to his vehicle.

"Wait!" Tanya said. "Please Duncan, wait."

Duncan turned back and looked at her.

"My name is Master Warrant Officer Kovaks, Ma'am. I would thank you to remember that. You are my employer, not my sovereign or my ruler. The only allegiance I owe you is that stipulated in my contract. I have been contracted to eliminate your enemies using whatever means I find necessary to do so. I intend to do that, Ma'am. Once I have finished my assignment, if this fool wishes to pursue this further, I assure him, I will meet him anytime, anywhere."

"Please Master Warrant Kovaks. Excuse my cousin," Tanya said. "He has been on the other side of the planet and is unaware of all you have done for us. I also apologise for my own actions the day of the battle. They were uncalled for. I was not myself, Mr. Kovaks."

"Very well," Duncan said. "What do you require of me, Ma'am?"

"I would like my people to accompany you, Mr. Kovaks. I know we are not many, but they are good troops. They are my best people and they have been trained by you. They will report to you Mr. Kovaks. Not me. My niece will be in command of them and my cousin her second in command."

Duncan looked at them for a few moments, especially the haughty aristocrat. He noticed the change in rank badges on Katerina's uniform.

"Very well," he said. "Commander Horshack, have your people bivouac with the Marauders."

"Sir!" Katerina said and saluted.

"Sub-commander, you are in an active war zone under arms. Any disrespect or dereliction of duty and I will shoot you. Is that clear?"

The man mumbled something.

"Sub-commander," Tanya said. "Your commanding officer just asked you a question." Then she pulled out her own pistol and pointed it at him. "If you do not answer correctly I will shoot you myself."

The man drew himself up to attention and saluted. "Yes, Ma'am!" he said. "Very clear. Master Warrant, Sir!"

"Very well, Sub-commander,' Duncan said. "Commander, clue this idiot in as to how we operate. I have no time for this bullshit. Carry on!"

Both saluted and walked back to the vehicles, leaving Duncan and Tanya alone. Tanya put her pistol away. She reached out her hand and touched Duncan's shoulder, looking into his eyes.

"Please Duncan, I am very sorry," she said. "I reacted badly. After, it was worse. If you can understand? I…I really cannot explain it."

"Welcome to the brotherhood, Tanya," Duncan said. "I was nineteen when I made my first kill. It was not a very big firefight and it was at long range. But still. The first one is the worst and yours was very intense, up close and very personal. Lucky for you, my people are very well trained. Otherwise, your very pretty body would have a large number of holes in it."

He was smiling now.

"Why thank you, young man," Tanya said smiling back. "You are definitely my type, even being so young. But I think Karen would scratch my eyes out, and if she didn't, Dianne would."

Now Duncan laughed. "Ya, all these females seem to be overprotective. You have some time? Come on, we have some beer and vodka."

Tanya put her arm around him and kissed him on the cheek.

"Well, now that we are friends again, why not?" she said. "I planned on staying the night in any case. My niece tells me you have a proposal for me?"

He had his arm around her waist now, and they were making a show for the Wind Riders as they came toward them.

"We'll talk in a minute," he said.

"Hey, hands off, you floosy," Karen said as they came near, but she was smiling. She gave Tanya a hug, then invited her to sit down, but not before planting a big kiss on Duncan's mouth. "He's mine, all mine."

"A girl can dream, though?" Tanya said.

"Dream yes; touchy, touchy, no," Karen said as she handed Tanya a beer.

"Oh poo," Tanya said. "Can't you just loan him to me for a couple of days? Or weeks?"

"Not a chance, honey," Karen said, now she draped herself over Duncan as he sat down.

"Not even if I were to sign over control of those two sectors you are going to take back for me?" she said. There was a twinkle in her eyes now.

All talk stopped now as the Wind Riders looked at Tanya.

"This is what you wanted to talk to me about, yes?" she asked playfully. "Don't worry Duncan, I was just joking. You really are too young for me, pleasant as it would be for a few days. Katerina tells me you have a proposal for me that I will like. But she did not know all the details."

"We checked into your system of government," Duncan began. "What we are proposing will fit. Carol's people back home operate under the same system we are proposing and it has worked well for almost two hundred years now. In return for complete control of those two sectors, we will pledge allegiance to you and your rightful descendants. We will remit to you ten percent of any taxes we collect. We will provide our own infrastructure. In addition, we will provide one battalion of troops for the planet's defence. We will maintain and equip this battalion at our own expense. Once you have called us into active service, you will pay all expenses incurred and provide all supplies and make good any equipment losses. We also reserve the right to offer our services for hire to other interested parties, as long as those parties are not in conflict, directly or indirectly, with Your Highnesses."

"This is much like the agreements we have in place with our other noble houses," Tanya said. "You have this proposal in writing for me?"

"Yes, Ma'am," Duncan said. CT handed her a file folder. Tanya glanced over the documents quickly, then looked up. "Some Washka, I think?" Then she put her head down and continued to read.

Scott produced a bottle and filled a glass for her.

"Glasses for everyone, I think," she said and went back to her reading.

Scott and Amanda rushed back to Duncan's LAV and brought back some more bottles and glasses. Once everyone's were filled, Tanya put down the file and stood, picking up her glass with her.

"I believe this agreement to be beneficial to me and my realm," she said. "My niece tells me you have a way of sealing an informal agreement?"

She stuck out her hand to Duncan, who jumped up and grasped it.

"So, we have an agreement in principle," she said. "To take effect after this war is over and the current people occupying those lands are removed from power."

"Yes, Ma'am," Duncan said. "Thank you, Ma'am."

"We will take this preliminary draft back with us to the capitol in the morning," she said. "We will have our solicitors clean up the language and send it back for your approval.

"Now a toast. To the uniting of our two peoples!"

Everyone raised their glasses and drained them. Tanya tossed hers to shatter in the fire pit. Carol was the first to follow suit, then Duncan remembered the significance of that gesture and tossed his to shatter as well. The rest of the Wind Riders followed suit.

Then Carol came up to Duncan saluted and went to one knee in front of him.

"I am Carol, Daughter of Hines, Canadian born. I renounce my allegiance to Andreas Host and pledge allegiance to my new ataman, Duncan, House of Kovaks. I pledge this in front of God and man." She made the sign of the cross and stayed down on one knee.

The response words came to him from the back of his memory. He had heard his mother say them many years ago. He took her by the shoulders and raised her up and turned her around to face the crowd.

"This is Carol, daughter of Hines. What is done to her and hers, is done to me and mine. So say I in front of God and man."

Dave came next. His grandfather had been a member of Andreas Host.

"I am David, son of Burt, House of Kline. What is done to Duncan Kovaks and his is done to me and mine. So say I in front of God and man."

Barb was next, followed by Megan.

Everyone else was just looking. They knew something important had just happened, but were not sure exactly what.

"This is an old ritual," Tanya said. "We have the same ritual. The wording is a little different, but I think yours is truer to form. Those four have just committed themselves and their families to Duncan and he has committed himself and his family to them. To protect each other in times of need. Duncan will in turn pledge himself to me and my people. Not now Duncan. The war must be concluded first or the Planetary Counsel and the Guild will not approve.

"I understand that the rest of you come from democratic institutions and are unfamiliar with our form of government. I will leave it up to these five to explain it to you.

"Now, thank you for your hospitality. I have a lot of reading to do tonight and you have an early departure. Good evening all."

She strode off toward her encampment and Duncan was faced by twenty-four questioning faces.

He explained to them that this was the original intent of the old feudal system and was not all that much different from the system of government they were all familiar with back home, the Canadian system of a constitutional monarchy. Carol, Dave, Barb and Megan, had just elected him to be their leader.

"Carol was kind enough to provide me with the constitution and bylaws of her people and the agreement they have with the Canadian people and the Crown. I will upload it to your vehicles' computer systems and you can review it. We will have a meeting tomorrow night and I will answer your questions at that point. CT, can I talk to you for a minute?"

"Count me in, Duncan," he said. "I've already read it. It makes more sense than the system of government I am used to. I will talk it over with the other Americans."

"Thank you, CT," Duncan said. "I appreciate the vote of confidence. Now, can you still reach Shelly? I really need her to take a look at the final agreement."

"Ya," CT said. "Text is easy, if you're not in a hurry. Voice has a twenty second delay, though."

"Okay, send her an encrypted message telling her that, and that I will be hopefully in contact with her in a week's time."

Barb, Dave and Megan were in deep discussion with most of the Wind Riders. Karen, Jane, Bob, Amanda, Dianne, Scott and Brett were waiting for him. Carol was also there.

"We already know how the colony operates," Jane said. "We have been pumping Carol about it for a few years now."

"I don't want a commitment now," Duncan said. "Please read the material thoroughly. Think about it. Tomorrow is soon enough."

Karen came up to him, turned him so they were sideways to the group and put her hand above his heart.

"I am Karen, daughter of Jane,' she said. "This is Duncan, my husband. What is done to him and his is done to me and mine; so say I in front of God and man." Then she made the sign of the cross.

Duncan placed his hand over her heart and pledged himself to her and made the sign of the cross on her forehead, lips and chest.

"So say I in front of God and man."

"So say I," Carol said.

"No more tonight," Duncan said. "No more. Please, look over all the documentation. You are not just committing yourselves, but your future families. The others knew what they were doing. Karen had no choice, she is my wife. The rest of you, no. Talk it over among yourselves. You have until Tanya and I formalise the agreement."

"They really have no choice, Duncan," Karen said later. They were snuggled together on a cot in their own tent. This would be their last night together for a long time. Starting tomorrow, there would be no tents and each crew would be sleeping with their machines.

"You always have a choice, Karen," Duncan said. "But if they want to stay here as members of our new community, they will have to. You didn't have to either. I thank you for it, but you didn't have to do it. We are already married."

"No Duncan, I had to say it," she said. "Even though everyone else knows it, even though we are already husband and wife, I had to say it. We only had a civil ceremony, Duncan. I didn't know you were Catholic or we would have had a church wedding. I said something similar in my heart the day we were married, but now I have said it aloud and pledged myself to you in front of God. As you have me."

"Well, I am not a very good Catholic," Duncan said. "The last time I was at mass was for my father's funeral. I was deployed overseas for my mother's. Besides, I think religion causes a lot of problems."

She didn't answer because she agreed with him. She pulled him very close and they began to make love. She would tell him about the baby later.

The column was forming just as the sun broke the horizon to the west. It was cold enough to see breath and even though the locals were all bundled up in warm clothing, the Wind Riders had theirs undone. It was chilly, but not cold for them. So far, the vehicles' heating systems had not come close to being overtaxed. But he heard a lot of complaints from the locals and Marauders about how cold it was.

"What are you guys going to do once it really gets cold?" he overheard Amanda say to one of Katerina's people. "This is nothing."

Three aircraft landed just then, blowing snow everywhere and making everyone duck away. Even his people were swearing now. Without preamble, Tanya and three guards jumped into the centre one and, as fast as they arrived, they were gone.

Two troopers from Katerina's troops, one from each vehicle, joined with one of Duncan's vehicles; the sub-commander was one of them. He had been assigned to Karen's all-female crew.

"It will do the spoiled brat good," Katerina said. "He, like most of the male aristocracy, think we females are somehow less worthy than they are. I am sure Karen and especially Ann will clue him in. I would like a chance to speak with you in private tonight, Duncan. It is personal."

'Can't do it tonight, Kat," Duncan said. "We will be across the border by then and I won't have any time. If I clear my crew out and we both turn off our radios, we can talk for the next four hours, until we stop for lunch. Don't worry about Bob. This thing is too noisy for him to hear anything up there in the driver's compartment."

She agreed and Duncan banished his dismounts to the other LAVs. He put Jane in charge of the column. There was lots of room in his vehicle now, so he removed his headset and sat down, relaxing. Katerina did the same and the LAV jerked into motion. Soon the road and vehicle noises increased in volume. Katerina made to speak a number of times, but then stopped herself. It was clear she was struggling with what she wanted to say. Duncan let her be. She would talk when she was ready. He was almost falling asleep when she began to speak, first so low and hesitant that he had trouble hearing her. She saw that and began to speak louder.

"Aunt Tanya had an attack of conscience just before your meeting, Duncan. She was most distraught, not only about what she had just witnessed, but what she herself had just done. My stupid second cousin decided to take command at that point. It was he that ordered you to be treated that way. I was with my aunt at the time, doing what you have done with me. It took her two days to calm down. By then you were already gone and were not replying to any of our radio messages."

Kat had convinced Tanya that this was standard procedure for Duncan. That he would only be using the short range tactical radios and those infrequently. She had convinced her aunt to allow her a small force to make contact with Duncan, and Tanya had insisted on coming along.

"I had been eavesdropping on your conversations while I was serving with you, Duncan. I will not apologise for it. You would have done the same in my position. I knew you would never be allowed to go back home and were formulating a plan for my aunt about making one here. Carol also told me much about her people. How they were different from others in your country. She told me about their system of government, which is very similar to ours. So, I recommended to Tanya that she propose a similar agreement with you. I see that you had already thought of that yourselves and were very prepared for it."

She went quiet then for a time, once again reflecting on what she wanted to say.

"Duncan, I am the only member of my family still alive. We are a minor branch of the family and are not landed aristocracy. All we share is the name. Aunt Tanya will make sure I am well looked-after and she will probably arrange a marriage for me to some buffoon like that sub-commander. But I will never have anything of my own and my offspring will be looked down on, for they will not be true aristocracy.

"Carol told me how her people would take in deserving people, making them full members of the community. Will you be doing the same?"

"Depends," Duncan said. "Depends on what the person has to offer, if the other members of the community agree and if they can find two members to vouch for them. It helps if I like them, but it is not a requirement."

"I would like to join," she said. "I have proven my skills as a soldier and a commander. I have good managerial skills. I managed my father's interests for many years. I think I will be a good asset to your community, Sir."

Duncan sighed deeply and took her by the hand.

"Yes, you have proven to us you are a good soldier and commander," he said. "That alone will fast-track you into membership. But you still have to find two members to sponsor you. Karen and I cannot. In these matters, we have to be impartial. You convince two members of the community to sponsor you, and I will hear your request. That is all I promise. So, now here come the mandatory requirements, Kat.

"You will have to serve five years as a minimum as a trooper on active duty. If we are at war during that time, it will be extended. After that, you may choose to go in the active reserve for ten years, or stay on active duty. You will spend two weekends a month training and will be on active duty for three months a year until your five years are up. At any time, during an emergency, you can be placed on active duty during that five-year period. After that, if you do not choose to remain in the army, you will be placed on the inactive reserve list and will only have to serve one month a year for the next ten years, but you will have to qualify with minimum standards every year to maintain that status. There are a few perks involved, but we will get into that later.

"Some last thoughts, Kat. You will be swearing loyalty to me and through me, the community and only after that to your aunt and the planet. In addition, you may be allowed to marry after three years of service, but in no way will you be allowed to have children during that first five-year period. If you do, you will lose your status."

"I understand, Duncan," Katerina said.

"Okay, so find two sponsors and get back to me if you are serious. Now, let me get some sleep until lunchtime, because I don't think I will be getting much after that."

Katerina was amazed at how fast these people fell asleep when they were not on duty or during a rest period. But she felt her eyes start to droop and, before she knew it, she too was asleep, thinking about what they had just discussed.

Duncan's eyes snapped open as the engine changed pitch and they began to slow down. He put his headset on.

"What's up, Bob?"

"Just stopping for lunch, Boss," Bob said. "Do you think Brett can take over this afternoon? I could use some shuteye myself."

"Ya, he's probably been sleeping like a baby over there," Duncan said. "I'll take over as gunner for the rest of the day. No, I don't want to be vehicle commander today. Tomorrow is soon enough."

Duncan climbed up out of the gunner's hatch in the cupola and surveyed the area. They were in a large field that was not covered in snow and the temperature was somewhat warmer now.

As Bob levered himself out of the cramped driver's compartment, Katerina let herself out via the man-door in the rear ramp. Duncan watched her hurry over to Carol and they began a conversation.

"Getting a little chunky there, Bob," Duncan said.

"Rub it in, you young punk," Bob said giving him the finger. "I'll be happy when I get back in my nice cozy Cougar. In the back, not driving it."

Then he made a beeline to Jane. Both Coyotes had raised their surveillance masts and Duncan just leaned back and enjoyed his last few moments of silence.

"Nothing but us and some large animals around, Ghost," CT reported. "The little bird shows a border guard post up ahead. There are ten armoured vehicles and about a hundred troops manning it."

"Okay, have someone keep an eye on it,' Duncan said. "You go get some lunch and I want you rested up for tomorrow."

"Will do, Ghost," CT said.

Duncan looked over to Katerina and saw her hugging Megan and then she jogged over to her own vehicle, the same one she had used before.

"Voice," Duncan said. "Get your sorry ass over here and bring some hot coffee with you. All my bloody troops have gone AWOL."

"Step into my office," he told Barb as she came up, two travel mugs in hand. Then he slid back down into the LAV, pulling the gunner's hatch shut behind him.

"Ah, nectar of the gods," he said taking a sip of coffee from the mug Barb had handed to him.

"So, my oldest and best female confidant," he said. "My turn. Does Megan understand all that is required of her?"

"Yes Duncan, she is aware," Barb said.

"Are you sure? She is mature for her age, but she is still a young female, Barb. As far as I know, there is no birth control around here."

"Oh, I can assure you," Barb said. "Our little girl is no blushing virgin and hasn't been for a while now. She knows what is what and, so far, nothing has come along to tempt her. Yet."

"Okay," Duncan said. "Everything else all right?"

"I miss the boys sometimes, Duncan, I won't lie to you. But there is nothing I can do about it and I think we made the right decision." She kissed him on the cheek.

"You make sure you come to me if you need to talk," he said. "You know I will be coming to you at some point. I always have."

She patted him on the cheek and walked back out, leaving him to his brief period of solitude. All too soon it was over and they were on the move again.

Just before sunset, the border crossing came into view and Duncan loaded high explosive rounds into the 20mm gun, arming it and the coaxial machine gun. Then he began tracking targets and he and the other LAV began to fire at eight hundred yards distance. They didn't even slow down as the targeting systems kept the barrels level and aimed as they moved. The vehicles and buildings were in smoking ruins as his LAV smashed through the flimsy barrier that was strung across the road. He did not concern himself with the troops on the ground. The Marauders were taking care of them with their weapons and he didn't want to waste his precious ammunition supplies on people, yet.

An hour later, they found a suitable camping spot, just outside a small village, and formed up in their defensive postures. There would be no tents set up from now on. Full defensive posture was put into place. Listening posts and foot patrols were established and each vehicle had one person manning the vehicle's weapon. Those not on duty would find a place to sleep inside or under the vehicles.

The villagers rushed to their vehicles and vacated as fast as they could, taking only what they could carry. The village was empty in short order.

Katerina approached him and saluted.

"Master Warrant," she said. "The full army is following us. They are two days behind. Her Highness would like it if you postponed the attack on the city until they can join us, but it is not an order, Sir."

"If they can catch us, no problem," Duncan said. "Otherwise, too bad. I am not slowing down or stopping to wait for them. Speed is everything now."

"I will tell Her Highness Sir," she said.

"And Commander, no further radio communication from here on in. No sense in making it easy for the enemy to track us, eh?"

Duncan called a staff meeting after supper and let everyone know they would be two miles outside the capitol by nightfall the next day. They would blow right through any villages or towns on the way. They could return fire if fired upon and were to run over anything that got in their way. But other than that, not to bother. The army following could handle controlling the inhabitants. They had no time. Then everyone but James and his second in command left.

"A few of the locals have been speaking to some of my people," James said. "Is it true? That Her Highness has granted you these two districts for a home?"

"We have an agreement in principle," Duncan said. "But nothing formal at this point. I am sure Her Highness will honour her word, though."

"You will need troops to comply with the agreement, then," James said. "My people and I would like to be those troops, Sir. We are aware of the commitment and are willing to comply, Sir."

"Take some time to think it over, James," Duncan said. "It is a lifelong commitment, not only for you, but your descendants."

"Yes, Sir, we are aware," James said. "We have all seen the requirements sir and have studied them."

"Let me guess," Duncan said. "It just happened to appear on all of your computers. CT, I'm gonna kick your ass!"

"It wasn't him," Karen's voice came over his earpiece. "I did it."

Duncan sighed; he would talk to Karen after this.

"Okay, I have to speak with my people first," he said. "After that, come and see me."

Once they had left, Karen and the other four community members came up and stood behind him. Then, one by one the rest of the Wind Riders came up and said the words pledging themselves to him.

"Okay, time for some beer," Duncan said. "No party though; that will have to wait."

"No, Sir," Carol said. "We are not finished yet. Candidate, front and center!"

Katarina came forward and saluted, staying at attention after Duncan returned it and Carol came along one side of her and Megan the other.

"Ataman," Carol said. "Katarina Horshack has asked to join the host. She is a strong and powerful leader, Sir, a good warrior and I vouch for her. Sir!"

"Ataman," Megan said. "I have been in battle with the candidate. I count her as my friend and will die for her, Sir!"

Then Dianne stepped forward.

"Ataman, I have not been asked by the candidate, Sir. I will vouch for her, Sir!"

Karen made to join them, but Duncan held her back. Barb did come forward, as did Amanda, Anne and Jane, along with all the other females. Duncan turned and looked at the male members. As a group they all walked over and stood by Katerina.

"Sir," Dave, as the ranking male member, said. "We all agree, Sir."

"Candidate, step forward," Duncan said. "The band has accepted you. What say you?"

Katerina went to one knee in front of him and said her vow. Duncan raised her up and turned her around, placing his hands on her shoulders.

'This is Katerina, house of Horshack. What is done to her and hers is done to me and mine. So say I in front of God and man."

"So say us all!" the others responded.

"You are out of uniform, trooper," Duncan said. "Somebody find her a uniform and a beret."

Carol placed a beret on Katarina's head and handed her a beer.

"Okay, you are still in command of your people at this point," Duncan said. "After this is over, I am putting you with Dianne's section. Ah shit, now what?"

The Marauders, all five thousand of them, were marching up in columns of eight and then split up into battalions and companies, coming to a halt in front of them and saluting.

"Sir!" James belted out. "The Marauder Regiment wishes to join with the Wind Riders, Sir!"

"What say you, my brothers and sisters," Duncan asked his people.

Jane marched forward and saluted.

"Ataman, the Wind Riders agree to the request, Sir!"

"Very well, Colonel," Duncan said. "Commander Bishop, front and center. Commander, we do not have time to have each of your people swear to me individually. They will place their right hands over their hearts and go to one knee, while you say the words for them."

Almost as one man, all five thousand of them, did just that, and James said the words. Then they all stood to attention once again.

"I am Duncan, your Ataman. What is done to you and yours is done to me and mine, so say I in front of God and man."

"So say we all!" the Wind Riders belted out behind him.

"Well, I know for a fact we don't have enough uniforms for you all. Nor am I sure if we have enough beer; in fact I know we don't. The party will just have to wait."

"This was enough, my lord," James said. "We will die for you, my lord."

"Well, I pray that will not be necessary," Duncan said. "We are in the middle of enemy territory, people. We can't afford any mistakes and we leave at first light. So, don't overdo it tonight. Now, will somebody please give me a bottle of beer or am I going to die of thirst over here."

Scott tossed him one and he made a big show of chugging it all down. He pulled Karen to him and hugged her close.

"I couldn't let you go to her, Karen," he whispered in her ear. "We are the leaders and can't be seen to influence a decision made by the band members one way or another. I explained that to her already. Now go to her and let her know we love her, eh?"

The sub-commander and a few of her troops were watching the proceedings and the cousin did not look pleased. Duncan walked up to Carol and spoke into her ear.

"You keep that asshole close," he said. "You have my permission to blow his ass away if he gets out of line. Let me worry about Tanya."

Carol nodded her head and Duncan walked away, grabbed his sleeping gear and tossed it under the LAV. Another night spent on the cold hard ground, he thought, as he climbed in and was soon asleep.

Chapter Eight

THE SUN WAS JUST HITTING the tops of the mountains to the east as they stopped and formed their laagers for the night, two miles outside of the capitol city. Some city, Duncan thought — more like a small town back home. Duncan was standing on top of his LAV, binoculars to his eyes. Enemy troops were abandoning their outposts and hurrying to the large fortress in the center of the town. The walls were tall and armoured with towers mounted and manned on each corner. Two towers flanked the single entrance into the fortress and CT reported that was the only exit point.

Amateurs, Duncan thought. He would have both drones flying tonight, one watching the fortress, the other the town and its perimeter. Both Coyotes' surveillance units would be manned all night. He wanted no surprises. Foot patrols and listening posts would be doubled, watches changed every two hours. Duncan had no intention of being taken unawares.

CT had taken control of all the enemies' transmitter systems and Duncan had contacted the renegade leader and offered him an honorable surrender. He received a blunt refusal, complete with the obligatory insults to himself and his family and graphic details of the horrors that would greet him after he was defeated. CT blocked any further communication from leaving the fortress and gave Duncan a signal when he had control of the civilian radio frequency.

"I am Duncan Kovaks, commander of the troops loyal to Her Highness, Tanya Horshack, ruler of this planet. People of New Paris, your self-proclaimed ruler, Napoleon the seventh, has pulled all of the troops protecting your community into his fortress, concerned only with his own welfare. Let it be known that, two hours after dawn, we will attack your town and the fortress.

"We have no wish to make war on unarmed non-combatants. You have until we start the attack to come forward and surrender yourselves. I personally guarantee your safety if you do. However, I cannot and will not, if you do not surrender. When the attack begins, we will kill anyone with a weapon or who gets in our way. If we are fired upon from a dwelling, we will destroy that dwelling and everyone in it. We will not go out of our way to harm you, but will do what we must.

"Two days behind us, ten thousand of Her Majesty's troops are coming. After what they have suffered from your soldiers, they have no love for you people. Anyone who has not surrendered to me before I begin my attack tomorrow, I will not protect. You will be on your own to persuade Her Majesty's troopers that you are innocent of any crimes. I will not intervene on your behalf.

"This offer is extended to all far reaching and remote communities. Come in and surrender before we find you. Otherwise you will be hunted down and killed."

Duncan removed his headset then and walked outside. There was a bite in the air, but it was warmer than it had been a few days earlier and there was no snow on the ground. His commanders were all waiting for him and he commenced his briefing. CT was following along, projecting a hologram of the city streets and the route they would take to the fortress. Anything that had a weapon was fair game in the town. Anything that got in the way would be run down or gunned down. No surrender of townspeople would be allowed once the invasion began. Nothing was to slow them down on their way to the fortress. The LAVs would take out the guard towers, the Coyotes the gates. Both would attempt to create breaches in the walls, but nothing was guaranteed. They just did not know how thick they were or what kind of armor was protecting them. All Wind Riders vehicles would enter the compound, and all of Katerina's. A maximum of one thousand of Bishop's people would guard any townspeople who surrendered prior to the invasion, and the camp area. The rest of his people would be split into two groups. One would guard their backs to the town, the other would take control of the yard. They would be joined in the yard by Katerina's people. The Wind Riders would assault on the residence. No one else.

"We have extensive training in this type of operation," Duncan said. "We will be killing anyone with a gun who does not have the proper identification, and that means all of you as well. None of you have compatible equipment for us to determine if you are a friend or foe. It is much easier for us this way.

"Any troops who throw down their weapons and surrender, I recommend be allowed to do so. I leave it up to your discretion. The so-called emperor and his inner circle will not be granted that option. If there are no questions? Very well, outline the plan to your people. Wind Riders, you stay."

After everyone else had left, CT projected an interior schematic of the building. Current infrared images showed where the guards were at that time. CT, Barb, Jane and Bob would be monitoring the situation in real time. Each of them would have one of the four teams to handle. There were four entrances and stair wells and three floors to clear. D Troop would take the first floor, C the second, A and B the main residence on the third. Anything with a gun was fair game on the first two floors and anything that moved was on the third.

"Full personal loads, people," Duncan said. "Carol, keep that asshole out of the way. Yes, he comes with you. Katerina is one of us now. She goes with Dianne's gang. Karen, you're with me. Crew gunners, lose the machine guns and take your C8s instead. Make sure all of you have fresh batteries for the IFFs and night vision equipment. There are almost two hundred tangos in there, people. Be safe, come home alive."

Then he pulled out his last case of beer and passed it around. Others were found and each of them began their pre-battle rituals. Clips were emptied and cleaned. Bullets were cleaned and reinserted into the clips. Rifles and pistols were taken apart and cleaned. Sharp knives were sharpened again. Grenades and flash-bangs were hung on the weapons harnesses. The vehicle gunners prepared their weapons. Drivers filled the fuel tanks to overflow and checked engine compartments. Then there was nothing left to do. The married ones broke away in pairs to spend a last night together.

The rest of them, Duncan and Karen included, stayed together, swapping stories until the beer ran out.

"Fuck it," Duncan said. "Who wants to live forever, anyway? I'm off for bed."

Karen watched him walk away, then she chased after him. She had only told her mother she was pregnant and she would tell Duncan after. He would not let her come tomorrow if she did. They both held each other close that night, lying face to face. There would be no sex tonight; they were both too keyed up for that. But they held each other tight until they fell asleep.

"Duncan, promise you will stay safe today?" Karen said. "Promise me you will come back with me."

"You know I can't do that, luv," Duncan said. "I'd be lying. Nor can I ask that of you. It is all in God's hands now. If he wants us to die, we will. All we can do is our best, my love. Kill them before they get a chance to kill us. I love you with all my soul, Karen. I will do my best to keep you safe, but the mission comes first. If we don't think that way, all of us may die."

"I know, Duncan. I love you with every fiber in my body. I will do everything I can to keep you safe, too."

Then they kissed and after, he held her at arm's length, brushed a stray lock of her hair back behind her beret and smiled. "God, you're beautiful," he said. Then he turned and walked away, loading his weapons and making sure everything was in order.

"God, please let him come back to me," she whispered. Then she followed him, making the same preparations he had just done. Now came the false bravado they all put on, making stupid jokes and laughing, while, deep inside, each of them was grappling with their demons and their fears.

It looked like most of the townspeople had come out. They were being watched closely by Bishop's men, weapons at the ready. All the troops were boarding their transports and Duncan took his place in the commander hatch, loading a belt into the machine gun mounted on it and chambering a round. She lost sight of him as she entered the LAV and sat with the others and the ramp closed, leaving them in darkness. Alone with their fears.

"IFF check," Duncan said and he turned his on. As he listened to CT report everything was operational he took a last look around. Every machine was manned. The roof gunners or commanders were looking his way. The sun was shining; not a cloud was in the sky. He keyed his mike.

"This truly is a good day to die," he said. "Crank 'em up, people."

Starters whined and vehicles came alive, the sound of engines vibrating the landscape. He waited a few minutes and keyed his mike again.

"The hunt's afoot," he said. "Tally ho!"

The LAVs would take the main street. Bishop's people split up to take other streets leading the same direction. Duncan was in the lead, the other three LAVs right behind him. The two Coyotes brought up the rear, followed by Kat's people. Duncan kept his head on a swivel, but he really did not want to waste ammunition out here. They would need it more against the fortress. Kat's people had enough firepower to handle anything the locals would throw at them and proved it more than once along the way. They were almost at full speed when he had CT hit the open channels and the PA systems and keyed his mike.

"We are the wind rustling through the leaves and the grass, bringing fresh air and comfort.
We are the babbling brook, bringing refreshment and soothing.
We are the sun in the sky, bringing warmth and sustenance.
We are the Wind Riders, bringers of Peace, Hope and Justice.

We are the torrent that rips trees from the ground.
We are the raging flood waters that destroy homes.
We are the burning sun that devastates crops.
We are the Wind Riders, bringers of Despair, Death and Destruction."

As he spoke the last word, his gunner opened up with the cannon, as did the others behind them. The guard towers were destroyed almost before they knew they were under attack, the gates blown off right after. The walls turned out to be ceramic and they blew apart quickly, creating huge gaps in them. Duncan fired a few bursts at troopers foolish enough to stick their heads up and soon weapons were flying off the walls as troopers threw them away. Duncan ignored everything but the residence once they were inside the compound. He was stitching the walls with his machine gun. The cannon was blasting away at them, too, and the gunner was firing the machine gun as well.

Then he dropped inside, the vehicle slid to a stop, the rear ramp crashed down and Duncan joined the troops running for the door, his rifle and theirs firing into windows as they ran. He fired a grenade into the door before they got there and the vehicles stopped firing as they entered the building and dashed up the stairs. Duncan was in the lead, taking two steps at a time. Gunfire broke out on the floors below and Duncan came to a stop at the stairwell door. He slowly tried the door, finding it unbarred and unlocked. Then he took a flash-bang from his pocket, armed it and tossed it through the door. He waited for it to explode, then he flung the door open and stepped inside, shooting a trooper holding its head. Lasers were firing back; these were well trained troops, Duncan thought, but they had to expose themselves to fire. Duncan and his people just fired into the walls and doors as they came by. Suddenly, Karen shoved him aside and took a shot meant for him. It was at close range and Duncan buttstroked the trooper, smashing the helmet and contacting the head beneath it. Then he brought the weapon forward again and shot another trooper who had exposed himself.

Four men were stationed behind sandbags in front of the last set of doors and fired at them bravely, but it was not enough as multiple grenades were tossed over the barricade. The explosions not only killed the brave troopers, but blew the door itself apart. Inside, the leader was cowering behind his wife and children. It didn't help him. They were all cut down, then Duncan spun around as he was hit by a glancing shot. Another brave man was pointing his weapon at him, waiting for it to recharge. Three others had tossed away their weapons and were on their knees with their hands behind their heads.

"Give it up, son," Duncan said. "Nobody else needs to die today."

The poor man had eight rifles pointed at him. He looked over at the leader and his family, then back at Duncan.

"You did your duty, son," Duncan said. "Drop the weapon."

The weapon had finished charging and the man kept looking at it, then Duncan, and finally the leader. Then with a sob, he tossed the weapon away and sank to his knees. Tears were running down his cheeks.

"Third floor clear," Duncan said. "You did a good job here, son." He clapped the young man on the shoulder and lifted him up. "No one could ask for anything more. You were outgunned, son, you had no chance, no chance at all.

"Wind Riders, take any of these brave people who survived into custody; we'll sort it all out after."

Then he walked out into the hallway and saw what had happened to his two missing troopers. Karen was lying on the floor, her eyes wide open. She wasn't breathing. A blood-soaked Amanda was working on the trooper he had buttstroked. By the long hair, she was female and still alive.

"Bishop, get your people in here and help us police up the wounded. Bob, secure channel now!"

"Ya Ghost, what's up."

"Karen is dead, Bob. I'll be down in a minute to talk with Jane."

"Fuck," was all Bob said.

As the rest of the assault teams reported in, Karen was the only casualty.

"A Team has one KIA," Duncan said. "Secure the area. Wind Riders will be exiting the building with prisoners. Four of you grab the wounded prisoner, the other four grab Karen. Come on people, get your heads out of your asses. The mission isn't over yet."

The last he said without keying his mike, so only the two fire teams could hear. It was a quiet and solemn crew that left the building. The cheers that were erupting stopped on the spot as they saw the body coming out.

"Who was it?" Jane asked as Duncan came into her Coyote.

"Karen," Duncan said. Then he got out of the way as Jane ran out of the Coyote to be with her daughter. Bob was looking at Duncan.

"Go to her Bob, If she ever needed you, it's now."

Duncan came back outside and looked around. The courtyard was full of his troops, just standing there looking.

"Get your fucking heads out of your asses!" he yelled. "This area is still not secured! Commanders, get your people under control and back doing their jobs, God dammit! CT, get me a channel to Her Highness, stat!"

"Your Highness," Duncan said. "All resistance has been eliminated. The fighting has stopped and we are securing the area. We have four wounded and one killed, Ma'am. Your relatives are unharmed, Ma'am."

"My God, Duncan, already?" Tanya said.

"Yes, Ma'am. It was not much of a fight."

"I will be there in two hours. Good job, Duncan."

"Yes, Ma'am, thank you, Ma'am. Now, if you will excuse me, we still have to secure the area for your arrival, Ma'am."

Jane, Bob and Barb were still with Karen. Jane was crying uncontrollably. Amanda was still bandaging the soldier he had buttstroked and Duncan walked over to her.

"Is she going to live?" Duncan asked.

"I think so," Amanda said. "Her skull isn't caved in, but until a real doc gets here I can't be sure."

"Keep her as comfortable as you can Amanda. Brave girl like her deserves to live. I need people like her, Amanda. Do whatever it takes to keep her with us, okay. Enough brave people have died for that asshole emperor."

"The town and the compound are secure, Duncan," James said "I've got my medical people working on the wounded and Her Highness is bringing some more with her. The full hospital will be here when the main column arrives. Other than the ones you people shot, most of the wounds are light."

"Good. As I told Amanda, these were all brave people. I can use people like them. Keep them all safe for me, James."

Then he saw the sub-commander standing to one side by himself and he walked over to him.

"Not exactly all roses and glory, is it?" Duncan said. "People get hurt and killed in this job, son. This is nothing compared with what Her Highness faced. Now get your shit together and get your people back to work."

"How the hell can you be calm?" the man asked. "Did you not love your wife? Are you that unfeeling?"

"I don't have fucking time for that shit right now!" Duncan said. "If I fucking lose it now, the rest of you will fall apart. The troops are looking to us for guidance. Now get back to work!"

Duncan walked away and as he walked he clapped troopers on the back and told them they had done a good job. Even troops he did not know he praised, and he left smiles behind him. Karen's body had been covered up and taken from view by the time Tanya arrived. Jane had herself under control and met Tanya as she exited the aircraft. She gave her a tour of the battle. The bodies had been removed from the interior of the house, but fresh bloodstains, bullet holes and splintered walls and furniture told their own story. Jane visibly faltered and shuddered as they passed one large blood stain on the floor on their way to the room where the emperor had met his end.

"Where is Duncan?" Tanya asked.

"He is touring the positions, Ma'am," Bob said. "And Karen is indisposed. Kat should be free by now, Ma'am; I will take you to her. The colonel's presence has been requested on another matter, Ma'am. I will take over for her, Ma'am."

"Of course, Major. You must all be busy right now and here I am wasting your time."

"Not at all, Ma'am," Bob said as he escorted Tanya out of the building and to Katarina. Then he hurried back to Jane who was barely hanging on as Barb walked her out of the house and toward her Coyote.

"Oh my God," Tanya said after Katerina told her about Karen. "You must take me to her at once."

They had placed her on a stretcher and covered her with a blanket. Two troopers from B Troop were guarding the door to the small building in which she was being held. Four female troopers, one to each corner, were standing. Their arms crossed over rifle butts, barrels on the ground and their heads bowed. Tears were streaking down the dust on their cheeks.

Amanda entered behind them and she peeled back the blanket so Tanya could see. Karen was still fully clothed; the shot had taken her square in the chest and exited out her back.

"I was right behind her, Ma'am," Amada said. "She spotted the shooter before I did and pushed Duncan aside and took the shot herself. She was dead before she hit the ground, Ma'am. Duncan was too close to the shooter, but he buttstroked her, Ma'am. Hard. I am not sure she will survive without brain damage, Ma'am. Both of them are brave women, Ma'am."

"Duncan is unharmed?"

"He took a shot in the arm at the end, Ma'am. It was a glancing shot, Ma'am. He commended the young man who shot him for doing his duty and talked him out of committing suicide, Ma'am. If he would not have dropped his weapon, he would have been riddled with bullets, Ma'am. Enough people had died already. And, Ma'am, Karen was two months pregnant."

"Did he know?" Tanya asked.

"No, Karen wanted to be with him and he would have made her stay in a Coyote if he had known."

Two of the guards were sobbing openly now. No one had known about the baby.

• • •

He had turned off his radio and his IFF. Try as he might, CT could not find him. Duncan was living up to his nickname. But those who knew him well found him. He was sitting under the eves of a small outbuilding on the edge of town, his back against the wall, looking up at the stars. Dianne sat on one side of him, Megan on the other. Brett and Scott sat outside of them. No one said anything. They all just sat there.

"Why her?" Duncan finally said. "Of all of us. Why her? Twice today I should have been killed, but was not. I promised to come back to her and to keep her safe. She made the same promise. She only kept part of hers and I only kept part of mine. What kind of shit deal is that? She shoved me out of the way and took the shot herself."

"She was two months pregnant, Duncan," Dianne said softly.

"Ah, fukin shit!" Duncan tossed the stone he had in his hand as far as he could throw it. "Fuck, Karen, why didn't you tell me?"

Then he did break down, badly. They stayed with him all night and he finally cried himself out as dawn approached. He shook himself twice and stood up.

"Okay, enough of this shit," he said. "Crying is not going to bring her back. Did Tanya make it in safely?"

"Yes, Duncan," Scott said. "The rest of the army pushed through all night and should be here mid-morning. Tanya said we are all to stand down when they get here."

"No way," Duncan said. "I promised those people they would be safe if they surrendered."

"Tanya promised to honour that, Duncan," Megan said.

"I don't give a shit what she says," he said. "Until we see it with our own eyes, we will not stand down. What's our status?"

"Vehicles have been refueled." Brett said. "We did not use very much ammo and are okay that way. All the other wounded were minor and they are all back on duty now. Except for one bonehead Canadian who is refusing treatment."

"What, this little shitten thing?" Duncan said pointing to his forearm. "I probably won't even get a scar out of it. Okay, take me to some coffee, then our glorious leader."

"Speaking of pompous asses, what did you say to that shithead?" Dianne asked. "He has been a model officer ever since you talked to him. Hell, he might even turn out to be an okay guy."

"Some people just learn a little slower than others," Duncan said. "Carol didn't kill him, so I thought he was worth some effort."

The five of them walked back through the deserted town to the town center, where the LAVs were set up in the large square before the mansion.

"If your glorious leader does not have a hot cup of coffee in his hands in five minutes, the cook will be shot," Duncan said as he came up to his LAV.

"CT, tell Bishop I want another thousand of his people and at least ten vehicles guarding the townspeople. All the LAVs but mine are to head over there as well. Hell, send mine as well. Then I want your Coyote over by the infirmary and all of Katarina's people and vehicles. Set up a perimeter. Any hostile moves against any of my prisoners, you shoot the perpetrators, clear?"

"Get Bishop and the sub-commander over here right now. And Dave. Kat, you stay."

"Her Highness wants to see you right away, Ghost," Katarina said.

"Not until I have something to report to her. Oh heaven in a cup." He took a deep pull of the coffee.

Once everyone had arrived he began his debrief. Bishop had filled a water tanker and sent it and two of his field kitchens over to where the townspeople were being held. Luckily it was warm for this time of year, but the night had been chilly. Some form of shelters for them would be needed before long. Fuel supplies for his vehicles was plentiful and he had enough rations to last a week.

The sub-commander reported the same and that the enemy wounded were progressing as well as could be expected under the conditions the small local hospital had to offer. The local doctors and all the medics were still working hard.

Fuel supplies were low, but not critical, Dave reported. All the vehicles and jerrycans were full and the tanks trailers were still a quarter full. Ammunition was not an issue yet, but they needed a resupply. Food and water were good for a week.

"Right," Duncan said. "Our first priority is to get those townspeople back to their homes and jobs. CT is to get our computer people working on vetting all the townspeople so we can start releasing them. Two priorities. First, we need to release all people needed for critical infrastructure operation: electricity, water, sewer, medical staff. We also need some heavy equipment operators, because we need to bury these bodies ASAP. Next, we need to isolate any ardent supporters of the old regime and any of the political leaders. Then we need to begin releasing regular folk. First, anyone with anything to do with food distribution; next, people with children or the elderly; finally, military prisoners. Find me some officers who are not fanatics first. I will want to talk with them myself. Okay, off you go. Dave, you and Kat stay."

"Dave, we are a major short. Find me a replacement and then do whatever juggling of the officers you need to do to fill in the blanks. As of now, Kat is a full member of the Wind Riders. Have her take over Megan's slot for now. Dismissed."

Duncan contacted CT and told him to find a replacement for Karen. They needed another computer hacker. They didn't have to be as good as Karen was — that would be hard to match — but they needed someone with decent basic skills.

Then he finished his coffee, and stood motioning Katerina to follow him. After a few steps, he stopped and looked her over. He adjusted her beret so that it was sitting properly, then nodded and started walking again. His first stop was at the small hospital. It had about twenty patients. Some were in the process of being discharged. Some had lost a limb or broken one and they would be a while rehabilitating. Five of them had no hope and would die soon. These would be kept as comfortable as possible. The arduous work, that of patching them up, was completed now and the overworked medical staff were taking rotating rest breaks. The doctor he had been talking with was local.

"Thank you for all your hard work, Doctor," Duncan said. "You and your people have done well. Help, a lot of help, should be here shortly. Then you and your people can take some time off. I have a personal interest in one of your patients. The one with the head trauma?"

"She's tough, that one," the doctor said. "We had to sedate her and put her in her own room. As soon as she woke up, she was trying to help."

The doctor led them to a single room. She was lying on her back. Her head, except for her eyes, nose and mouth, was completely covered in bandages. Both her eyes were the black-yellow shade one gets when punched too hard. Her skull was cracked but not broken, and she had a massive concussion. Brain swelling was under control and, as far as they could tell, other than the pain, she had not had any further damage. The left side of her face had been reattached, but she would be scarred. Her hair had been removed to deter infection. The doctor felt she would recover physically. But an attractive young woman who had just been scarred badly on the face? Well, there would most likely be some mental consequences.

"Get her whatever help she needs, Doctor," Duncan said. "Like I said, I have a personal interest in this young lady."

"So, Kat," Duncan said as they left the hospital. "That also is part of your education as an officer and a leader. Luckily, none of our people was injured severely, but we need to make sure the wounded are properly cared for. After all, it was our orders they were following that got them injured, so it our responsibility to look out for them. Just because they are our enemy, does not mean they are not people, Kat. They followed their orders and did their best.

"Now, gird up your loins, girl. We are off to see your aunt and I don't think she is going to be pleased."

They were only kept waiting a few minutes and were then ushered into Tanya's presence. Today she had two aides in attendance and her broad smile changed to a noncommittal one when she saw the beret Katerina was wearing.

"Master Warrant Kovaks and Ensign Horshak reporting as ordered, Ma'am!" Duncan said, then he bowed his head.

"First, let us congratulate you, Master Warrant, on your successful conclusion to this unfortunate war," Tanya said. "We are in your debt, Sir. We would also express our deep condolences on your loss."

She snapped her fingers and an aide handed Duncan a large file folder.

"That is our agreement for you and your people to take control of these two districts. We have already signed and sealed it. Please look it over, sign and return our copy."

"Leave us," she said to her aides. Duncan handed the file folder to Katerina.

Once the aides had left, Tanya rose and came up to Duncan hugging him.

"I am so sorry, Duncan. Karen was a special person and I loved her almost as much as I love Kat."

"Yes, Ma'am, thank you, Ma'am."

Tanya looked up at his eyes and saw he was staring at the ceiling and his eyes were wet. She released him and gave Katerina a hug. Then she took a step back and looked her up and down.

"What is the meaning of this, niece?"

"Ma'am," Katerina said. Her eyes were focused above Tanya's head as well. "The Ensign asked for and was granted admission to join the Wind Riders, Ma'am. The Ensign formally resigns her commission in Her Majesty's service, Ma'am."

Tanya was shocked but said nothing.

"I will withdraw if you wish to speak in private, Ma'am," Duncan said.

"No, Duncan, you stay. Look at me, child. Why?"

Katerina took a deep breath, held it and then slowly let it out. Then she lowered her gaze to look into her aunt's eyes.

"Aunt Tanya, you have been so good to me, especially after my parents died. But I am not landed gentry. I know you would have made sure I was well looked after and arranged a good marriage for me. But I, and my children, would never be equal and you know it.

With Duncan and his people, I can be whatever I want to be. I can make my own life, not have one dictated for me. I was not forced, Aunty. In fact, Duncan and Karen tried to talk me out of it. I am sorry I have disappointed you and I will understand if you cut me out of your life. But I must do this, for myself and my descendants."

"What is done is done," Tanya said. "Now leave us, child."

"Do try and keep her safe, Duncan? She means much to me. Unfortunately, appearances must be kept, but you can expect a visitor tonight. Tell me of your plans."

Duncan told her of his immediate plans of getting the townspeople back in their homes and resuming normal lives. He also told her of his offer for amnesty to all the outlying areas and what he proposed should be done with the hard core radicals. Until that was done, nothing further could be done.

"I agree, Duncan. The sooner we can get everything back to normal, the better. I will issue orders for my people to assist yours wherever possible. We have extensive files on all the malcontents and I will be contacting the Interplanetary Counsel and the Guild, informing them of the end of hostilities.

"Once again, thank you for everything, Duncan."

She and Duncan hugged, then he left her room and her aides rushed back in. Jerking his head, he and Katerina stepped into the street. This time she had the beret positioned properly.

"That went better than I expected," he said. "Of course she is disappointed, but she loves you a lot, Kat. Officially she has to make it look a certain way. Unofficially, she is very happy for you. Now you will begin training as a real Wind Rider. It will not be easy, Kat, not if you want to do what I do. There is a reason why most of us are young. Bob is still at the top of his game, but physically, he can't hack it anymore. Not the tough stuff. He's still better than average for regular infantry duty, but not for the challenging work we do."

They were entering their camp now and Duncan spotted Jane and Bob sitting quietly by themselves. He told Katerina to find Carol and to have her issued a full weapons complement. Then he walked over and climbed into CT's Coyote.

"Send all this stuff to Shelly, CT. Have her go over it and schedule a call with her. Dave is in charge until I tell you differently. I have to go talk with my mother-in-law now."

"Hey Jane, how are you making out?" Duncan said. Tears started again and Jane jumped up and hugged him.

"Oh Duncan, I am so sorry," she said.

"Hey Bob," Duncan said releasing Jane. "Please tell me you have some beer left."

Bob reached into the cooler under his chair and tossed Duncan a beer. Duncan sat down in another chair, took Jane's hand and looked her in the eyes.

"We had just entered the last hallway leading to the leader's residence," he said. "I was in the lead, Karen right behind me. The enemy had been resisting well but we had better training, weapons and tactics, so the issue was never really in doubt. As I stepped into the hallway, a trooper came from the side. Karen knocked me out of the way and took the shot that would have taken me in the back. The trooper was too close to shoot, so I buttstroked her hard and carried on. Amanda stayed with her, but she was dead already. The shot took her in the chest and it was through and through."

"Amanda told me Karen was dead by the time she reached her, Duncan. What of the girl who killed her?"

"She is recovering from her wounds, Jane. I don't hold it against her. She was doing her job and she did it well, expecting to die. The doctor feels she will physically recover well, but she will be scarred for life on her face and possibly in her mind."

"I do not share your view, Duncan. I will never forgive her for killing my daughter."

"I loved Karen with all my heart and all my soul, Jane. Even when I thought she had betrayed me, I still loved her. I treated her badly and lost all those years I could have had with her. Yet, she, and you, forgave me. That trooper was doing what any of us would have done. Trying to protect her commander, willing to give up her life, like Karen did. Chances are we will never see her again, Jane, but I will not punish her for doing her job.

"How long did you know about the baby?"

"Only a few weeks, Duncan. She was going to tell you after this battle. She needed to be with you Duncan; you can see that, can't you? She loved you dearly, Duncan. She knew, as do the rest of us, that without you we are doomed. Not back home, where we would survive without you. But here? Here, you are or only hope. By saving you, she saved us all, Duncan. I will never say, why her and not you. She made that choice, Duncan. Please honor her sacrifice. She wanted you to live. So live, Duncan, live."

Duncan nodded his head and sat still for a few moments, then he finished the beer and stood.

"I need both of you back on the job as soon as you can," he said. "We have a community to build and the Guild is sending some bad guys our way to get us under control. We need a plan to make sure that doesn't happen. So, the sooner you guys are back to work, the better."

As he walked away, Amanda was walking forward. She had her rifle at the ready, as they all did, but she was clearly tired. Her uniform was bloody and her face haggard. She had bags under her eyes and she was shuffling more than walking. She grabbed the first sleeping bag she found, threw it under the Coyote, wrapped it around herself and passed out.

Duncan keyed his mike. "CT, Amanda is passed out under the Coyote. Don't run her over if you have to move. Are any of our people free?"

"Nope, we are all busy, Dunc."

"Hey Bishop, you up?"

"Yes Mr. Kovaks, I hear you."

"I wonder if you could delegate some people to look for some kind of building for us. The mansion is a write-off, and so are the onsite barracks. Maybe there is another barracks or an armory somewhere? Some of our people, especially the medics, are worn out and sleeping under a vehicle is not exactly the best accommodation. Also, we will be needing an administration building. I would prefer not to commandeer it from the local population. Also, we need to find a suitable place to set up your temporary camp."

"I'll have my quartermaster look into it, Duncan. They had a fairly extensive military complex when we were here at the beginning. It should be able to hold all of us easily."

"Sounds good," Duncan said. "CT, Dave is in charge until I get back. I'm going to have a look at the prisoner compound."

Duncan started walking down the main street, headed for the prisoner compound two miles away. The streets were deserted and quiet and the further he walked the lower the generator noise from the Coyotes was, until only his footsteps and the birds could be heard. Well not just his footsteps. Brett and Scott had joined him.

Both men had their personal weapons with them, pointed at the ground but ready to be used. Weapons harnesses were fully equipped, which reminded Duncan he had not replenished his ammunition yet. He only had one grenade left for his launcher and had used two clips of his rifle ammunition. He made a mental note to stock up once he reached his LAV.

To the casual observer, it looked like three soldiers taking a stroll down the center of the street. But their heads and eyes were in constant motion, ears and noses alert for any unusual motions or sounds.

"I say, my good fellow," Brett said effecting an upper crust British accent. "I wonder, is there a suitable pub in town?"

"I shouldn't think there would be one for persons of our stature, old chum," Scott said in the same manner. "I fear we will have to make do and libate with the lower classes, dear me."

"I suppose there is no billiard or card club, dear me," Brett said. "Oh, the privations we must endure, old chap."

"Well I did find a suitable area for a cricket pitch, my good man," Scott said. "With plenty of room for a tennis court."

"Jolly good, old chap," Brett said. "I found a beautiful area for a polo grounds. Now, if we could only find some good ponies. Dear me."

"Where exactly are you two peons planning on getting the cash to pay for all that stuff?" Duncan said.

"Well, me lord," Brett said. "We just happened to stumble on the previous lord's stash."

"Was a sub-basement, under the sub-basement," Scott said. "It took us most of the night to even find the entrance. It's loaded with silver, Dunc."

"Any room left for our stash?" Duncan asked.

"We can probably get half in it," Brett said. "It's pretty full. It has the same footprint as the main floor of the mansion and is ten feet high. It's loaded to the roof, Dunc."

Duncan whistled. "Somebody was making, or stealing, a lot of money. Hey CT, we need to find out where the previous owner was getting his cash from."

"One of the girls is on it, Ghost," CT reported.

"I sure hope there is some decent cashflow coming in," Duncan said. "All this is going to take a lot of cash to get up and running. How bad is the mansion?"

"I'm no engineer," Brett said. "But I think it is structurally sound. A few holes in the outside walls, busted windows and doors. The worst of the damage inside was on the third floor where you guys were."

"Tanya probably has some engineers with her bunch," Duncan said. "I'll ask her. We should probably use the mansion and complex for our admin center. Bishop is checking out the old regime's military base. We'll probably barrack there. It'll be better than sleeping in tents or on the ground under a vehicle."

"Well, at least we have decent gear," Scott said. "Not like those poor saps in that compound there."

The Marauders had been busy. They had erected a ten-foot high wire fence around the ten acres. While it wasn't overlarge, the people were not overcrowded. The people were huddled up under whatever protection from the elements they could muster. Some had rigged lean-to shelters and tents out of tarps or blankets. Others just had blankets wrapped around themselves.

One LAV and two Marauders' vehicles were on each of the four sides of the compound and two fire teams were patrolling on foot on each side, outside the wire.

"Good morning, my lord," the sub-commander in charge said as they walked up. "We are just beginning to call up and release the first of the townspeople."

"Good," Duncan said. "Keep at it until they are all gone. Have you a figure on the numbers that will be left? The fanatics and military types?"

"Roughly a thousand undesirables and their families, my lord, and about a thousand military personnel. I have included the undesirable military people in with the other undesirables, Sir."

"Right, muster the military types and march them to the old base in town at your shift change and get the others under canvas for tonight. Also, if you could supply one of my comms people with a list of tradespeople I would appreciate it, Sub-commander. We need to rebuild the mansion complex.

"You have done a good job here, Sub-commander. Let your people know I am happy with their work."

"Oh drat," Brett said. "Would you look at that, there goes the polo grounds all to hell."

Tanya's advance guard had arrived and pulled off the road into the field opposite the prisoner compound. They quickly set up a perimeter defensive line and the main body arrived and started setting up the main camp.

The commander's vehicle and his guard vehicle pulled up to where Duncan was standing and stopped. The commander stuck his head and shoulders up out of his roof hatch.

"Good morning, My Lord Duncan," he said. "I wonder if you could direct me to Her Majesty."

"Sub commander," Duncan said. "If you would be so kind as to provide an escort for the commander to Her Majesty?"

"Any problem on the trip, Commander?"

"Not after the first day, My Lord," the commander said. "We finished off what was left of the enemy troops. That was it. Nice and quiet. I see you have everything under control here."

"We are just in the process of releasing the townspeople," Duncan said. "Her Highness will have to decide what to do with the thousand or so that will be left."

"It's always the poor civilians that take it in the neck," the Commander said. "Some idiot takes it upon himself to start a war and the rest of us have to pay the price. Ah, my escort has arrived. I will catch up with you later, My Lord."

"When is your shift change, Sub-commander?" Duncan asked.

"19:00, Sir. We run twelve hour shifts, Sir."

"Will you be done releasing the townspeople by then, do you think?"

"I should think so, Sir," he said.

"Very well," Duncan said. "I think we will have our friends across the way take over from you at 19:00. Estimate how many tents you will need for those who are left and ask Commander Bishop to send them up to you. Just put them inside the wire. They can set them up themselves. Escort the prisoners to the base. Tonight, you and your boys should be sleeping in a real barracks for a change."

"We are going to appreciate that, My Lord," the sub-commander said. "We have been under canvas for a year now. Ever since we got here."

Duncan slapped him on the shoulder and then he and his two self-appointed guards moved out of his way to let him do his job. After an hour of watching not only the prisoner release but Tanya's army, it was time to go. He was hungry.

"Wind Riders," he said keying his mike. "Enough of this. Crank 'em up and head back to town. A Troop, pick me up. Brett is complaining about his pedicure."

"I suppose he'll be wanting a bubble bath and massage after," Dianne said.

"Only if you're giving it," Brett said.

"In your dreams, lover boy," Diane retorted.

Duncan and the two guys were laughing their heads off as his LAV pulled over and they jumped in the back.

"Who the hell is the commander of this wreck?" Duncan asked. "Somebody should take him out and shoot him. What a mess."

Scott and Brett grabbed a can of beer each from the cooler stashed under the seating bench, shook them vigorously and popped them so they sprayed all over Duncan.

"Your word is our command, My Lord," Brett said.

Duncan was still wiping the beer off as the three laughing men fell out of the vehicle, having stopped beside CT's Cougar.

"That's it, where's the boss?" Duncan yelled. All the other crews were piling out of their vehicles. Each of them had a can of beer in their hands and were shaking them. Tanya, her army commander, Bishop and the Guildsmaster watched as Duncan was sprayed with beer, drenching him and his uniform. He had a beer of his own and was trying to fight back.

"Mutiny! Mutiny!" he yelled. "Kill 'em all, kill 'em all."

It didn't help as troopers piled out of the Coyotes, ran and added their beer and laughter to the already soaked Duncan, howling with laughter at the good-natured fun. Al was the first to see the visitors.

"TENHUT! Flag officers on Deck!"

"Oh fuck," Duncan said, coming to attention. The Wind Riders formed a line behind him all at attention.

"Wind Riders all present or accounted for, Ma'am!" he barked out.

Tanya returned his salute. Then he saw the smile on her face, heard a few suppressed sniggers from behind him and saw the beer dripping off the arm he was saluting with and collapsed on the ground rolling, laughing his head off.

More beer was found and Tanya and her commander joined in. Bishop just stood there and laughed.

"Enough, enough already," Duncan spluttered out between laughs. "Shit, you're wasting all the good beer, you dummies."

Duncan's beer bath had turned into a mini beer war. Everyone, except the Guildsmaster and Bishop, who had made sure they were out of range, was soaked. Duncan took his shirt off and wrung it out, pouring it into his mouth.

"What the hell are you guys looking at?" he said. "I'm not wasting all this good beer."

Tanya turned sober as she saw all the scars Duncan had on his upper body. Two of them still red and one on his arm, very fresh.

The other Wind Riders stripped off their shirts and were wringing them out as well. All of the men had battlescars, as did Carol. Dianne had one behind her ear, normally covered by her hair. Young Megan had a long one on one side, which was fresh. Katarina's on her right shoulder blade was also fresh.

"Oh my God," she said to her commander. "We have just been playing at being soldiers."

"It looks like Duncan, Dave and Al have used up a few lives," Bishop said. "I've been at this almost twenty years and don't have that many scars. Here, we only get minor burn marks or we are dead. From what I have seen firsthand, their weapons are far more devastating than ours are."

"Barbarians," the Guildsaster said. "All of them, barbarians."

"My Lord Kovaks," Tanya said. "We came only to invite you and your troopers to dinner this evening."

"Well, Ma'am," Duncan said. "I am afraid we only have field uniforms, Ma'am."

"That will be just fine, Duncan," Tanya said. "Just make sure they are clean and dry."

"No shirt, no shoes, no service," Al blurted out and all the Wind Riders started laughing again.

A disheveled Amanda rolled out from under the Coyote, "Can you guys hold your bloody orgy someplace else?" she said seeing all the shirtless people. "I'm trying to get some sleep here."

Then she emanated a high pitch squeal, as she was immediately drenched.

Tanya shook her head, smiling as she and her entourage walked away, shaking the beer off her arms as she went.

Amanda stood up, removed her shirt, and wiped her face and arms with the dry back of it. "Damn," she said. "You assholes got my sleeping bag all wet."

She picked up the soaking wet sleeping gear and watched as the beer pored off it onto the ground.

"Oh, hey," she said seeing the name tag on it. "Jokes on me. This is Brett's sleeping bag not mine. Oops."

"Glorious Leader," Bishop said. "We have found a barracks for you. One set has two-room married quarters and the other, the more standard long, single room with many beds. They are linked together and there are separate male and female washroom facilities, including showers. My people found a large laundry facility and a few of them have volunteered to run it. So, we can wash those beer-soaked uniforms and that sleeping bag for you and have them back in time for the dinner tonight."

"What are you waiting for, my good man?" Duncan asked. "Lead on. Mount up, gang. Hot showers and a soft, warm bed tonight!"

Jane banished Bob to Carol's LAV and dragged Katarina by the arm to her Coyote as Katarina was struggling to put her very damp shirt back on. She tossed a duffle bag at her as they started to move. It had Kovaks, written on it.

"You're about the same size she was," Jane said. "There is a complete spare set in there, including boots, which may not fit. Just remove the name tags and rank insignia. I think you will appreciate the bra. It is much more supportive than the one you are wearing."

Katarina just looked at the duffle bag and then back up to Jane.

"Don't worry Kat, they have never been worn," Jane said. "It was a fresh set from the spares at the warehouse. Karen is not going to need them anymore."

"Okay," Katerina said. "I don't mean to sound stupid, but I am still trying to learn some of the words you use. What is a bra?"

Jane reached over and pulled the straps of Katerina's. "That would be good enough for the bedroom or under a sexy blouse, luv. But your boobs would be killing you after a half a mile of jogging."

"Oh," Katarina said. "Well, usually our armour holds the goodies in place."

"And such nice perky goodies they are, too," Barb said. "The nipples standing out and such. Would have distracted all the boys to no end, had they been paying attention."

"Yes indeedy," Anne said from the driver's compartment. "Why, I might just have to rip the rest of my man's clothes off him as soon as we get our new room, just to get him to forget what he saw."

"Ah, you're just hot and bothered from seeing all that bare man flesh," Barb said.

"Ladies, please," Jane said. "You are making poor Kat all uncomfortable with your dirty talk. But I must admit, my nipples got hard seeing my Bob's big chest and arms all shiny and wet."

"Oh baby," Barb said in her low sexy voice. "Oh, you turn me on so much. I just can't wait for you to spank me."

She had her arms around herself, caressing her back and making kissing noises. "Oh, baby you make me so hot!"

"Ah Jayzus!" Katarina said. "Can it already! You guys are going to at least get some tonight."

"Oh my," Jane said. "The goodies bounce ever so nicely. too."

Kat picked up a rag from the floor and hit Jane with it.

• • •

"That's the spirit, luv!" Barb said. "The lads enjoy a good cat fight. Get it? Kat fight."

Knowing she would never get one-up on the older women, Katarina just shook her head and took the ribbing. She had been accepted into the tribe.

Chapter Nine

THE MILITARY COMPLEX was enormous. It encompassed one hundred sixty acres bordering the eastern edge of the town, alongside the road leading toward the snow-capped mountains.

A fifteen-foot tall wall surrounded the complex, which was square and had an entrance in the center of each side's walls. Guard towers flanked each entrance and were placed at fifty yard intervals along the walls. The neighborhoods leading up to it slowly degraded as they approached and changed to light industrial until the final two blocks, which became the seedier section of town. The group saw bars, pawnshops, brothels, thrift shops and liquor stores. These led right up to the complex's walls.

The four-lane road ended at the gate complex with a small guardhouse at the entrance. An unkempt hundred-yard space led to the first of the warehouse buildings. The complex was laid out in a grid pattern with a boulevard-lined two-lane road between the blocks. All four roads converged on the center, which was ringed by two blocks of barracks. A large open parade square was in the exact middle of the complex. Administration buildings were located on the eastern side.

The barracks themselves were U-shaped, with the open end of the U facing the road. They were single-storied. One side held forty bunks, and the opposite side was divided into small one-bedroom apartments. The washroom facilities and company administration offices were in the center.

The Wind Riders were escorted to the barracks closest to the administration buildings. They parked their vehicles in the open square, shut them down and exited them, collecting their person gear and weapons.

The nine couples headed to claim their apartments while the unmarried troopers claimed bunks. Carol claimed the four bunks closest to the center wing for the four females, while the guys spread themselves out around the remainder of the empty spaces. Leaving two troopers behind, everyone headed to the showers with their somewhat clean spare uniforms in hand. The two left behind organised their own lockers and spaces, then, as the first returned from the showers, headed that way themselves.

There were two commanders' quarters in the administration part of the barracks and Duncan claimed the largest for himself. As well as the bedroom, it had its own washroom with a shower. A second room was an office and it had a large living area with a small kitchen and refrigerator. Stripping off his beer-soaked clothing, he had a fast shower and shave and, wrinkling his nose, put on his less soiled spare uniform. Then, grabbing his beer-soaked garments in a bundle, he headed to the single troops' barracks and added his bundle to the other pile of brewery-smelling bundles.

Once that was done, he joined the others unloading the vehicles of personal equipment and snagged his portable computer. CT had commandeered one of the administration offices for himself and was busy arraigning it. A two-troop guard rotation kept an eye on things and everyone else started organising their personal spaces and cleaning weapons. Two Marauder troops showed up in a vehicle, gathered up the clothing, tossed them into the back of their vehicle and headed off to the laundry.

Verifying that everything was in order, Duncan said he was going to grab some rest and, leaving Dave in charge, headed to his apartment, shut the door and collapsed shaking into a chair. The shaking became more severe as he slowly lost the battle to hold in his emotions. He could not stop replaying the sight of Karen shoving him aside and taking the blast meant for him. The loss of his love, his unborn child, his best friend and his future tore him apart.

Katerina was heading back to the barracks from her shower and heard the muffled sobs coming from his room. She stopped and was about to open the door to comfort him, when a pair of hands grabbed her shoulders gently. She looked behind her to see Barb's tear-streaked face.

"Let him be, Kat," Barb said. "You would just embarrass him. I've known Duncan for most of my life. He is a strong and proud man. If we go in there now, he will shut his emotions down again. He needs to grieve, Kat, and he will not do it with other people around. Let him get it out of his system. Bob, Dianne or I will go to him if this goes on for too long."

Three hours later, the now fresh and clean uniforms were back from the laundry. Only one pile was left on a spare bunk while everyone else changed and piled the next batch of dirty ones on the floor in front of it.

Carol gently took up the unclaimed clothing and walked to Duncan's door. Taking a deep breath, she slowly let it out and knocked on the door. Duncan was composed when he opened it, but his puffy eyes betrayed what had been going on.

"Clean uniform, Duncan," Carol said quietly and handed them to him. "They are waiting for your next load. Bishop says the prisoners will be here shortly."

"Okay," Duncan said, taking the clean uniform. "Have the prisoners muster on the parade ground. Have our people in formation by the road as they march in."

In short order, Duncan entered the main barracks room, handed his dirty uniform to the waiting trooper and joined his lounging troopers by the road. Everyone was in improved spirits. Hair was shiny, beards were gone, boots were as shiny as they could be made. Battered but clean weapons were slung over right shoulders. Only pistols were on the weapons harnesses for once.

Hearing the tramp of boots in the distance, the Wind Riders lined up in front of two LAVs parked sideways across their small open space, small gaps between their sections. Duncan and Jane stood in front of the formation.

Duncan shifted to the at-ease position and the rest of the Wind Riders followed his example, a few hushed comments instructing Katarina in the proper procedure. As the prisoner formation came abreast, they saw a line of twenty-eight Wind Riders, their two officers standing in the center. They wore black berets squarely on heads just above the eyebrow, crisp tan uniforms, pant legs stuffed into clean combat boots. Their feet were shoulder-width apart, rifles held on the ground by their left feet with the rifles held by the barrel at an angle from the body, right hands tucked into the small of their backs and eyes staring straight ahead.

The long line of prisoners walked by in ten groups of one hundred, with an armed vehicle in front and behind and three spaced out along each side of the column. They were walking, not marching, but they were in formation. Their uniforms were dishevelled and dirty, they were dejected, and no one was talking.

As the lead vehicle reached the edge of the Wind Riders formation, Duncan brought them to attention and thirty right legs crashed to join the left and rifles were snapped tight to left sides, right arms rigid to the sides. Then Duncan had his troops perform the rifle salute and thirty rifles were placed in the center of their bodies, barrels in front of faces.

As the lead vehicle reached Duncan, the commander, standing at attention in the turret hatch, returned the salute. Instinctively, the walking troops, after seeing the Wind Riders, drew themselves erect and started marching in step. By the time the end of the column passed by, they looked like soldiers again. The column was marched to the center of the large parade square and formed up. The guard troop dismounted from their vehicles and formed up alongside. Then the commander of the guard troop approached the senior officer of the prisoners and they marched back to Duncan and the Wind Riders. They both came to attention and saluted. The Wind Riders were at ease once again and Duncan returned the salute with a crisp hand gesture.

"Gentlemen," Duncan said. "Welcome. Sub-commander, in a moment you will release your charges to their officers and you may be dismissed to barracks. Commander, you have been assigned the ten barracks opposite ours to billet your troops. You will not be under guard, but I expect you and your officers to maintain discipline. In four hours, we will be conducting a ceremony to honour the fallen. It would be a privilege if you and your troops would join us. It would also be an honour if you would choose one of your troops to join with one of mine to make the presentation, Sirs.

"Sub-commander, if you would be so kind as to pass on my invitation to Commander Bishop? And if he would also provide one trooper? Carry on, gentlemen."

As the two men walked back to their troops, Duncan brought his to attention.

"Sunset ceremony in four hours, people. One set of boots, weapons and helmets from each of the deceased combatants, if you please. Ensign Horshak will be our representative. CT, inform Her Majesty of the ceremony and that it would be an honour if her people would participate. Dismissed."

"Dave," Duncan said. "Karen's boots, beret and rifle please. CT, get Bishop for me."

Everyone dispersed to the barracks at that point and Duncan followed CT into the communications office they had set up and was quickly put through to James.

"James," Duncan said. "In four hours, we will be conducting what we call a Sunset Ceremony. This is to honour our fallen comrades. We will be placing a single representation from each of the combatants in front of the assembled troops and will conduct a fast memorial for all the fallen. I will need a pair of boots, a firearm and a helmet from you, and one of your people to present them. It can be a member who has distinguished him- or herself, or whoever you choose, as long as it is not yourself. I plan on using my most junior officer. Have your people form up on the right side of the square, if you please, and they are not to be under arms."

After he had finished his conversation, Duncan told CT to tell Tanya's people the same thing he had just told James.

"No prob, Dunc," CT said. "Also, Shelly will be online in an hour. I can send it to your quarters, Sir."

"Right, make it happen," Duncan said and he walked away and to his living quarters and laid down on the bed. It seemed like only seconds later, when Duncan's eyes snapped open as the loud shrill of the intercom system woke him up.

"I've got a good link up with Shelly," CT said. "Video as well as audio. The lag is really good, only about two seconds."

Duncan sat himself in front of his computer monitor and it came alive to show Shelly. She was in her office and the lights were on, which meant it was night. She was also dressed in a T-shirt, which meant it was well after hours.

"Where the hell are you, Duncan?" she said. "Everyone has been frantically looking for you. I have been telling everyone you are on a secret mission for an undisclosed government, but it is getting hard to keep up the story. And this document, Duncan. Is this for real?"

"You are looking well, Shelly," Duncan said. "We are doing well too, mostly. Calm down. Yes, the document is for real. The situation is far too complicated to explain right now. We will not be coming back, Shelly. Ever. The document should have made that clear. Is the document okay? Are our asses covered?"

"The language and form is a little archaic, but yes, it looks fine, Duncan," Shelly said. "Can you at least give me a brief version of what is going on?"

"Okay," Duncan said. "Keep an open mind, though."

Duncan ran through a brief version of how things had come to pass.

"So, essentially," he said. "We have been given a very large area of the planet to govern as our own. It's about the size of the province of Alberta, or, a little larger than Texas. Right now, there are less than one hundred thousand people in this district. In fact, this planet has only been colonised for a little over a hundred years and there are not too many people on the whole planet. And yes, they are people. They are not little green men. They are more advanced than we in some ways and less in others. For instance, our computer and communication skills are better than theirs, but their equipment is better than ours. The whole planetary system of government seems to be like our old feudal system. The rulers have the ultimate say in things. We will be implementing our Constitutional Monarchy system here in our district."

She asked him what it was like there and he explained that it was much like his home, but that things were slightly different. The sun rotated in the opposite direction, the days were a little longer, the vegetation was a little off in colour and the wildlife was different. The common language seemed to be English-based and the local language had a Russian base. The insurgents spoke a form of French, but, as yet, Duncan had run into no German or Arabic speakers.

"It sounds like a wonderful opportunity, Duncan," Shelly said. "Kind of a more sophisticated and romantic version of the Old West. I would love to go there."

"Believe me," Duncan said. "I could use you. I am at my limits with all this, Shelly. All of us are. We have some decent local help, but the major part of the workload setting all this up will be on us."

"I would jump on it in a minute," she said. "Things are really getting stupid in the States now. Massive unemployment, civil strife and the government is losing control."

"You know," Duncan said. "If you are serious, I think I could make that happen. The Interplanetary Council has authorised us to bring one more contingent of no more than thirty people to join our military force. I could really use you, Shelly. Also, a few of your people, no more than ten. Paralegals, support staff and maybe a financial person would be useful. Single people with no ties would be best, and, oh ya, there are absolutely no black people here. So, not to be racist, but the people involved should be warned."

"I am in for sure, Duncan," Shelly said. "You know I have the physical and shooting skills, so the army part shouldn't be a problem. Let me put out a few feelers. How much time do I have?"

"I think we have about three months, Shelly."

"What should I pack? How will all this happen?" she asked.

"Don't worry about it right now," Duncan said. "Just assemble your team and give me the names and addresses. We will take it from there. Look, I have to break this down now. So far they don't know we have this capability and I would like to keep it that way."

They signed off and Duncan laid back on his bed again.

The passing of vehicles and the increasing hum of many voices woke Duncan up before CT knocked on his door.

"We are almost ready to go, Dunc," CT said.

"Have you thought about what I said about finding some help for you, CT?" Duncan said. "Shelly has asked to join us and she will be looking for ten of her people to come along."

"I have two I am looking into," CT said. "A female and a male. One is a self-taught Canuck and the other is hiding out at the University of Alabama."

"So, bring them both," Duncan said.

"Well…" CT replied. "They are both, um, a little different."

"Ya, like you're not," Duncan said. "The concern will be if they can meet the physical requirements."

"One of them is an active hunter, Duncan. The other one is…well, should be okay is all I will say."

"Bring both of them then," Duncan said. "Dave, everything ready?"

"Yes," Dave said. "I have explained what needs to be done to the four presenters. Her Majesty will be attending with her guards, but has not committed to say anything."

"Right," Duncan said. "If you would inform the colonel the regiment is ready to join the formation?"

Duncan and CT walked out of the barracks. Once again, the Wind Riders were lounging around, the jokers of the group doing their thing. Everyone saw Duncan come out, but nobody stopped what they were, or were not, doing. Then Jane, Bob and Dave came out and everything changed. The joking stopped and everyone gathered in their fire teams and sections, adjusting uniforms and berets. Bob and Dave joined their fire teams and Jane joined Duncan who was standing casually in front of the single line of Wind Riders.

Duncan grabbed Jane's hand and squeezed it.

"This going to be hard, Jane," he said. "We both have to keep it together. Our people will understand if we lose it, but these others? They will see it as a sign of weakness. We can't have that, Jane. Not with our circumstances here. It is just a pair of boots, a rifle and a beret, Jane. That's all. We have to be strong, Jane. We have to be."

She squeezed his hand so hard he thought she might break it. Then she let it go.

"Take them out, Master Warrant," she said.

"Regiment, Attention!" he yelled. "Regiment in column of four, right face!"

Then he and Jane marched to the front of the small column.

"Regiment! By the right! March!"

The other brigades were arranged in front of a small temporary stage. In the center, in their black uniforms, was the remnants of the enemy army. Their walking wounded were with them. On their right, all five thousand of the Marauders were assembled in their grey uniforms and on the left were five thousand of Tanya's army, in their light blue uniforms. Tanya was in uniform on the stage with ten armed and armoured guards standing behind her.

Duncan led the Wind Riders along the edge of the parade ground and marched them in front of the stage. He snapped his hand up in salute as he came abreast of Tanya, who rose quickly from the chair she had been sitting on.

"Eyes Right!" Duncan bellowed. Every Wind Rider head snapped right at the order and kept them there until they had passed Tanya, then snapped them in unison back to the front. The formation passed to the end of the lines, then wheeled about and marched back until they were in the center of the formation and, in a smooth transition, split into columns of two, stopped and turned to make two ranks of fifteen with Duncan and Jane in the center. Then Duncan put them at ease, marched forward and mounted the stage, coming to attention before Tanya and saluting.

"Formation is present, Ma'am," Duncan said.

"Very well, Master Warrant," she said. "Carry on."

Duncan spun around and surveyed the formation. All of them were in their respective army's version of the at-ease position. It was deathly quiet. Not even the birds were singing. Instead of the expected four stands made up to hold the rifles, there were five. A large contingent of civilians was on the outskirts of the parade ground, all of them standing quietly.

Then, led by a light blue uniform, five people marched up to and onto the stage. The second of the five was a civilian female dressed in black. Instead of the rifle the others had across their arms with the boots and head gear on top, she had a shovel. The five stopped in front of their stand and placed the boots first, then the rifle and finally the head gear on the stands. The rifles on their barrels stood between the boots and the helmets of the local troops, but Karen's beret was placed on the rifle butt. The civilian placed the work helmet on the handle of the shovel, which had its blade behind the boots.

Once the last was in place, the five took two steps back, saluted, turned and joined their formations, leaving Duncan and Tanya alone on the stage. Duncan was avoiding looking at the C8 between Karen's tan combat boots with her black beret on the butt. He glanced at Jane and saw she was swallowing repeatedly and he quickly shifted his glance and walked forward. CT had rigged a PA system to pick up his throat mike and Duncan came to a stop in front of the memorials, just back from the edge of the platform.

He went to one knee and the Wind Riders were right behind him. After a slight pause, all the other formations followed suit and when he made the sign of the cross, many went down on both knees and most followed suit.

"Heavenly Farther," he began. "We ask you to console the loved ones of those lost. We ask you to help them to grieve and to understand. We ask you to help us forgive past enemies. I ask you to absolve all those who killed your children by my orders. I ask you to help them come to grips and to have healthy minds after what they have experienced. I take full responsibility for their actions and beg you to absolve them."

Then he stood and replaced his beret on his head.

"It is the soldier's burden to do the fighting and the killing," he began. "Often it is the civilians who bear the brunt of the fighting. Civilians who had no say in what the leadership decided. Who had to endure privation, loss of life and property. We soldiers have the training and the tools to affect the outcome of what we do. Civilians have not.

"We soldiers believe we will never be killed. It will be someone else, not us. Those of us standing here today are proof of that. We did not die. Others did. All of us here suffered a loss. A brother or sister. Mother, father, good friend.

"I ask you today, right here and right now, not to remember them with sorrow, but celebrate their lives, their accomplishments. Their sacrifice. They did their best for their cause."

"Armies of Oaken, Attention!" he gave a quick motion with his left hand behind his back for Tanya to join him. He took two steps back, turned around, and had Tanya stand beside him.

"Armies of Oaken, Present Arms!" Then he brought his right hand smartly to his forehead in salute, while Tanya smashed her right clenched fist against her chest. Then the five presenters marched back on stage and stood at attention behind their stands. Duncan walked up to the first stand, bowed his head, then came to attention and saluted the memorial. He went down the line doing the same. At the center stand was the black uniform. The presenter, her head still covered in bandages so only her eyes were visible, was at rigid attention. Duncan saw no anger in her eyes, only sadness. He looked her right in the eyes as he saluted. Then he gave her a quick smile before he turned to the next. Katerina had tears streaming down her cheeks as Duncan came to her. This time he was very quick. He could not afford to linger. Tanya, however, stopped and went to her knees, crossed herself and prayed a moment.

When she was done and had risen, Duncan led to the front and the center of the stage to stand alongside of him.

"Now is the time for us all to come together as one," he said. "The war is over. The fighting, killing and dying are over. We must unite. We must rebuild our lives, our homes, our families. We all share this land, this planet.

"Her Majesty, Queen Tanya, has asked my people and me to rebuild this district; to make it and its people viable, profitable and prosperous. We have accepted. It will become our province. Bishop's Marauders have asked to become members of this new community. This has been granted. I ask any of you here present to consider joining us. We hold no animosity toward anyone for events of the past. We will accept anyone who is willing to agree to our terms and conditions."

Then he turned and faced Tanya who turned and faced him. He removed his beret and went to one knee in front of her and bowed his head.

"Your Majesty," he began. "My people have pledged their allegiance to me. I, Duncan Kovaks, pledge myself and my descendants, my people and their descendants, to serve and protect Oaken, the citizens of Oaken, and Queen Tanya and her descendants, against all enemies."

Tanya took his hands between hers and bowed her head.

"I Tanya, Queen of Oaken, pledge myself, my descendants, my house and their descendants, and the people of Oaken and their descendants, to serve and protect Duncan Kovaks, his house, his people and all their descendants."

Then she took him by the shoulders and made him stand, refusing to let him put his beret on.

"People of Oaken," she said. "This man and his people were brought here to this land against their will. They agreed to help us, people they did not know. They tried their very best to stop the bloodshed, to stop the fighting before it started. When they could not, they were always in the thickest of the fighting, willing to sacrifice themselves, for us, whom they had no reason to love - or even like.

"This young man has sacrificed much for us. In the final assault, his young wife sacrificed herself and her unborn child, so he might live. I have seen his people do this repeatedly. When they fight, they are demons. When the fight is over, it is over. He threatened to kill us, and myself in particular, to protect Bishop's Marauders after they had surrendered to him. We, and I, have much to learn from this young man and his people. I count him as one of my own and love him as a brother.

"My niece, the Lady Katerina, was the first to join his people, such is her admiration and love for this man and his people. I would ask that all here heed his words. The fighting is over, the war is over. It is time to reunite as one people, one planet."

Then she nodded to Duncan and stepped back. Duncan put his beret back on and came to attention.

"Armies of Oaken, Dismissed!"

Then he saluted Tanya and made his way down the line of presenters once again, shaking each person's hand and thanking them for the job they had just done. He bypassed the black uniformed trooper and Katerina, but came back to the bandaged woman. He saluted her instead of shaking her hand.

"I hope I have not caused you too much harm, Commander," Duncan said. "I am sorry for the pain, Ma'am. You and your people fought hard, Ma'am. I commend you and them on your courage, Ma'am. I would consider it an honour if your people, and you specifically, would join us, Ma'am."

He saluted her again, turned and without a look back, left the stage and the parade square, returning to his room in the barracks. He didn't see the tears begin to stain her bandages or hear her muted crying as he left.

Duncan sat on his bed and quietly cried for a while. Then the tears stopped and his mind drifted to times long ago. Karen was the star center of her college basketball team. How beautiful she had looked at their graduation ceremonies. He laughed when he remembered her shock when she realised she would be riding a normal horse in a western saddle for the first time, instead of the pampered show animals she was used to. How she looked wearing blue jeans and plaid with hiking boots and a baseball cap on her head. Her antics in the barn loft that had been changed to a mess hall the night she first met the Wind Riders. Her short red designer dress, long earrings and high heels contrasting with the T-shirts, blue jeans and sneakers of the others. How everyone had adopted her as their sister and loved her, right from the start.

Her joy at rough camping in the mountains back home, traveling by horseback for days and eating the trout she caught in the glacier-fed streams. Her ready laugh and her weird humour. His mood had already changed from the sorrow he felt at her loss when he heard the others trooping into the mess hall section of the administration part of the barracks. He stood and walked to his locker. Inside was a box holding his last four bottles of Canadian Rye. He picked it up and left his room, headed for the mess.

"Okay, you bums!" he yelled. "Who's got the glasses?"

Helping hands rushed to the cupboard that held the shot glasses and handed them out as Duncan handed out the bottles, pouring himself one before handing the last one out. He waited until the last glass was filled then raised his above his head. As he did, he saw that Tanya had entered, as had James and a black-uniformed commander.

"Absent comrades," Duncan said and he shot the glass back, then filled it back up again. "Karen!" and they drank again and once again he filled his glass. This time he looked each person in the eye before he spoke.

"The best fucking Regiment in the universe! Wind Riders forever!"

The room erupted in a yell and drained their glasses. Then in the silence that followed, Barb began and everyone joined right in.

"We are the wind rustling through the leaves and the grass, bringing fresh air and comfort.
We are the babbling brook, bringing refreshment and soothing.
We are the sun in the sky, bringing warmth and sustenance.
We are the Wind Riders, bringers of Peace, Hope and Justice.

We are the torrent that rips trees from the ground.
We are the raging flood waters that destroy homes.
We are the burning sun that devastates crops.
We are the Wind Riders, bringers of Despair, Death and Destruction."

The room fell silent after that.

"Okay," Duncan said. He had a weird look in his eyes. "Some assholes have drunk the last of my booze! If I don't have a bottle of beer in my hands in the next thirty seconds, I'm gonna hang somebody!"

"Here, you grumpy asshole," Al yelled and tossed him a bottle.

"Ah," Duncan said, spinning off the twist top and taking a long pull. "Nectar of the gods. You live to hang another day, Al."

"As if," Al said. "I run faster scared than you do mad."

The party was on.

"Where is Amanda?" he asked Barb.

"When Jane came up and shook that Black Shirt's hand, she lost it, Dunc. She kept repeating that she was sorry and wouldn't let Jane's hand go until Amanda came and settled her down," Barb said. "I think Amanda took her back to the hospital."

"Ya she kind of lost it when I talked to her, too," Duncan said. "Shit happens. I hope she makes it. We can sure use her."

"You pissed at Kat? You've been avoiding her." Barb said.

"Avoiding, yes," Duncan said. "Pissed, no."

Barb turned him around and shoved him in Katarina's direction. She was standing just to one side and to the rear of Carol and her gang. She was there, but trying hard not to be noticed. Somebody, probably CT, had found a way to pipe music into the mess and a slow country song came on just as Duncan came up behind Katerina and tapped her on the shoulder.

When she turned around he bowed. "May I have this dance, my lady Katerina?"

"Wha..what?" she said and Duncan grabbed hold of her by the waist and right arm and started to dance with her.

"Kat, I am sorry I have been avoiding you," Duncan said. "You did a great job. It couldn't have been easy for you."

She let her head sink so she was looking at the floor and, when Duncan didn't say anything else, she looked up and saw him staring over her head, tears welling up in his eyes. She took her hand from his and pulled his head down to her shoulder and put hers on his chest. They stayed that way for a while, feet barely moving, taking comfort from each other. Then Duncan raised his head.

"Goddammit, CT!" he yelled. "You're making the Lady Kat cry! Enough of this slow shit! Come on ladies, it's time to show Lady Kat how to line dance!"

A fast country tune came on and all the ladies jumped up and, placing Kat in the centre, formed a line. They were soon all laughing as Kat tried to match their moves. They laughed even harder when Tanya joined them.

Duncan made his way to the bar and grabbed another beer out of the fridge. James, with the black-uniformed sub-commander in tow, approached him and he gave them both a beer.

"Nice party," James said. "I like being with you guys already."

"Ah shucks, thanks," Duncan said. "What did you think, we are all bloodthirsty all the time?"

"Not me, I know better," James said. "But the sub-commander here, well, he thought sure you were going to truss him up and roast him for the main course at dinner tonight."

"Rest easy, sub-commander," Duncan said. "You're too skinny. Now Bishop here, on the other hand…"

The sub-commander came to attention and saluted.

"Sir, on behalf of myself and my troops, I would like to say how sorry we are about your wife. Sir," the sub-commander said. "Our commander regrets her actions, Sir and is waiting your judgment and execution, Sir."

"What the hell did you tell this guy, Bishop?" Duncan said. "We don't do that kind of shit! No wonder the bloody woman is a wreck!"

"Hey, not me, boss," James said. "That's how these guys operated."

"Well, we don't operate like that, Sub-commander," Duncan said. "I meant what I said. The war is over, you guys fought well, that's the end of it. But if I find out any of your people ever take part in atrocities, that will be a different story. You make sure you tell your commander, I meant every word I spoke to her."

"Thank you, Sir, I will, Sir."

"What the hell is all this sir shit? I ain't no officer, Sub-commander, I work for a living. You got another name besides sub-commander, Sub-commander?"

"Yes Sir, LeFlame, Sir."

"You want to become a Wind Rider, LeFlame?"

"If it could be arranged, Sir."

"What the fuck, are all you guys so prim and proper all the time? No matter, you'll get the hang of it soon enough.

"Yo, Brett you fat ass! Get your fat ass in motion and bring a couple of bottles of the good stuff over here. We have a candidate to initiate."

Brett reached under his chair and grabbed a bottle from the box there. He walked over and handed it to Duncan, who spun the top off of it.

"Okay Candidate, Sub-Commander LeFlame, this is how it is done," Duncan tilted his head back and took a deep pull, then handed the bottle to LeFlame.

"So, Mr. Flame," Duncan said using the English pronunciation of the name. "You will now finish the bottle in one go, or we might string you up and roast you for dinner."

LeFlame, tilted the bottle up and made short work of it.

"What say you, brothers and sisters?" Duncan asked.

"He ain't puked yet," Brett said and handed LeFlame another bottle, making sure he drank the first half himself, of course. Duncan beat a hasty retreat.

Chapter Ten

It was a week after the sunset ceremony and a lot had happened. A long supply column had been dispatched to the secret supply depot and all the spare equipment and vehicles had been brought into the military complex and warehoused. Workers had been recruited and work begun on repairing the old mansion into offices and a meeting area. The walls were being torn down and the barracks turned into office complexes. The province was becoming theirs.

A local automotive firm was working on ways to convert the Wind Riders vehicles to the local propulsion systems. One of the original G-Wagons was the first to be worked on as a test and progress was well under way.

Brett had taken a burnt-out Minimi barrel to a local machine shop to see if the machinist could replicate it. Research had been conducted on the materials required to manufacture their own ammunition. The raw materials were abundant on the planet and had been ordered. A tool maker in the planet's capitol city had been contracted to make the various machines that would be needed and several warehouses in the military complex were being converted to manufacture the various components that would be needed to produce the diverse types of munitions required.

Suitable land away from the town had been purchased and builders hired to construct a gunpowder factory. All of this had to be done in secret to keep the knowledge from reaching the Interplanetary Council and the Guild.

The biggest problem was in recruiting potential workers for all this manufacturing and building. The capitol city and the region in general had a large unemployment rate, but the loss of ten thousand able-bodied workers killed in the war was telling. Most of the shortfall could be replaced by women who had lost their main wage earners.

But that created another problem: what to do with all the underage children?

The previous rulers had frowned upon employing women outside the home, so few had skill sets other than that of homemakers. Schooling for the lower classes had been almost nonexistent, especially for females. None could read or write and few had mathematical skills. Few could speak the common language and the few who did spoke it badly.

Katerina said this education problem was planetwide. Only the upper class had higher learning and only the wealthiest of the middle classes had any schooling. Jane, Katerina and one of the troopers from G Troop who had been a teacher's aide back in California took it upon themselves to set up a school and daycare system.

They were spending money rapidly. Fortunately, most of the income the province generated was from agricultural pursuits and it was substantial, if seasonal. Farmworkers had been exempt from military service and few had volunteered to serve. But, from what Duncan had observed, all the work in the fields was done manually, both in his province and throughout the planet. Machinery was available from off-planet manufacturers but it was expensive. Duncan ordered one of each model to test on one farm and CT was hacking into farm equipment manufacturers' databases back on Earth to steal designs.

It would take time, but they had a few years. The farmworkers were essentially slaves. They did not even own their own homes, let alone the farms they worked on. Landowners had either been killed in the war or had been exiled off-planet. In any case, the new charter granted all the land to Duncan. Bishop had been delegated the task of inventorying the farmland and his officers and senior non-commissioned officers were busy at that task.

The province's civilians had jumped at the chance to become citizens once the rules and the benefits were explained. That meant that a lot of new, smaller farms would come into production in five years, as people finished their mandatory military service. Priority for land would be given to the existing farmworkers, but there was a lot of non-productive land.

Katerina had used her contacts in the other districts and five young geologists, two forestry engineers and two mining engineers were on their way. All of them were like Katerina, minor aristocrats, who owned no land and had no future beyond that of working for someone else. They were university graduates, intelligent, young and eager. They had also served in the military for five years already, so the rules could be bent slightly.

Requests to join the new province were flooding in, especially from younger members of Katerina's class. But it had been decided that every position would be filled by the citizens of the province first. Only then would outsiders be considered.

The hardest task the Wind Riders had to face involved Karen. She had been cremated and Jane had remembered a place that Karen had loved. It was a hilltop that overlooked a river valley leading to a lake in the distance on one side and an unobstructed view of the tree-covered mountains on the other.

The Wind Riders and a few dignitaries, Tanya included, attended as Karen's ashes were spread on the hilltop. Tanya proclaimed that the whole hill would be declared a nature preserve and was to be left in its natural state for all time.

Duncan had disappeared for a few days after that. Even now, a week later, he was not really himself. But he was back to work, for the work had to be done and there was a lot of it.

He had just come into his office for the morning and the first of two surprises greeted him. The first was from a Commander Isabelle, who, on behalf of her battalion, asked that they become members of the brigade. The whole battalion. The next came right after that as Megan crashed into his office.

"Duncan, you have to come right away!" she blurted out. "There are fifteen people sleeping on the mess hall dance floor."

Duncan rushed behind her to the mess hall and true enough, fifteen people were spread around the dance hall asleep. They were all dressed in Canadian Army desert pattern uniforms, had full duffle bags and a C8 rifle lying beside each of them.

Duncan quickly ordered the rifles removed before the sleepers could awaken. When that was done, the Wind Riders gathered and sat on tables or chairs, sipping coffee, watching the sleepers.

Shelly was the first to awaken, but the others were not far behind. They were all confused and a few were frightened, but most of them knew each other and things quieted down a bit, then someone saw the watchers watching. All of them dressed in army uniforms and fifteen of them with rifles.

"Welcome to Oaken, people. My name is Duncan Kovaks and I am your new boss."

Shelly's eyes went very large and she rushed into his arms, giving him a big hug, then she held him at arms length and looked at him.

"How?" she asked. "I went to sleep last night in my own bed. How did I get here?"

"Beats me," Duncan said. "We woke up in a clearing in the woods. At least you guys are inside."

The newcomers were still looking around at their surroundings. Nobody knew anyone but the members of their own group, as no one but Shelly had met Duncan before, and she only knew Duncan. There were two exceptions. One was female and the other male. The male definitely looked out of place in his uniform. He had an orange Mohawk haircut and a few rings imbedded on his face. The female had copper-coloured short hair, but wore the uniform as if it was normal attire.

"Okay people, settle down," Duncan said. "You volunteered to come and here you are. How you got here, I don't know. This room was empty an hour ago, that's when we closed the mess. One time only, the mess will reopen so you can have breakfast. Breakfast will be scrambled eggs, pork sausages, white toast and coffee. If you don't like it, don't eat it, but get used to it, because that is all that is available. After breakfast, we will assign you bunks, show you where the showers are and take you outside for a bit. Things are a little different here. The sun came up two hours ago and we should all be at work right now. You will be split up into groups of five and one of my people will provide orientation for you. Shelly, if you would follow me?"

Duncan took her to his office and had her sit down.

"Okay, you will be their officer for now," he said. "This is a meritocracy. You earn your station on merit. For the first few weeks, your group will be barracked separately from us. You will be assigned a training officer and a training instructor. Their jobs are to make sure that you are fully indoctrinated into the military lifestyle and that you pass minimum qualifications. Consideration will be made that you are all civilians. That does not mean we will be going easy on you, it only means we will not expect you to perform to our standards, yet. The accommodations are sparse and they are co-ed. The whole purpose of this training is to get you civilians to work as a team. Is all this clear, Candidate?"

"Yes, Sir!" Shelly said sitting at attention.

"You don't call me sir, candidate, I work for a living. You call me Master Warrant or Mr. Kovaks."

"Yes, Master Warrant," Shelly said.

"You'll get the hang of it Shelly; it's not all that different from the corporate world. All of us have our rank insignia on these little patches velcroed to our chests. Right now, you are all recruits, so below everyone else in the pecking order. Questions?"

"Yes, a lot of them, but they can wait," she said. "Where is Karen? Will I have a chance to talk with her soon?"

"Karen is dead, Shelly," Duncan said quietly. "She was killed in the last assault of the war. Now, if you can find your way back to the mess hall, Candidate? I have a lot of work to do."

Shelly was stunned, but Duncan was ignoring her now and she stood and left his office. Barb was waiting for her.

"He is getting over it, hon," Barb said. "But it is still a sharp wound and we don't talk about it to him unless he mentions it first. Come on, I will tell you about it over breakfast. This morning will be easy for you, but after that? Well, you are a mere candidate and below the notice of a captain such as me."

The training syllabus had been established previously. Megan, now second lieutenant, would be the officer in charge and Amanda was the assigned training sergeant. Today would just be for establishing bunks and familiarisation. It would be somewhat friendly. The candidates would be rudely kicked out of their bunks at dawn the next day. After a fast breakfast, the real work would begin with a one mile run, followed by close order drill. They would be formally inducted along with the black-shirt battalion in three days and needed to at least know how to walk in step and stand in line by that time.

Bishop had five classes of a hundred in training, four of farmworkers and one of townspeople. They had been at it for a week already and it would be interesting to see the difference in the two training classes. Bishop's group would be inducted at the same time.

The next morning, all the Wind Riders were casually waiting for the candidates to come tumbling out of the barracks in various stages of undress, Amanda haranguing them at every mistake. There were a lot of chuckles and smiles at the newcomers' expense as they tried to form a straight line and stand at attention. Then Megan trooped the line looking each of the candidates up and down with a frown on her face. Two of the men had clearly had some level of training before, as they were fully dressed and standing properly, eyes avoiding contact with Megan's or Amanda's as they were scrutinised. The girl with the copper hair was also fully dressed and standing somewhat the right way.

The candidate that received the most scrutiny was the one with the orange Mohawk haircut and the facial piercings.

"Pretty," Megan said looking at him nose to nose. "Pretty ugly." Then she walked away.

"What a disgusting bunch of humanity!" Amanda yelled. "I am going to the Master Warrant right now and ask him to please shoot me. I cannot stand the humiliation! You two big galloots there and Copperhead, stay behind! The rest of you get your sorry asses over to the mess hall for breakfast. You have half an hour, now get!"

"I expect the three of you to get the rest of this sorry-ass group up to snuff, so they can at least get dressed properly in the morning!" Amanda yelled at the three still standing at attention. "In two days, we will be marching in front of the Master Warrant and the other training groups. I have been promised promotion to Master Sergeant after this and if you yahoos do anything to jeopardise that I will not be pleased; is that clear?"

Both the men barked out, "Yes Sergeant!" The girl said Ma'am.

"Do I look like a pussy officer to you, Candidate!" Amanda was nose-to-nose with the girl now. "I work for a goddamn living, Candidate! You call me Sergeant, Candidate!"

"Yes, Sergeant." The girl said.

Amanda put a dumbfounded look on her face, looked away and dug a finger in an ear.

"Speak up, Candidate, I can't hear you!" she yelled.

"Better," Amanda said. "Now get your asses over there and get breakfast."

She waited until they had run into the mess before she laughed.

Amanda was yelled at and asked if there was something wrong with her watch by Megan as they lined up after breakfast in front of the barracks in running gear.

"I said half an hour, Sergeant!" she yelled, nose-to-nose with Amanda. "Not forty minutes! Half an hour! I am not pleased, Sergeant! Not pleased at all! This will not look good on your report, Sergeant! Now get these people out of my sight and on the trail!"

"Yes, Ma'am!" Amanda barked out. "Sorry, Ma'am! Won't happen again, Ma'am!"

The Wind Riders were lounging around, packs and rifles at their feet, howling in laughter as the gaggle of candidates started to jog, Amanda yelling at them the whole time. She put her right hand behind her back and gave them the finger, which only made them laugh more.

They were joined on the road by the five other training groups, who, while not in step, were at least jogging in formation. About halfway down the two-mile course heavy thumping could be heard coming from the rear that got louder as it came nearer. Twenty-nine Wind Riders caught and then passed the jogging groups of candidates, and Megan was with them. The Wind Riders had full packs on their backs and a rifle in one hand. They were in columns of four with officers to the sides. Each foot hit the ground in unison and it sounded like one large person running down the street because they were running, not jogging.

To make matters worse, they reached the turn-around point before the other groups and were laughing and blowing kisses at the sweating recruits as they passed them. The worst of the lot was diminutive Diane, who was almost dwarfed by her pack. She hurled insults at the recruits as they went by.

Every move the candidates made was watched by the Wind Riders, who would wait until the close order drill was done each day, then do it themselves in front of the candidates. To make matters worse, they always did it with full packs and weapons loads and made it look easy. Which it was for them; they could do it in their sleep.

In the mess, the candidates were ignored. So were Megan and Amanda who were always sitting apart from the rest of the Wind Riders, like they had been banished; not part of the group who were always laughing and joking around. Until the candidates had been released for the day to collapse in their bunks, that is. Then the laughing was done while Amanda related the latest stupid stunt someone had performed.

"CT," Megan said. "I think you should have a talk with Metal Head."

"Is there a problem?" CT asked. "He should be okay. He was part of a Civil War re-enactment troop."

"Ya well, he's not acting like it," Megan said. "He seems to think he is above it all. And he has got to lose all that metal on his face. You know what kind of hygiene shit that will cause in the field."

"Ya, okay, I'll have a talk with him," CT said and headed for the candidates' barracks.

"Tenhut!" one of the men with military training yelled out as CT walked into the barracks. Everyone piled out of bunks and stood in front of them at attention.

CT went down the line a look of disgust on his face as he looked each one of them up and down. He had put on his one pair of full pants for this and his combat boots.

"You with the Mohawk! Outside! Move it! Move it!"

He made the man stand at attention for a whole minute before he put him at ease.

"I personally picked you to come here," CT said. "I need someone to back me up in what I do. Your skills are almost as good as mine. Yes that's right, almost, I said. I was hacking your shit for the last year. You never even knew it, did you? This close order drill shit should be easy for you. Hell, you should be helping the other candidates, not acting like the worst candidate out here. Hell, I didn't even know how to walk properly when I joined. You haven't earned the right to be different yet. Lose the metal in your face. You know it is going to get infected when we go in the field and we do that a lot, man. You will be running a lot of sophisticated electronic warfare equipment in the field. Essential equipment. They rely on us for the information we provide. If they don't get it, they will die, which means we will die, get it?

"These people will die for you. Or they might just as easily kill you if they think you are getting in the way. I have been with that little Diane humping those heavy packs for weeks at a time. So, don't kid yourself that this is all for show.

"Do you know who you are replacing? Karen Kovaks, that's who. You do know who she was don't you? The second-best computer geek in her Stanford class. Wanna know why you are replacing her? She was killed three weeks ago as the second person in an assault team, that's why. Our second job is computers, numb nuts; our first job is being a soldier.

"So, lose the attitude and get with the program. Or I will shoot you myself. Oh. and by the way, the first in that graduating class that Karen was in? Master Warrant Duncan Kovaks, and he did shit in Afghanistan for five years that would make your hair curl and that was before he went to Stanford. Dismissed."

CT left him standing there and was so distraught with the conversation he forgot to put on his flip flops and shorts when he went back in his office.

"Hey, you're a Canadian, right?" Metal head asked the copper-haired girl. "What do you know about the Master Warrant?"

"What, just because I'm Canadian I'm supposed to know everyone in Canada?" she said. "That would be like me saying you know everyone at Georgia Tech. But ya, I've heard of him. He applied to Cal Tech, MIT and Stanford. All of them wanted him. He chose Stanford and they were going to give him a full academic scholarship and an athletic one. Yes, both. He was wanted by every Tier One football college in the States and a bunch of NFL teams. But he paid his own way and he passed with honours at the top of his class. If you have not figured it out yet, he was the top computer geek in North America, if not the world. I tried to hack into some of his shit once and he wiped out my computer for me. I couldn't even stop him. I heard CT got a little further, but not much.

"The army shit is even more impressive."

"That's not all of it," Shelly said, inserting herself into the conversation. "I have known the Master Warrant for many years. He was wealthy before I met him. He made me and all my people here a lot, and I do mean a lot, of money. I expect to do the same here. Hell yes, we could get killed doing this shit. But the way things were going back home? Hell, it's probably safer here. Now get the hell to bed before that bitch sergeant comes in here and makes us all do twenty push-ups or something."

Amanda had just been about to do that when she heard the conversation, but instead smiled and walked away.

It had been arranged that the Wind Rider candidates would enter the parade ground last. They were the least senior. The first were the black-uniformed battalion. They were led by a tall woman whose face was heavily bandaged. The whole battalion marched in perfect step. Their uniforms were spotless, boots and buttons gleaming.

The next were the five hundred being trained by the Marauders. They were not as precise as the first battalion, but still looked better than the Wind Rider candidates when they marched in.

Duncan, Bishop and their command groups were formed up in front of them. First the woman commanding the full battalion marched forward and saluted, then she went down on one knee, as did her battalion behind her. They raise their right hands as she pledged her allegiance. Then Duncan raised her up, shook her hand and handed her a file of papers.

The next was the leading candidate from Bishop's group. They performed the same ritual, but did not receive a file folder. Finally, Shelly approached on behalf of the Wind Rider candidates and pledged her allegiance.

Then, in the same order they had arrived in, they all marched out. This time the Wind Riders did not berate them when they returned. In fact, the candidates would have preferred it if they had. They were just looked at; not a word or gesture was made. It was clear to them that they had disappointed the veterans.

Chapter Eleven

THE FOLLOWING MONTH, the candidates worked hard. The Wind Riders no longer ran with them every morning. Nor did they march with them at night. Except for the weekly Saturday morning run, in which the whole Brigade participated, they were on their own. The Saturday runs were conducted in running gear, not uniforms, and each battalion or regiment had its own T-shirt design made in a local shop.

The fronts of the T-shirts had a crest or other insignia on them that designated them as different from the others, all but the Black Shirts, who ran with black running gear and T-shirts.

The Wind Riders had white T-shirts with a trooper brandishing a C8 in one hand astride a wolfhound in full flight. They were cheap T-shirts, but the candidates loved them. They were still running at the back of the formation, but they were allowed to wear the regiment's crest on their chests and that made them feel special.

It had been decided that they had progressed far enough to be issued their own rifles. After a few days of learning how to take them apart and put them back together again, and practicing over and over, they were led to the shooting range, where they were instructed on the proper operating methods the Wind Riders used.

Thirty of the Black Shirts were also being instructed and the Wind Rider candidates resigned themselves to being humiliated once again. It was anything but a humiliation. The Wind Riders almost to a trooper had all passed minimum qualifications on the first round. Four had passed expert level. The two that had not passed minimums on the first round passed on the second, and two more passed expert on the second round. Few of the Black Shirts even hit the targets, let alone passed.

The next day, Bishop's group was already shooting when they arrived. They were even worse. Maybe one in ten hit the target at all.

Two more Wind Riders qualified expert and the six experts were taken to another range where targets were placed further away. The rest of them went through familiarisation with the light squad automatic weapons.

The rest of their days was spent in learning tactics and practicing them. They were now running, not jogging, the two miles each morning with their weapons. Slowly more gear was added each day, until they were finally running with full combat loads and gear. That's when the Wind Riders joined them each morning again. Still they pushed them hard and still they beat them.

It was the last Saturday of the month, the day the whole brigade would march ten miles with full combat loads and gear. Once again, the Wind Rider candidates, as the junior of them all, started last. By the time they had reached two miles they had passed the Marauder training group and two of the Marauder battalions. They had passed all the Marauders and were gaining on the Black Shirts at the half way point, when the Wind Riders passed them on their way back. They were still in step and still striding strongly, which made the candidates work harder. They had caught up to half of the Black Shirts by the end of the march, but they were spent.

The Wind Riders were all sitting on their packs hurling insults at them as they came in, but then helped them to their barracks and even bought them a round of beer in the mess after. Things might be looking up, they thought. Until Monday.

• • •

"What the fuck?" Somebody was banging on Duncan's door Monday morning. It was still dark out and Duncan snapped a light on and he yanked his door open. CT was standing there.

"Remember that gang the Guild was bringing here? Well, they just left their barracks planet," CT said.

"How much time do we have?" Duncan was grabbing his uniform now.

"Friday morning," CT said.

"Okay get the command group together in the board room," Duncan said. "But page them; don't go banging on their doors. I'll put the coffee on."

Duncan emailed Bishop to call him as soon as possible and sent another one to the Black Shirt commander to do the same. Then he filled up the big coffee urn and began a brew. It would be a long morning.

"Sorry for getting you up so early," Duncan said. "That mercenary group will be here Friday morning. The members are from Earth and they are all SF types. We have allies with them, people. CT has been in regular contact with Karl. He was with us for that Saudi job, so his people will be on board. So should the JTF people, the Yank SF types and the SAS. The wild cards will be the Russians. The largest faction is about a four hundred Foreign Legion types. They have complete control and the Sergeant Chef who has taken control is a real work of art. Major nasty asshole, that one. Just like the assholes we took out here."

"CT, I know we are still blocking most traffic into and out of the planet. Block everything starting now. All of it. Jane, make sure the LAVs and the Cougars are ready to go. Barb, grab those two new geeks we have and get them up to speed on the surveillance suites. I'll have Megan and Amanda start familiarising the new people on the LAVs, but the crews will still be our people. Get to work, make it happen."

The rest of the Wind Riders were up by then and breakfast was being made. Duncan called Amanda and Megan to his office.

"Show time, kiddies," he said. Then he outlined what was happening and what he wanted them to do for the next few days. He dismissed them as his phone began to ring.

"Good morning, Commander Isabelle," he said. "Sorry to disturb you so early this morning, but I need your help."

"Good morning as well, Master Warrant. How may I be of help?"

"The Guild is sending fifteen hundred very nasty people to make a visit to our happy little province. The visit will not be pleasant. All of the troops are from my planet and are very good warriors."

There was silence on the other end of the line.

"That does not sound good," she said finally.

"Ya well, we have a couple of things going for us," Duncan said. "For one thing, they don't know that we know they are coming. For another, they don't know you are with us, so we are more than just thirty now. Do you have fifty people competent enough with our weapons to help out?"

"Yes, Master Warrant," she said. "I have ten qualified expert, and forty minimum."

"Okay, send them over as soon as you can," Duncan said. "I will have my people put them through some advanced training. Next, these guys will be coming in on their own space transport. I know next to nothing about those things. Where will they have to land? Things like that."

"We can help with that, Master Warrant," she said. "We have experience in those matters."

"Good," Duncan said. "These guys also think we don't have any functioning weapons systems, that they have all been used up or destroyed. We will let them continue thinking that. They will be using the same weapons systems you guys do. But I need the landing area to be near someplace where I can deploy my LAVs and long-range rifle people without being seen."

"Yes, Master Warrant, I understand," she said. "I will have a suitable location for you by the end of the day."

"Do you have any people who know how to pilot those little air vehicles?" Duncan asked. "And can we mount weapons on them?"

"Yes, Master Warrant, I have five vehicles and pilots," she said. "I believe we can modify them easily to accept our vehicle weapons systems. But I would caution against using any of yours, Master Warrant. I think the recoil from your weapons systems would affect the vehicles' safe operation and we don't have the time to train for it."

"I agree," Duncan said. "Can I also ask you to provide troops for a backup reserve, Ma'am?"

"Of course, Master Warrant, it would be an honor, Sir," she said.

"I told you already, Isabelle, I work for a living; you address me as Master Warrant or Mr. Kovaks," Duncan said. "I am not an exalted officer type like you are, Isabelle."

"I am sorry, Mr. Kovaks," she said. "I will remember that in the future."

"Very well, Commander Isabelle," Duncan said. "Carry on, I am expecting a call from that bandit Bishop anytime now."

Well, at least she can carry on a conversation with me now, Duncan thought. Then his phone rang again.

"Sleeping in, are we Bishop?" he said.

"Hey, not all of us are machines like you, Kovaks," Bishop said. "Some of us are real human beings who need our sleep."

"Okay, you got me there, Bishop," Duncan said. "Look, I need a favour, James. I've got a battalion and a half of very nasty guys coming here Friday morning. They are all from my home planet and have almost as much training and experience as my people do. What they lack in weaponry they make up for in numbers."

"Holy shit," Bishop said. "I think I know who you are talking about Duncan. The Guild uses them for all the really hard jobs."

"Ya well, they are using local weapons systems and don't know we still have all of ours fully functioning," Duncan said. "So, we may have a bit of an advantage on them, but they also use the same tactics we do, so it could get interesting."

"So, what do want me to do?" Bishop asked.

"I've got the Black Shirts backing me up here," Duncan said. "They know the terrain and have made great progress in their training. What I would ask of you is to get all your people, and I mean all of them, the hell out of here before Friday. We are blocking all communications and electronic signals in and out of the planet. So, all you need do is prevent being seen by eyeball mark one. If things go sideways, I would like you to take those assholes out for me and carry on the work we have started here."

The line went quiet. Duncan could not even hear Bishop breathing.

"You have my word of honour on that, Duncan," Bishop said softly. "I will wipe those assholes off the map, Duncan, count on it."

"I am, James, I am."

• • •

From intel CT had obtained from the Guild, Duncan was able to paint a picture of what he wanted to do. The Marauders had moved to a wooded area thirty miles to the west and drone flights confirmed they were well hidden.

The Black Shirts had prepared positions along the buildings fronting the landing zone. They would have to sprint a hundred yards to get into weapons range for the bulk of their troops, but the thirty troops armed with C8s would be able to cover them.

Duncan's people would arrive with Black Shirt vehicles. Their rifles would be propped against the vehicles on the side away from the landing zone and they would have local weapons in their hands. They would be stationed two hundred yards away and in the open with an open field behind them, making an L shaped ambush with the Black Shirts.

The LAVs and Coyotes were placed out of sight in a warehouse complex two blocks away, and three snipers were placed in offices located in the buildings the Black Shirts were using. The snipers were well inside the offices and would not be observed.

Friday morning, the arriving ships asked permission to land and to begin negotiations respecting the Wind Riders joining this battalion. Permission was given and the ambush was put in place.

As the five transport craft came to a hover and landed, the ten Wind Riders deployed in the two vehicles and parked, exiting the vehicles and lining up at their rear. Ramps unfolded from the front and the rear of the transports and troops rushed out and formed up a hundred yards in front of the transports and a hundred yards away from the Wind Riders.

Three men came forward and Duncan walked toward them. The only weapon he had was his Sig pistol holstered under his left arm. All three of the men approaching him had Glocks on hip-mounted holsters. They stopped ten yards apart.

"Whiskey Romeo, Alpha Five," came over Duncan's ear piece. "Anyone standing or holding a weapon will be killed."

"Good morning," the man in the center said with a French accent. He was a tall wide man. His nose had been broken at some point in the past and not been fixed properly. He had a large knife scar ranging from his right eye down to the jaw. His right hand was casually resting on the pistol grip.

"My name is Sergent-Chef Leclair and I am the leader of this battalion."

Duncan looked past the man at the troops. They had split up into two groups. The group on the left were slowly going to their knees, placing weapons on the ground and linked hands behind heads. The other group had weapons ready.

"Welcome to Oaken, Sergeant Chief Leclair. I am Master Warrant Kovaks, the leader of the Wind Riders. It seems we Sergeant Chiefs have a knack for command." Duncan replied in French.

The man across from him laughed. "Well, stupid officers don't really know much about leading now, do they? You are a few people short. We were led to believe that you were thirty and that you had just received fifteen more. Yet I only see ten."

"Well, when one is facing odds of ten thousand to one, casualties do happen," Duncan said. "The last bunch were just untrained clerical people, and they didn't last more than ten minutes."

"But still you won, eh? That is good. We need people like you."

"What's in it for us?" Duncan asked.

"We pay top rates," Leclair said, continuing in French. "Five pounds of silver per month in garrison, eight on active duty. We provide barracks and mess privileges for a small fee. We split ten percent of any spoils with the troops."

"What's in it for me?" Duncan asked.

"Ah, a man after my own heart," Leclair said. "I will give you six pounds per month and eight on active duty."

"Not interested," Duncan said. "Have a good day."

Leclair's hand pulled out the pistol and he shot Duncan in the chest knocking him from his feet. Micro-seconds later all three men were thrown from their feet as the high caliber sniper rounds hit them. The ten Wind Riders reached behind the vehicles, took their weapons in hand, went to one knee and started shooting the troops on the right who had begun advancing toward them, firing as they came.

The group on the left was now all face down laying prone on the ground, hands on heads. The snipers were shooting as fast as they could and the Black Shirts advanced, riflemen firing to cover.

The attackers were well-trained veterans. They split into five-man fire teams and spread out, making tougher targets and forcing the Wind Riders to scramble behind the vehicles and use them for cover.

Then a 20mm cannon opened up on full auto, decimating attackers wherever it found them. It was joined by another and still another as the four LAVs and two Coyotes joined the fray. They stopped three hundred yards away and the vehicle commanders perched outside the cupolas started firing their machine guns.

Three air cars, with a high caliber laser mounted on each, circled the grounded transports, ready to fire if they gave a hint of lifting off.

By this time, the Black Shirts had come in range and added their fire to the fray. Enemy troops were falling everywhere.

Suddenly, the remote weapons systems on the LAVs came alive. They rotated to the left and elevated, the fronts popped off and as the first four specks in the air came into view, one air-to-air missile from each LAV left the pods and streaked to join with the specks, blowing the approaching aircraft from the sky in spectacular explosions.

"Five inbound enemy transport, escorted by four fighter craft," CT said. "They are headed to land two miles west of the city."

"Roger," Duncan gasped out. "All mounted Wind Riders to advance to that landing zone. Hold them as long as you can. Bishop, get your people moving. Hit those assholes in the rear. Team one and two disengage and proceed to landing site on foot. Black Shirt fire teams to assist."

"If team five and his friends could help, Ghost?" came across in German.

"Right, all Black Shirts disengage and join the assault on the next landing zone. Our new friends will finish up here. Kurt, get the flight crews off those transports and secure them or blow them up of they try to take off. Brett, you got my C8?"

"Coming, Boss."

Duncan stood and pulled his Sig from its holster. Leclair was still alive, barely.

"I've got friends everywhere," Duncan said pulling his shirt open to show the vest underneath. "About half of your people, in fact. Too bad. I could have used your Legionnaires but such is war, eh?"

Then he shot him in the forehead. The other two were already dead.

"If I don't see any live Legionnaires after this, Kurt, I will not lose any sleep," he said in German. Then Duncan grabbed his rifle and weapons harness from Brett and started running toward the next battle.

The surface-to-air missiles mounted in the remote pods on the LAVs took out all four fighter craft and one transport. The other four landed successfully and eight hundred troopers deployed and spread out. The LAVs stopped three hundred yards away, dropped their loading ramps, and started engaging with the cannons. Now the coaxial-mounted machine guns added their fire to the cannons and the cupola-mounted machine guns.

The fifteen rookies split into three five-man fire teams and opened up. Hesitantly at first, but when laser strikes started coming closer, the firing intensified.

Now the Black Shirts saw the reason for the Wind Riders' obsession with running. The Wind Riders doubled the pace they normally used for the long distance runs and their loping gait soon left the Black Shirts behind. They formed into their four-trooper fire teams and spread out across the street as they ran. The fire teams staggered one on the left side of the street, the next on the right, with five yards of separation between them.

The firefight settled down to measured shots as each side went to ground and Duncan swung his people over a couple of blocks so he would outflank the attackers. As soon as they broke cover, the sniper team deployed. They were eight hundred yards away and fired single shots, taking out officers and senior enlisted men.

At five hundred yards' distance, Duncan's fire team went to a knee and started firing while the others continued to advance. At four hundred yards, Diane's team went to a knee and Duncan's team rose, went twenty yards to the right and ran forward again.

The attackers were kept under constant fire while the Wind Riders advanced. Duncan fired his first grenade from his launcher as soon as he was in range and the other four joined him. Every few seconds a grenade would impact near a group of enemy. The Wind Riders ran out of grenades just as the Black Shirts entered the fray, lasers crackling and rifles firing.

The Black Shirts advanced as they had been trained, in a long line, but their fire was effective. The 20mm cannon exhausted their ammunition and one by one fell silent, as did the machine guns. Then their crews joined the fight on foot with their rifles.

Just at the point of ordering a withdrawal, Bishop hit from the rear, his vehicles firing as they came. Duncan's people picked up their rate of fire as the Marauders' dismounts swung into action. Suddenly it was over. First in small groups, then in large, the enemy surrendered.

Bishop's vehicles surrounded the grounded air transports and Duncan's vehicle crews headed back to their vehicles. While Bishop's troops collected the few prisoners, the Black Shirts and Wind Riders stood and took stock.

Duncan's teams started to report in. They had a few minor injuries and everyone was short on ammunition. Except for ammunition, Isabelle's Black Shirts reported the same. Bishop's people hadn't even sustained any minor injuries.

The same could not be said for the attackers. Only a hundred were unhurt or had minor injuries. The rest were dead, dying or severely wounded.

The weapons pods on the LAVs came alive again.

"Three airborne inbound, Ghost," CT said. "One Guild small transport and two fighter escort. They are requesting a ceasefire."

"Ya okay," Duncan replied. "Send a message to Her Majesty on all this."

"Already done, Ghost."

"Area secure, Wind Rider One," Kurt said. "No friendly casualties. No enemy survivors."

"Roger, Wind Rider Five," Duncan answered. "Do I presume you have agreed to our terms, Wind Rider Five?"

"On behalf of my comrades we pledge allegiance to Duncan Kovaks and the Planet of Oaken," Karl said.

"Consider yourself under my protection, Karl," Duncan said. "We'll formalise all this later. Keep alert for any more surprises, but I think we are clear now."

The two fighters had the same markings that the transports did, but the small transport was a Guild machine. As soon as they landed, they were surrounded by Marauders' vehicles and covered by the vehicles' weapons systems.

The Guildmaster and two others exited the transport and he angrily stalked up to Duncan.

"You will release all these prisoners immediately and all of the transport ships!" he said. "You will also release the Guild member's prisoners and their transports immediately. This was an unprovoked act of war and the consequences will be severe!"

"Well, you are correct in one thing," Duncan said. He was holding his rifle pointed in the Guildmaster's direction but at the ground. "It was an unprovoked act of war against the Planet of Oaken and its citizens. I, Sir, and my people, are citizens of Oaken. You, Sir, are my prisoner, as covered under the Acts of War legislation enacted by the Interplanetary Council.

"The planet of Arial and the Mercenary Guild, by this action, are now in a state of war with the people of Oaken. You are correct, Sir; the consequence will be severe. The Guild and Arial have conducted an illegal action. Her Majesty has sent a strongly worded message to the Interplanetary Council demanding immediate censure of the Guild and the Planet of Arial."

"You and the crews of the transports and the fighters may go. The ships themselves may not."

"You cannot do this!" the Guildmaster said. "Do you know how much power I have! I will crush this puny planet! Now you will release all the Guild members, those prisoners there and all our transports!"

"Well your so-called Guild members have just pledged allegiance to me and the people of Oaken," Duncan said. "As such, they are now citizens of Oaken and at Her Majesty's beck and call, not the Guild's. These other people conducted an act of terrorism on the people of Oaken and will be held for trial as such.

"As I am the acknowledged ruler of this province for Her Majesty and as you and the people of Arial have committed an act of war against me and my people, I am now in a state of war with the Guild and the people of Arial, which means that Her Majesty is now in a state of war with the Guild and the people of Arial.

"The Guild and Arial intervened illegally in an internal affair and you have now created an interplanetary war. Congratulations."

"I will crush you!" the Guildmaster yelled. "I will muster the full might of the Guild against you!"

"You do that," Duncan said. "Do I look worried? You know what? I changed my mind. The transport crews are now prisoners and are to be held. I will honour the ceasefire and allow the crews of the fighters to return with you, but not the machines. Now go, before I change my mind again and kill all of you!"

The four crew members of the fighters quickly exited and ran to the small transport as the Guildmaster and his two escorts joined them. The machine took off, tracked the whole way by the weapons pods.

"Tanya has just placed the whole planet on war alert, Duncan," CT said. "All armed forces are placed on active duty. District and province commanders and the armed forces leaders are to report to the capitol on Monday for a conference."

"Roger," Duncan replied. "Bishop, escort our prisoners to the compound. Place guards around these machines; we will deal with them later. Send some people to escort our new candidates to the complex and find them some barracks. Kill those fucking wounded terrorists; I refuse to waste resources on them.

"Get some backhoes and bulldozers over here and dump these bodies and those Foreign Legion fucks in the holes and cover them up. Commanders' meeting in an hour in my barracks; that means you too, Karl.

"Good job everyone, massive damage to the enemy, none to us."

Duncan refused the offer of a ride and, accompanied by Brett, Amanda and Scott, he walked back to his barracks.

Duncan tossed his rifle and weapons harness on his bed, then walked to the board room and sat down at the head of the table. One by one the people arrived and arranged themselves around it. Bishop had the only clean uniform; all the rest were dirty and sweat-stained. Kurt was welcomed by the Wind Riders and introduced to Bishop and Isabelle. Her lower face was still wrapped in a now very dirty bandage.

"Right," Duncan began. "Again, well done everyone. Those Arial troops were well trained and it looks like they had body armour. Not that it helped them any. Speaking of which, I think I am going to have sore ribs for the next month." He laughed and pointed to the hole in his shirt.

"Okay Karl, tell me what you've got."

"One company made up of Commonwealth people. JTF, SAS and Australian," Karl said. "One European, which consists of French, Italian, my people and Russian. One American: SEALs, Delta, Marines and Air Force. One support company, all locals. Transport crews and pilots."

"We don't have enough weapons for you, Karl, so you'll have to make do," Duncan said. "Set up a training schedule. I want your people back up to standards as soon as possible. Get your support people going on that as well; you know how we operate. CT?"

"No way the Guild can retaliate for at least a year," CT said. "All their troops are committed elsewhere on contracts for at least that long. Arial does have about forty thousand troops, but we have thirty percent of their transport capacity here. I don't think we will have a problem for a while from them."

"Bishop?"

"The new recruits are shaping up nicely," Bishop said. "My people are training in your tactics and coming up to speed. We should have another thousand new candidates next month. The training should be easier this time as we have all learned your methods and what needs to be done."

"Isabelle?"

"Our troops trained in your tactics and weapons did well," she said. "We will train the rest of our people in your tactics. This fight showed us the value, Master Warrant. We will not disappoint you in the future. Arming the small aerial vehicles was successful and tests have proven that our large weapons can be used accurately. We will be testing the crew weapon you provided us to see if it can be used successfully. I would like to add another battalion and a support battalion, Master Warrant."

"We don't have the numbers yet, Commander," Duncan said. "But I will put you on the list. Bishop, give her the thousand new people after their initial training. She can give them the advanced training. I think our numbers are going to rise dramatically after this, but time will tell.

"Jane?"

"The big guns and automatic weapons were using local ammunition, Duncan," Jane said. "They performed as good as or better than the original. We have rearmed already and have plenty on hand. More is being made and stockpiled. The locally manufactured barrels for the guns performed well. We are giving them the spec to chrome the barrels and they should be ready for testing by the end of the month. As yet, we haven't found anyone with the skills or machinery to produce the weapons themselves, though, and carbon fiber for the stocks will be a big problem.

"Dave and Bob have been working on something, though."

"Okay Dave, lay it on me," Duncan said.

"Bob and I were a little bored," Dave said. "So we bought some metalworking stuff and made a couple of AK 47s. As you know, the Soviets mass-produced them back in the day. They are easy to make and make cheaply."

"What about AK 74Ms?" Duncan asked.

"Much like our C8s," Dave said. "Complicated firing mechanisms and carbon fiber stocks. The AK 47 is easier to make and maintain. They may not be quite as accurate or have as rapid a rate of fire, but they are robust and easy to use. Shit, more than half the world back home is still using them and they quit making them twenty years ago."

Duncan's mind was racing back to the manuals he had studied in the past.

"How about RPKs?" he asked.

"Same thing," Dave said. "Cheap, easy to make and reliable. Uses the same ammo."

"Speaking of which?"

"Not a problem, Duncan," Dave replied. "We change the dies for the brass and the primers. Make new bullet molds. The link belts might be a problem; we have a hard enough time making ones that work for our stuff. We use fifty round magazines instead. We can ramp that up easy."

"What do you think, Kurt?" Duncan asked.

"I would prefer the smaller caliber," Kurt said. "But yes, the AK is a reliable weapon in every condition. It is easy to train on, use and maintain. It's a little heavy with the wooden stock, but not that much.

Unlike our weapons, we can opposite-stack two magazines together for a quick change. They are just as accurate as a C8 at the ranges we will be using them. I say do it."

"If I get the proper machinery and maybe fifty people, Duncan," Dave said. "I can be pumping out a thousand a week. Well, the metal parts anyway. The wooden stocks might be a different story."

"No shortage of wood around here, if you failed to notice, Dave," Duncan said. "Find a local woodworking shop. We will fund all the tool-up costs they need. If not, I am sure somebody on this planet can do it. I've already got somebody in the automotive sector working on making us LAVs and Coyotes. Dave, maybe work on developing the cannons for them. CT has already put together a team to make the electronics. That stuff we keep in-house, people. Otherwise, this province needs the cash flow.

"Okay, we are digressing. Dave, make that shit happen and let me know what you need. Everybody else, step up training. Okay everyone but Jane get out of here, have a shower and clean up. Take the rest of the day off."

"Jane," Duncan said after everyone else had left. "You and Bishop will be coming with me to the capitol. While we are there, I want you to find a clothing manufacturer. I'm tired of all the different uniforms around here. It's time to come together. Black berets and black stripes are ours. Find out what Bishop and Kurt want. Tell Isabelle I am sorry, but that is the way it is. They can use black for formal mess and informal gym clothing, but she is going to have to find another colour for the beret. Also make some unit flags and badges.

"Send copies of tables of organisation, unit strengths and designations to everyone but our people. We will also be using Canadian ranks and protocols from now on. The Wind Riders are to be the only Recon brigade. Everyone else is to be classed as cavalry or infantry. I think the Marauders are to be infantry."

"Will do, Duncan," Jane said. "I'll have Kurt and Commander Isabelle decide on whether they want to be classed as infantry or cavalry. You want to keep the King's Own badges?"

"For now," Duncan said. "I'll clear it with Tanya, but I think it should be alright. I kind of like that wolfhound's head, don't you?"

Jane smiled. "Yes, I do, and so do the rest of us. I'll have Chris make me up a mockup. She did a great job on the vehicles."

"Once you have suggested designs from the other brigades," Duncan said. "Have Chris make up some designs for them as well. Badging also."

He dismissed Jane, walked into CT's office and closed the door.

CT didn't need to be asked.

"They have five hundred thousand troops," CT said. "Like I said, all of them are committed but the few they have on garrison duty. We have at least a year. They still don't know that we are producing our own ammunition. They figured out we had hidden our spares and have calculated we will be almost out of ammunition now. They are right, we would have been."

"I am more worried about that transportation rig they have," Duncan said.

"It's broken right now and they don't know why," CT said. "I don't either; it wasn't me. The thing seems a bit finicky and breaks down all the time. A big load like they carried resupplying us takes a lot out of it and it generally takes a month to get it up and running again. Which is why we were only getting resupplied every month or so. I've downloaded the specs, but haven't had the chance to work on it yet."

"Have you found out where it is?" Duncan asked.

"But of course, my commandant," CT said. "It is at their headquarters, on Arial."

"It all comes together now," Duncan said. "The plot thickens, my good man. Well, I don't know how far away this Arial is or how long it will take us to get there, but I think a raid is in order. I want you and your two new buddies getting me every last bit of information on that machine that you can find. Down to the type of bolts holding it to the floor. Then I want a full plan of the building and base it is in. Defences, troop strengths, everything, that and the planetary stuff.

"But not today, my good man. I do believe a wee shot of brandy is in order?"

"Why I believe you may be correct, Guv'nor," CT said as he swung his flip flop-clad feet out from under his desk. "I do hope there is a decent vintage of claret on hand."

"Well, the establishment is not known for its fine wines my good fellow," Duncan said as they entered the mess arm and arm.

"Barman, good fellow," he said. "Some of your best brandy for my companion and me, if you please."

"Who let the two jackass limeys in here?" Al, the day's bartender, asked.

"Well, I never..." Duncan said. "Come CT, we will take our trade elsewhere."

"Who allowed you bloody Colonials in this establishment?" a real British voice came from the door.

"Oh, my goodness," Diane said. "Look girls, some real soldiers for once."

"Have no fear, luvs, the Southern Cross has arrived," another said.

"Oh shit!" Duncan said. "We got enough beer? Those fucking Aussies drink like fishes."

"Not a problem," Kurt said. "The master race always comes prepared." Three of his troopers had beer kegs on their shoulders.

Others arrived with boxes on shoulders and the party spilled out into the open U space of the barracks as there were too many people now for the mess to hold. Everyone but the Russians and Duncan's new people had worked together before or knew of each other. Everyone but Katerina was from Earth and she was fitting in nicely. The rookies were all grouped together watching this gathering of super troopers with wide eyes.

Duncan looked over at them and smiled. Then he grabbed Megan and spoke into her ear. She smiled as well and grabbed a few Wind Riders and they disappeared back into the barracks. When they returned Duncan whistled loudly, getting everyone's attention.

"For the first time in a long time, the Wind Riders have taken in some rookies," he said. "They have been subjected to every humiliation possible. They have had their asses kicked and their feet run off. They have been kicked out of their bunks in the dead of night and force-marched twenty miles with full loads.

"Candidates! Front and center!"

The fifteen candidates ran to form a line in front of Duncan. Megan slipped a black beret unseen into Duncan's hand behind his back and then joined her fellows standing behind the candidates.

"Today," Duncan continued. "These wet-behind-the-ears babies in diapers saw the elephant for the first time! Today they joined the most powerful brotherhood in the world! Today they became soldiers! Today they became Wind Riders!"

He strode forward to Shelly who was standing in front of him and placed the black beret on her head. Then he stepped back and saluted her. All the others had theirs placed on their heads from behind.

"But!" Duncan said before bedlam broke out. "You have not fully earned those berets. Gentlemen?"

Bottles of vodka were produced, tops spun off and the bottles handed to the candidates.

"Get at it, rookies!" Duncan said. "Ya can't wear the beret until it is broken in."

Almost as one, the bottles were tipped back and drained.

"People!" Duncan yelled out, holding his bottle of beer high. "I give you B Squadron Wind Rider Regiment!" With a lot of hooping and cheering, the rest of the gathering drained whatever they had in their hands.

"A few more things and then we can party," Duncan said. "First, in order for us to keep our special status on this planet we must field a fully trained and equipped Brigade Group. We meet that qualification, barely. The Marauders and the Black Shirts currently are carrying the biggest burden of that requirement. Ultimately, I want a full division, but that is going to take time. The Marauders, the Black Shirts and you new people will be the Brigade Groups. The Wind Riders are not, nor never will be designed for that function. They will remain what they are, a Recon Regiment.

"This division will be uniformed and organised like a Canadian Army Division. Why? Because I am the boss and I say so. For you Earth people, this should not be a problem. Our armies all have similar ranks and formations. You Oaken people will have to make only slight adjustments in your organisation and uniforms.

"Now you will notice I only have forty-five troopers. That is a troop and a half. I need two and a half more troops to make up a full squadron and Colonel Jane is insisting on a full squadron. To that end, we will be holding a qualification to fill the open slots next Saturday.

"The competition is open for everyone except two people, Brigadier General Bishop and Lieutenant Colonel Isabelle. Bishop, because you are too old, fat and ugly. Isabelle, because you are not and I need you where you are."

The last comment got a lot of laughs.

"There will be one more exclusion," Duncan continued. "Whoever you new Earth people decide is going to be your commanding officer. I was only using Kurt because we did an op together once and I know him. All of you guys know and have worked with each other. Right now, that person will only hold the rank of Major, because of your numbers. As I said, work it out for yourselves.

"Now, before all you Special Forces types get too cocky. Some of Bishop's people, especially the new recruits, are good, and the Black Shirts are very good. I guarantee some of them will be with us. Highest score wins, people; I don't care who they are.

"Okay, that's it. My beer is empty and I am dying of thirst."

Duncan made a beeline to Isabelle.

"Look Colonel, this is definitely not personal," he said. "I know it's a bit of a demotion, but that is only temporary. You'll be getting the next batch of recruits and your rank back at that time. I meant what I said. I really need you where you are. You are the heart of your Battalion and I want you to be the heart of your Brigade Group. I don't need you wasted as a recon trooper; I have enough stupid he-men for that already."

"It is an honour, my lord," she said bowing her head. "I take no offence. I know what you are trying to accomplish, my lord. Thank you for the drink, my lord, but I must return to my troops and begin to get them prepared for the competition."

"You make sure you tell them I said you did a good job today, Colonel; a very good job, thank you."

She bowed her head and she and her command group moved off.

"Very serious lady," Bishop said. "Thanks for the promotion."

"What promotion?" Duncan said. "It's actually a demotion. You were a Major General before."

"So what; not as much fun though," He replied laughing. "Now you get stuck behind a desk, not me."

"Not me," Duncan said. "That's what Colonels are for. I am just a lowly Master Warrant Officer."

"Ya and I'm a duck," Bishop said.

"Quack, quack, quack," Duncan replied. Bishop whacked him on the arm.

"Go play with your friends, Duncan," Bishop said. "You guys did all the work today. Like usual. We just mopped up after. I've got everything under control."

"Ya, I need to unwind." Duncan said. "We have a Monday afternoon meeting in the capitol, James. We'll use those three air cars Isabelle has to get there."

"Hey Ghost, you finished sucking up to the brass yet?" Bob yelled. "I've got a bottle of vodka with your name on it. The rookies don't believe you can back up all your big talk."

"Rookies are to be seen barely, and heard from never," Duncan said. He tilted the bottle back and killed it in seconds slamming the empty bottle on the bar. "Good enough? Work on it, rookie." He patted the male computer tech on the shoulder and walked away.

"Okay," Kurt said to Carol in German. "What's with Duncan and the colonel in the bandages? And where is Karen?"

"Karen is dead, Kurt," Carol said. "The Colonel killed her and the bandages are from Duncan buttstroking her as he went by. She's lucky she is alive. He hit her pretty hard."

"Typical Duncan," Kurt said. "Try to kill your enemy, then make them your friend."

"I don't know that she's our friend," Carol said. "She respects us, and that's good enough. Her Black Shirts were the Imperial Guard. They are very good, Kurt. Very professional, and you know that's all that really matters. Oh, and Kurt, I have been training them, so when I say they are good, you can bet your ass they are good."

CT's new computer people sauntered into his office. As usual, he was wearing Bermuda shorts and flip flops.

"So," he said. "Yesterday you found out what it was like to have real bullets flying past your heads. Well, not bullets exactly, but you know what I mean. You killed something for real yesterday. Now you know why we were pushing you so hard. We didn't really do all that much, we just held them for Duncan. He did all the hard work and they ran the whole two miles to get there. Those guys are the real pros. We just back them up.

"Now we find out how fast you can put some more stripes on those shoulders, or crowns. Those two computers over there are yours. I've hacked into the Guild's systems, or rather Duncan has. We have full access. This is what we are looking for. We need to find every single component that is used to make this thing," he said, pointing to a picture onscreen of the transport device. "What the component is made of, where it is made, how it is made. Everything. Get at it, children, time is money."

Chapter Twelve

"SHELLY," DUNCAN SAID. "You are now a second lieutenant. You can look up what that means later. Right now, it means that you will be coming with me to the capitol today. I might need your legal advice. Jane will be looking at your organisation table and figuring things out when we get back, so you might get a promotion. It's up to her, she's the support groups' commander. Before you go, get your people working on the province's financial aspects. Don't bother CT with that; he is working on another project. Link up with Ann; some of her ladies were gathering info and they can point you in the right direction. We have hacked into the interplanetary banking system so you can find whatever you need. Then get back here; we leave soon."

Shit, the faster these people get up to speed, the faster I can focus on other shit, Duncan thought.

They had to split up to fit in the small airships. Duncan and Shelly got in one, Dave and Jane in the second and Isabelle and Bishop in the third. The ships were small but fast. The trip by ground would have taken thirty hours, but this took three. They landed in the palace courtyard and were escorted into what looked like a large library where a table of light foods was laid out. Uniforms and rank badges had been found for Bishop and Isabelle so that all of them wore the same uniform and, while they were clean and pressed, they were dull compared to the others in the room. The desert tan contrasted with the rich blues, reds and blacks of the other officers.

None of the others made a move to approach them, but Duncan ignored them anyway. Over time, more people entered, all ignoring the tan-uniformed people. The large double doors at the end of the room were eventually opened, revealing a large banquet room and table. The table was bare, except for water pitchers and glasses. Everyone filed in and was ushered to a seat at the table. Duncan and his party held back and were the last to enter, sure they would be seated as far from the head as possible. Instead, they were ushered right up front to the six seats next to the head on the right side.

"Wow," Jane whispered. "You could fit your whole barn in here."

"Horses wouldn't like all the gold, or all the stuffed shirts," Duncan said. Jane almost choked on the water she was trying to drink.

A door hidden in the far wall opened and everyone rose as Tanya swept into the room. She was dressed in her scarlet red uniform today and she quickly took her seat and told everyone to sit down.

"Friday morning our loyal subjects were attacked by a combined aerial and ground assault made by the Guild and the forces of Arial. This attack was unprovoked and stopped dead in its tracks by my lord Major General Kovaks and his combined army. We have expressed our deep concern to the Interplanetary Consul and our displeasure to the Guild and have, in fact, declared war on both."

The room erupted into shouting, most of it directed at Duncan.

Tanya rose and banged her hand hard on the table.

"Enough!" she yelled. "Arial was supporting the rebels! I have proof! If that was not enough, they destroyed one of our supply bases during the rebellion. They are working together to take this planet away from us anyway they can. Get your fat oversized heads used to it!"

"But, Your Majesty," an older man in a bright blue uniform with lots of brass on it said. "The Guild has many soldiers at its disposal. Why, even Arial itself has a bigger army than ours."

"Duncan, if you would address this?" Tanya said.

"Yes, Ma'am," Duncan said. "Arial has forty-five thousand combat troops. Well, forty-four thousand now. We have captured one third of their troop transport capability and we have also captured the troop transports used by the mercenaries, giving us nine fully functioning troop transports capable of transporting two hundred troops each.

"The Guild has five hundred thousand troops at its disposal. All but five thousand are fully committed in conflicts for the next year. The five thousand uncommitted troops are mostly support troops located in their headquarters complex on Arial."

"How many soldiers do I have, General?"

"Thirty five thousand of your own troops. Ma'am, seven thousand of mine, Ma'am. All fully trained and equipped, Ma'am. I cannot speak to these other gentleman's capabilities, Ma'am."

"So we already match Arial's manpower and all of our people are combat veterans, correct, General?"

"Yes, Ma'am," Duncan said. "I would caution on any offensive attacks, Ma'am. We will need many more troops to take control of Arial, Ma'am."

"I agree, General," Tanya said. "I think more in the line of the type of work you did against our last enemy? It was very effective."

"Possibly, Ma'am," Duncan said. "I have my people working on it, Ma'am."

"Do you see, my lords?" Tanya said. "Do you see how a real soldier operates? He has anticipated Our needs and is planning accordingly. By my order, this planet is now on a war footing. All manufacturing and production is to start on equipment needs for our armies. Each of you, my lords, is required to provide us with ten thousand troops fully equipped at your expense. If you need assistance in organising that, I am sure my lord Duncan can provide it. Now, everyone but my lord Duncan and his people, out! Get to work! We have no time!"

"Pompous asses," Tanya said after all but her personal advisors had left. "They make like big brave soldiers. I will wager you, Duncan, that they spent all their defence budgets on buying new toys for themselves."

"No wager, Ma'am. I'd lose," Duncan said.

"My people tell me they are having trouble communicating off-planet Duncan. Do you know anything about that?"

"Who me, Ma'am? I just a poor lowly Master Warrant Officer, Ma'am. I leave that kind of thing to the real officers, Ma'am."

"Stop it, Duncan," Tanya said, waving her arm in a cutting motion. "You are now a member of the landed nobility and of high stature. As such, you are at least what I have been calling you, a Major General. These are my friends, Duncan, and we are in an informal setting and I classify you as my friend, so you can stop all the ma'am talk as well."

"No Ma'am," Duncan said. "No disrespect, Ma'am, but this is not an informal setting, Ma'am. This is a serious discussion of topics to do with national security, Ma'am, and should be taken as such. You may address me as you wish, Ma'am, but as my ruler I am bound by convention, Ma'am."

"As you wish, Duncan," Tanya said. "Now, back to my communication problem?"

"Yes, Ma'am," Duncan said. "We did not want, and still do not want, our enemies or suspected enemies to discover our plans, Ma'am. We have been jamming and blocking all forms of electronic surveillance and transmissions in and out of Oaken, Ma'am."

"You can do that?"

"Yes, Ma'am," he said. "Your electronic equipment is much more powerful than mine. It was no great feat."

"Knowing you, you were eavesdropping as well," Tanya said. "Maybe not you yourself, but I am sure CT was."

"Yes and no, Ma'am," Duncan said. "We have automated systems set up to do that for us, Ma'am."

"You surprise me more each day, Duncan. Besides learning of the Guild and Arial's plans, what else have you discovered?"

"Two of your noble houses are in bed with either the Guild or Arial. They are much the same anyway. The older gentleman who spoke and his neighbor, Ma'am."

"Dammit, I knew it!" Tanya said. She turned to one of her advisors. "Arrest both of them and their staffs immediately. Trading secrets to the enemy. Do it in front of all the others and tell them what they are being arrested for in front of everyone, too."

"How do you do all this, Duncan? Are your people that much more advanced than ours are?"

"No, Ma'am," Duncan said. "I would say the opposite, Ma'am, to be honest. Your computer hardware and designs are very good, much better than ours. Our software is slightly better. Well, our normal software is better. CT's is much, much better and mine is better than his. Karen was better than CT, too, and Jane is not that far behind us. We have two new people that will be as good as CT soon."

"Way beyond me, Duncan," Tanya said. "Have you some names for the districts and the province for me yet?"

"The one by the mountains, Mountainview, Ma'am, the other, Skyview. I hadn't put much thought into the province's name, Ma'am. I am open to suggestion."

"What was that name you had on your shoulder when you first came here, it was catchy."

"It's the name of the country we come from, Ma'am," Duncan said. "It means village in the original people's language."

"Stanista," Tanya said. "It has a nice ring to it. The Province of Stanista. So it shall be. And what of that symbol on the arm?"

"It is the flag of our country, Ma'am. The centerpiece is a leaf from our national tree, Ma'am. The leaves turn scarlet in the fall."

"Hmm…I think not," Tanya said.

"If I may be so bold, Ma'am," Jane slid a piece of paper face down to Tanya.

"Yes, just so, thank you, Jane," Tanya said leaving the paper face down. "This will be my gift to you, Duncan. I will give it to you at your graduation ceremony. Oh, surprise! Do you think you are the only one who has spies? Now, you have other things for me?"

"If we could expedite the manufacture of our LAV models, Ma'am?" Duncan asked. "We can really use them. Also, I want to use common uniforms for all my people, Ma'am. If someone could suggest a manufacturer?"

"Yes and yes," Tanya said. "See to it, Vitally. Anything else?"

"Yes, Ma'am, a personal request, Ma'am."

Tanya gestured to him to continue.

"Our regiment is called the King's Own Regiment, Ma'am. We would like to keep the name, Ma'am. It has a long and honorable history, Ma'am."

Tanya just looked at him for a minute but did not respond.

"So," she said finally. "You have two people here I have not met, Duncan. Who are these two lovely ladies?"

"Lieutenant Colonel Isabelle and Second Lieutenant Shelly, Ma'am," Duncan said. "The Lieutenant Colonel is the commander of the Black Shirt battalion, Ma'am. The Second Lieutenant is my legal advisor, Ma'am."

"And your new formation? Where is their commander?"

"They are determining that, Ma'am. They are all the best soldiers of their countries back home, Ma'am. Very professional, Ma'am."

Tanya picked up Duncan's beret and fingered the crest on it.

"This is your regiment's symbol?"

"Yes, Ma'am," Duncan said. "Each regiment has its own, Ma'am."

"I don't much like Black Shirts, Colonel, nor do I like Marauders, General. You may continue to use them informally among yourselves as the Wind Riders do, but I will issue you your official names and crests."

She tossed Duncan's beret back at him and motioned for Bishop's. She unpinned the badge from it and tossed it back to him.

"You are not a Wind Rider General and, as a General, nobody will say you are out of uniform. I need this for a sample. Jane, your designs please? I will see to it myself."

Jane slid the whole file folder over to Tanya.

"My lord, Duncan," she continued. "I wish to pattern my army after yours. Please send your table of organisation at your convenience. If there is nothing more?"

All six of them rose and bowed. Then they exited the room. They were escorted back to the court yard.

"Sorry, guys," Duncan said. "She's the boss."

"I didn't want to hang around with all these assholes anyway," Bishop said.

"Looks like they don't want us hanging around either," Duncan said as their air cars approached.

Duncan contacted Barb on the way back and had her send a table of organisation and a brief summery of uniform requirements, ranks and symbols to Tanya's people.

Duncan had an official email from Tanya waiting for him when they returned.

> *We hereby name our Reconnaissance Brigade Group, the King's Own Regiment. They are designated cavalry and will wear black berets and black striping.*
>
> *Tanya, by the grace of God, Queen of Oaken.*

He had a follow-up email.

You can be such a stuck-up ass sometimes, Duncan. No fun at all. You owe me a beer and a steak.

Tanya

The next week was a blur. From dawn until dusk, Duncan and the entire command staff were busy. Doing research, compiling reports, implementing policy. He needed a bigger staff, Duncan decided.

Bob said he had found a local woodworker who could pump out the rifle stocks they needed as fast as they needed them. They were superior quality and the new rifles were being issued to the new guys first, then the Black Shirts. The Marauders would be last. Ammo was not a problem and one day a week they would manufacture RPKs and distribute them.

Duncan sent a message to Bishop telling him to schedule training on the new weapons. Then he sent one to Isabelle telling her to return the C8s and C9s, as they would have the new weapons shortly.

All too soon it was Saturday. Test day. There were almost a thousand soldiers waiting to test for the seventy-five open positions. They were divided into groups of a hundred. Each trooper had a GPS/IFF unit. This would not only keep track of where they were, but their start and finish times. All of them had rifles and full packs and combat loads. Duncan had shortened the distance from ten to five miles. The groups of a hundred would leave in ten minute intervals. It was going to take all day to complete this test as it was, let alone at the normal test distance.

Duncan waited until half the test group had left, then he and the rest of his section took off in their brand new, locally produced G-Wagon. Scott was harassing the struggling troopers as they labored under their heavy packs from his perch in the roof hatch. Well, everyone else was, too. Duncan would let off the odd flash-bang as they went along, scaring the hell out of anyone nearby. Amanda tossed out a smoke grenade once in a while to make their lives even more miserable. All the while, the Wind Riders were laughing and having a great time.

They even backed into a small clearing until they were out of sight in one of the gaps between groups and waited. Then Scott booted it and they came blasting onto the trail, Brett firing his C9 on full auto, Duncan tossing flash-bangs, Amanda tossing smoke grenades and Brett tossing insults and holding the horn button down to sound continuously.

They were in position twenty minutes before the first group came struggling into the firing range. They had parked so that the tailgate was facing the target range and were sitting on it, legs swinging, sipping cold beer from a full, iced stash in a cooler behind them.

The fifteen Wind Riders at the finish kept walking up and down the firing line harassing the shooters, firing rifles over their heads and tossing flash-bangs. Anything to distract them.

As each group finished, Duncan and his crew saluted them with their beer and laughed as the tired troopers made their way to the waiting transport vehicles and the buckets of cool water awaiting them.

Not surprising was the fact that half of the candidates dropped out before the finish line. It was a tough test, especially in the hottest part of the day for troopers used to traveling around in vehicles instead of walking. Duncan was amazed that any of the Earth people finished at all.

"Good job guys, have a beer," Duncan said to his troopers who had been manning the finish line. "All the scores tabulated?"

"Okay, guys, fun time!" he said after he had received a positive response.

All of his fire team advanced on the targets in a line and started firing as they walked. By the time they reached the firing line, their rifle clips were empty and they let their rifles drop to hang across their chests and pulled out their pistols and emptied them walking backwards toward their vehicle.

"Ta ta, rookies!" Duncan yelled as he jumped into the vehicle. "It was a fun day."

Then the four G-Wagons tore off back down the trail, everyone laughing like crazy.

Duncan knew who had passed and what their scores were before he reached the barracks. Most of them were Earth people but ten were not. Three of Bishop's rookies had passed and two of his regular troops. Five Black shirts, one of them the original sub-commander informally inducted earlier, had passed.

Duncan waited until all the trucks had unloaded before he transmitted the pass signal to the GPS units of those who had passed. This was the final test. To see who had kept their units on. All forty-five passed. They grabbed their packs and gear and headed to the Wind Riders' barracks.

As they entered they saw all the Wind Riders lined up against the bar. All of them had a bottle of vodka in hand and ten, Duncan one of them, had two.

"Before you can wear one of these, you have to prove you have earned it," Duncan said holding a beret up. "Sub-commander you know the drill, so show the other rookies how it's done."

The sub-commander, a huge grin on his face, came forward, took the bottle out of Duncan's hands, spun the top off and killed the bottle. Then Duncan plunked a beret on his head.

Jane did the next one. Carol kept moving back until one of the Russians came forward, then she stepped up and handed him his bottle. He drank it down with much panache and turned around after he received his beret, making to hug Carol when he saw what was on her collar and stopped. He muttered something under his breath.

"Why, thank you, Corporal," Carol said. She had a big smile on her face. "My mother did wear army boots. In fact, she taught me everything I know."

She patted him on the back and laughed as he walked away to huddle with his two comrades. He pointed at her and talked fast.

Diane, too, had been waiting for someone and she came forward as the man did.

"Ah fooking hell!" the man said with a strong Welsh accent. "I shoulda fooking known. Hand the fooking bottle over, luv. I fooking earned it this time."

Duncan waited until the last trooper came forward. She was one of Bishop's recruits. She was not as small as Diane, but almost, and she was very shy and frightened, but she came anyway.

"Dianne, get your scrawny butt over here and show this rookie how it's done!" Duncan yelled.

Diane approached like a blushing virgin, looking down and sideways and batting her eyelashes.

"Yes, me lord, anything you say, me lord," she said. Then she grabbed the bottle Al had in his hand, spun around so she was facing the crowd, spun the top off it and downed it in ten seconds flat. Then she tossed the bottle back to Al, wiped an arm across her chin and laughed.

"Just like having sex, luv," she said. "Ten seconds of pleasure and whoosh, he's done."

The girl, no more than eighteen, turned beet red, quickly grabbed the bottle out of Duncan's hands and with some difficulty finished her task. Diane took her by the waist after Duncan had put the beret on her head and walked her away.

"Now you really must stay away from men like him," she said. "He is a frightful brute."

Duncan tossed a bottle cap at her and she turned around and stuck her tongue out at him.

"You can share my tent anytime, Diane," the Welshman said.

"Oh really? Diane said sweetly. "Why thank you I'll remember that while I'm shoving your ass all over those mountains over there for the next two months."

"Oh fooking hell, not again!" he said hanging his head.

"Ha, dis nutting," the Russian said pointing at Carol. "What she put us through, I never see before. Dat eagle on her collar make her one tough lady."

"Well Duncan, Barb and Dave can wear one, too," Carol said. "But they don't. This hat and this crest means more to them. And the next two months, Anatoly? They are going to be way worse than what I put you through."

"Is she an EBB, Ghost?" one of the JTF guys asked. "I took that training and it was a fucking killer."

"Ya, she is," Duncan said. "And most of them can't pass what we do. She did, but she was trained for it. They only have about twenty that can do what we do."

"Okay you guys, listen up!" Duncan yelled. "Yes, we are special. Yes, we are tough. We have to be. How the hell do you think you Super Troopers got all your intel? From us or somebody like us. I am called the Ghost for a reason, people. You will never see me or any of my people unless we want you to. That is our job, people. See but not be seen, hear but not be heard. The only thing tough about our training, the only thing different about our training, is learning that.

Well, and how to not be bored out of your minds sitting on some hilltop for days on end looking through a spotting scope."

"Okay enough. It's party time, but take it easy. I have it on good authority that Her Majesty will be here tomorrow to hand us our colors."

He grabbed two beers and headed over to Tanya, who was standing beside Barb. She was dressed like they were, in a desert tan uniform.

"So where is my beret, Duncan," she said. "As Colonel in Chief I think I deserve one, heh?"

Barb had one in her hand and a bottle of vodka in the other.

"Well I don't give a shit if you're the Colonel in Chief or the Goddamn Queen herself," he said. "Nobody gets a beret without earning it."

Barb thrust the bottle in her hand.

At first Tanya was shocked, then she realised what was going on when Barb started twirling the beret in front of her face.

"You are such an asshole, Duncan!" Tanya said. Then she yelled and downed the bottle as Diane had earlier, in ten seconds flat. Then she grabbed the beret out of Barb's hand and put it on the crown of her head.

"But such an adorable asshole," she said, kissing then patting Duncan on the cheek. "But still too young for me."

"Aunty!" Katerina said, grabbing Tanya in a big hug. "Oh, you look so marshal in that beret and uniform."

"Well, I fucking earned both," Tanya said. "First this asshole won't let me kill any more bad guys, then he makes me drink a bottle of that horrible rot gut they brew here."

Duncan walked away as Jane came up and let the four women catch up. He rotated around the room for a while until he spotted the small girl sitting by herself in a corner. He grabbed two beers and sat down beside her. He handed the beer to her, breaking her concentration.

"You ok, trooper?" he asked.

"Ye…yes, my lord." she said putting her eyes down. She had a heavy French accent so Duncan switched to French.

"So, what's the problem then?" he asked.

She took the beret off her head and caressed it and the crest, then made to hand it to Duncan. He refused it.

"You earned it, love," Duncan said. "You keep it."

"But I don't deserve it my lord," she said. "I am a farmer's daughter, and I can barely read and write. Not like all of you."

Duncan smiled. "I am only a lord because her majesty made me one." He said. "My dad raised cows. See those four women standing with their husbands? They are just like you. No military background. They were poor townspeople. In fact, I would bet most of the people in this room are just like you. What's your name, trooper?"

"Hanna, my lord," she said.

"Hey Carol," Duncan called waving her over. "Young Hanna doesn't think she belongs here with us. Just like somebody else I heard about a long time ago."

Carol swung a chair over and sat right in front of Hanna and picked her chin up so she could look her in the eyes.

"We are who we wish to be, Hanna. I was like you: poor, wearing old hand-me-down clothes. I probably had it worse than you. Here all but the very rich are poor. Not so where I come from. But I have pride. God help me, I have a lot of it. So, I confronted my leader in front of everyone and asked him why I couldn't have one of these eagles, why I couldn't be an officer. Because only the rich people got the eagles and were officers.

"He told me to quit feeling sorry for myself. If I wanted an eagle bad enough and I wanted to be an officer bad enough, I could be. And I am. The uniform, Hanna, anyone can get the uniform. This beret and this badge? You have to earn them. Yes, we make you drink a bottle of vodka. That is just initiation, it is just proving you are willing to be one of us. To accept us, not that we accept you. You passed that test all on your own. Half the people that started gave up, Hanna. Half. You came in fifth overall, Hanna. Fifth out of a thousand who started! I'll fight beside you any time, anywhere, kid."

"What is all this, Duncan?" Tanya asked, sitting down beside them. "Trying to take advantage of a young innocent girl, are we?"

"Well, you keep telling me you're too old for me," Duncan said. "I have to take advantage of someone."

"No, I have never said I am too old for you, Duncan," Tanya said. "What I said was, you are too young for me. There is a difference, you know. Men, they are quite daft sometimes, don't you think, young lady?"

"I suppose so, I guess," Hanna said.

"Did I hear right? You came in fifth overall, Hanna?" Tanya asked. "That is quite an accomplishment for someone as young as you. Most of the people in this room are accomplished veterans with much skill."

"Oh, I don't think so, my lady," Hanna said. "I just got lucky."

"What were her shooting scores, Carol?"

"Expert marksman, Tanya," Carol said. "If she would have been thirty seconds faster she would have come in first. She had the best shooting score."

"What?" Duncan said. "She lost by thirty seconds?"

Duncan picked her up by the waist, swung her around and put her on top the table, then whistled.

"Hey!" he yelled. "This little pipsqueak just beat my score on the rifle range. She beat all your asses. You know why she only came in fifth? Because she was thirty seconds slower than four of you assholes. That's why."

Diane jumped up on the table with her and hugged her. Then little Hanna was swarmed and she was crying. But she was no longer blushing or keeping her head down, she was smiling.

"Keep up the good work, Duncan," Tanya said rising and patting him on the shoulder. "I'm counting on you and her to make more just like her." Then she walked out.

Chapter Thirteen

A MONTH HAD PASSED. Uniform shipments were slowly coming in. The Black Shirts now had regulation field uniforms. They had been officially named the Queen's Own Cavalry. Their berets were dark blue, almost black, and they were all armed with the locally produced firearms. Every morning, they practiced on the firing range or out on the field range practicing tactical assaults.

The new Battalion comprised of the SF people also had been issued new uniforms and weapons. Kurt had been confirmed as their commanding officer. They had been named the Prince Igor Guard, for Tanya's oldest, her thirteen-year-old son. Their berets were dark brown. Already they were being called the PIGs and had embraced it. Their jogging T-shirts were emblazoned with a tusk-sporting pig's head.

The Marauders had been named the Prince Stephan Foot after Tanya's eleven-year-old son. All of them had dark green berets, but only the new recruits and senior officers had the new uniforms at this point. The new recruits and training cadre had the new weapons and, in order of seniority, weapons were being distributed company by company as they became available.

In addition to the one thousand local candidates, one thousand volunteers from other districts had arrived. The Marauders were also training these people and they would be posted to the PIGs once their initial training was completed. The locals would be posted to the Black Shirts.

Duncan had capped the volunteer numbers at five thousand. That would be enough to flesh out the PIGs. Weekend training had begun for the active reserve. These were mainly townspeople at this point. Each of the four battle groups had been assigned a minimum number of reservists. The Wind Riders would wait for a competition to choose their final members, but they had taken it upon themselves to train the rural reserve people in their initial training phase. The support staff had all volunteered to do this.

Deliveries of what they were calling GW2s were at fifteen per month. It took a week to transport them from the district in which they were made. They arrived three per truck in large enclosed trailers. These trailers were then loaded with produce, frozen animal carcasses and an increasing number of wood products.

All of the existing G-Wagons had been mothballed as it was not cost-efficient to convert them to the local engines.

Four LAV4s and two Coyotes per month were arriving the same way. Two Coyotes could fit in one truck, but only one LAV could. Once they arrived, they were fitted with the locally made machine guns. Bob was still working on the cannons for them. CT had perfected the arming systems and communication suits and Duncan had funded a local company to produce the electronic suites and systems required.

Another firm was created to install them and still another to produce the surveillance modules the Coyotes needed and the portable versions the Wind Riders needed for the GW2s.

First starting off as a hobby, Al and the other three marines had developed a sniper rifle. It was bolt-action and used the same cartridges as the AKs. Duncan tried it and was satisfied, even using the open sights and the factory ammunition. He placed an order with them to supply all of the sniper teams with the weapons. All except the Wind Riders that is. They would continue to use their own.

Shelly had set up a corporation for them and the new bank that had been established lent them the funding to buy machinery and to lease one of the unused warehouses in the military complex for manufacture. They worked after their duty hours were over at first, then hired four local women to work during the day. That left their nights open and they began to work on weapon enhancements, first on long-range scopes for the rifles, then spotting scopes. The only problem they had was in obtaining the lenses for them. They had to come from another district and had the same delays in shipping that everything else had.

Dave had consulted with the five transport crews who had stayed with the PIGs. The Arial transports were well-suited to be converted to cargo carriers. They had a large rear ramp and massive interiors. Testing had shown that two LAV4s and three Coyotes could fit, with room left over. The trips would be faster and more cost-efficient. So, the interiors were converted to cargo configuration and a weekly schedule of flights set up.

The benefits were substantial and more of the province's goods were being shipped. Everyone had a job, good paying jobs and the capitol, now called Wind City, was a hub of activity.

The farm machinery Duncan had ordered from off-world had proven successful in tests. A local woman had suggested to one of Duncan's people that she could build these vehicles, if she could get drive systems and funding. A joint venture was formed and in a month the first vehicle rolled out the door.

It was sold to one of the farmhands on the test farm and he and his family started to lease land on that large farm from Duncan, with the understanding it would be theirs after their son finished his five years in the army. The same deal was made with every farmworker in the province and loans were arranged so that they could buy the machinery as it came off the line. Priority was given to those families with children already in, or training to be in, the army. The waiting list was long.

Tanya had arranged for troops from her other districts to be trained in the new tactics. The training would be two months in duration and the Marauders would organise it. The trainees would be using local weapons and vehicles and the Marauders had plenty of both.

The training classes were limited to a maximum of five hundred troops, conducted at a special complex set up in a remote area. Even so, Al and his buddies had been spotted hunting with their new rifles and the aristocrats were clamouring for rifles to hunt with. Al developed a lighter version with a shorter barrel, single shot only. They priced it and its ammunition astronomically high, hoping to discourage sales, but this had the opposite effect. It seemed everyone who was anyone just had to have one. They made more money from five of these toys than they did from five hundred sniper rifles - and the profit margin for the sniper rifles was good.

But, even using air transport, supply delivery was a problem. Trucks could only hold so much and there were only so many drivers and not many of them wanted to drive the long distance required to reach their remote end of the planet.

One of Duncan's people contacted one of Tanya's people and Duncan, Shelly and George, the financial man, were summoned to the Palace for a meeting. There, at first with Tanya's legal and financial ministers and then with the transportation, labor and land ministers included, they developed a plan to make a railway. This was a new concept . It was not until the manufacturing minister joined that the benefits of a railway were fully understood. Then everyone became excited. Until the costs were tabulated.

George demonstrated that, within a few months, the railway would be generating income and that after the first year would be almost breaking even. Tax revenues would increase as delivery times for goods would decrease, which would drive up demand for goods that were either too large or time-sensitive to transport by road over long distances. Stanista Province was willing to pay for half of the cost of laying the rail line to Stanista, even though only a tenth of its length would be in Stanista itself. In return, Stanista wanted a thirty percent share of the railroad and three seats on the board of directors.

It took a week to hammer out all the details. Most of that time, Duncan was left on his own. But his nights were full. The young, rich, newly single, good-looking new ruler was much in demand as the high fliers paraded their unmarried daughters in hopes of arranging a profitable marriage. Their hopes were repeatedly dashed. Duncan was polite and courteous, but aloof to all the maneuverings and pandering and the sometimes outright sexual proposals.

Tongues started wagging when Duncan was spotted having lunch every day with his stunning blond legal advisor and even more so after the grand ball Tanya gave Saturday night in celebration of completing the deal for the railroad. Shelly arrived draped on Duncan's arm wearing a gown that highlighted her features. She caught every eye, male and female, and she made no bones about her claim on Duncan.

She was seated next to Duncan, who was seated next to Tanya at the head table. The couple made a show of holding hands and whispering to each other.

"Oh, stop it you two," Tanya said. "You are making it too obvious."

"Pardon, your majesty," Duncan said in all innocence. "Her Majesty wouldn't be getting jealous, now, would she?"

"I keep telling you, you're too young for me," Tanya said. "I did have hopes for you and Katarina, though."

"Not going to happen," Duncan said. "She's got her hooks into Brett big-time and he loves every second of it."

"I see," Tanya said. "I suppose you arranged for Shelly to come because of your past relationship? I don't blame you. She is very stunning, has a fantastic mind. You make a good-looking couple."

"Oooh, are you kidding me?" Shelly said. "He's too old for me."

"Can't flippin' win around here," Duncan said. "Too old for one, too young for the other. None of the other women around here even interest me, or come close to either of you in the brains or the personality departments."

"The way to a woman's heart," Tanya said. "Complimenting her on her brains and her personality. Is something wrong with the way we look?"

"Never really noticed," Duncan said. "Don't look at me like that. Sure, you're both beautiful. Any guy would do anything to be with either of you. It's just…Well, you know…"

"Karen, Tanya," Shelly said. "He won't say it so I will. When I met him he loathed her, hated her, wanted to kill her, but, try as I might, he wouldn't touch me. He still loved her, badly. When he met you, the two of them were madly in love. So, we both became his friends, good friends.

"Yes Tanya, I love Duncan, but not that way. He is and probably always will be my best friend. But never my lover and never my mate."

"I agree," Tanya said. "It's not often that women like us find a man who only wants to be our friend. Not that I wouldn't mind a quick roll in the hay with him now and then."

"Oh I've seen him naked, Tanya," Shelly said "Vava voom!"

"Ah, Cheerist," Duncan said. "Please get me back in the field, Lord, and away from all these lecherous women. Pleease!"

• • •

Duncan had decided to take the afternoon off. His workload was much lower now that Shelly and her gang had taken over all the office duties. He had just reviewed the financial report for the last month. They were still bleeding cash, but nowhere near as badly as they had been. Even though the taxes they levied had been reduced by two-thirds, tax revenue was up. The joint ventures were paying dividends and profits, loans were being repaid and military equipment purchases were dwindling. Unfortunately, the railroad was taking a lot out of the cashflow, but as it made its way across the landscape and the benefits were realised, the revenue was starting to come in.

They had run through about half of the silver stash, but CT had finally found the secret bank accounts the previous ruler had hidden and transferred that money into their own accounts. They were using those funds now instead of the silver.

So, with nothing to do for the afternoon, Duncan put on one of his old uniforms and went for a walk through town. Everyone was busy. The roads were filled with delivery trucks. Shops were displaying their goods and trade appeared to be good. Restaurants and bars were busy with business meetings or friendly lunches. The people looked happy and were all well-clothed. Quite different from when the Wind Riders first arrived.

He made his way into a residential area. The streets and yards were clean and the homes in good repair. He stopped and watched children playing at lunch break in a school yard. They were also well-clothed and looked well-fed and happy. Until the bell rang, of course, and they had to go back inside.

He came to one of the daycare centers that had been set up and watched for a while. Again, all the children were well looked after and happy. He was struck by the attention these young children were getting by the staff, especially from one young woman.

She was laughing and playing tag with her group of four-year-olds and would listen intently when she was asked a question or spoken to. It was a bright, warm day and she gathered her charges around her and pulled out a book. As soon as she did that, all the other kids came running and sat all around in front of her and listened intently as she read.

Duncan's head dropped and his eyes teared up as he remembered Karen and how she had also adored children. He was still like that, his arms draped on the fence and his forehead on his arms, when the young woman came up to him.

"Is everything all right, my lord?" she asked.

His head snapped up and he stood straight.

"Ya, everything is good, Isabelle," he said. "What are you doing here?"

She was wearing civilian clothing. A tasteful sleeveless blouse with the top two buttons undone was tucked into a calf length skirt. She had white ankle socks in sneakers and her shiny auburn hair reached just above her shoulders. She swiped the right side of her hair behind her ear and smiled at him. Wow, what a smile! It lit up her whole face and her green eyes twinkled.

"Not the picture of the ultimate warrior queen, I guess?" she said and giggled. "I don't have much to do in the afternoons, so I volunteer here. What about you, my lord, out slumming?"

Duncan was looking at her face and she began to blush. She really was beautiful, he thought. This was the first time he had seen her without bandages. There were two thin scars on the left side. One just below the cheek, the other along the jaw that disappeared behind her hair.

"You should get out more often," he said. "You look good in real clothes. Me, well, same as you. I don't have much to do in the afternoons anymore and got bored hanging around the base and decided to take a walk. Those kids really like you."

"And I really like working with them," she said. "Like you said, it makes me feel like a normal person. At least for a little while. Get off-base and do normal people things, you know?"

"Na," Duncan said. "I haven't been normal people for a long time. Hell, look at what I'm wearing. I don't even own any normal people clothing."

"That's not what I heard," she said. "I hear you broke a lot of hearts in the capitol."

"Not likely," Duncan said. "All stories. Hey, I've got an idea. You know anyplace around here a guy can take out a cute girl for a normal meal?"

"There is a good steakhouse just a couple of blocks over," she said. "You and Shelly would have a great time there."

"I am sure we would," Duncan said. "Unfortunately, she has a hot date tonight with one of your guys so I am out of luck. No, I was wondering if you weren't busy? You know, we have never really had a chance to talk. Bishop and I hang out all the time."

"Well…I'm not sure," she said.

"Ah, come on," Duncan pleaded. "We work together all the time. Hell, I might even buy, this time. Come on, give a guy a break."

"Why not," she said. "I have nothing to do tonight anyway. Just give me a few minutes to make sure the kids are all headed home for the day. Meet me out front?"

"Woo hoo, Kovaks has a date with a hottie tonight!"

"Be nice, or this hottie will kick your sorry ass for you," she said, walking away.

Duncan walked to the front and stood off to the side. He was enjoying watching the moms pick up their kids and the kids excitedly telling them of their day. A few of the women recognised him and made a little curtsy as they passed and he smiled and waved back. Then Isabelle came out and the kids coming behind her all said goodbye as they went by her. She was clearly liked by all the kids and the moms.

"Enchante, Mademoiselle Isabelle," Duncan said offering her his arm.

She took it and turned red as a couple of little girls giggled and whispered, or so they thought, to their mothers. "Look, Miss Isabelle has a boyfriend."

"Well, my lord Kovaks," Isabelle said in English. "Shall we?"

"But of course, Miss Isabelle," he said affecting a high-class accent. "Such a lovely day for a stroll, don't you think?"

"So, I know you know my name is Duncan," he said. "And it really is a pain in the ass to call you Colonel or Miss or just plain Isabelle. I do presume you have a first name?"

"Marlene," she said, she was blushing again. "Marlene Isabelle."

"Marlene: a beautiful name for a beautiful girl. You sure clean up nice."

"You don't look so bad yourself without that ugly black beret on your head," she said and she dropped his arm and they walked down the street together, as if they were normal people and not the leaders of the army and city.

"Well, if I get some more time off, I should probably invest in some civilian clothing," he said. "So, what else do you do besides being in the army and hanging out with kids?"

Just then a gust of wind hit them and blew her hair back from her face. She quickly raised her hand to pull it back to cover the left side, but not before he had seen what her hair had covered. Duncan stopped and turned her to face him, brushing her hair back so he could see.

The two thin scars changed to thick ones just behind her eye and the whole area from her eye to her neck was one massive blotch of wrinkled scar tissue.

"Oh my God!" Duncan whispered. "I am so, so sorry, Marlene."

She pushed his hand away and let the hair fall back down.

"It's not so bad," she said. "I'm getting used to it. My troops say it makes me look bad ass."

"I really am sorry, Marlene," Duncan insisted.

She looked him in the eyes and saw he was serious.

"Does it hurt much?" he asked.

"At first," she said. "A lot of headaches, and my neck was sore for a long time, but everything is fine now. You should have killed me, you know. I would have."

They had not moved and were still facing each other. She had her guard up; he could tell by the tone of her voice. She had become the professional again.

"I do what I do and I am damn good at it," Duncan said. "But that does not mean that I go out of my way to cause someone harm. I remove the threat as fast and as efficiently as I can in order to complete my mission. Would I have shot you given the chance in that particular situation? Yes. But I didn't have the time or the space to do that, so I did the next best thing. Believe me, I held back on the stroke. But I still don't have to like it, Marlene, and I don't."

"What's with you, Duncan?" she was dropping the walls now. "I killed your wife and unborn child and you are still worried about me? If I was you, I would hate me with every ounce of my body, but you want to be friends?"

She put her right hand on his chest above his heart. "I hurt you here," she said. "My scar is visible and is a badge of honor. The pain was brief. Your wound was here and can't be seen and the pain will never go away."

Now a tear came out of her left eye and ran slowly down her cheek. Duncan took his left hand and brushed it away and held her hand on his heart with his right hand.

"You were only doing your job, Marlene, and Karen was doing hers. Had I known she was pregnant, she would not have been on the assault team. That is not your fault, it is mine."

He let his right hand drop and they stood like that for a time. He with his hand on her left cheek, she with hers on his heart.

"I tell you what," Duncan said finally. "I will buy you dinner and a beer to apologise and you buy me a dinner and a beer to apologise and we will call it square."

She looked up at him and the twinkle came back in her eye. Then she pushed him away with the hand on his chest.

"No way," she said. "You're not getting off with just buying me a beer. You buy a lady a glass of good wine to apologise, not a beer. You lower classes have no taste."

"Oh, I go from My Lord Duncan to lower class, do I?"

"Well you are new nobility you know," she said sticking her nose in the air. "I, on the other hand, am of noble birth."

"Well that would explain the holier-than-thou attitude," Duncan said. "And the oh-so-superior walk and grace."

She had just stumbled on the curb she had not seen with her head stuck up.

They made it to the restaurant without further incident and were seated away from everyone else, the young soldier and his young girlfriend not being the type of clientele the owner wanted in his establishment. The service and food were good, but not overly friendly.

"So, back to our original conversation," Duncan said between mouthfuls. "What does a pretty girl do around here on her days off?"

"Well," she said. "I used to go out to the farm and do some riding. That was before the new boss made me the commanding officer of a new battalion. I haven't seen my mom for almost a year now and my horses probably have gone wild."

"So, explain horses to me," Duncan said.

"Four-legged animals that you ride," she said. She opened her purse and dug through it for a bit and came up with a small photo album. "Here, horses."

"Very nice," Duncan said. Yup, real horses, he thought.

"Oh, ours are not that nice," she said. "They are just work horses, not like the rich people. They have nice pretty horses. We use ours for cattle work."

"You don't say; how interesting!" He said. "So, big rich landowners, then?"

"Ha, far from it," Marlene said. "My dad was from the big city. His people were minor nobility with a lot of money but no land. My mom's family had a lot of land but no money. So…"

"Everybody wins," Duncan finished for her. "Your mom's family gets access to a lot of money and the prestige of your father's old name, and your pop becomes landed gentry."

"In theory, anyway," Marlene said. "The old folks got the money and the prestige. My pop was lazy and just wanted to hang around with the big shots. My mom had to run the farm and try and make a go of it."

"Where is your dad now?" Duncan asked.

"You or one of your people killed him," she said matter-of-factly, "in the first raid you made on the invasion column. He was one of the commanders."

"Shit, things just keep getting better and better for me here," Duncan said. "Almost kill the daughter and do kill the father."

"Oh goody," she said. "Does that mean I get off the hook for buying you an apology dinner? You owe me two for one.

"Just kidding, Duncan. No loss killing dear old dad. He was rarely around, and when he was it was just to demand more money from Mom."

"So, have you heard from your mother lately?"

"Oh yes, I call her every night. Well, when I can, anyway. She's doing fine. That new law you passed let her keep the land. Her daughter seems to be a full-time soldier. Between the money I send home and the rise in price for cattle, our debts are being paid off and she has a few pounds to spend on herself for once."

"What does she owe money on?"

"Back taxes from the old regime," Marlene said. "Especially for the two years before the war. They jacked up the taxes to over sixty percent. It's no big deal; we will have it paid back in a couple of years. A lot of us are in the same boat. The way you lowered the taxes right away was a big help."

"Good," Duncan said. "Glad to see something we are trying to do is working out."

"Your currency idea is good, too," Marlene said. "It's a lot easier to buy and sell things now. Before it was always such a hassle storing and shipping different sizes and shapes of silver bars. The bank transfer system you have established works well."

"Thank you," Duncan said. "I would like to take the credit, but George and Shelly set all that up. And before you say it, yes, that is the real reason Shelly is here. She was doing all that for me back home."

"What's it like where you are from?" Marlene asked.

"A lot like here," he said. "With a lot more people though. The climate where I come from is a lot like here. The colors are greener and the sky is bluer. The sun rotates east to west instead of west to east. Our day is twenty-four hours long, not thirty-two. The tilt and rotation of the planet around our sun make the summers hotter and the winters longer and colder. Where I lived, anyway, we had very long summer days and very short winter ones. We grow a lot of the same crops and livestock."

"Greens and blues," she said. "I am not sure I would like that."

"When we first arrived here," Duncan said. "We thought we were going to have a bad storm. Your normal sky color is the same as what happens when a bad storm is coming for us."

They had finished their meal and had been talking for an hour and the owner was glancing their way often. Not that it was busy. There were a lot of empty places.

"Well," Duncan said. "I guess we should be going before my lady gets a bad reputation for staying out late with a common soldier."

He looked at the bill and tossed enough coin on the table to cover it and a hefty tip and they left. It was a nice night. The sun was just going down and families were out in their yards. A lot of the children knew Marlene and ran up to her and alongside of them as they walked, chatting away briefly before their moms called them back.

A short time later they were back on the base, walking down the middle of the quiet streets. There were no children playing in the married quarters' yards here. The few children that had been born were not even toddlers yet.

Marlene's barracks were just down the block from Duncan's and they both stopped in front of it. She had both hands on the strap of her small purse holding it down by her waist and he had his hands in his back pockets.

"Well, I guess this is it then," Duncan said. "No more normal people. Back to the army again."

She just nodded her head.

"You know what?" Duncan said. "It's Wednesday. I haven't had any time off for almost a year. How about you?"

"No, what with the war and the preparations for the war and everything else," she said. "Except for the time I was in the hospital, no, not me either."

"That's against regulations," Duncan said. "Even though we are the bosses, we are still allowed time off. We both have efficient staffs that don't really need us around that much. I know I don't have anything big coming up. Do you think your mom would mind if you came home for a week or ten days?"

"She would love it!" Marlene said. "But can I afford to be gone that long?"

"Well it's time to find out if your majors can get by without you for a while," Duncan said. "I know my people can. They have been bugging the hell out of me to take some time off and relax. Do you think your mom would mind if I tagged along? I could sure use some time away from all this and get back to nature for a bit."

"She won't mind at all," Marlene said. "But are you kidding me? You being who you are?"

"Well, could you just tell her I am one of the people you work with?" Duncan asked. "I really am just a normal guy. All this other boss shit is new to me. I would just like to have some time away and be a normal person for a while. Not a lord or a commander or a soldier or a boss. Just a normal guy."

She saw he was serious. He had his head down and was looking at the ground.

"I can do that," she said. "I'll just tell her my friend Duncan from work is coming to chill out at the farm with me. We have a couple of guest houses and there are a lot of hiking trails you can go for walks on. I'll settle one of my gentler horses down for you and maybe we can go for a short ride if you want to."

"Outstanding!" Duncan said. He was smiling now. "You set it up so you don't have to go to the daycare for…um…two weeks and I will cut orders, ordering you to take time off. How much time will you and your mom need to get ready?"

"I could go tomorrow," Marlene said. "All my clothing is still at home. But we should give mom a couple of days to get ready. Friday afternoon?"

"Done," Duncan said. "How far way is it?"

"Five hours by road," she said.

"I know you can fly one of those air cars," Duncan said. "As a Colonel, you have to be able to return if you are needed. So, I think the General is going to insist on your taking one, as well as insisting that you take time off. Of course, you will need the requisite understaffer along to handle anything that would happen to become necessary for your immediate attention."

"Now I know why Jane calls you a pain in the ass sometimes," Marlene said. "You always know a way to bend the rules."

"Hey, I'm the guy who makes the rules now, I will have you know. Okay, I'll be here at noon sharp on Friday. Don't be late or I will leave without you."

"How are you planning to manage that, smart ass? You don't know where it is you're going."

"You do have a point, Colonel," Duncan said. "Well, if you are not waiting for me, I will just have you arrested and dragged out in irons."

They were laughing when they took leave of each other and everyone noticed the spring in Duncan's step as he strutted through the mess on his way to his rooms. The new people had never seen it and his old crew hadn't seen it for a long time.

The first thing Duncan did when he hit his office was to schedule a department head meeting for the next morning. Then he kicked of his clothes and had the first good night's sleep he'd had in months.

"Right," Duncan said as he breezed into the board room and took his chair. "It has come to my attention that Colonel Isabelle has had no time off for a year. Not only that, but she should have been given time off after getting out of hospital for her injury. Unacceptable, people, unacceptable. Colonel, the second this meeting is over you are on leave. No excuses. If your 2IC can't cut the mustard it's time to get someone who can. Is that clear? We can't have our commanding officers burnt out. Just make sure you let CT know where you are going to be in case we need you. Now get out of here."

Marlene just looked at him.

"I mean it Colonel, get the hell out of here! If I see you on this base after noon tomorrow, I will have you thrown in the brig for disobeying orders!"

Marlene grabbed her file folders and all but ran out of the board room.

"Duncan!" Jane said.

"If I wanted any input from you, Colonel, I would ask for it!" Duncan said. "Our people need time off whether they want it or not. Otherwise they burn out and make mistakes! Someone should have brought this to my attention before I found out about it! I am not happy, people. Colonel Isabelle is one of our best people and we need her operating at peak all the time! That goes for the rest of you, yahoos!

"It has also been brought to my lord's attention that one of his generals is well past burn out and has not had a day off for over a year! Unacceptable people! Bishop! You will hold down the fort! Karl, you are 2IC. Jane, you take over the Wind Riders!

"One of the local land owners has offered his lordship an offer to stay for a two-week holiday in the back and beyond and his lordship has accepted. I am outta here, people. Have fun. I'm gone, too."

249

He thumbed his nose at them as he left.

"That's it," Barb said, as they all sat shocked around the table. "He's found a girl."

"Who, Duncan, chasing women?" Dave said. "Not in this lifetime. They do the chasing, not him."

"Well something has certainly gotten into him," Barb said.

"Probably sick of seeing Bishop's ugly face every day," Kurt said.

"Ha ha, funny guy," James said. "More like he's had enough of that stuck-up Black Shirt; he sure tore a strip off her."

"She must have done something to piss him off," Jane said. "I don't see what, though. Like Duncan said, she's a hard worker and one of our best people."

Duncan spent the rest of the day picking up "normal people" clothing. A pair of sneakers, a pair of sturdy work boots. Several polo shirts and two work shirts, three pairs of work pants and one casual pair. He also bought a baseball cap. They had become big sellers after everyone had seen the Wind Riders wearing them while off-duty. This one was bright red.

All his stuff was in a duffle bag. He was bringing his sniper rifle with him. Maybe he could get some hunting in and if not, he needed the practice anyway. He placed his stuff on the floor and walked into CT's office. He was wearing the bright red cap, a polo shirt and the casual pants with sneakers on his feet.

"Woah, casual Friday," CT said. "Woo hoo!"

"It's casual Friday every day for you, CT," Duncan said. "Okay, I'm out of here. I will turn my comms on for exactly one minute every morning at seven. Unless the world is coming to an end, I don't want to be bugged. Got it? I don't care if Tanya calls herself. I'm not available. If she doesn't like it she can fire me. I didn't want to be the boss anyway."

"Sure, Boss," CT said. "No problem."

"I mean it, CT. If you guys can't handle all this Mickey Mouse shit, I'll get rid of you and find somebody else to do your job."

"Get the fuck out of here, Duncan," CT said. "You're starting to piss me off with your micro-managing."

Duncan kissed him on the top of his head, grabbed his rifle and duffle bag and headed off down the street. He tossed his stuff inside, then climbed in himself and waited.

Amanda, Bob, Barb, Brett, Dave, Megan, Diane and Scott were standing outside, watching. Then Marlene, also in civilian clothing and with a small bag, came out of her barracks and tossed the small bag inside and climbed in, shutting the hatch and taking off.

"I told you it was a girl," Barb said.

"No way," Bob said. "They can't stand each other."

• • •

"Ha ha ha," Duncan said. "Had them going Thursday morning. They think we hate each other now. My, do you pout nice."

"You did pour it on a bit thick," Marlene said. "I wasn't sure you were joking."

"Ah, I can tell the Colonel has never had the pleasure of training new recruits," Duncan said. "We have a hell of a good time jerking them around and then laughing about it after."

"Do you people ever take yourselves seriously?" she asked.

"All too often, Marlene. All too often. Life is seldom easy where we come from."

He took in the scenery for a few minutes and then turned to her again.

"I used to fly an airplane back home, once in a while," he said. "Nothing at all like this thing. If you have some time, do you think you could teach me to fly this thing? I kind of miss it sometimes."

"I am not sure you have the skillset, Duncan," she said. "It takes many years of training even to get the most basic of skills. You normally have to spend many hours in a simulator before taking the controls for the first time."

"Oh, ok." He said. "I just thought I'd ask."

She laughed and took her hands off the control column.

"Got you, rookie," she said. "It's easy. This thing mostly flies itself. I'm just here for show. If Mom leaves me any free time I'll take you up a few times."

By then, they were coming up on the farm and as soon as Duncan saw it he became a little homesick. It was much like his family's farm back home: a modest home with a few guest houses. Machinery sheds and a big barn were nestled in a clearing with a view of the mountains in the distance. Cattle were grazing in pastureland and crops were growing in the fields. The yard was well-kept and flowers were planted around the house.

Marlene maneuvered to land in front of one of the machine sheds and shut down. Men and women and some older children ran up as they shut down and exited the vehicle. Marlene was in the center of the group of laughing and hugging people. Duncan unloaded her small bag and looped his rifle onto the duffle bag and slung it up on his left shoulder and picked up her bag with the other hand and waited.

An older version of Marlene ran out of the house a few steps and Marlene ran into her arms. Then her mother took her hand and stroked the left side of Marlene's face and Duncan had to look away. He heard his name being called and he looked up to see Marlene waving him over and her mother wiping tears from her cheeks.

"Mom, this is my friend Duncan. He is from the city," Marlene said. "Duncan, this is my mom, Magdalene."

As Magdalene made no move to greet him Duncan bowed his head.

"Pleased to meet you, my lady," Duncan said. Magdalene returned his bow with one of her own.

"Well met, sir," she said in French accented English.

"The pleasure is all mine," he returned in French.

"A man of breeding, then," she said to her daughter. "No, we will speak in English please. I seldom have the chance to use it. Your family is of the nobility? Your French betrays you, Sir."

"I wish," Duncan said. "No, my lady has been tutoring me, Ma'am."

"Gaston," Magdalene said. "Take Duncan's things to his guest house. You have not had lunch I hope? Come, then, the table is laid."

The furnishings, like the house, were good but not opulent. The food was home-cooked and plentiful. Duncan felt himself relaxing almost at once.

"You are in the army with my daughter?" Magdalene asked.

"Yes and no, Ma'am," Duncan said. "I have the pleasure of serving with the King's Own Regiment, Ma'am. I provide information for the Colonel and her regiment, Ma'am."

"Now Duncan, what did I say?" Marlene said. "We are on holiday and off-base."

"Yes Ma'am, sorry Ma'am," Duncan said.

"Duncan?" Marlene was pointing her finger at him and frowning. "You are my friend and we are not on duty, and you know Lord Kovaks frowns on all this deferring-to-betters nonsense."

"Humph," her mother said.

Marlene changed the subject and asked about things on the farm and Duncan contented himself with being ignored. He was just sipping his lemonade, lost in his own thoughts, when Marlene interrupted them.

"Duncan," she said. "Why don't you get Gaston to show you where your cabin is and do some exploring while Mom and I catch up? I'll send someone for you at diner."

Duncan excused himself. Gaston was waiting for him and escorted him to the cabin he would be using for the week. Like the house, it was modest but well-kept. It had a bedroom, a washroom and a sitting room with a large roofed porch at the front door. He changed into work clothes and boots and packed his other things in the dresser and closet. He removed the bolt from the rifle and stuck it under one of the shirts.

He wandered around the yard for a while, just taking in the sights, the workers watching him and nudging each other. He was obviously a big-city guy making like a farmer in his new work clothes. A white rail fence enclosed the farm yard and Duncan made his way past the garden and leaned against it and just stared at the snow-capped mountains, basking in the afternoon sun above the trees. He was trying like hell not to be homesick and was losing the battle.

Then he heard activity at the barn behind him and walked over. Marlene was up on a horse putting it through its paces in the corral. She was a good rider and Duncan could tell she had spent hours in the saddle.

The horse was black and not overly tall, maybe fifteen hands, but broad. He was a gelding and while not pretty, he had good tone and muscles and was not a plough or draught horse. He was well-trained and moved well as Marlene put him through his paces. Then she rode over to the barn, dismounted, and mounted another black horse. This one was younger and more spirited, but she had control of him quickly and settled him down, then started working him in the corral.

While he was watching her ride, a black and white farm dog came and sat beside him. He nudged him a few times on the leg and Duncan reached down and scratched behind the ears. It reminded him of one of the Australian herd dogs he had back home.

"I see you have made a friend," Marlene said. She had ridden up while Duncan had been scratching the dog.

"Well, at least somebody doesn't mind me being a city dude." Duncan said.

"Dude?" she asked. "Is that like a duke or something?"

Duncan laughed. "Or something," he said. "You look good up there."

"After breakfast, we will go riding," she said. "You will ride the first one I was riding. He is very gentle. This one is a little too spirited for a novice. We won't go far."

She flung a leg over the fence and dismounted to stand next to Duncan. She bent down and scratched the dog and rubbed his chest.

"Sam was just a puppy when I left home," she said. "If he is half the dog his mother was, he will be a good dog. I'm going for a shower. Dinner in half an hour."

It was another awkward meal and Duncan excused himself early and went to his cabin. Sam was waiting and escorted him to the cabin. Duncan walked inside and left the door open but Sam stayed just outside the door. Rummaging around, Duncan found a coffee pot and some coffee and brewed up a pot, then filled a cup.

Then he turned off the light and stepped back outside, dragging a high-backed chair onto the porch. He moved it to the edge and, after a few adjustments, sat down and perched his feet up on the railing, leaned back and took in the night stars.

He woke up the next morning still on the deck with his feet up on the rail. Sam was lying beside the chair. The yard was busy with people headed for work as Duncan went in his cabin, had a quick shower while a fresh pot of coffee was brewing, and changed clothing. Then he perched himself back on his chair with his feet up and watched all the activity. Sam disappeared for a while then came back and laid down beside him.

"This is the life eh, Sam?" Duncan said. "Warm weather, sunshine and pretty girls to watch. Not a care in the world."

He had dozed off again until someone hit the bottoms of his feet. He cracked open an eye and lifted the baseball cap high enough to see.

"Come on, lazy bones," Marlene said. "You missed breakfast. The horses are waiting."

The horses were saddled and waiting when they arrived. Duncan let Marlene show him how to mount and sit and how to hold the reins. Then she adjusted his stirrups for him and they started off riding side by side, he made like a rookie rider, holding onto the horses mane and sitting off-balance. Sam was trotting easily beside him.

Then the trail narrowed, forcing Duncan to drop behind. He relaxed in the saddle, loosened the reins and started to experiment a bit with his knees. The horse responded and Duncan smiled and looked down at Sam, who seemed to be laughing at him. He put a finger to his lips. Both he and the horse were sitting in the bush and now both of them knew it, as the horse's ears and raising of his head let him know.

The trail widened back out again and when Marlene looked behind her to motion him to come forward, Duncan was once again off-balance and the horse had its head down plodding along, going through the motions. Sam was laughing and wagging his tail.

They rode for about an hour, mostly in single file. Once in a while Duncan let a tree branch whack him in the face and dutifully swore after it did. He knew damn well Marlene was doing it on purpose, as he could see her holding the branch back before letting it go. He had done the same to dudes many times himself.

They came to an open clearing with a creek feeding a nice little pond created by a natural dam. Marlene dismounted first and Duncan could tell she had not ridden in some time, but she held it well. He, though, almost overacted when he came sliding off his horse as she held the halter for him. But not much, since he had not been on a horse for a while himself.

They sat by the pond and as she reminisced about coming here as a child. Sam took off, doing whatever it is dogs do when they take off, and the horses grazed on the plentiful and lush grass.

Duncan just laid back on his right side facing her as she talked and leaned his head on an elbow. Her voice was very soothing, he thought, as he looked around, drinking up the forest and hearing the birds sing. He came back to himself as he realised she had stopped talking.

"You were very far away," she said.

"I was just thinking about when I was a cadet," Duncan said. "In the summer, we used to pack into a place much like this and spend a week camping. There were fish in the pond and the stream and we had fresh fish for breakfast every morning. The water was very cold and the pond was created by animals we call beavers. They make dams by cutting down trees and blocking a small stream like this. Then they make a lodge in the center of the pond with the entrance underwater. No predators can get at them, summer or winter. They eat the tree leaves and bark. They have two very large front teeth and cut down the trees by gnawing with those teeth."

"We have fish, too," she said. "Mom used to take me here some days and we would sit like this and she would fish and tell me stories from when she was a girl."

Sam came back and sat beside him.

"Well, now that Sam is back, I suppose we should head home," she said.

She checked and adjusted the horses' tack, then helped Duncan mount and they headed back to the farm. Duncan and his horse played the same game they had on the way out. Duncan was not playacting all that much, though, as he staggered his way over to his cabin to clean up and change for supper. Looking back, he chuckled as he saw Marlene gingerly walking, too.

Gaston removed Duncan's saddle and then looked over at him as he made his slow way to the cabin. There were no rub marks on the horse's back or where the cinch had been. He had deliberately left the cinch loose. There were also no sore spots on the horse's mouth from him fighting the bit.

Once again, Sam was waiting for him when he left early, but tonight Duncan slept in the bed and he did not wake up until Marlene was banging on his door the next morning.

"Come on," she said. "The only cure for a sore butt and thighs is to get in the saddle again."

This time when Duncan mounted, the girth was so loose he almost pulled the saddle over when he mounted. Once Duncan was up, the horse looked at Gaston and grumbled, then looked forward once again.

Today, they went in the opposite direction and were soon out of the trees and into the farmland beyond. Marlene was busy chatting away about the various types of crops and how they were grown and harvested and didn't notice that Duncan was riding relaxed and was only holding the reins with one hand. Nor had she noticed that he had untied them from each other and that they were in a loose loop, not being held taut like hers were.

Every once in a while, Sam would go tearing off in a field chasing something. Marlene always rode on his left, keeping her scarred face away from him. She had her hair tied back in a ponytail and out the back of her battered old cap. He enjoyed listening to her talk of her childhood. He knew so little of this place or its people.

They came upon a small cattle herd and Marlene was just getting into how they were bred, when Sam took off down the road at high speed and Duncan's horse's ears went forward and he raised his head, nostrils flaring.

A portion of the fence was down and ten cows were headed for the barley field. All pretences by horse and man vanished as they swung into action at the gallop. Duncan tore across the barley to head the cows off and started waving his cap and whistling loudly, while Sam blocked them from going down the road, barking and nipping at heels.

Duncan took off his shirt, guiding the horse with his knees when he needed to and waving the shirt in a circle and snapping it at a cows' heads now and then, yelling his cowboy yell and whistling the whole time. It took about ten minutes to chase the cows back into the pasture. Then Duncan flipped off the horse, letting the reins drop and roughly jerked the fenceposts up.

"Son of a bitch!" he said. The two posts were rotten and had broken right at the ground. He looked around and found some sticks, rejecting the first two. Then he walked up to the first good post and started to tighten the wire just in front of it until the top wire was tight again. He did the same for the middle wire.

"Who is in charge of this herd?" Duncan said as he came back to where Marlene was waiting with the two horses. She was holding Duncan's reins. "Son of a bitch should be fired! You could have lost that whole goddammed herd!"

He wiped the sweat off his face and chest with the shirt, then put it on, only buttoning up the bottom two buttons and leaving the tails out. Now he rolled the sleeves up above his elbows, bent down and gave Sam a big hug and told him how good a boy he was and did the same with the horse, hugging his neck. The horse brushed his forehead up and down on Duncan's chest.

Then Duncan pulled the cinch tight, grabbed the reins out of Marlene's hands, mounted, and without looking back, cantered toward the farmyard.

He rode right up to Gaston who was standing in the middle of the yard and, as the horse was sliding to a stop, Duncan was out of the saddle and had grabbed a handful of Gaston's shirt front, lifted him on his tip toes and started yelling at him in French.

"Are you the slack-ass foreman in charge around here? The posts on that pasture fence are so rotten they are busting at the ground! The fucking fence was down and ten cows were heading into the barley field. You're lucky I was there and had a good horse and dog with me or you would have lost all ten cows, you fucking asshole! The next time I catch you saddling a horse like you have been, I'll whip you with the goddammed cinch and see how you like it, you prick. Now get to work doing your job and fix that fucking fence! Or do I have to that for you, too?"

He threw the man from him, gathered up the reins, mounted and took off at a canter toward the little pond in the woods, Sam chasing after him.

When she found him, he had taken the saddle off his horse and was brushing him down with a handful of long grass. He looked up when she approached and with a little slap on the neck he stepped away from the horse and let him wonder away to graze. Marlene just sat in the saddle looking at him.

"What?" he asked. "If that asshole was one of my people I'd fire him! Useless sack of shit is what he is! No wonder your mom is losing money with asshole employees like that!"

Magdalene came riding up next and had heard his last comment.

"Fuck!" Duncan said. "That's all I need now. Some self-important play farmer telling me how to do my business."

He walked right up to her and stared her down.

"Look lady, I run a thousand head of cattle back home and a hundred head of horses. I am not some asshole city boy. My family has been ranchers for ten generations. I don't need no lecture from the likes of you, got it? It's a good god-damn thing we are here to show you idiots how it is done or we'd be losing more money than we already are.

"Fucking joke is what you are! Megan could run a better operation than you guys are here and she's only twenty-four! Back home, Barb and Dave are my neighbors and they have more land and cattle than I do. Cheerist! And you guys are trying to tell us how to be ranchers. I've forgotten more than you know!"

He took a few breaths to calm down while both women looked at him.

"Fuck me," he said. "Pasturing cows next to a barley field is bad enough, but with a bad fence? Do you guys have rocks in your heads or what?"

"Are you finished now, young man? Magdalene asked. "May I speak now?"

"Ya, say your piece," Duncan said. "I'll walk back and somebody will be waiting to fly me back."

"No," she said. "I wish you could stay longer. You are right, Gaston is not the right man for the job. But he is all I have. My fool of a husband took the best men with him and they were all killed in the war. Now can I get down off this horse so we can talk like real people? And put your damn shirt on. It might impress my daughter but all those scars on your body distress the hell out of me."

Duncan shrugged on the shirt, doing the buttons up to mid-chest. Then he took off his cap and rubbed his hair. Sam came and sat beside him.

"Sam has always been a good judge of character, I should have paid attention, hey Sam?' Magdalene said rubbing his chin. "Don't sit there all gaga like a little schoolgirl, get down here and join us. Just let your reins drop, he's not going anywhere."

"I apologise for my behavior, Duncan," she said sticking out her hand. "My daughter told me you were a Wind Rider before you came and I was upset because of that. I should have known better. You could not possibly have killed my husband and even if you did, it was in the heat of battle."

"No, Ma'am," Duncan said. "If he was the commander of that first group we hit, I definitely killed him, Ma'am. I took him out with my first shot. Just like I was the one who gave your daughter the scars on her face, Ma'am."

He was rewarded by a slap on the face for that one. Then he got another and would have got another had Marlene not grabbed her mother's hand.

"It was war, Mother!" she said. "I had just killed his pregnant wife!"

That sobered her up.

"I thank you for my daughter's life," she said softly.

Duncan shrugged his shoulders. "Like your daughter said, Ma'am, it was war. She was just doing her job. It wasn't personal."

"Come on, let's all sit down and calm down," Duncan said. "I forgot how hot-headed you French girls get."

"Like you Englishmen are not," Magdalene said, but she was smiling.

"I'm not English, Ma'am," Duncan said. "My mom was Russian and my dad German."

"Russians, I have heard of," she said. "But what is German?"

"A calmer Russian and a colder Englishman," Duncan said and laughed.

"So, you say you have expertise that could help us? Why then has Lord Kovaks not done so? We need the help."

"Not for lack of trying, Ma'am," Duncan said. "You old noble types are rather stubborn, Ma'am. The ex-servants who have gotten their own lands are already out-producing you and we have not had to teach them much at all."

"Yes, but all my farmhands went off and were killed in the war. All I have is house servants like Gaston and underage boys, and I will be losing them as soon as they turn eighteen."

"But the wives are still here, yes?" Duncan said. "They know how to do the work and probably did it when they were young. Ask them. We have women doing all kinds of things in town. Being military commanders and, well, ranch owners, Ma'am."

"Don't push your luck, young man," she said but she was smiling and had a twinkle in her eye. "I can still twist your ear if I have to."

"I have heard Barb say the same thing to him, Mom," Marlene said, "and he blushes just like he is doing now."

"You must have had a good mother, then. I assume you can saddle that old nag? We should head back. We still have six hours of daylight and can at least fix that section of fence that is down before the day is out."

"I didn't know old Buster still had it in him," she said to Marlene. "He was a good cow horse in his prime."

Duncan flipped on the saddle, punched the horse in the gut as he tightened the cinch, then lengthened the stirrups before he mounted.

"Yes, you are no novice," Magdalene said. "I should have noticed."

Then Duncan grabbed the reins with both hands, pulled them tighter and wobbled on the saddle. Buster lowered his head and plodded along looking at the ground.

"Smart asses," she said and slapped Buster on the neck. "Both of you."

Buster shook his head up and down as Duncan laughed.

"We were born at night, me lady," Duncan said. "But not last night."

Some young boys were loading shovels and fence posts in a wagon when they rode into the yard, being supervised by some women. Magdalene rode up to the women and spoke to them briefly, then they took off, headed to their homes. They returned wearing work pants, gloves tucked into the belts and headed to the corrals and saddled horses for themselves. They all headed out to the bad fence and tut-tutted when they saw its condition.

Duncan got to work digging a hole next to the first broken post. The ground was soft and it did not take long to rebury the post, the soil being tamped down every few shovelfuls. They had six new posts with them and by dark the new posts were in place and the wire pulled tight.

Everyone was tired but in good spirits when they returned to the yard. Duncan ate heartily that night and Magdalene pumped him for information until she saw he could hardly stay awake. Then she sent him to bed.

Marlene found him the next morning taking inventory of fenceposts with one of the women.

"You're going to need more posts than you have here," Duncan said. "There is a sawmill about ten miles from here. Call over and order some up."

"I'll have to see if we have enough money, Duncan," she said. "Posts are expensive."

"Not anymore, my lady," the woman said. "They are a lot cheaper now. We can get four for what we paid for one before. A good haggler can probably get six."

"What?" Marlene said. "But Gaston?"

"What does Gaston know?" the woman said. "He is a glorified cook, my lady. Best he goes back to doing that, my lady, and leaving the farming to the farmers."

"Well we had best get at it, then," Duncan said. "We are burning daylight."

"Burning daylight?" the woman said. "Oh, I see. Wasting time. Yes, you are right. I like that expression. Burning daylight. But if you don't mind, sir? We have enough bodies to fix fences, but not many good riders to herd. We need to move those cattle a pasture over so they are not tempted by the barley. If my lady would not mind helping? Your lady mother has already said she will be coming along."

"I've never done anything like that before," Marlene said.

"You take Buster," Duncan said. "He knows what to do. I'll take your horse. He needs a little training; you are spoiling him."

Duncan looked around the barn and found some work saddles. He grabbed two and tossed them and two bridles on the top rail. The he walked back in the barn and found a strong rope about ten feet long and as he walked back to the corral, fastening a lasso on one end of the rope. As he suspected, Buster came right up to him as he climbed into the corral and Duncan quickly had the bit and halter on him, the reins tied around a fence post.

The other horse was standing at the far end of the corral, watching him. He started to run around the edges of the corral as Duncan approached, trying to lose himself in the other horses as he started them running, too. Duncan started swinging the rope back and forth as he came to the center of the corral and pivoted while the horses ran circles around him. Then he started swirling the rope around his head and it was soon whistling and the horses ran faster. Then with a quick flip of his wrist the rope snaked out and went around the target horse's head.

Duncan braced his feet and held the rope tight against his butt as the horse tried to pull away and dragged him a few feet. The horse gave up and just stood there with wide eyes as Duncan walked toward him talking softly to him as he came. All the while he was walking, he kept coiling up the rope, keeping it tight as he did so.

"Well at some point somebody trained you well, bucko," Duncan said quietly rubbing the horse's neck while he spoke. Then he fashioned a quick halter with the rope and slipped it over the horse's head, talking to him softly the whole time, telling him how good a boy he was. Then he started rubbing his side and his back, moving around him, touching him and talking to him the whole time, until the horse had stopped quivering and was standing calmly. Coming to the horse's left side, Duncan leaned on his back with his forearms on and off for a couple of minutes, then levered himself up on his back.

He kicked him in the ribs with his right foot to get him to move to the left toward the waiting saddles and saw he had an audience. Marlene and two teenage boys were watching at the fence and Magdalene was smiling, standing behind them.

"Piece of cake," Duncan said jumping down and tying the rope to a post with a slip knot. "Carrot please."

Magdalene reached over a boy's shoulder and handed him one.

"Good carrot," he said after taking a bite out of it. Then he gave the rest to the horse.

The other six horses came up to the fence wanting their carrots. But they didn't get them until four of them had bridles on and were tied to fence posts.

Duncan supervised as the teenagers and Marlene saddled their horses. He saw that Magdalene knew what she was doing. But Marlene need at bit of help. The boys were saddling like it was second nature. Duncan quickly saddled his horse and adjusted his stirrups while he was standing on the ground. He had Marlene stand up, then lengthened hers two notches and had her stand up again and ran his hand between her butt and the saddle and nodded.

Then he grabbed the reins out of her hands, took the knot out of them so they were free and handed them back to her. The boys were smiling at him. They had already done that and were leaning forward on their hands, braced on the front of the saddle waiting for him.

Duncan removed the rope harness from the horse and with a quick tug undid the rope from the post. Then he pulled the lasso off the horse's neck, coiled it up and tied it to the saddle. He mounted and rode to the gate, opening it and closing it after the last rider had left the corral.

They walked out of the farm yard in a loose gaggle, then Duncan came to a trot and stayed that way until they came to the pasture gate. Sam was running alongside him the whole way.

"Any of you done this before?" Duncan asked. Magdalene nodded her head.

"Where you want these cows, Ma'am?" he asked. She pointed at the fence line about a mile away.

"Okay, this is how this is going to work." He said. "Cows are pretty stupid and stubborn. Just like some high-born women I know." Marlene stuck her tongue out at him. "I want one of you to ride up to the fence over there a bit and wait. The rest of us will start pushing them toward the fence. Sam here will be helping us out. Once they start moving down the fence line, two of you stay in the back pushing them forward. The other three of us, me, my lady and one of you young fellows, will be riding alongside. Marlene, as soon as you see those cows coming your way you start riding forward. They will probably follow you. Once we get close to the gate, I want you to open it wide and get the hell out of the way.

"My lady, you, me and Sam here have the hardest job. We have to keep them from breaking back into the pasture behind us. The horses probably know how to do this better than you young guys do, so let them do their job. Same with you, Marlene. Buster knows his job. Loosen up those reins a whole bunch or he will start fighting you. Okay guys, off we go."

They spread out in a line. Duncan untied the rope, shook it out and started swinging it up and down the horse's side slowly. The cows saw them coming. The ones that had been laying down got up and, after watching them for a while, they all started heading toward the fence line where Marlene was waiting. Sam was trotting from side to side head moving all the time, whining in anticipation, his tail wagging frantically in his excitement.

"Okay, boys," Duncan called out. "Start getting in behind them. Make sure they don't get behind you." He nodded at the young fellow with him to start angling toward the front and Magdalene started angling the rear. Duncan kept moving forward. Sam went with the boys to the rear. Then the cattle hit the fence and turned to face them. That's when Sam sprang into action, barking and nipping at heels. He got them moving forward and Marlene started walking forward. The next few minutes were intense as cattle attempted to break past on the side, and Duncan started whistling and yelling. He swung his rope as he guided his horse up and down in quick spirts every time a cow made to turn and come his way. Magdalene, too, was busy sprinting this way and that. Sam was busy helping her. The young fellow didn't have much work but was keeping a sharp look about.

The next problem occurred when they came to the corner at the far end. But the cattle soon got the idea and followed the fence. Duncan, as he knew he would, had the most work. He and his horse were in constant motion, heading off stubborn cows that kept wanting to return to the pasture and away from the fence. Marlene sprinted up to the gate and made to dismount.

"No!" Duncan yelled. "Just lean over and undo the latch! Buster will push it open for you. Then get the hell out of the way so you don't get trampled over."

She got clear as the first cow broke through the gate and ran for the far end of the pasture, followed by her buddies.

Duncan waited until Marlene had come back in the pasture, then he closed the gate and latched it.

"See, told ya," Duncan said. "Piece of cake."

His horse was sweated up badly. Duncan patted him on the neck and dismounted.

"Good job, boy," he said. "All of you, good job, guys."

Sam was sitting beside him, panting, with his tongue lolling out one side of his mouth. Duncan scratched behind an ear and chucked him under the chin, then he was headbutted by Buster.

"Ya, you too, you old coot," Duncan said and rubbed him between the eyes.

"Well what about us girls?" Magdalene said. "Didn't we do a good job, too?"

"Don't see no girls here," Duncan said. "Only see cow pokes and all cow pokes is called guys. If ya didn't like that, ya should have staid home in the kitchen barefoot an pregnant. My lady."

"Oh you!" she said shaking her fist at him. The young boys were all laughing.

Duncan coiled up his rope, tied it on the saddle and started walking toward the road across the pasture. Sam saw, heard or smelt something that interested him and took off headed for the barley field.

"Damn dogs always amaze me," Duncan said. "Look at him go."

He opened the gate for them as they came up to it and closed it before remounting again. He waved at the women working on the fence and headed back to the yard. Magdalene rode over to talk with the women.

"That was fun," Marlene said. "You had a lot of work, though."

"Ah shucks, Ma'am, it was nothing," Duncan said and laughed. "Try doing it on your own sometime. Now that's fun. Not!"

"Hey guys, keep those horses at a walk," he called, as one of them started to trot. "They will be too hot when you get back to the yard and you will have to walk them around until they cool off or they will founder."

He and Marlene kept to a slow walk and were soon riding alone.

"Your parents were lords and ladies at your home and yet you still worked like a common labourer?" she asked. Duncan laughed.

"Well, who else was going to do all the work?" he replied. "All the peasants revolted and ran off."

He looked over at her and saw she thought he was being serious.

"No Marlene, I was just joking, sort of," he said. "The aristocracy back home are just figureheads. Technically, they hold all the power, but the reality is much different. Every person has a say in how the country is run. No one has any more than one vote. No matter how rich or poor. Each vote counts."

The only sound was the horses' hooves for a while.

"But how was your family able to amass all that land and cattle?" she asked.

"By working our asses off for ten generations," Duncan said. "Nobody gave us anything; we had to work for it. When my ancestors came to that country there was nothing. It was all wild land. They had to clear the trees, construct the buildings, tend their herds and grow their crops. A lot of people died. Mine didn't. We all left countries that were governed like this one was. Some were worse. Constant warfare and revolution. We all came together in that new land, speaking different languages, with different cultures and religions. You learned to rely on yourself and your neighbours and you helped your neighbours when they needed it. The climate was too severe, it would kill you if you didn't help one another out."

It was quiet again for a while.

"I think I understand what you are trying to do now, Lord Kovaks," she said. "It will be hard. The nobles will try and hold onto their power."

"What are they going to do when the middle class all moves here, Marlene?" he said. "They are going to, you know. This is where all the money will be soon. All the jobs. They are going to lose their workers, too. If they crack down on them, well, there are way more common people than there are nobles."

"Are you not worried they will band together and come at us?"

"Well look what thirty of us did, Marlene. What do you think ten thousand of us would do? People will fight and fight hard to keep their freedom."

"I will speak to Mother on this," she said. "I already think she sees the wisdom in what you are saying."

"So does Tanya," Duncan said. "Why do you think she agreed so readily to my ideas? She had no choice. She had no army. We showed them how to fight using simple, nonpowered weapons and they destroyed the Marauders. Not us. Ten thousand of them wiped out fifteen thousand Marauders using nothing but hammers and spears. Common people, Marlene, not nobles."

The rest of the trip was made in silence.

Duncan grabbed some food from the kitchen and ate by himself that night. Magdalene and Marlene came later and joined him on his porch. Marlene had a cooler of beer with her.

"I will speak in French tonight," Magdalene said. "This way I know I will not make a mistake when I talk. My daughter says you know Lord Kovaks well?"

"As well as any," Duncan said. "Less than some."

"What do you think his plans are? How good a ruler do you think he will be?"

"He doesn't want to be a ruler at all," Duncan said. "He wants the people to rule themselves. To nominate leaders to govern for them in the peoples' best interests."

"How can this be?" she said. "The common man has no idea how to be a leader."

"Then you have not been paying attention," Duncan said. "That woman took control of the situation and led yesterday. All of them are leaders in their own houses."

"I understand that," she said. "But how can they lead a district or a country or even a village? Or this new concept I am hearing about, a province?"

"Education," Duncan said. 'They are taught what needs to be done and then they do it. That is why Lord Kovaks is insisting that every man and woman know how to read and write. So they can learn and make their own decisions."

"How did you become so smart at such a young age, young man?"

"Education, Ma'am, education. Everyone where I come from must attend school until they are sixteen, Ma'am. Even us dummies learn something in that amount of time."

"You are far from dumb, young man."

"When I was those young cowboys' age, I was more interested in fishing, hunting and playing around, Ma'am."

"Add chasing boys and you have my daughter, Duncan," she said then she smiled. "Me too. But my mother broke more than one wooden spoon on my butt until I got the right idea."

"Shit, you guys use wooden spoons here, too?" Duncan said. "My mom damn near pulled my ear off a couple of times."

All of them rubbed their ears as they remembered. Then they all laughed. Marlene reached in and pulled out three bottles of beer and handed them out.

Magdalene raised her bottle up. "Absent comrades, my daughter says."

"New friends," Duncan said for the next toast.

• • •

"So, young man," Magdalene said the next morning, standing on his porch. "My daughter tells me you have one of you wonder weapons with you. Would you show me how it works?"

"Sure, but not here," he said. "It can cause a lot of damage."

"How about the pond? Is that safe enough?"

"As long as we shoot towards the mountains it shouldn't be a problem, Ma'am."

"My name is Magdalene, not ma'am. You make me sound like an old lady, young man."

"Yes, Ma'am," Duncan said.

"All right, point taken, Duncan," she said. "We will be waiting for you by the horses."

Duncan walked back in the cabin and grabbed his rifle. He loaded two clips, put one in it and the other in his pants pocket. Then he removed the bolt from his dresser drawer and inserted it in the rifle, ensuring he didn't chamber a round when he did so, and walked toward the corral.

The saddle he had used the day before was on Buster's back and Duncan just made sure everything was rigged right and the cinch tight before he slung the rifle across his back and mounted.

"I'm just going to make sure the sights are fine first, ladies," he said. "Here, put these in your ears; it is going to be loud."

He handed them each a pair of earplugs and screwed a pair into his own ears. Then he pulled the rifle off his back, extended the bipod from under the barrel and laid down behind it, flipping his hat so the brim was at his back. He sighted on a tree stump two hundred yards away, jacked a round into the chamber and fired. A big hole appeared in the stump and splinters blew out of the back of it. He rapidly fired four more times hitting the same mark. Then he put the gun down and stood up.

He pulled the ear plug out of one ear, so did Marlene, and Magdalene followed suit.

"My God, that was loud," she said.

"Hence the ear plugs," Duncan said. "Okay Missy Black Shirt, your turn. This is a much bigger cartridge and has a lot more power than you are used to. Keep both eyes open and your cheek on the cheek-piece. Hold the stock tight against your shoulder. Got a target? Good, take a deep breath and slowly release it, and as you do so, caress the trigger."

Boom! The gun went off, bouncing off the ground.

"Holy shit!" she said. "This thing kicks as hard as a horse!"

"You were two inches to the left and one high," Duncan said. "Try it again."

This time she was way low and off to the right.

"You closed your eyes and yanked the trigger that time," he said. "Do it just like I said. Hold the butt tight to your shoulder, keep both eyes open, take a deep breath, and caress the trigger like you would do to you lover's nipple."

She looked back at him and frowned, then went back to the scope and shot.

"Close, half an inch high and left. Again, faster."

She let off four fast rounds and then stopped and stood rubbing her shoulder.

"You want to try?" he asked Magdalene.

"No, thank you. That thing would probably break my shoulder."

Duncan folded up the stock, brought the rifle up, wrapped the sling around his left arm and jammed the elbow into his hip. He fired five rapid shots into another stump around three hundred yards away. Then he put the rifle down and grabbed a beer out of the saddle bag he had on the back of the saddle.

"Barrel needs to cool down," he said. He took the clip out of his pocket and pulled a bullet out of it and handed it to Magdalene.

"Is this what you shoot with, Daughter? That is a very big projectile."

"No. Mine is much smaller and not as powerful, Mother," she said. "Only a few special people are good enough shooters to be trained to fire that weapon. Duncan is one of them."

Duncan sat quietly sipping his beer while Marlene explained the difference between her rifle and Duncan's. Movement caught his eye on the other side of the pond about six hundred yards away. It was one of this planet's large predators. It was a very large cat, much like a lion from back home. It had spotted them and the horses, was downwind and creeping forward around the edge of the pond. He kept his eye on it as it made its way toward them.

"Were those last shots the distance you shot my husband from? Madeline asked. "That's about triple the distance our weapons can fire."

"No Ma'am; yes Ma'am," he said as he slowly stood and picked up the rifle, his eyes on the big cat. He folded down the bipod and laid down again. He found the cat by watching the tall grass move as it crept along. It was taking its time and stopping often. Then Duncan spotted its tail waving above the grass and followed it.

Marlene saw he was concentrating on something and was not going to offer an explanation.

"He means, no, that was not the distance he shot dad from and yes, it is triple the range our weapons can fire."

Then the gun went off, scaring them both. One second later a spray of blood erupted and the grass was moving around like crazy as the big cat died.

"That's about how far away I killed your husband, Ma'am," he said, ejecting the clip and the empty cartridge and standing up.

"Let's let that big cat be for a bit to make sure it's dead, then we can go look at it."

"Cat, what cat?" Marlene said. "I didn't see any cat."

"Which is why I am a Wind Rider and you are a Black Shirt, Colonel, Ma'am," Duncan said as he picked up all the spent shell casings and put them in his pants pocket. "To be honest, most of the Wind Riders would have missed it, too. Which is why I am the Ghost and they are not.

"Okay, it should be dead by now, you can look if you want," he said.

"Are you sure, Duncan?" Marlene asked. "Those cats are dangerous."

"Ya, I hit it in the lungs. Probably blew the spine out of it, too."

He sat sipping his beer as both women walked over and had a look. Magdalene put her hand to her mouth and then looked back at Duncan. Then they made their way back. She was still very white when she returned. Duncan slung the rifle back on his back, put the empty beer bottle back in the saddlebag and mounted.

It was a quiet trip back to the farm.

Three of the boys were waiting for them when they got back and took the horses from them when they dismounted.

"If it's any consolation to you," Duncan said. "It takes about two seconds from the time the bullet leaves the barrel until the sound hits the target. I hit your husband in the head. He was dead before they even knew they were being shot at."

He walked away and headed to his cabin, pulling the rifle from his back as he went. He cleaned the rifle as the coffee was brewing and had it stowed away by the time the coffee was ready.

He was looking at the stars in the dark when the two of them came up and sat down.

"Got some coffee in there if you want some," he said.

They both held up their hands showing a beer bottle.

"Thank you for telling me," Magdalene said. "There is always a doubt at the back of your mind when you don't see the body."

"No problem," he said. "Glad I could help."

"Was it fast for your wife, too?" she asked.

"No Ma'am," he said. "She died as I was walking up. She was in massive shock and most likely didn't feel any pain. Besides, we have something called morphine, it's a pretty powerful painkiller. Amanda would have given her a couple of shots of it."

Marlene was wiping her eyes.

"If we don't talk about it, it never goes away, Marlene," he said. "Was she your first kill?"

All he could hear was her whimper. He stood up and walked toward her and knelt down and hugged her close. She wrapped her arms around him, buried her face in his chest and wailed.

He just squatted there and stroked her hair and she kept saying she was sorry, over and over again. Finally, she stopped and just sat there, holding him tight. He picked her head up and saw her face in the moonlight. Then he wiped her tears away with his fingers, kissed her cheek on the scar, stood and walked away into the yard.

"Go after him, damn you!" her mother hissed.

He was standing with one foot on the bottom of the corral fence, his arms draped on the top rail looking at the horses, when she came running up.

"Are you okay, Duncan?" she asked.

"Ya, I'm fine," he said. "She has been dead almost a year now. Nothing you or I can do to change that, Marlene."

"No, she wasn't my first, Duncan," she said. "To be honest I never really thought much about it until I heard she was pregnant. That bothered me a bit. She was a soldier and she died protecting what she loved. As it should be. No, I am crying because I have come to love you, Duncan, and I have hurt you. And there is nothing I can do to undo that."

Duncan was looking at the horses again and after a few seconds she turned to walk away. He reached behind him and grabbed her arm.

"Don't go," he said, almost a whisper. "She was not much like you. She had to work at being a soldier, not like us. She really should not have been up there with us. But she insisted. She was supposed to be the last in the line, not the second. I don't know why she did that. Good thing she did, though. But I don't think you would have killed me anyway, love. I had seen you out the corner of my eye and was turning before she hit me in the back and tossed me out of the way."

He went quiet again for a minute and she thought he had finished talking and made to break away from him, but he pulled her to him and turned around so they were face to face.

"I think I fell in love with you when I saw you working with your kids," he said. "That was the real you. Nobody was watching you but those kids. You were so tender, so loving, so unlike Commander Isabelle of the Black Shirts, the cold unfeeling human killing machine. But I have to be sure first, Marlene. I have to be sure this is real love. I really, really do not want to hurt you. You are too precious. What you have, your tenderness, your caring, is a rare gift. I would never forgive myself if I caused you to lose that."

He hugged her so tight she though he might break her ribs then he pulled back from her, looked her in the eyes and kissed her on the forehead and walked away into the darkness.

"What happened?" her mother asked her when she came back in. "Did you find him?"

"Yes, Mom, I found him," she said. "I found him and he said he was falling in love with me. But that he wanted to be sure. That he didn't want to hurt me. Then he kissed me on the forehead and walked away."

"Give him some time, Daughter," her mother said and pulled her close. "Give him some time. You already have more with him than I ever had with your father."

"Who makes and repairs your saddles for you?" Duncan asked the next morning at breakfast.

"There is an old man in the village who does that for us," Madeline said. "It is half a day's ride to the west from here."

"Can that air car handle two of us and four saddles?"

"It will be at maximum limit," Marlene said. "But yes."

"Alright," he said. "We are going flying today. I will buy dinner, okay? Go get ready. Chop, chop."

He walked back to his cabin, found a piece of paper and drew a quick sketch. Then he went over to the barn and found four old work saddles, brought them over one by one to the air car and dumped them into the back. By the time he had done that, Marlene was walking toward him.

She was wearing thigh length tan pants and sneakers today, with a blue and white striped polo shirt. Her auburn hair was tucked behind her right ear, but long on the left side, and she had a dangly earing clipped to her right ear.

She came up to him, grabbed his right arm in both of her hands and kissed his cheek, then let him loose.

"Mom says to go on without her, she is tired and wants to have a snooze," Marlene said.

Including starting, taking off and landing, it took ten minutes to fly to the village and she landed in front of the saddle maker's little shop .

It was cluttered with work tools, benches, pieces of wood and leather and it smelt like new leather and wood. A tall, thin man of about seventy emerged from an office in the back, looked them over and at the old saddle Duncan had tossed on a work bench.

"Whatcha need?" the old guy said. "That there saddle done seen better days, that's for shore."

"I would like the tree replaced and a modification made to it," Duncan said. "I would also like a higher cantle, a rear cinch, the ties lengthened and D rings mounted on the front and on the front cinch for a breast strap."

"Don't want much, do ya?" the saddle maker said.

Duncan passed the sketch he had made over and the old guy glanced at it. Then he walked into an enclosed area at the back of the shop. They heard some rummaging around and some muttered cursing and the old man returned with a saddle draped over his shoulder and dumped it on the counter.

"Good old western cow puncher's saddle," the man said with a Texas drawl. He had been speaking French before.

"Exactly," Duncan said in English. "Don't need all the fancy silver work and geegaws though."

"Ya, this is a Mexican saddle," the old man said. "I got a couple regular cowpuncher saddles up in the rafters there. Where you from, boy?"

"Place called Alberta, Canada," Duncan said. "You probably never heard of it."

"Hell ya," he said. "Won a bareback buckle at the Calgary Stampede when your mom was a twinkle in your granddaddy's eye."

"I'm an hour north and a little west of there," Duncan said.

"Around Olds? Served in 'Nam with a guy from there. Big family, Germans like me."

"Well Oppa," Duncan said in German. "It seems we know some of the same people, then."

"Haven't heard or spoken that for nigh on thirty years," the old man replied in accented German. "Suppose the Guild snatched you up like they did me."

"Something like that," Duncan said. "Look, this lady has a ranching outfit just up the road a bit and they have these crappy saddles. Can you modify them for me?"

"Hell, would be easier to make new ones, these is all wore out," he said, returning to English. "Tell you what, you get those two saddles down from the rafters there, I'll sell them to you, build you four more for ten pounds. I'll even throw in four saddle blankets."

"Six saddles, four blankets, ten pounds," Duncan said in French.

"No," Marlene said. "Too much. Six saddles, six blankets, eight pounds, and you know that is still too much, John, but he wants them in a hurry."

"He he," the old guy said. "Well, ya can't blame an old guy for tryin'. You go grab that ladder over there, young fella, and bring them two saddles down over here."

"So, back from the Army, young Isabelle? How's your mom?"

"I'm just on leave," Marlene said. "My friend Duncan is here on holiday, too. Mom is, well mom is."

"That Duncan Kovaks?" the old guy said. "I knew his mom back in the day. One tough lady. His pop was a real go-getter."

Duncan dropped the saddles on the table.

"Your mom's name Ilse, Duncan?" he said in German.

"Ya it was. She died about ten years ago." Duncan said.

"Sorry to hear that, she was a good woman. She was my instructor for frozen hell. Your pop must miss her."

"Dad died a couple of years later," Duncan said. "I suppose he missed her. I was deployed overseas when they both died."

"Funny how things work out," the old man said. "Why don't you go bring those other three crappy saddles in here, I'll take them off your hands and knock a couple of pounds off the purchase price."

"What is that language you were speaking?" Marlene asked as Duncan left. "His regiment speak it a lot."

"German," he said. "His people, they got a crest with a bear on one side, eagle on the other, and do they wear an eagle or a bear on the left collar?"

"One does," she said. "A female, but the rest do not. Although I hear three of them, Duncan for one, could wear an eagle if they wanted to."

"Last time I saw him, he was a gawking thirteen year old," the old man said. "Turned out to be a looker. Got his mom's eyes. Special people, his mom's people."

Duncan came back in and dumped two saddles on the floor.

"Why don't you take young Isabelle here for lunch or something," he said. "I'll have these two saddles oiled up nice for you by then."

"How come you don't wear your eagle like your mom, son?" he said in German.

"Eagles are guard dogs," Duncan said in English. "The King's Own are Russian Wolfhounds. I don't guard or herd, old timer. I kill for a living."

"Special breed, those recon guys the Canucks have," the old timer said as Duncan went for the last saddle.

"Oh, his section is even more special," Marlene said. "They are called the Wind Riders and he, the Ghost in the Wind. He gave me this for a present." She pulled her hair back to show the scar.

"Yup," the old guy said. "Special, just like his mom's people. Knock you on your ass hard, then help you up and hand you a glass of vodka and shake your hand."

"You filling Lady Isabelle's head up with lies, old timer?" Duncan said walking back in.

"No Duncan, he is not," she said. She grabbed his arm, kissed his cheek and looked up at him. "Now, you still owe me one more apology lunch."

"No way," he said. "I bought the last time."

She was still draped on his arm as they walked out the door.

Duncan had a new saddle slung over each shoulder and he hung them on the top rail of the corral fence. As he was doing that, Marlene ran into the house to change.

"Morning, Ma'am," he said to the ranch forewoman as he walked in the barn. "If you have a free hour or two, I would like to show you something. Could you bring those four boys along, too?"

As he walked into the corral with two bridles, Buster and the horse he had ridden the other day came right up to him. He saddled them both quickly with the new saddles. Then walked back in the barn and collected the lasso he had made and rummaged around until he found a length of soft cord, which he stuck in his shirt pocket. He hung the rope in the loop made for it on the saddle and waited.

Once everyone was saddled up and waiting, he pointed to his horse.

"This is a new type of saddle you will be using," he said. "It has been designed for cattle work Four more of them are coming shortly. It is designed for your comfort and your horse's comfort. I have ridden for days at a time in a saddle like this. You will see the reason for the extra equipment and the high cantle shortly."

Magdalene and Marlene came out of the house wearing work clothes. The boys ran back in the barn and grabbed another saddle.

They rode over to the cattle pasture and Duncan told them all to dismount. Marlene held Sam by the collar. This was going to be hard enough for Duncan on his own with a horse that had not done this before, without Sam yapping and scaring cows.

Duncan focused on the calf he wanted and headed over, unclipping the rope and shaking it out as he slowly walked up to the herd. He took the short rope out of his shirt pocket, put it in his mouth and clenched it with his teeth. He started breaking the calf away from the herd and every time it tried to turn back, it found the horse blocking its path. Slowly it was being pushed further and further away and it became frantic, dodging this way and that to get around. Then finally it began to sprint away from the horse who sprinted after it.

Duncan swung the rope a few times around his head then let it fly so the open loop landed in front of the calf, he jerked it up and caught the two hind legs. Then he wrapped the end of the rope around the saddle horn a couple of times and pulled back hard on the reins. The horse squatted and slid to a stop and the rope jerked tight, pulling the calf off its feet.

Duncan flung himself off the horse and grabbed the rope, keeping it tight. As he reached the calf he flipped it over on its side, took the short rope from his mouth, pulled a front leg back to the two rear ones and quickly tied them together with a slip knot. The horse had figured out what it needed to do and kept tension on the rope as Duncan watched the calf struggle for a minute to get free then settle down.

Now Duncan jerked on the lasso rope, having the horse come forward a few steps. And he undid it from the saddle horn and walked to the calf, coiling the rope and finally removing it from the legs. He waved the others to join him.

"So, this calf is completely under our control now," he said. "If it had an injury, or a stone caught in a hoof we could fix it without too much risk of hurting ourselves or it. That is the reason for the high cantle, the rear cinch, the breast strap and most of all, the horn. If you work in teams it is easier, and once Sam here has seen it done a few times he can be a great help.

"So, when we go back, I want you young fellas to make a rope like this and practice catching fence posts. Then you can start on other things, and then doing it mounted and at the gallop. This knot here is just a couple of loops around the ankles and a slip knot.

They all bent down and had a look, and then Duncan released the calf to run back to his herd and they rode back to the farm yard.

"We have been using these techniques for hundreds of years, Ma'am," Duncan said in answer to Magdalene's question. "Even with modern motorised vehicles, you still have to go by horseback sometimes."

The rest of the week, he spent the mornings doing small fixup jobs around the yard and the afternoons with Marlene riding or just sitting and talking. After a few days, they were holding hands as they walked. Finally, Magdalene saw him kiss her for the first time when he walked her home from a late-night walk, and she smiled.

Chapter Fourteen

Duncan strode up the middle of the U of his barracks complex and entered the center section through its own outside door. He walked to his room and tossed his duffle and rifle on the bed, then walked over to the comms office. It was Sunday evening and he expected everyone to be lounging in the mess and was surprised to see the comms manned.

"Hey Cheryl, what's going on?" he asked. Cheryl was one of the wives. She was about eight months pregnant and he didn't expect to see her on duty.

"Welcome back," she said, holding her arms up for a hug. "Not much; it's quiet in here, so I come here to read and relax. How was the holiday?"

"Relaxing," he said. "Nice to be a semi-normal person for a while. Need a coffee or anything?"

"Nope," she said lifting a full glass of something up. "I've got my prego lady beverage, thanks."

He kissed her on the forehead and squeezed a shoulder, then walked into the mess and behind the bar and grabbed a beer out of the fridge. Everyone was seated at the tables in conversation or playing cards or board games and no one had spotted him yet.

That didn't last long as Diane spotted him as she came to the bar.

"Welcome back, boss," she said loud enough for everyone to hear.

The whole gang was soon clustered around and either peppering him with questions or wanting to report things to him. Finally, he whistled and raised an arm.

"Yes I am back, my unruly mob," he said. "As you can see, I am still off duty and still on holiday until tomorrow morning, so I don't want to hear about work. Let me enjoy my freedom for one last night.

"As you can see, I got a bit of a tan, did some horse riding, fishing and hunting. Met some new people, regular people, not like you yahoos. Fresh air and all that rot. What's that roster sheet I see on the wall there?"

"We've been challenged to a football game," Brett said. "Flag, not tackle. Those Yanks seem to think they have some hotshot ball players."

"Probably do," Duncan said. "Put me down. I used to play a bit in high school."

He grabbed Brett and put him in a head lock and the war was on.

Barb looked at Jane and smiled. He was back to himself.

"I was right," she said to Megan. "He's found a girl."

"Na, Mom," Megan said. "He's just relaxed. Got away from all that pressure for a couple of weeks. I didn't know they had horses here. I miss riding."

• • •

"Good morning everyone," Marlene said as she walked into the board room. She was in uniform, but it was not the severe crisp it normally was and she had her hair down, not up under her cap like normal. She was also smiling and started a conversation with a shocked Barb.

"Right, let's make this fast, I want to do an inspection this morning and I want to be out of here by one," Duncan said, breezing into the board room with his full travel mug in hand.

Jane stood as he sat down and opened a thick folder.

"If that is not your homework for tonight or a novel, I don't want to hear about it," Duncan said, forestalling her. "It's called a briefing for a reason, Colonel. It would be called a dissertation otherwise."

"Yes, Sir," Jane said and she closed the folder. In less than five minutes she was finished updating him on overall training status.

Everyone else took their cue from that and the Monday briefing was over in less than an hour. Duncan scheduled a more detailed briefing of his own people for the next morning and was out the door.

Marlene stayed for a few minutes and had a coffee with Jane and Barb. She was pleasant and smiling and she had a spring in her step when she left.

"Wonder who melted the Ice Queen?" Jane said. "You sure that was Colonel Isabelle?"

"Looked like her," Barb said. She saw Duncan jump into the passenger seat of his GW2 and then she looked at Marlene strutting down the street to her own HQ.

"You don't think??" Barb pondered looking at Jane.

"Nah." They both said at the same time.

"No way," Jane said. "Like combining a match and gasoline."

•••

"Okay," Duncan said as he sat down at the board room table the next morning. "Only one item of business this week."

All of his officers were present and they all had a list of items they wanted to present to him.

"Regimental party Friday night, people," Duncan said. "We've been here damn near a year and not had one yet. We have all these fancy new uniforms, time to put them to use. Field grade officers and plus-ones from the other battalions are invited and any visiting officers. Also invite the mayor and any other big shot government types in town. Let them know it's a formal affair. Everyone, and I do mean everyone, CT, from the regiment will be there in the proper uniform and decorations. Non-military plus ones will be in formal attire. Now flutter away, my little chicks, and make it happen."

"CT, your office."

"What's going on with that transport gizmo?" Duncan said sitting across from CT at his desk.

"We have identified every component, boss," CT said. "I have copied all the specs for everything. Most of the stuff we can source on-planet and we can manufacture everything else right here. I even downloaded the room specs. Everything but the most common items that break down all the time have not been accessed for years and most of the companies that made those components are long gone. There is only one hardcopy of everything and it's all stored in one room just down from the machine itself. Once you give me the okay, we'll wipe all the specs from the memory banks and they are toast, boss."

"You have all the defences mapped out?"

"Ya," CT said. "They are pretty lax over there. Same with the planetary guys. I'll have all the surveillance grid down when we need it, boss."

"Good work CT. Look, CT, I mean it. This party is a big deal, don't piss around."

"I know, General," CT said. "Tradition, honour all that stuff. I get it. Besides I look pretty good in the uniform."

"Attaboy," Duncan said slapping him on the shoulder. "Besides, the chicks really dig the fancy uniforms."

"Cheryl? See if Kurt is busy, will you? Ask when it would be convenient for me to drop by. On second thought, just tell him to give me a call when he can. I'll be in my office and, if Jane is not busy, ask her to come by my office."

Jane entered just as Duncan was sitting down and the phone rang at the same time. Duncan pointed at the coffee pot on his bookshelf and then at a chair and then picked up the phone.

"Hey, Kurt," Duncan said. "I've got something in the works that is right up your guys' alley. Can you and your people come by tomorrow morning? Majors and above, Kurt. Good; see you then."

"I want to conduct a raid on the Guild HQ, Jane," Duncan said. "CT has the defensive plan. I need you to plan the operation. Coordinate with CT, Kurt and Dave. Kurt will be doing the bulk of the work. A Troop will be going and B Troop will provide intel overwatch.

"Tomorrow will just be a preliminary background session, so keep it brief, okay?"

"Sure," she said. "So, the holiday was good?"

"Ya real relaxing," Duncan said. "I have been micro-managing for too long. Only so much of me to go around, you know."

"The capitol has been giving us fits," she said. "Calling every day about the stupidest of things sometimes."

"Cut them off at the knees, Jane. Get them to put whatever it is they want in writing and let the staff handle the dumb stuff or, better yet, just trash it. I'm only responsible for this province, not all of their territory. Everything seems to be falling into place nicely. I read your reports, Jane, and it's faster than you reading them at briefings. Flesh out the Black Shirts first with the new recruits, then Kurt's group after."

"Will do," she said. "Bob wants a minute when you get time."

"As long as it's before lunch. I'm busy after that."

"So, nothing interesting happened while you were on leave?"

"Nope," Duncan said. "Just a nice relaxing time in the backwoods. Now get going; you have a party to plan."

Bob arrived a couple of minutes after.

"I think I've got the cannon figured out, Duncan," he said. "We have conducted a couple of tests and it looks good. When can you come by and have a look?"

"Now would be good," Duncan said. "I have to go see the land administration people on another matter this afternoon after lunch. That give you enough time?"

"I'll have my guys take the LAV to the range," Bob said. "We can meet them there. I'll drive you."

"No, I'll have Brett drive me," Duncan said. "Then he can drive me over to the palace complex after."

They arrived at the firing range before the LAV and Bob explained that he had found, or rather CT had found, the original blueprints, and Bob had manufactured a few prototypes before getting the bugs out. The LAV rolled up just as Bob had finished his explanation and the vehicle fired a series of shots, stopped for a minute and fired again. Then it started to move, the cupola and barrel tracking the target as it moved. It fired five shots while moving. These were not as accurate, but close enough. Then it fired off a series of grenades, smoke and high explosive, from the grenade launchers mounted on the cupola. That ended the demonstration.

"The first cannon shots were with our original ammo," Bob said. "The rest were with our local stuff. The grenades were all local manufacture. CT is still working on the firing system, but it should be okay for operational use as is."

"Okay," Duncan said. "Outfit two LAVs and two Coyotes with them and do some heavy testing under operational conditions. Let me know when they pass."

"How are these GW2s working out, Brett?" Duncan asked as they were driving back to town.

"Carol and Diane have been running the shit out of them," Brett said. "They seem to be okay."

"Not asking Carol or Diane," Duncan said. "I'm asking you."

"Me? I think they are great," Brett said. "Lighter, faster and a lot quieter than the old ones. Scott says the firing platform is superior and Amanda says the electronics are fine. We have taken ours on some fairly hard cross-country unofficial trials and it worked okay."

"Just park in front, Brett. I shouldn't be long," Duncan said.

Duncan climbed out and walked into the land administration office. It was in one of the old barracks buildings in the palace complex and had been converted into offices.

"Good morning," Duncan said. "Who would I speak to regarding land accusations?"

"Fill out this form here," she said passing a piece of paper across the counter. "Make sure you put your military rank and time of service in the right places and when your five years is up. Then bring it back."

Duncan filled it out in a couple of minutes standing at the counter and then called the clerk back.

"What happens now?" he asked.

"Now we see what is available and will issue you your allotment after a review," the clerk said. She had not even looked at it yet.

"Right," Duncan said. "Thank you for your time."

"Ya right," the clerk said, then sat back down at her desk.

"Excuse me?" Duncan said.

"Look I'm busy, soldier boy, go away."

Duncan vaulted across the counter and picked up the phone receiver on her desk and dialed his HQ.

"Hey Cheryl, get the land minister down to meet me at his reception desk right now. Thanks, Cheryl."

"Oh you're in big trouble now, soldier boy," she said and called security.

"What seems to be the problem here?" the security officer said when he arrived.

"This soldier came bursting in here and started hitting on me," she said. "Then he grabbed my phone and called his girlfriend. Can you imagine?"

The security guard started walking toward Duncan with menace in his eyes.

"If you want to have a broken arm and jaw and your balls kicked up your arse, keep on coming, buddy," Duncan said. "Now calm down and let's all talk this through, shall we?"

"What in hell are you doing?" The minister came bursting into the room. "Back away now! I am sorry, Lord Kovaks, there must be some misunderstanding."

"Ya, more than one," Duncan said. "You need more training, bud. Coming at a trained soldier by yourself is a very bad idea. You, lady, grab my piece of paper and follow us to the minister's office.

"Sit down! Both of you!" Duncan said and he slammed the door shut. "Now that I have your attention, would you do me the honor of reading my piece of paper, lady?"

She read it and turned even more white than she already was.

"You got kids at home, lady?" Duncan asked.

"No, my lord," she said barely over a whisper.

"There is a military vehicle parked out front," Duncan said. "Get in the back seat. You are now in the army!" She scurried out.

"Okay," Duncan said. "Please have your people trained better, minister. You are public servants. Remember that. The public does not serve you, you serve them. Turn that computer on and punch in the coordinates on that piece of paper."

"Anybody own it?" he asked after the minister had said he had it.

"No, Lord Kovaks," the minister said. "The Isabelle holdings are the last in that area. It is very remote and not much good for anything."

"Just what I want," Duncan said. "I am requisitioning all of it then. See to it. Also, send that woman's files over to the Marauders' administration office in care of General Bishop with a note attached saying I authorise it. What's her story, anyway?"

"I hired her as a favor to her mother," the minister said. "They were minor nobility from the old regime and I am afraid a little over-indulged."

"If they don't work, get rid of them," Duncan said. "We can't afford people like her working in places like this. What's the mother do?"

"Well nothing, my lord, the girl was doing the work."

"Get the minister of labor to find her a job," Duncan said. "We can't afford to have able-bodied people sitting around doing nothing. I will call him myself for a little chat tomorrow morning. Thank you for your cooperation."

"What's with the babe, boss?" Brett asked.

"The little princess has just decided to join the army, Master Sergeant," Duncan said. "I thought that the least we could do was to escort her over to the Marauders' admin office ourselves, as we are headed that way anyway."

"Sure General, no problem, Sir," Brett said and they headed back to the base.

"You know what, I've changed my mind, take us to the Black Shirts instead," Duncan said as he picked up the microphone clipped to the dash.

"Hey Cheryl, I've changed my mind, get Bishop to send those records to Isabelle when he gets them and let her know I'm coming by with a new recruit for her."

"Okay Master Sergeant, go find something to do for the rest of the day and leave the vehicle here. I need it for some personal things. Come on, miss, your new home awaits." Duncan took her by the arm and more or less dragged her into the administration offices.

Marlene looked less than pleased when they walked in.

"Colonel Isabelle, I have a new volunteer recruit for you," Duncan said. "Please see to it that she receives the very best of training Officer?"

"Yes, my lord," Marlene said and nodded at a very large male corporal who escorted the girl away.

"The transport you requested for your next meeting is waiting for you outside whenever you are ready, Colonel. That young lady needs an attitude adjustment and a job and you people are going to do both for me."

It was close enough to be after lunch, so Duncan drove to his barracks, had a shower and changed and was back parked in front of Marlene's with the driver's seat reclined having a snooze. The door opened and she jumped in and whacked him on the arm.

"That's for dumping that princess on me," she said as Duncan brought his chair back up to normal. Then she whacked him again. "And that is for giving me no time for your stupid party!"

She was wearing a short skirt that rode up nicely on her bare thighs today and a polo shirt with all the buttons undone.

"Nice view," Duncan said, then he started the vehicle and drove toward the gate. She grabbed his hand, looked quickly round, and gave him a fast kiss on the cheek.

"That little princess needs to get with the program," Duncan said. "She was working as a receptionist at the land office and doing a piss-poor job. Her stupid mother still thinks she is a noble and sent her out to work so she could laze around at home. So, I fixed both. She is from your class, so I figured you guys were the best ones to clue her in."

"Okay, I can live with that," Marlene said. "Well, not me. Somebody else gets to have that fun. But really, Duncan, four days' notice for a fancy party? I have to find a gown, get my hair and nails done, find a pair of shoes and a bag. That all takes time."

"You have two choices," Duncan said. "Pants or long dress. You have both. The tunic, under jacket and blouse you already have. You were issued them. This is a regimental party. Mess Dress is the only option, especially for a colonel."

"Oh," she said. "But I still need shoes."

"Two choices," Duncan said. "Pumps for the dress, wellingtons, with or without spurs, for the pants. Also, both issued."

"Oh, then just my nails and hair," she said.

"No nails, subdued hair and makeup," Duncan said. "Read the regs, love. You guys will be allowed to wear your original decorations if you have them."

"Oh, that makes it easier then," Marlene said. "But I still have to find a date."

"Optional," Duncan said. "I am not taking one."

Marlene took her hand from his and looked out the window.

"Why would I?" he continued. "I happen to know a very cute Ice Queen Colonel who will be attending solo. In the interests of inter regiment cooperation it is only fitting that I ensure she has a good time."

"You can be such an asshole sometimes, my lord," she said frostily, still looking out the window.

"Only sometimes now?" he said. "Things are looking up. My lord thinks the colonel may be melting a bit."

They were a block outside the base gate when she leaned over and put her head on his shoulder.

"I really think I should be getting back to the daycare soon," she said. "I miss my kids."

"Tired of hanging around with me already?" Duncan said. "It hasn't even been a week yet."

"It's not that, Duncan," she said. "You guys can be so dense sometimes. No, I miss the kids and the work and they can really use me there. It is so hard to get help now."

Duncan drove through some pleasant residential neighborhoods as Marlene rolled her window down and let the wind go through her hair. Duncan kept glancing over at her as she watched the neat yards and homes go by and, as she played with a lock of her hair on the left side, a whimsical look crossed her face. It was quiet in the neighborhoods, the hustle and the bustle missing during the middle of the work day. A few older women were out and about, keeping a watchful eye out while they looked after toddlers. There were more than a few homes on every street where the unkempt yards betrayed abandonment.

After about an hour, Duncan pulled onto the street leading to the local restaurant they had come to before going on holiday and he found an empty spot to park. As they entered it, he saw a payphone in the entry and had an idea.

"Why don't you find us a table?" he said. "I need to make a call. I might be a while, so order something for me, will you?"

He deposited the required coin and dialed the number for the labor ministry, identified himself and asked for the minister. It took a few minutes but eventually the minister came on the phone.

"That woman I had sent to you?" he said. "I think that maybe sending her to work at that child care center up on Elm to work might be a good idea. They are short-staffed. Do you have any idea if there are any more layabout old nobility around?"

"More than a few," the minister said. "They are all a lot like that mother, getting their kids to work for them and bumming money from old friends. Men and women, I am afraid."

"There are a lot of manpower shortages all over," Duncan said. "Get them all out there working someplace at something. I am also seeing a number of empty houses in some of the residential areas. How about talking with the minister of lands and making those empty homes available to the young people of those nobles to occupy at a reasonable rate. But only if the parent stays in their own home. That will solve a couple of problems for us."

They had been given slightly better seats this time in the middle of the restaurant and the service was also a little better. They had timed their meal just right: after the lunch rush, but before the after-work crowd. There were some patrons, but the place was nowhere near full. Marlene was more relaxed this time, smiling and being very pleasant. Duncan just sat back and enjoyed watching her.

"What?" she said, finally realising he wasn't talking, just looking at her and smiling.

"Nothing," he said. "Just admiring the view is all."

"Well I am tired of talking," she said. "You say something for once."

"Well," he said. "I met a girl you know. She is very smart, brilliant in fact, and has a very nice personality."

"Oh really," Marlene said. "I suppose she is beautiful and has a lot of money and connections as well. Was that who you were talking to on the phone?"

"No that was business," he said. "Speaking of which, I am going to be busy in the afternoons for the rest of the week. Probably most of the nights as well. That will free you up to spend more time with your kids."

The rest of the meal she was still pleasant, but the sparkle was gone and it was a quiet ride back to the barracks.

I guess I was just a rebound for him after all, she thought as she tucked herself into bed.

• • •

"Good morning, people," Duncan said as he walked into the board room. Kurt and his second and third in command were with him sitting at the table along one side. Jane, Dave and CT were along the other.

"As I mentioned to Kurt yesterday, I have a job that is right up you people's alley," he continued. "We will be hitting the Guild's HQ on Arial. Hit and run. Jane?"

"We have identified a target of very high value in the HQ complex," Jane said. "The primary mission is to destroy that target. Secondary mission is to destroy as much of the Guild communications ability and the last, basically to damage anything and anyone we come into contact with. One Wind Rider troop will land ahead of your main assault and establish current on-the-ground intel, and the rest of us will be providing real time telemetry for you.

"CT has worked out the defensive arrangements the planet and the Guild has and will be defeating all remote, or electronic detection, means. He also has building drawings and plans for you to base your mock-ups and training around, as well as numbers of defenders and types of weaponry.

"Dave will be planning the air and transport requirements, so coordinate with him on what you need to have happen for you. You will be deploying all your Earth personnel. Leave the rookies behind for this one."

"Without even looking at the proposal," Kurt said. "I can tell you that I will be needing a big training area, away from prying eyes."

Duncan hit a button in front of him and an aerial shot of a wilderness area was projected in front of them.

"This is about six hours from here. It is very remote and very secure. We have complete control of one hundred square miles of wilderness. Your nearest neighbor is thirty miles away."

He hit another button and the display zoomed in on an abandoned complex of some type with an equally abandoned small town right alongside.

"This is an abandoned mine," he said. "The buildings are in fairly good shape and you can use the town site to practice your urban warfare skills. You won't have to worry about hostages or friendlies. Anything that is moving in your sectors will be fair game.

"You will have about two months to train and make your plans. No, make it two months at least. After two months, expect the go signal at anytime. Questions?"

"Ya," one of the majors said. "I hear some hot shot DB ringer is going to play Saturday."

"Well you heard wrong," Duncan said. "As much as I would like to, unfortunately something has come up and I can't play. Maybe next time."

"Are you sure, Duncan?" Jane asked as everyone left. "It might be good for you. Let off some steam."

"No, I just bought a house in town and want to move in on Saturday. You and Bob should look into it. There are a lot of really nice empty houses in town."

"But what about the residence at the palace?" Jane said. "You were supposed to move in there. The rooms have been extensively renovated and we paid a lot of money to make that happen."

"I think we will just leave those for visiting royalty, Jane." Duncan said. "Besides, we will be moving the entire base to that remote area very soon. I want to separate the military from the civilian. Not only that, but we can run around and make all kinds of noise without having to worry about the neighbors.

"I have CT looking for another area just as large out west in the flatlands to make another base. And Jane, let everyone know this is a secret operation. The Marauders and the Black Shirts have no reason to know what we are doing. Nor is the queen to find out about it, until we are actually deploying. She has too many ears around here."

Then Duncan went to his office, dug through his laptop bag until he found the external hard drive he was looking for, plugged it in and accessed a set of files he had not looked at since Africa.

As he had predicted to Marlene, Duncan flung himself into his work. The mornings were spent reviewing evaluations of equipment and manpower, while in the afternoons and late into the night he was in his office working hard on his personal old laptop. Some nights, he only had time for a fast shower and change of uniform before the next work day started.

He was totally engrossed in a schematic and trying to figure out how to use local components to replace the ones in the circuit, when someone banged loudly.

He looked up and saw Barb leaning against the door frame. She was dressed in her Mess Dress and had her arms crossed against her chest.

Duncan looked at his clock in the corner of his computer and swore.

"Yes, oh shit," Barb said. "You have an hour to get ready and get to the party. I bet you don't even know where it is being held, do you?"

"Just leave me the address," he said, frantically shutting down everything. "I'll be there in time!"

"You look fabulous, by the way," he said.

She had opted for the long formal dress and it fit her well. She made a curtsy, then slapped him gently on the cheek.

"Thank you, my lord," she said. "Now get your ass going!"

Duncan tore out of his office and headed down the hall to his room. Everyone else was already in their fancy uniforms that made up the formal Mess Dress and his dark green normal uniform clashed with theirs. He slammed his rooms door behind him and began to strip off clothing as he hurried to the shower, just letting things drop where they fell.

Ten minutes later, he walked out naked and began to don the multiple garments that made up his formal attire. As a General officer, he would be wearing the peaked hat tonight instead of the beret. It was optional, but he felt it was more appropriate. He looked in the mirror and made sure everything was where it should be, straightened out a few badges and, with a final tuck at the seams of the small jacket, opened the door and walked out.

"Holy shit!" Brett said. "Where's my sunglasses? I've never seen so much brass and gold lace."

"I could say the same for you," Duncan said. The formal uniforms were anything but practical and were very colorful. The short midnight blue jackets covered a yellow cummerbund in Brett's case and a yellow under-jacket in Duncan's. The large lapels were black. Shiny silver chainmail epaulets replaced the normal shoulder boards. Campaign and honours ribbons were on the left breast, qualification and unit badges on the right.

Gold thread rank insignia was on both sleeves. As a master sergeant, Brett's were on the upper part of the sleeve, while Duncan's were down by the cuff. Duncan also had General Officer braid in swirls running down the lower part of the sleeves.

Both men had midnight blue trousers with a wide black stripe down the inseam over shiny black Wellington boots with silver spurs attached at the heels. Where Duncan had the peaked officer's cap with two rows of braid on the brim, Brett wore a black beret with a shiny brass unit badge centered over his right eye.

"Christ," Duncan said. "The Taliban would see us coming for days dressed in this getup."

"You got that right," Brett said. "Come on, my lord's carriage awaits. If we hurry we should make it."

A large banquet room in the center of the business section had been rented and their timing was perfect as all the guests had just been seated when Duncan and Brett paused at the entrance, ran a hand over their hair, having surrendered their head gear to the cloak room attendant. Brett looked at Duncan, who nodded.

"Attention!" Brett yelled out and the whole room rose and turned to face the door.

As Duncan marched up the center to the head table, Brett scurried over to his seat. Duncan reached his seat and sat down, then everyone else did as well and the meals were handed out.

"Typical Duncan," Bishop said leaning out so he could address Duncan. He was seated next to Dave who was on Duncan's right. "Call a party and then forget to come."

He was dressed the same as everyone else, but his lapels and under-jacket were green.

"Canadians, especially high-ranking ones, always make you wait," Kurt said. His lapels and under-jacket were a dark maroon. He was seated next to Barb, who was seated next to Jane on Duncan's left.

"Well, sorry," Duncan said. "Somebody has to redo all the work you incompetent unit commanders do, or the world would surely come to an end."

Marlene didn't say anything. She was sitting next to Kurt and her second-in-command was sitting next to her.

The four-course meal was excellent, as was the wine. The conversation was, as always, witty and light. The room was abuzz. Most of the room was filled with Wind Riders and their guests, but the heads of all the government departments were there with their spouses as well as majors and colonels of the other regiments and their guests. At last, the dessert was finished and the wine glasses refilled.

Katerina as the lowest ranking officer rose with her glass in hand. "To Queen Tanya," she said. Everyone rose and took a sip of wine.

Scott, as the senior noncommissioned officer, raised his next. "To My Lord, Major General Kovaks," he said. Everyone but Duncan toasted.

Bishop was next. "To the King's Own Regiment."

Now it was Duncan's turn. "Absent comrades," he said and he drained his glass and turned it upside down laying it on the table.

"Thank you all for coming," Duncan said. "This party is not just for the members of the Regiment. It is also to honour our new homeland and the people in it who have welcomed us. To honor past enemies who are now friends, old friends reunited once again, and new friends. Enjoy the rest of the evening. Party is on!"

Servers scurried around removing dishes, while others took drink orders. Duncan headed to the bar while everyone else from the head table dispersed to be with friends. A band began to play and Duncan made his way from table to table, making sure he spent time with everyone. Everyone but Marlene, that is, who always managed to be on the opposite side of the room from him, no matter where he was at the time.

He went to the bar for another beer and she took to the dance floor with one of the civilian government officials. She had opted for the trousers instead of the long skirt. Her hair was down instead of being tied back and the uniform looked good on her. She was laughing at something her dance partner had said and from what Duncan had seen she was enjoying herself.

He went to the end of the bar and hooked his elbow on it, watching her dance. She stayed with the young civilian even when the band took a break, going to his table of friends. She was soon laughing along with them. When the band started back up, she returned to the dance floor with the same man, clearly enjoying his company.

Well, I guess that's the end of that, he thought to himself. She is back with her own people and class now. He grabbed two more beers and joined his fire team at their table and was soon involved in the joking and ribbing. Megan came by and dragged him on the dance floor. She was also wearing trousers instead of the long skirt and was making the most of showing off her figure every chance she got.

"Go find someone your own age to play with, Daughter," Barb said, grabbing Duncan away from Maegan.

"So, what's going on, Duncan?" Bar asked. "You mysteriously take off on leave the same time Isabelle does, then mysteriously come back the same time she does. She is no longer the Ice Queen when she gets back and you two were spotted hanging out together off base. Now you won't even talk with her?"

"Hey, she is keeping her distance, not me," Duncan said. "Besides it looks like she has found a guy from her own station anyway. Look at her, she is having fun."

A slow waltz started to play and Barb dragged Duncan over to where Marlene and her friend were dancing.

"Excuse me, young man," she said. "I really like this song and My Lord Duncan is a horrible dancer. Would you mind?"

She shoved Duncan at Marlene and spirited the young man away. Marlene looked at the two of them and laughed, then turned and looked at Duncan and the laugh stopped. She was still smiling, but not as broadly.

"It really is a nice song," Duncan said. "Would you do me the honor, Colonel Isabelle?"

He took her in his arms and they began to dance, but she kept her distance and would not look at him.

"You look beautiful tonight, Marlene," he said. "I have missed you these last days."

She snapped her head back to look at him. She was not smiling now. "As if," she said. Then looked away again.

The song was concluding and they stopped dancing.

"Thank you for the dance, my lord," she said and started to walk away. He grabbed her arm and held her in place. "Is it my lord's pleasure to dance some more?"

"Yes," Duncan said. Another slow waltz came on and while she danced in step and was beautifully graceful, she made no eye contact and no attempt to talk. Now he was getting pissed off.

"Look, Colonel," he said. "I don't know what I did to piss you off. I can understand you dumping me to be with your own people. But I thought we could at least be friends. Whatever I did, I am sorry."

She snapped her head back and while she wasn't smiling she wasn't frowning either. She looked him right in the eyes this time.

"I'm serious, Marlene," he said. "I thought we had something special and I guess I was wrong. I apologise, I should not have pressed myself on you like that."

"You can be such an asshole sometimes, Duncan," she said, then she pressed herself into him, drew his head down and kissed him.

It was the third dance now. Even though it was a fast song they were still dancing slow and she had her head on his shoulder.

"You know what?" she said. "Why don't you introduce me to your friends? Are you ashamed of me?"

"Hell no," he said. "I thought you wanted to keep us a secret?"

"Well I somehow think the secret is out," she said. "Come on, let me meet your friends."

She dragged him over to the table.

"Trust Ghost to pick up the cutest girl in the place," Scott said. Katerina punched him on the arm.

"You told me I was the cutest," she said.

"Ya, you are," Scott said. "But you're my girlfriend so it doesn't count."

Duncan made the introductions, held a chair for Marlene to sit down, then went to the bar and grabbed a tray full of beer and brought it back. Marlene was laughing at something Brett had just said. She had brushed her hair back behind both ears, which told him she was comfortable with all of them and they with her.

"You know what?" Brett said. "You just cost me a hundred pounds, Duncan."

"I told all of them you two had a thing going on," Barb said. "They bet me you didn't. Easy pickings." Barb stood and made her way to the washroom and Marlene went with her.

"I didn't think we were that obvious," Marlene said as they were freshening up.

"You weren't," Barb said. "But I have known Duncan all my life and I can tell. I also have a daughter, if you haven't noticed. A mother knows these things, so does a sister, and Duncan is the brother I never had."

"And he is the son I never had," Jane said. She had just come in and heard the last part. "You have made him happy and I can see he makes you happy. That makes me happy."

"But, Karen was your daughter," Marlene said. "You should hate me!"

"No dear, I don't," she said. "As long as you remember Karen will always be in his heart? It is big enough for the both of you."

It took the three of them a long time to return to the table.

It was getting late, and some of the guests had already left. Duncan stood and beckoned Marlene to join him.

"Time for some fresh air," he said. "Don't worry about us. It's a nice night out. We can walk home; it's not far."

Instead of turning right to the barracks, Duncan turned left and after a few minutes they were walking down a residential street. He really wanted to put his arm around her, but regulations would not permit it in uniform. So, they contented each other with just holding hands as they walked.

The streets were empty and most of the lights were out in the houses. He turned up the path to one of them and walked up to the door. He dug out a key, unlocked it and motioned Marlene in. The second the door closed he pulled her to him and kissed her.

"Welcome to our new home," he said.

They were soon banging against walls as he guided her to the bedroom, kissing and removing clothing as they went and their passions rose.

Duncan woke up and found he was alone in the bed. He looked around and saw that the sun was barely up. A noise in the en suite bathroom drew his attention and he saw Marlene, a towel wrapped around her, brushing her hair. He walked up behind her and put his arms around her, kissing her neck. She took his head in her free hand and held him there and purred.

"No time," she said and pushed him away. "I have to get back to my barracks and change."

"No, you don't," Duncan said. "I bought a pair of jogging pants and a couple of shirts for you. We can get the rest of your stuff later."

She turned around and kissed him and he pulled the towel off and hoisted her on the vanity and they found out it was just the right height.

Later in the afternoon they walked back to the barracks. Now that they were not in uniform, they had their arms around each other's waists. They stopped in front of her barracks and kissed.

"Why don't you get your stuff together and take it over to the house?" Duncan said handing her a key. "Then come back to the athletic field. The PIGs and us are having a little game tonight. It should be fun."

Duncan watched her jog into her barracks and then made his way to his own. No one was there, but he didn't expect anyone to be. They would be on their way to the game. He found his small cooler and put six beers in it, then made his way down to the large field they normally used for PT and drills. A small set of bleachers lined the sidelines and Duncan saw that the Wind Riders not playing were all sitting together. He headed up to them.

"Where did you disappear to last night?" Barb said. "As if I don't know. Are their barracks as nice as ours?"

"They were not there last night either," Marlene's second-in-command said. "I thought they were at you guys'."

"Oh my," Barb said. "A hotel room. How romantic. Was it nice?"

"None of your business," Duncan said.

"Oh my," she said. "A little grumpy today. Not get enough beauty sleep last night?"

"Too much beauty, not enough sleep, more like," Cheryl said.

Duncan just smiled and pulled a beer out of the cooler. He wouldn't win this argument, so didn't try.

The game started and at first the Wind Riders did well. They were faster, lighter and more agile than the mostly American people they were playing. The game was also being played under Canadian rules, which were different from American ones.

By the halftime break, the Canadians were up by seven points. Marlene arrived just at that time and the ladies elbowed Duncan out of the way and surrounded Marlene.

"So how was the walk last night?" Barb asked. "It must have been a long one."

"Oh yes it was," Marlene said. "It was very pleasant. Duncan showed me the new house he just purchased in town and asked my opinion of the furnishings."

"Oh?" Barb said. "And has he good taste?"

"Oh yes," Marlene said. "He tastes very sweet. The bed was oh so comfortable and springy. The en suite bathroom counter is just the perfect height."

"Really?" Barb said, then looked over at Duncan who was innocently looking the other way, pretending not to hear.

"Tonight, we plan to see if the couch is as comfortable as the bed was," Marlene said.

Barb had nothing to say.

"That's a first," Duncan said and he handed Marlene a beer and they clinked bottles. "The Voice with no comeback."

"Well, I never…" Barb sputtered and she was the brunt of the jokes after that, leaving the two lovers off the hook, for now.

The game started again and Marlene asked questions about how it was played and, after Duncan answered a few, the ladies took over the explanations. Duncan's answers were either too in-depth or too vague to be helpful.

The PIGs had listened to the advice of their few Canadian players and were pushing the Wind Riders hard, first tying the score and then going ahead by a touchdown. But with three minutes remaining in the game, their lack of knowledge of the differences in the game rules came to the fore and the Wind Riders scored two touchdowns while holding the PIGs to no gains. The Wind Riders won the game!

Now the post-game party began and the steel drums converted into barbeques came alive. The area was soon saturated by the smell of steak, ribs and chicken being barbequed. Huge pots of chilli were being prepared, all by the losing team members as had been agreed on.

The quarterback of the PIGs, a captain, came up to Duncan and Marlene as they were making the rounds.

"Good thing you decided not to play," he said to Duncan. "I am getting the hang of the passing game now, and I will destroy you guys the next time."

"If I would have been playing," Duncan said. "I would have picked you off at least three times, two of them for touchdowns. You telegraph your moves and you always have."

"You played?" the captain asked. He had been a highly rated American collage player before he joined the army.

"The last four games of the season in my senior year at high school," Duncan said. Then he walked away.

"Don't let that answer fool you," Marlene heard CT say to the captain. "He was at Stanford the whole time you were at Texas A and M. You know how good those teams were. They guaranteed him a starting position as safety his freshman year and he turned them down. Seattle, San Francisco and Oakland wanted him to turn pro, too."

"Holy shit!" the captain said. "He was that good?"

"What does that mean, Duncan?" Marlene asked.

"In his country, this is a very popular game and you can make a lot of money playing it," Duncan said. "A lot of universities provide full scholarships if you are a good enough player. The schools make a lot of money from the game that funds other programs. I had high enough marks and enough funding that I didn't need a scholarship and I wanted an education, not to play football."

"Okay, you bums!" he yelled out. "Have fun tonight, because Monday your asses are mine, all mine."

"Ah shit!" the captain said to CT. "I didn't know you guys were coming!"

"Oh, did I forget to send the memo?" CT said. "Bad me."

"What did you mean about Monday, Duncan?" Marlene asked. They were lying entwined together naked on the couch, the clothing strewn from the door to the couch.

"Not to worry, love," Duncan said. "Two months of training in the bush integrating what we do with what they do. Most of us have worked together in the past, but not to this degree. Next year we will pick the Marauders or the Black Shirts to work with."

"Oh," she said. "Two months apart."

"That's the army for you," Duncan said. "It wouldn't matter if I were staying anyway. You and the Marauders will be training together for two months as well, but in the new base we have just established in the middle of the district to the west. The Marauders will be based permanently there, the PIGs in the base to the west along with the Wind Riders. The Black Shirts will be garrisoned here."

"Oh," she said again.

"Also, you need to groom a replacement for yourself," Duncan said.

Marlene pushed herself away from him and looked at him with a frown on her face.

"If you think I am giving up the army to be with you, think again!" she said.

"In the next year, one of two things are going to happen," Duncan said. "You are going to get pregnant, which means you will be pulled out of front-line command. Or, you will become a Wind Rider."

"What?" Marlene said.

"If you think the woman I love is going to serve as infantry you are sadly mistaken," Duncan said. "I expect you to compete and pass qualification this spring to be a Wind Rider. That might be difficult if you become pregnant, but?"

"Do you actually think this is my first go around?" Marlene said. "I don't know how this works for your people, but here, we have very safe ways for females preventing pregnancy. I would have tried out last year if you would have let me."

"You probably would have passed, too," Duncan said. "But I really did need you where you were. Now that your people have had time training in the new methods and weapons, I can use your mind and you with us. But only if you pass."

"Oh, I will pass Duncan, I will pass." She said.

"And I meant what I said about the other, too," he said holding her close. "Never again will I let the mother of my unborn children fight in the front lines. After, sure, if you still want to, I won't stop you."

She held him close too, then she kissed his chest and stood.

"There are two other bedrooms with two other beds we have to test," she said, then took off running for the nearest and he was chasing her.

Chapter Fifteen

MONDAY MORNING FOUND DUNCAN supervising the PIGs as they loaded their equipment and tested systems on their brand new LAV4s. The vehicles were heavily laden both inside and out with tents, sleeping gear, personal gear, spare fuel cans and ammunition, but an hour before midday, the first vehicles moved out and shortly after that, their part of the base was empty.

The Marauders had been more organised and had started leaving at daybreak. By midday they were all on the road. The Black Shirts had followed.

Except for the Wind Riders and a battalion of Marauders to provide security and services to the base, the base was empty two hours after midday. The Wind Riders loaded all their equipment on their vehicles and moved them to a warehouse, where sections of telecommunication towers were fastened to the Coyotes and GW2s. Those that did not have towered sections had reels of wire or weatherproof boxes full of electronic components strapped to them.

It would be an uncomfortable and cramped five-hour journey the next morning.

As the sun was breaking the horizon, each Wind Rider vehicle had a five hundred gallon tanker trailer attached to it and they moved to the refuelling station and filled them all. The Wind Riders were on the road headed east towards the mountains strung out along the highway two hours after daybreak.

During the initial planning stages, it had been decided that the assault teams would use the war hammers developed by Tanya's people. They would be highly effective at the close ranges of combat expected and, while the assault troops would have their firearms in case of need, most of the work would be done by the primitive weapons.

The first few days, both regiments would be busy setting up camp, then the assault troops would begin training with their new weapons and the Wind Riders would begin erecting the communications towers and setting up the communications center.

For now, everything would be under canvas tents. Plans had been made to begin construction of permanent buildings and the base itself, but not until the attack had been made. Right now, everything had to remain secret. A landing area for a transport ship had been cleared by the end of the first week and on Monday the first one landed, bringing more food, ammunition and a small brush clearing machine with a dozer blade in front. Dave was sent back with them to supervise their initial training, while the Wind Riders began to remove trees and undergrowth to expand the landing area to hold six of the craft.

The next week, along with the food delivery came refrigeration units and generators to run them as well as a small backhoe. The next day it was back with large fuel and water tanks and the Wind Riders started installation of temporary piping and pumping stations for both.

Water was not a problem. The original mining complex had tapped into a natural spring, so fresh water was plentiful and just needed to be pumped into the new storage tanks. The fuel came on the next supply transport and between what the Wind Riders had brought along and what the transport had delivered, the holding tanks were full.

Ammunition, explosives and spare weapons were temporarily stored in the mine itself. It was under cover and dry. Now that all the work on the base was done and the telecommunications set up, tested and working, the Wind Riders began their training, fanning out in troops and single units to operate by themselves as they were designed to do.

CT stayed behind to train his two new technicians and the other new people on how to operate, maintain and monitor the systems and they were finally beginning to operate as they should: independent intelligence gatherers.

By the middle of the next month, the two brigades began joint operations. Wind Riders were deployed and doing their tasks supporting the PIGs. The final Saturday, all six transports arrived and, for the rest of the last week, dry runs in ever-increasing complexity were conducted. On the last Friday, a full-blown insertion from orbit was made. They were ready to go.

It was a three-day trip to Ariel from Oaken. CT was cloaking their departure and arrival. The ship reserved for the Wind Riders broke orbit and landed on the outskirts of the Guild base, far enough away not to be spotted by eye. The Wind Riders spread out and began to complete their tasks.

CT and his technical teams were busy collecting data and updating building plans and troop strengths. The Wind Riders had completed their secondary tasks and were in position to provide up-to-the-second intelligence and support.

And then it was time.

At a predetermined moment, CT relayed a transmission from Duncan on the ground to Tanya in her palace back on Oaken.

"Your Majesty," he began. "The Stanista Army Division is in place and will be conducting offensive operations on Ariel in the next half an hour. I would advise you to inform the Interplanetary Counsel of this. Regardless, we attack in half an hour."

The five transports holding the assault team spread out and waited. CT watched the time closely and began a countdown. At one minute, every electronic device on ships and on the ground were turned off.

Duncan waited on the ground with his team. He pointed his sniper rifle at a guard in a tower as they waited. He counted to himself the seconds and at the end of the first minute a visible shimmering went through the atmosphere as the huge electronic pulse CT sent through the atmosphere hit Arial. Three minutes after that another hit the planet. Then Duncan put his eye to the scope and counted. At the thirty second mark he fired, knocking the sentry from the tower. Other rifles fired immediately after his. Then he turned his electronics back on and keyed his mike.

"Wind Rider Alpha One to PIG Alpha One, have begun operations," he said as he sighted on another sentry on foot and fired.

Now the transports entered the atmosphere and as they came in, automatic rifle and machine gun fire began to rake the compound and anything moving that could be spotted anywhere near the landing zones or in the open. The noise of the rifles and grenades going off was deafening. Very few shots were returned, as bewildered defenders were cut down, most of them sprinting from barracks to armouries.

The transports started firing their internal weapons as they came in range, causing more havoc, As they approached the ground, the shots began to take their toll on the buildings themselves. Soon they had landed and troops were pouring out, entering the buildings and killing anyone they contacted.

The biggest group entered the main building and Duncan began receiving information from CT on troops approaching and directions to the main targets.

The Wind Riders maintained their suppression and defensive fire, keeping the landing areas secure, but soon had no targets, as the defenders either went to ground or were dead.

One by one the assault teams returned. Some did not reboard the transports but set up defensive positions around the landing zones.

"Wind Rider Alpha One, Wind Rider Gulf One, disengage and proceed to extraction point Bravo," CT said.

Duncan acknowledged and rebroadcast the order to the rest of his teams, slung the sniper rifle on his back and picked up his C8. He began to walk backwards along with his fire team until they were far enough away, then they turned and jogged to the extraction point.

"Wind Rider Gulf One, Poppa Alpha One, all primary and secondary objectives complete, Poppa disengaging and proceeding to LZ." CT acknowledged the withdrawal and, as the Wind Riders established a defensive perimeter, their transports flared and landed, the ramps opening before they hit the ground.

As the five main transports rose, their armaments fired at everything in the surrounding area until they were out of range. Then the explosions began. It started in the transport loading areas, as the explosives the Wind Riders had placed the day before went off on the fuel tanks and pumping stations, but quickly the whole loading area and the transports themselves were on fire, flames shooting hundreds of feet in the air.

Shortly behind those came the explosions in the Guild complex. Entire buildings, especially the main complex, were exploding, their flames added to those of the surrounding town as more and more buildings caught fire. Nothing could be done. All electronics were nonfunctional as the massive EMP pulses that CT had generated had wiped them all out on this side of the planet and any that were housed on the back side of the planet in *on* mode. The Planet of Arial was essentially defenceless and helpless.

Except for casualty reports, they travelled home as they had come, silent, unseen and unheard.

They landed at their new base on the mountains and dispersed to their tents. They set to work unloading and cleaning weapons or, for those designated as cooks, starting the first fresh meals in over a week. Section commanders reported to troop or company commanders, who in turn reported to senior officers, who converged on Duncan's tent. One by one they made their reports.

Their casualties were light and easily treated by their own medical people. But estimates of enemy casualties were extremely high. They had been caught totally unprepared.

"Well I think somebody has been taught a lesson," Duncan said. "Don't piss us off! Well done, people!"

He let them bask in what they had just accomplished for a few minutes, then got their attention once again.

"Now," he said. "I do not plan to inform, or even make contact with, Her Majesty or anyone else for two days. Once I do, I fully expect that we will all will be summoned to the capitol and have our asses handed to us. I will take full responsibility and try to shield all of you as much as I can. But…"

"Ya well," Kurt said. "If you go down, we go down with you, and I don't know about the Wind Riders, but I can tell you the PIGs will kick some serious Oaken ass if you or I go down."

That sentiment was expressed by everyone else in the tent.

"I don't think it will go beyond a wrist and peepee slap," Duncan said. "But you never know with these people. I won't go down without a fight, I assure you. Now enough of this talk! Get back to your people, tell them I am extremely happy, and they are to relax for the next couple of days. It will take a couple of months for any Guild response, if one ever comes. We hit their command and control really hard. Now get out of here. Not you, CT."

"Totally destroyed boss," CT said. "We wiped every bit of memory anywhere before the explosions wiped out the machine. The room the hardcopies were in was wiped out with phosphorus charges. If anything survived, it won't be much. All of the techs and scientists were killed. They won't be rebuilding that thing. I won't say forever, but I would say pretty damn close."

"Fantastic, that's a load off my mind," Duncan said. "Now there is no way they can surprise us by infiltrating troops using that damn machine. Send my team in as you leave, then go celebrate."

"Okay guys," he said when they came in. "Before we party, we have one more job. Brett, grab the GW2, the rest of you, personal weapons. We are going on a little trip."

They made the trip to the small town in just under an hour and Duncan had them stop in front of the saddle maker's shop. It was still open as the work day would not end for another hour.

"Hey old timer, get your ass out here," he yelled out in German as he came into the shop.

The angry retort the shop owner was going to make died in his mouth as he saw Duncan. Duncan was dressed in his combat uniform, black beret on his head, weapons harness with all of its pouches filled with munitions, and rifle slung to hang barrel-down across his chest.

"Grab your jacket and close this shithole up," Duncan said. "It's party time."

Brett, Scott and Amanda were standing by their doors and townspeople were congregating around the vehicle but keeping their distance.

"Front or back?" Duncan said pointing at the vehicle.

"Where's she sitting?" the old guy asked. Amanda pointed at the back and the old man got in the back, moving to the center.

They all laughed and got in and were soon on their way back to base.

"What's all this about then, young fella?" the old man asked. "Am I in shit for something?"

"I don't know what Lord Kovaks has in store, old man," Amanda said reaching under her seat and bringing up a bottle of vodka. "But you better have a shot of this just in case."

"Ya well, if you don't leave anything in that bottle," Duncan said, "I can for sure tell you Lord Kovaks will kick your cute little butt out and make you walk home, Sergeant."

The old man looked from Amanda to Duncan and back a few times and Duncan laughed and stuck his hand between the seats and toward the old man.

"Duncan Kovaks, at your service," he said.

The old man sat straight up at attention in his seat.

"Master Gunnery Sergeant Hendrix, Company A Force Recon, reporting for duty, Sir!" he belted out.

"Semper Fi, Gunney," Duncan said. "You going to shake my hand or what?"

"Sorry Sir," Hendrix said and took Duncan's hand.

"Next to you with the bottle is Master Sergeant Amanda, on the other side is Warrant Officer Scott. Next to me is Master Warrant Brett. We all have the privilege to be members of the King's Own Regiment, recently of the Canadian Army, now members of Her Majesty's First Stanista Division. We do the same job you used to do, Gunny. And I am not kidding, if you guys in the back seat don't leave anything in the bottle for us up front, Brett and I are going to make you walk home."

"No fear of that, boss," Brett said. He reached into the cargo pocket in his door and came up with another bottle and handed it to Duncan.

"Oh great," Duncan said. "Now some stupid cop is going to arrest us for driving under the influence."

"Hell, there ain't never been any cops out here," the old guy said taking a deep pull of the bottle. "Sheeit! Good hooch! Where we off to?"

"Got some jarheads, SEALs and various other malcontents stationed not far from here," Duncan said. "I figured it was time you reunited with some of your own people."

They came blasting into the camp a short time later with every driving light and head light blazing and Brett holding the horn button down. Everyone in camp came running and were soon surrounding the GW2, most of them armed but most in T-shirts.

The occupants exited the GW2 and lined up in front of it.

"Stand To!" Duncan ordered and the others lined up in their companies and troops before them.

Duncan brought Hendrix up with him to face the assembled soldiers all at attention with rifles grounded beside them.

"This is Master Gunnery Sergeant Hendrix, Company A Force Recon!" Duncan said. "I told him that we were not the almighty fierce warriors he was used to, but that he was welcome to party with us. So, don't let me down people. Welcome home, Gunny."

As Duncan walked away, his own ex-marines were the first to come up to the old man, salute him and shake his hand. The old man had tears in his eyes as he was reunited with the brotherhood of warriors.

Two days later the Wind Riders and senior commanders of the PIGs were on the road back to the main base in their command vehicles. They were headed toward the province's capitol city, which they had begun to call Sundry. It was as good a name as any and better than New Paris, its former name.

Duncan took a deep breath and began the radio call to Tanya's communication center, breaking the radio silence they had been operating under for the last two weeks. As expected, he was ordered to report to Tanya, along with his senior officers, immediately. What was not expected was that she was at the palace complex in Sundry.

A large contingent of her own troops was waiting for them as they came into town and the senior command was escorted to the palace as they were, not being allowed to change uniforms or clean up. They were marched into the large ballroom and lined up before a seated Tanya. She was in her ceremonial uniform as were her two sons, one standing on each side of her. Ranged behind her, also in their ceremonial uniforms, were her war cabinet and senior generals.

A few civilians in formal attire stood alongside the two boys. No one was smiling and Tanya made them stand at attention for over a minute, not a word spoken the whole time. She looked over each of them and finally stared at Duncan for a full ten seconds.

"Explain yourself, my Lord Major General Kovaks," she said quietly. She didn't have to talk loudly; you could hear a pin drop in the room.

"Your Majesty," Duncan began. "We identified an opportunity to conduct a punitive raid on Your Majesty's enemy, Ma'am. We planned and conducted the operation, Ma'am."

"Why were we not informed of this plan, my lord?"

"Your Majesty, we had evidence that members of your inner circle and advisors were in collusion with your enemy, Ma'am, and we could not risk having those plans divulged to the enemy, Ma'am."

"You have proof of these allegations, my lord?"

"Yes, your Majesty," Duncan said. "I would have presented them to you had I been afforded the opportunity to prepare, Ma'am."

"I assume they can be transmitted to me?" Tanya said. "Make it so."

She consulted the small computer screen in front of her on the table for a few minutes. Then she called the commander of her guard to her and whispered into his ear. In minutes, a troop of her guards entered the ballroom fully armed and roughly dragged three of the uniformed advisors out of the line and frog-marched them out of the room.

"What were the results of this so called punitive raid? And how much of our slim stock of silver was spent?" Tanya asked.

"The operation was a success, your Majesty," Duncan said. "The headquarters of the Guild of Interplanetary Mercenaries was damaged severely and all command and control centers destroyed. An estimated seventy percent of the garrison are casualties. All electronic devices on that side of Arial are destroyed and we estimate sixty percent of all other electronic equipment on the planet was destroyed. The main transport loading and unloading facility on the planet has been largely destroyed, as well as half of Arial's remaining transport ship capability. The cost of the operation was borne by the coffers of the Province of Stanista, Ma'am."

"Which will result in a drop of tax revenue for this year," she said. "And what of our losses in valuable troops and material?"

"Other than the reduction of ready ammunition and fuel for the transports, no losses in materiel, Your Majesty. The injuries sustained by your soldiers were not substantial and no loss of life was experienced, Ma'am."

"Very well," Tanya said. "Leave us now. We will consider this information. Hold yourself ready to hear our judgment on this matter."

All of them bowed their heads, took two steps back, pivoted and marched out of the room.

"That went better than I thought," Duncan said. "Okay, I think the worst is over for you guys. Go get cleaned up and relax. I'll let you know how all this turns out."

Duncan drove his personal GW2 to his home and let everyone else do the unloading. He showered quickly and made sure his regular uniform was ready to go, then dressed in gym attire and relaxed, waiting for the call.

"What have you done, Duncan?" Marlene said as she rushed into the house. She was dressed in combat uniform, as the Black Shirts had arrived back two days before.

"We have been on alert for a week now," she continued. "All leave was cancelled and we have been placed under Her Majesty's command."

"Nothing much," he said. "Give us a hug?"

It was rapidly developing into more than a hug, but Marlene pushed him away.

"Her Majesty is reported to be very unhappy with you, Duncan," she said. "You just can't go off planning and conducting operations on your own, Duncan. Shit! What the hell were you thinking?"

She paced the living room for a while, then stopped in front of him and touched his cheek. Tears were in her eyes.

"For the first time in my life, I am truly in love and very happy. How could you do this to us, Duncan? She has every right to strip you of everything at the very least and perhaps to imprison or execute you."

"Well I wouldn't care too much about the first part," Duncan said. "I can always work for your mom and I don't really need all this command BS anyway. As far as the second part? Unlike your previous boss, my people would never let that happen and, I can tell you right now, we would decimate this planet and be in complete control in a very short time."

She pulled him to her and held him tight. Then things did get heated and they made it to the master bedroom, barely. It was mid-morning two days later when the doorbell rang. Duncan got out of bed and threw on a pair of jogging pants and, bare-chested and barefoot, opened the front door. Tanya, with two guards behind her, was at the door. Other guards were stationing themselves around the yard. She was dressed in, what were for her, casual clothes.

"Are you going to stand there all day, Duncan, or are you going to invite me in?" she said.

Duncan got out of her way and she entered, leaving the guards outside.

"Who was at the door, hon?" Marlene said as she walked into the living room dressed only in Duncan's Wind Rider T-shirt which came to mid-thigh on her.

"Oh my God!" she said and she dropped a curtsy as well as she could in the short garment. "Your Majesty."

"She turns such a lovely shade of red, don't you think?" Tana said. "Oh, stand up, Marlene. I wouldn't turn down a glass of beer or something if you have one."

Duncan walked into the kitchen trailed by Tanya who plunked herself on a chair and Marlene rushed into the bedroom. She still had Duncan's shirt on when she came back a few minutes later, but they were tucked into a pair of blue jeans and she had socks on her feet and she had run a brush through her hair quickly. She tossed a polo shirt at Duncan and he pulled it on.

"First things first," Tanya said holding her hand out for the beer and taking a sip of it.

"It would have been nice to have more than a half-hour notice, Duncan," she continued. "I barely had enough time to composed and transmit a message so I didn't look like a complete ass. You could have at least told me, Duncan."

"With the small number of troops we had, I couldn't take the risk of your telling someone," Duncan said. "I also couldn't tell you about the traitors. You would have arrested them on the spot and that would have alerted the Guild that something was up. Sorry, Tanya."

She sat staring at her beer, then nodded her head.

"Apology accepted," she said. "Christ, you really knocked the shit out of them. Nobody anywhere has ever experienced what you did to them. The amount of destruction and devastation with minimal resources and time. Bang! you were there; bang! you were gone.

"CT sent me all the reports and real-time data and video. I don't mind telling you, you people scare the shit out of me and I am glad you are my friends. More importantly, everyone else is scared shitless of us now. You would not believe the number of offers of friendship I have been receiving from all over."

She took another mouthful of beer.

"You and your people have made us safe, Duncan. Thank you."

"I have ordered Bishop to come here," she continued. "He should be here shortly. It is now Sunday. You have until Friday to plan and train for a full divisional pass in review. You will all be in ceremonial uniform. Including you, young lady. As beautiful as you are now, somehow, I don't think your mother would like to see her daughter dressed in her lover's T-shirt and nothing else. You have brought honor back to your house, Marlene, and I mean to show it."

"Now, how serious are you about this young lady, Duncan?"

"Um…Well, I guess pretty serious, Tanya, sorry," Duncan said. "I really love her a lot, Tanya."

"I keep telling you, you are too young for me Duncan," Tanya said. "Now you, Marlene. How serious are you about Duncan? He might be too young for me, but I still care for him deeply."

"I think my heart would crumble to pieces and I would die if he left me, Tanya," Marlene said.

Tanya looked from one to the other, then frowned.

"Can't have two lovers from prominent families living together unmarried," she said. "Bad for morals and bad for discipline. What do you two plan on doing about that?"

Duncan just looked at Marlene and shrugged his shoulders. She just looked back at him.

"Why are you always such an asshole, Duncan?" Tanya asked. "Or are your customs different from ours?"

"Huh?" he said.

"Well, here it is customary for the man to ask the woman to marry him. But I suppose it is different where you come from?"

"No, it's the same," Duncan said. "Oh shit, you idiot, Duncan."

"Oh, not an asshole then," Tanya said. "Just clueless or scared, like all men."

Duncan walked up to Marlene and took both her hands in his.

"Marlene Isabelle, I love you with all my heart. Would you marry me?"

"Took you long enough to ask, asshole," she said. "Yes, Duncan Kovaks, I will marry you." Then she kissed him.

"Good. My work here is done," Tanya said. "Great minds think alike, Marlene, and he really isn't that big of an asshole."

"Your mother will be here tonight, Marlene. She will be staying with me in the palace. I wouldn't put her in this man's pigsty if she were my worst enemy. Which she most definitely is not."

She went to the door, opened it and took a thick file from the guard at the door's hand. She tossed it at Duncan.

"Some light reading for you. Bye!" As fast as she had arrived, she and her guards were gone.

Duncan read the first few pages of the file and whistled. Then he picked up the phone and called his headquarters.

"Ask all the Division field grade officers to report for a meeting Monday at nine," he said. "Alert status is rescinded; have all units stand down. Uniform for all members to be regular uniform as of the next shift change until further notice. On and off base unless authorised otherwise."

"And what about my uniform?" Marlene asked after he hung up the phone. She was leaning on the bedroom door wearing only the T-shirt again and beckoning him with a finger.

Chapter Sixteen

"As you were," Duncan said as he breezed into the board room. The officers had begun to rise and sat back down again as he spoke the words.

He had two file folders with him, one thick and one thin. He opened the thicker of the two.

"Her Majesty has approved our actions, people," he began. "In fact, she is very pleased. She has ordered a divisional review to be held Friday at noon. Dress is ceremonial and I believe we will have the Master Gunnery Sergeant lead the review. He is owed that much. See to it that he is properly kitted out, Karl, and that he is up-to-date on our protocols. Start practicing today, people. Full dress rehearsal Thursday after morning muster.

"Next. The Guild and Arial have asked for and been granted a cease-fire. They have sued for peace, terms have been set and agreed upon. We are no longer at war, people. Congratulations.

"Arial will pay Her Majesty and the people of Oaken the sum of one hundred million pounds of silver. The Guild, five hundred thousand pounds.

"The Marauders are awarded one million pounds of silver from Arial and two million from the Guild. This is to be distributed equally among the original survivors of the Marauders. In addition, the Guild will repay funds lost during the civil war and pay fees owing.

"The PIGs will also be awarded the same amount of reparations and all wages until the end of the war will be paid. This also is to be spread equally among the surviving members of the original PIGs.

"The Black Shirts will receive five hundred thousand pounds of silver from Arial and one million from the Guild, also to be distributed among the surviving original members.

"The money will be held in trust by the Province of Stanista. Each member of the regiments named will receive one hundred pounds of silver credited to their accounts immediately. Half of the remainder will be released after their five-year commitment has been completed. The remainder will be credited to their accounts plus interest after the twenty-year commitment has been completed, or the member's services are no longer deemed to be required, whichever comes first. Interest will be accrued at the prevailing rate at the time, paid monthly and compounded monthly.

"Back wages can be paid in whatever means the unit commanders decide is prudent.

"Questions?"

Hearing none, Duncan passed out each Battle Group's orders and awards papers from the thick file and dismissed all but the Wind Riders.

"Get all our people in the mess ASAP," he said, then he walked to his office taking the thin file with him and sat behind his desk.

Ten minutes later, Brett was knocking on his doorframe and Duncan stood up and walked to the mess. He didn't need the file folder as he had its contents memorised.

"Attention!" Brett yelled as he and Duncan walked into the mess. They walked so that they were standing in the middle of the tables with the long ends of the tables going away from them. Duncan had them sit.

"Her Majesty has ordered a Divisional review," he began. "It will be held Friday at mid-day. Uniform is to be ceremonial. Officers and senior non-commissioned officers will be wearing pistols, not swords, and we will be wearing Stetsons, not berets.

"Officers will coordinate with the Master Warrant, and the Master Warrant will coordinate with Chief Master Warrant Hendrix, who is overall in charge of the review.

"Full dress rehearsal will be Thursday afternoon. Pre-review inspection, half hour after dawn Friday morning. Awards and honors will be handed out by Her Majesty at the review, but I have not been informed who, what, how many, or if any awards we will receive.

"Her Majesty has given each member of the King's Own a bonus of fifty pounds of silver. This has been credited to your personal accounts.

"The following is for all members of the King's Own, regardless of time in service or grade.

"The Planet of Arial will pay each member one thousand pounds of silver. The Mercenary Guild Interplanetary will pay each member five thousand pounds of silver. In addition, the Guild will pay retroactively, from the time the King's Own arrived on Oaken until last Friday, the sum of thirty-five pounds of silver for each month.

"The Guild will also pay each member relocated from Earth to Oaken a further three thousand pounds of silver.

"Of these funds, each member will have their personal accounts credited one hundred pounds of silver immediately. The rest of the funds will be held in trust for the member by the Province of Stanista. Current interest rates will be given and continually updated. The interest will be calculated and credited to the account monthly.

"Half of the original amount of the award will be paid to the member after completion of the mandatory five-year term of service. The other half, plus interest accrued, will be paid at the end of the member's twenty-year commitment or until the member has been honorably discharged, whichever is first.

"The Guild will also pay for equipment and materiel lost on the raid that was conducted on our supply base where all of our spare vehicles, weapons, ammunition and other supplies were destroyed. The Guild has also agreed to pay the King's Own the sum of five million pounds of silver for breach of contract and loss of esteem. These funds will be placed in a limited company to invest, or to start-up other companies. Each past, current and future member of the King's Own will be shareholders of this company as long as they are still qualified citizens of the Province of Stanista, or are working on their eligibility. Each shareholder will equally receive yearly dividends to equal one half of the yearly after-tax profit this company makes.

"Dismissed."

Duncan walked right out of the mess and to his personal GW2. He had a meeting with Tanya and he was late.

He was ushered into a sitting room where Tanya and another woman were seated in plush armchairs with a small table between them. Both women were dressed in expensive clothing, hair and jewelry adorned in the style of upper nobility.

Duncan stopped before Tanya, clicked his heels together and bowed his head.

"I believe you have met my cousin, Countess Magdalene Isabelle, Lord Duncan?" Tanya said.

"You are not the only one who keeps secrets, Lord Kovaks," Magdalene said. "You can be such an asshole sometimes, Duncan."

"Yes, Countess," Duncan said. "Her Majesty reminds me constantly of that."

"As is my prerogative," Tanya said. "As an explanation. Mags and I are indeed first cousins. We have been friends and almost constant companions our whole lives, until she married my husband's dreadful second cousin. Then she was banished to this backwater. How she has survived this long out here amazes me.

"First, to business. We will be promoting you to General of our armies and you are to be named Count. The Guild has had those managing directors and directors, not killed by your raid, arrested and incarcerated. You have been asked to head the Guild and all of your senior officers have been asked to be board of directors. What say you?"

"Your Majesty," Duncan began. "It is an honor that you have placed such trust in me, but I fear I must decline your offer to be General of your armies. I have neither the skill nor the experience to properly act on your behalf in that matter. I am sure others would be more suited to that task and, if I may make a suggestion, I believe that General Bishop would be the perfect man for the job.

"As far as being named Count," he continued. "The way we have set up the government of this province, the monarchy, while technically the head of state, in reality is comprised of figureheads. Again, I must politely decline."

"Speaking only for myself, I am not interested in heading or serving on the board of directors of the Guild. I will inform my senior officers of the offer and some of them may accept."

"As you wish, Lord Duncan," Tanya said. "As always, I defer to your judgment on these matters. You will, however, serve as my representative in the Province of Stanista. That is not open for discussion. Now to personal business."

"You and my daughter will not be allowed to cohabitate," Magdalene said. "What you do on your own time is your own business as long as it is discreet, but you will not reside under the same roof, is that clear?"

She did not wait for Duncan to respond.

"My daughter, as part of the royal family, will reside in an apartment set aside for her in this palace until such time as you two are married. She will be in the palace no later than eleven p.m. each night. If she is not here by that time, Her Majesty's Guard will find and forcibly escort her to the palace. Is all of this abundantly clear, Lord Kovaks?"

"Yes, Ma'am," Duncan said.

"My daughter is nervously bouncing at the doorway," Magdalene said. "Now go, before she has a fit or something and ruins our tea."

The two women waited until the lovers were out of sight before they started to giggle like schoolgirls involved in a secret conspiracy.

The rest of the week flew past. Marching, marching and still more marching. Preparing uniforms, frantically searching for last minute changes of plan or to find missing pieces of kit.

Each night, Duncan dropped Marlene off at the palace, usually late. Wednesday evening, she was an hour and a half late. Her hair and uniform were a mess, the blouse under the tunic was incorrectly buttoned, she had no hose on and her uniform skirt was crooked.

The two older cousins were standing in the hallway waiting for her as she came in, their arms across their chests and frowns on their faces. Marlene scurried down the hallway and one of the women couldn't hold it and snorted. Marlene stuck her right hand behind her back with the middle finger extended and both women howled in laughter.

Thursday was the day from hell. The Chief Master Warrant was never satisfied. Someone was always out of line or out of step. A uniform was not correct, a sword or rifle not at the proper angle. Over and over they marched. So far, the Wind Riders had not been singled out for special treatment - until the unfortunate incident with one of the PIGs' majors.

The poor man got his sword caught in the scabbard and when it finally did come clear, it sailed out of his hand to clank on the parade square. Hendrix was immediately in his face, nose to nose, screaming at the top of his lungs. Then he made the poor major pick up the sword and march in front of the lined-up battalions, yelling in his ear the whole time.

Unfortunately, one of the more colorful remarks was made right in front of Duncan who could not stop himself from smirking and an involuntary snort could be heard.

Hendrix immediately turned on him.

"Oh, the General thinks this is funny, does he?" Hendrix yelled right in his face. "No wonder you all march like a bunch of kindergarten pussies! How dare you laugh on my parade ground! This is not a party! This is not a comedy act! Do I look like a comedian to you, General?"

Duncan stood there, a blank stare on his face, looking above Hendrix's head for the whole five minutes Hendrix reamed him out. Each sentence became more colorful and more vulgar.

Finally, more due to the fact that he was running out of new things to say than anything else, Hendrix stopped his haranguing. He marched the unfortunate Major back to his position in the line and they began again.

When they stopped for a ten-minute break an hour later, Katarina approached Duncan.

"Are you going to let him get away with that, Duncan?" she said. "He can't talk to you like that!"

Duncan and those who had heard laughed, quietly, because Hendrix looked over at them and scowled.

"An officer may be in overall command, Kat," Duncan said. "But on the parade square, the ranking non-commissioned officer is in charge of the formation. It really is his parade square and if we mess up, it reflects badly on him. So, no, I will not be doing anything. Besides, between the hopeless major and myself, you guys got an additional ten-minute break from marching."

They kept at it until dark, then were dismissed. Brett drove an exhausted Marlene to the Palace. She was over an hour late, but nothing was said as the cousins saw she was in the special uniform with all the bangles and dangles and the sword banging on her hip.

She, like every other soldier that night, gently, lovingly pressed and brushed down the ornate uniform, shined every piece of metal until it shone brightly, then started on the leather, buffing and rubbing until she could see her face reflected. Then she climbed, exhausted, into her bed. Just two hours later a servant was banging on her door. It was time to get ready.

Hendrix and Duncan sat together in his barracks preparing their own uniforms. It was old hat to them and they went through the motions effortlessly.

"You took that very well today, Duncan," Hendrix said. "Pass me another bottle of beer; this one is dead."

"Hey Gunney," Duncan said passing him a fresh beer. "Until a year ago I used to work for a living. I was a Master Warrant Officer until some idiot by the name of Tanya decided I needed to be an officer."

"Ya, them Queens and Kings do shit like that," Hendrix said. "Take a perfectly fine soldier and make him a pussy officer. Makes me want to puke."

"Hell," Duncan said. "Just the other day she wanted to make me the general of the army and a count. Put my foot down on that one, I can tell you. Bad enough I can't serve in the line anymore as it is."

The men continued in that vein until they began to hear movement in the barracks. They consulted watches and began donning the intricate and immaculate uniforms. Taking soft leather shammies they rubbed fingerprints off buttons and boots. Then they stood, inspected each other, walked out onto the barracks' small parade ground and waited for the King's Own to form.

Once they were lined up in their troops and sections, they began their preinspection. Each trooper was carefully scrutinised. No crease was crooked, nothing was unpolished. Hendrix had just finished inspecting Carol and made to move away, when he turned back and looked at her collar and the gold eagle, wings outstretched on it.

"You authorised to wear that eagle, Captain?" he asked.

"Class of '05, Chief Master Warrant!" Carol belted out. Hendrix grunted and moved on.

Next was Barb. She did not hesitate. "Class of '96, Chief Master Warrant."

Nor did Dave. "Class of '95, Chief Master Warrant."

They began the second row and he stopped and looked hard at Megan. She had two mentioned-in-dispatches, a wound stripe and a parliamentary unit citation on her chest. She also had an eagle on her collar.

"Class of 2014, Chief Master Warrant," she said.

Hendrix just shook his head muttered, "Fucking babies now," and moved to the next line.

Now he saw globes and anchors on tunic collars. Two silver stars, a bronze star and the female had a navy cross. Each of them also had at least one purple heart.

"Semper Fi, Gunney," each said as he walked away. His eyes were misting over.

Then the inspection was over and they were off to the Black Shirts. This inspection was quicker and they went next to the Marauders, which took longer because there were so many of them, and finally to the PIGs, who also had chests full of medals, many of which Hendrix recognised. There was also one eagle, worn by a Welsh Master Sergeant.

It was elven-thirty by the time they returned to the Wind Riders. Almost time. The King's Own would lead the parade and would march past all the barracks and collect them as they made their way the long way around to the far side of the main parade square. Once again, they formed up in their troops and sections, Duncan at their head. Hendrix marched up to him, saluted him with his swagger stick and told him everyone was present and everything in order.

Then he dug into his right trousers pocket and brought out a gold eagle. "If the General wouldn't mind, Sir?"

Duncan took the eagle from his hand and fastened it on Hendrix left collar.

"Class of '72, Sir," Hendrix said.

Duncan smiled and dug into his right pocket and held the eagle his hand held out so Hendrix could see.

"Class of 2000, Gunny," Duncan said. Then he put the eagle back in his pocket.

"I shoulda' known," Hendrix said in German so only Duncan could hear. "You fuckin sneaky Canuck Cossacks. Always sittin in the bush."

"The eagles are guard dogs, Gunny," Duncan said. "The Wind Riders are Wolfhounds. We don't guard against wolves, Gunney, we hunt and kill them. Take us out, Gunney."

They marched out onto the deserted street, the only sound being of boot feet hitting the ground. Each barracks they passed added more boots and soon ten thousand boots were hitting the ground in unison, the sound echoing through the streets.

As the troops reached the wide boulevard leading to the parade square, the leading companies shortened their stride until they were barely moving forward and each column of eight moved out until they were marching in company- and troop-wide lines. Once all the formations were in place, the pace picked up again. They entered the parade square proper and saw the review stand was full of dignitaries in formal civilian attire or ceremonial uniforms.

Tanya and her two boys were dressed in the uniforms of the regiments of which they were Colonels in Chief, Tanya in the King's Own, Prince Eugene dressed in the Prince Eugene Mounted Infantry, Prince Ivan attired in the Prince Ivan Guards uniform. Magdalene stepped forward wearing the Queens's Own Regiment's uniform.

Portable stands had been constructed around the parade ground and they were full of people, while still more were standing behind barriers. The clapping started as the first column entered the square. The troops marched by the review stand, each line of heads snapping right as they came abreast of the reviewing stand and snapping back forward as they stepped past the end of it.

Hendrix marched them around the square counter clockwise and, as the lead formation reached the center, they wheeled to march directly for the review stand once again, shortening their steps as each formation spread out to right and left as they came in. Finally, as one mass block they marched the remaining distance to stop as one, five yards away from the review stand.

Hendrix had the mass formation form the rifle salute then put them all at ease. Duncan let his mind wander as he knew this would be long and boring. Local and regional politicians came up and made speeches, thankfully shorter than anticipated. Duncan let half his mind pay attention to Tanya's speech, more of the same pride-of-country stuff. Then individual awards were handed out. He perked up when Marlene was called up and she was given a wound medal. Then he glazed back over until the first of the Wind Riders was called up. Some, like Amanda received more than one decoration, then Jane was called up.

She was given a wound medal and a Distinguished Service Medal. Then she was promoted to Lieutenant General and was not allowed to leave.

An official came up with a largish box, opened it and took out a cross-shaped medal hanging on a neck ribbon. The ribbon was midnight blue as was the interior of the cross. The outside edges of the cross were a quarter of inch of solid gold and Tanya took it from the official and held it up for all could see.

"This a new award," Tanya said. "It is the highest award to be granted for bravery, sacrifice and dedication to duty above and beyond the norm. It is called the Cross of Queen Tanya. This is the very first time it has been awarded.

"During the final assault on the rebel redoubt, while being faced by an overwhelming and determined foe, Major Karen Kovaks, along with her team, pushed forward with grim determination under constant fire. Regardless of her personal cost, she pushed aside her commanding officer and sacrificed her life, so he might live. Her actions steeled the resolve of her teammates who cleared the final redoubt with minimal loss. Major Karen Kovaks died of her wounds.

"For her bravery and sacrifice, Major Karen Kovaks is awarded the Cross of Queen Tanya. On behalf of a grateful people I award her medal to her mother."

A muffled wail came from the front rank of the Black Shirts and Hendrix looked over with a frown, but Duncan put his hand on his arm.

"Let her be, Gunny," Duncan said. He had tears in his eyes as did all forty five of the original Wind Riders. "She is the one who killed her."

"Fuck!" Hendrix muttered.

Then Duncan was called up. He did not pay attention to the words spoken as several medals were pinned on his chest. Or when first Prince Ivan and then Prince Eugene hung smaller versions of Karen's medal with different interior coloring on the crosses around his neck. Nor did he pay attention to what Tanya was saying as she placed a wide sash to hang from his right shoulder to his left hip. All he was thinking of was when he could get the hell off this stage and parade ground and out of this uncomfortable and hot uniform.

He stepped back two paces at the right time, to stand at ease beside Jane, ready to endure more boring speeches.

Then Marlene was ascending the steps on the other side of the platform and moving toward him. She had recovered her composure, stomped to a halt across from Duncan and stood waiting. She was joined by her mother at her side. Everyone seemed to be waiting for something and Jane nudged him with her foot, then walked forward with him until they were almost touching Tanya who was standing separating the two small groups.

"You are such an asshole, Duncan," she said quietly so only they could hear. Magdalene cracked a smile.

Tanya stepped back half a step.

"Join hands," she ordered. When Marlene and Duncan grasped each other hands, Tanya put hers on top of both of theirs.

"Lady Marlene of House Isabelle, do you pledge to love and cherish Lord Duncan from this day forward?" Tanya said.

"Yes," Marlene said.

"Lord Duncan of House Kovaks, do you pledge to love and cherish Lady Marlene from this day forward."

"Yes," Duncan said.

"I, Queen Tanya, pronounce you husband and wife."

Both of them stood there with stunned looks on their faces.

"Don't be such an asshole, Duncan," Magdalene said. "Kiss her."

Duncan bent down and they had a quick brush of the lips.

"Ah for Christ's sake, Kovaks!" Hendrix bellowed out. "My five-year-old great grandson kisses better than that! You trying to embarrass us here, Kovaks! Are you a man or a mouse!"

Brett started to chant "Kiss her, kiss her!" and in seconds the parade ground was reverberating as the rest of the troops took up the chant.

Duncan shrugged his shoulders, tossed his Stetson away, grabbed Marlene's cap off her head, tossed it away, grabbed her and kissed her. Everyone on the parade square cheered and tossed their headgear in the air and the parade was over.

Two weeks later, grim looking Wind Riders in combat uniform formed a U formation around ten grimy, dirty and sweaty troopers standing at attention in a line. They faced the ten imposing Wind Riders at ease in front of them. None of the Wind Riders wore a smile. The ten facing them had fear in their eyes, except one whose eyes were smiling.

At a nod from Duncan in the center of the ten standing at ease, the mess began to recite:

"We are the wind rustling through the leaves and the grass, bringing fresh air and comfort.
We are the babbling brook, bringing refreshment and soothing.
We are the sun in the sky, bringing warmth and sustenance.
We are the Wind Riders, bringers of Peace, Hope and Justice.

We are the torrent that rips trees from the ground.
We are the raging flood waters that destroy homes.
We are the burning sun that devastates crops.
We are the Wind Riders, bringers of Despair, Death and Destruction."

One by one, a bottle was brought from behind a back and proffered to the one standing at attention opposite. One by one the bottle was drained and a beret placed on a head. Finally, only the one standing with the smile in her eyes was left and Duncan came forward and proffered the bottle. Marlene spun the top off it and drained it in fifteen seconds. Megan placed the beret on her head.

"Welcome to the Wind Riders, candidates," Duncan said. "Party's on!"

Several hours later, a GW2 came to a stop in front of a modest suburban home. Duncan came out of the driver's seat and opened the passenger door. He dragged a semi-conscious Marlene out of the passenger seat, slung her in a fireman's carry over his shoulder, hip-checked the vehicle door shut and walked her into house and flopped her on the bed.

He removed her boots and tunic then covered her up. Marlene opened her eyes, looked him in his and smiled.

"You are such an asshole sometimes, Duncan," she said. Then she passed out.

Also By RP Wollbaum

Cal's Quest Part One

Bears and Eagles Saga

Bears and Eagles
Eagles Claw
Eagles Talon
As Eagles Swarm
Bears Maul

CPSIA information can be obtained
at www.ICGtesting.com
Printed in the USA
BVOW06*2040161017
497822BV00003B/4/P